Praise for

"A very funny blast from the 1980s, tasting like the minty-flavoured freedom of our heroine's menthol cigarettes."
Peter Bradshaw, author and film critic at *The Guardian*

"A great cast of characters who ping and fizz around and off each other in an entertaining and moving story."
Jo Browning Wroe, author of *A Terrible Kindness*

"It made me laugh. A lot! But this book is more than just a humorous novel. It gets under your skin and you want to know more. The characters are all those multifaceted, flawed and believable people that we know, love and sometimes hate. A great read."
V A Gibbs

"Superb writing with spot on observational humour, warmth and joy. Prepare to be moved and to laugh. You're in for a treat."
Andrea Estelle (Author)

"The author at her effervescent wittiest. Laugh out loud funny – be careful where you're reading it."
Sarah L Wedd

"There is a mischievously observant eye and a sharply satirical humour at work here. A story about the secrets we all keep buried, it rings remarkably true."
Nicholas Bond

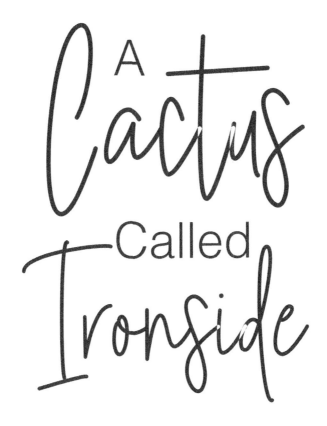

A Cactus Called Ironside

Kath Crew

To Mike and my fab four and all the other friends and relations who, despite their worries, do not appear anywhere in this story.

Truth is the most valuable thing we have. Let us economise it.

Mark Twain

Q. What is the difference between a misleading impression and a lie?
A. A lie is a straight untruth.
Q. What is a misleading impression – a sort of bent untruth?
A. As one person said, it is perhaps being economical with the truth.

Spycatcher trial 1986

Time shall unfold what plighted cunning hides:
Who cover faults, at last shame them derides.

King Lear (Act 1, scene 1)

Maybe someday you will rejoice to recall even this.

Virgil's Aeneid

'What's Past is Prologue'

When my knickers were hoist up the boathouse flagpole in the summer of 1983, I was delighted. Despite their age, size and colour and the fact that they were merely wafting limply in the breeze, I saw them as a pennant announcing my acceptance into a world I longed to join. In retrospect, they were a totem of the naïve and unmindful. Back then I was unquestionably both.

These days my underwear is regularly on display but I take no delight in it. My washing line is full of pants, blowing in the wind like spinnakers racing downwind of Cowes. A pair aloft indicating its force on the Beaufort scale always takes me back to that moment nearly forty years ago and the circumstances surrounding it.

Of course, it wasn't long before I realised I was mistaken. My pants up a pole were not the membership card to another tribe. At best their raising represented a half-hearted herald to the start of becoming an adult and the beginning of a process of self-realisation which is embarrassingly still incomplete.

Like most stories, my life is divided into three parts. It has a beginning, a middle and an end. The finale is about to start. I haven't got prior knowledge about my demise – who'd want that – but I know now that I've begun the last act, where things get resolved and conclusions are drawn.

My middle is an undefined, thirty-seven-year blob. Undoubtedly things have happened, but I struggle to ascribe exactly when and in which order. It's a busy grown-up melee of work and children which has passed rapidly, barely recorded.

If it hadn't been for the reunion, I may never have had a third part. I guess I would just have carried on existing in the middle, thinking it was the end – not angry or unfulfilled and for the most part content, filling in the unknown and the gaps with daydream and fantasy the way I always have. Like a football match, I'd be a game of two halves; I'd just have a beginning and an end. The blob would be my long drawn out second half decided by penalties, the winner booting me off to the crematorium.

I read about a French woman who lived to 122. If I live as long as her I'm not even halfway through. There will be sixty plus more years for the end part. A long-winded purgatory where I will have to confront my unspoken confession, where I will have to put things right and I will have to tell him. Yet time is irrelevant, counting days or years is pointless, they don't all pass at the same rate. I'm no physicist but even I can understand Einstein was on to something.

The Catholic ritual of confession and contrition is attractive for slate-wiping purposes. I have accomplished many of the sins on my Gran's list of those requiring confession. 'Lying by Omission' would be my most prolific. There are things I've obscured about the past but I'm not sure that's possible any longer. I'm not a liar but I have been, as they say, economical with the truth.

Looking back, sometimes it seems that three-year hiatus at the end of the beginning could have been a TV drama – or one of my daydreams: an interval between realities. After all, who'd imagine a bookie's daughter from Barking could end up in a low budget version of *Brideshead Revisited*?

But it happened. I have his letter, here in my hand. It's real enough. I can't avoid the truth any longer.

2

'In my end is my beginning...'

ow did I get talked into it? Want to come to a party where you're not sure who will be there, where you may have to spend the whole evening telling someone you couldn't stand forty years ago how glad you are to see them? Flatter someone you can't remember from Adam, that they don't look any different – whilst you know yourself that, without question, you are looking older, more tired, fatter and more unattractive than when they last saw you? I think not.

They're called 'alumni relations' these days, the office at the college which is full of people who claim they are desperate to 'catch up with me' so I can 're-connect'. The idea of doing so induces a state of panic rather than enthusiasm. They've stopped sending me e-mails about reunions, probably because there's a note on my file that says, 'thoroughly unpleasant and slightly unhinged alumna'.

I'd been rude to them during the telethon – a campaign whereby former students are cajoled into making donations to various projects. So now I'm on the list headed 'stingy fruitcake, don't bother' as well as the 'you'll not get any money out of that tight-fisted bastard' roll of honour. I can't help myself. It's because they don't get to the point. We all know why they're ringing.

The preamble to asking for your money or getting you to rush off to your solicitor and demand a codicil to your will is insincere chatter about your time at university.

"It must have been amazing playing for the squash team!" gushes some over-enthusiastic caller.

"Wouldn't know. I have never played the game."

"My notes say you were captain of women's squash, all those years ago."

"Well, your notes are wrong. I may be antique, but I can remember that." They should notice my irritation, yet they continue.

"Do you ever feel you want to give anything back?"

"I'm pretty sure I returned all my library books. I might still have an ashtray I nicked from the college bar. You can have that; I gave up the ciggies years ago."

"There's a non-smoking policy in college these days."

"Ah. Of course."

"Are there any memories you'd like to share?"

"I could look in the loft to see if there are any wax tablets or papyrus scrolls with historical records."

"The archivist is always happy to receive memorabilia."

The very last time the telethon included me the caller said, "Oh! I see from my notes that whilst you were here the boathouse burned down." That stopped my cheeky, smart-arse comments.

"What do your notes say about that?"

"Summer 1983: the boathouse burned down just before the Henley Regatta. Do you remember it? Were you there?"

This induced a flash of paranoia and the memory of my knickers flying from the flagpole but, predictably no donations to the latest campaign. Surely those inaccurate notes which had me champion of the squash ladder did not place me, or more alarmingly my underwear, at the scene? Had the archivist curated my pants in acid-free, preservation-grade tissue paper and displayed them in the college museum, the massive nametape still visible to tell everyone just who would wear such an item?

"Fuck off!" I demanded unreasonably and hung up. Who wants to be reminded of their youthful follies?

Unsurprisingly it was not 'alumni relations' but Mary who

sought me out and pressed me to attend the reunion of our college year group forty years after we had first met.

A call from her was a surprise in itself. In the thirty-seven years since graduation, I had had no contact with her at all. At university she had been a good and loyal companion, though not my most exciting friend, and shamefully there were others whose company I sought out in preference to hers. We had spent a good deal of time together but, for reasons never specified, we had not seen each other since we left. Perhaps it was time.

Recently, when we'd been through isolations and lockdowns, I had been thinking about all those people from that part of my life. I don't know if I was worried about the future or feeling nostalgic for simpler, happier times, but I'd caught up with friends I had, for whatever reason, shed along the way. My curiosity was pricked. Perhaps it was time to go back?

Mary had shown considerable perseverance to get hold of my contact details and had broken GDPR rules to do so. How un-Mary-like, I thought. She must really want to see me. She told me she still lived in Cambridge and was an academic. No surprises there. She was friends with someone in the alumni office who had slipped her the required information.

"Roni," she pleaded, "I really do want to see you. I need to see you." This sounded rather touching. Despite my cynical, hard-shelled exterior, I suddenly realised I wanted to see her too.

"Who's going?" I asked. She wasn't sure; the friend in the college office wasn't prepared to give that kind of information away. The only indication we had was that it was a reunion for the students of 1982-1985. We decided that a good number of girls from the concrete block of our first year were likely to turn up, and they would probably still be involved in some kind of cocoa-making rota.

We laughed about Binka and Bomber and the rest of the hideous 'in crowd' of which I had been desperate to be a part, none of whom would be included in this cohort. Would Julian Sousa still be playing his sousaphone and loud military music? I wanted to be a fly on the wall, to see without being seen.

There was someone I didn't want to encounter; someone I'd thought about regularly but had tried to put out of my mind. "I wonder if, oh what was he called? He had a stupid name… Webster Ferris. Do you think he will be there?" I asked, trying to sound casual. Mary didn't reply. "You know, Northern, a bit scary, read English."

"Who knows?" Mary replied eventually. "Don't tell me you had trouble remembering his name. You definitely remember him."

"I haven't seen him for 37 years!" I protested, truthfully but rather too emphatically.

Webster Ferris: the name alone sent a shockwave through me. I knew he had gone to the US when we graduated, and I expected and devoutly hoped that he would still be there and unlikely to make the visit. At least I thought I did. With some trepidation I found myself telling Mary that I'd come along.

What follows is mostly the story of just three years. That interlude between the beginning and the middle, when I thought I was an adult but didn't behave like one, a period with a disproportionate amount of influence and activity. It starts and ends with a child.

Finding 'that low door in the wall' [3]

I t's not an exaggeration to say Mrs Taylor changed my life. She gave me the opportunity to shape my future in a way that would never have been open to my parents.

No-one would have predicted that I would go to Cambridge University, this ordinary girl from an ordinary home. Mum had grand ideas about self-promotion and aggrandisement which centred mostly around our local area and in particular on Upney Lane, a road of large inter-war houses not far from our own. Dad kept quiet, happy with his lot. Neither of them would have considered university; it just wasn't in their orbit.

When I went to collect my A level results, Charles and Diana were on honeymoon. The former Lady Di, swinging a deceptively carefree leg whilst posing on a stile, was putting on a brave face about ending up with kilt-wearing Charles. At school Mrs Taylor, not dressed in the style of someone enduring a honeymoon in the Highlands but wafting about in layers of silky fabrics looking like a pink and purple hot house orchid, was waiting.

She thrust university prospectuses at me. No one argued with Mrs Taylor when she was in full bloom. I was filling in an UCCA form before the royal honeymoon was over.

Barking's Biggest Bookworm. That's how Mum described me to the clients in her salon, more as an explanation when she was asked if I had a boyfriend than because she was proud of the fact that I spent all of my time with my nose in a book. Mum's tone suggested that a love of reading made you oblivious to the charms of men. She spoke the word 'bookworm' very slowly as if it was a lifestyle with beliefs, like vegetarianism or communism. These were things my mother knew existed but didn't practise herself and wasn't entirely convinced were good for you.

Lack of a 'young man' was something Mum, poised with her scissors and comb, thought she should explain to the pinned and rollered women who looked inquisitively back at her in the mirror. She didn't want them thinking that no-one much liked the look of me or, more probably, that I just preferred print to passion. Mum did not equate a love of reading with an interest in real-life romance and convinced herself that spending time at the library was not a turn on for the opposite sex. She was ambitious for my future but did not see literature as the route to "getting on" – a programme which involved moving up the social scale, living in a bigger house than ours, married to a man who, even if he was a bookmaker like my dad, at least had more than one shop.

One of Mrs Taylor's booklets, glossy with a cover picture of scantily clad hunks in a rowing boat sweating it out on a river, caught my eye. My singular experience of rowing was on the lake in the park in a wooden boat with peeling paint and a slight leak. Dad, sinking ever lower down in the bow, took a while to manoeuvre the oars in the weedy water whilst I sat at the stern, raised up from the surface by the difference in our weights. We made slow and precarious progress like one of the Titanic's lifeboats hoping for rescue. No matter, gliding down the Cam in synergy with seven others wasn't the attraction the photo held. I had no intention of going in the boat.

Mum was wrong about my lust for romance. It was never far from my thoughts and these oarsmen could be a happy substitute for any fictional character. Not only that, they made an acceptable replacement for Donny Osmond and Bjorn Borg. It seemed increasingly less likely that those two were going to notice me if they passed through Barking to get their hair styled by Mum or stick a bet on at Dad's shop. Even I realised that my chances of being whisked off to the Osmond ranch in Utah or the Borg apartment in Stockholm were diminishing despite religiously kissing the posters of them on my bedroom wall goodnight.

If I wanted to include larking about with the Cambridge rowers on my list of potential universities, I needed to sit an entrance exam in the autumn. This, I was delighted to discover, involved reading my way through an inordinately long list of books beforehand. I plunged into the Woolworths 'pick n mix' of literary delight which the shelves of Barking library provided. Nirvana.

In recompense for coming to our house after school to teach me, Mrs Taylor spent hours under the dryer at The Mayfair Salon. She appeared from this free torture like an oversized Barbara Cartland. Being rolled and pinned then cooked until she emerged wearing a gravity defying white cloud of meringue on her head pleased her as much as doing nothing but read for three months pleased me. It was a symbiotic relationship, which surprisingly resulted in the offer of a place to read English at the University. I had a ticket out of Barking and Mrs Taylor had secured herself free hairdressing for life.

I'd read *Brideshead Revisited* and Mum and I had both watched the TV serialisation. Sebastian and Charles didn't do anything as exhausting as rowing but flounced about on bicycles and occasionally in a vintage sports car. They were quite clearly in Oxford not Cambridge, but I didn't disabuse Mum, who almost believed that I too would be waited upon by a college servant when joining them for elaborate lunches involving plovers' eggs (not available in Wallis' supermarket in Barking) and spending weekends at stately homes.

Place secured, I spent until the next October sweeping up hair or answering the phone at The Mayfair Salon or with Dad, chalking up the odds on a big board at McNamara Bros Turf

Accountants. In the summer I got a job in the ticket kiosk at the open-air pool in the park. I was only busy on the rare day when the temperature was high enough to encourage locals to imagine they were living in Biarritz rather than Barking.

Unofficially, I was Nan's carer, keeping an eye on her parked in the corner of the salon nattering on about the War, which in her mind was still very much ongoing. Mum's clients were tolerant of Nan, who lived with us but couldn't be left alone at home. I had returned from school several times to find her sitting under the stairs with a torch, complaining that she hadn't heard the siren sound the 'All Clear' yet. So Mum took her to the salon where she'd occasionally ask people if they'd been bombed out or had a husband or son posted overseas.

Mum was eager to broadcast about my forthcoming studies to whoever was listening. "It's where they do all those carols," she'd explain to those being permed, dexterously selecting a tranche of hair with her fine-toothed metal comb and wrapping a roller around it. The image we all had of Cambridge was largely based on the cover of an LP *Nine Lessons and Carols from King's College* which Dad would get out each Christmas for its annual spin on the record player: magnificent chapel and punts on the river. The photograph did not include a boathouse with a pair of pants flying from its flagpole.

After months of anticipation and discussion, the time came to begin the rest of my life. My Irish grandmother arrived on the bus from Mile End to see me off, with some advice from God's right-hand man, the parish priest at St Mary and St Michael, Stepney. When Gran was around, the spectre of Father O'Connor was never far behind.

"The Eyes of the Lord are in every place," she warned alarmingly, mysteriously adding, "Be sure your sin will find you out." She pressed a rosary into my hand, crossing herself as she did so, the look on her face suggesting she thought she was unlikely ever to see me again. She softened momentarily. "But it is enough that Our Lord knows," she whispered, "and there'll be no need to tell Father O'Connor everything."

Predictably, events did not proceed as I had imagined. For a start I don't recall either Lord Sebastian Flyte or Charles Ryder having a parent or grandparent with them when they arrived at their college. I had an escort of three and it would have been four if Mum hadn't banned Gran because she didn't want to listen to the wisdom of Fr O'Connor and the consequences of sin all the way up the A10.

Nan emerged from our house, coated, with her hair shampooed and set for the occasion. A light aircraft flew noisily overhead in the sunlit October sky. "Don't worry. I think it's one of ours," she advised. She noticed Dad checking the roof rack was secure for the tenth time. "Where are we going, Shirley? Are the Germans coming? Is it the Invasion?"

"Does she have to come?" I asked. It was bad enough having both parents coming along,

"Ron is just going away for a bit," explained Mum. "We're going to see her off."

"I didn't know you were being evacuated," Nan confided as Mum pushed her through the car door and towards me on the back seat of the Cortina. Dad caught my eye through the window. She drifted away at this thought until suddenly she was back in the present day, fussing about the sandwiches.

"They're in the bag with the Thermos, on the floor in the back." Mum was more patient than Dad or me.

"Don't have the egg," Nan whispered to me conspiratorially. "You can only get dried. I haven't had a real egg for years."

Were we the only family to take 'emergency rations' with us if we ventured more than ten miles from home? Dad had only to mention the Southend Arterial and the Tupperware and Thermos flasks were out.

Barking is in Essex – or was until someone invented some extra London boroughs. Even without going on the recently opened M11, it was less than 50 miles to Cambridge. You didn't need to take a meal with you, even if you were going there and back in a day. Wrapping and unwrapping greaseproof packets of unlabelled sandwiches to find the required filling was an accompaniment to even a short journey by road. As we waited in lay-bys for the discovery of the cheese and Branston, the car shook as it was overtaken by drivers of high-speed vehicles who seemingly had no desire to keep up nutritional requirements.

Leaving the Cortina anywhere was an issue. Parking it straight and the correct distance from the kerb, making sure it wasn't hemmed in, sticking out, near a corner or likely to be written off by a passing juggernaut took forever. The complex combination of leaving it both legally parked and in the least danger of wilful or accidental damage or, heaven help us, theft, was a regular feature of travelling in the vehicle. Once in Cambridge, even Dad realised we needed to get within carrying distance of the college. He acknowledged that he would have to break the habit of a lifetime and park not only halfway up a kerb but also on a yellow line. "Don't forget your gas mask!" called Nan as Dad locked her in the parked vehicle and we made off with my stuff. He reasoned leaving her inside might soften the heart of any traffic warden who might be looking to make a killing on penalty notices on freshers' arrival day.

The brutalist 1970s accommodation which greeted me was as huge a disappointment to my parents as it was to me. It was nothing like the rooms I'd seen when I came for interview. The brick and concrete block, its design more GLC housing scheme than ancient seat of learning or graceful Georgian example of the golden ratio, was right at the back of the college on a piece of land that had clearly previously been thought of as unsuitable for building projects. My tiny room and its functional furniture was not what I was expecting. "At least it'll be easy to keep clean," was as much as Mum could say about it.

Fortunately, the safety of the Cortina weighed heavily with Dad, and once he had helped me in with the bags he returned to it anxiously. No doubt drinking a Thermos of tea in the car whilst keeping an eye out for wardens would lessen his anxiety. Mum may have been feeling guilty about leaving Nan imprisoned in the back unable to escape without the key, but she wasn't so keen on leaving my room herself.

I'd already failed to prevent her introducing herself to some of the other girls on my corridor and giving them some styling tips for their hair. "A bubble perm is popular with my younger clients. Your face would suit that," I caught her telling a fresh-faced girl with long straight locks in the next room.

Mum had some parting advice for me passed on from a neighbour in our road. "Mrs Harrison's son Colin got one of those shaggy coats when he was at university. It smelt something rotten; she thought there were things living in it. She wouldn't let him leave it in the hall. He had to keep it in the shed." I'd heard about Colin's coat before and other snippets about his transformation from gawky schoolboy into hippy student. He couldn't get up in the mornings when he was back in the holidays. Mrs Harrison had thought he'd got some illness, perhaps caught from the coat.

"Don't come back with one. They're not hygienic," Mum insisted. No-one was still wearing an Afghan coat in the early '80s but my mother identified them with further education, along with sit-ins and "funny smelling tobacco." Fortunately, *Brideshead Revisited* had provided us both with a new student stereotype. She wouldn't be telling Anthony Andrews or Jeremy Irons not to leave their striped blazers in the hall. No coat hooks in the shed for them. They would be positively encouraged into the lounge in full outerwear for a Babycham or Mateus Rosé.

Eventually, when she felt unable to think of any more reasons why I might need her help, she left.

I thought for a while about what to write on the nameplate on my door. Very few people called me Veronica: Gran, doctors' receptionists and fractious teachers mostly – and Dad when he wanted to annoy Mum. My name had been his choice, won, appropriately for a man whose work involved gambling, at the toss of a coin. She'd borne a grudge ever since and always called me Ron, affectionate but with connotations of a plumber or someone putting a quid on a dog at Walthamstow. "Get Ron to do it!" she'd bellow from another room if she heard my father swearing at the new video machine. A passer-by would be forgiven for thinking a bloke with a toolbox and a pencil behind his ear was about to be summoned to mend something. Eventually, I settled on Roni thinking the i at the end made it sound trendy. Of course, it wasn't then and isn't now – but I'm stuck with it.

On the wall I stuck a reproduction poster of a large, green-eyed cat holding a suffragette in its mouth that I'd bought from a museum shop on a school trip. Mum wouldn't let me put it up in my bedroom because there was blood dripping from the cat's teeth. "I can't think why you'd want to look at that. It'll give you bad dreams." I'm not sure it was force feeding women seeking the vote she was referring to – nightmare inducing though that may have been. The poster was suitably intellectual with a message, I reasoned. Besides it was all I had. Donny, Bjorn and a picture of the West Ham goalie Mervyn Day had been left pinned to the Vymura on the wall in my room back at home.

Despite the concrete, the lino floors and the institutional design, I was a long way from crazy paving, through-lounges and Formica-topped kitchen tables. Mum, Dad, Wartime Nan, Irish Gran and the Mile End Lothario, my Uncle Pat, were back in East London.

The Mayfair Salon, with its outdated, buttoned and padded,

plastic covered desk, and its pale yellow and baby blue colour scheme, reeked of Sixties suburbia. To me it was redolent of what I considered the dull lives of our part of Barking's inhabitants. Now I was somewhere else.

I took out the box of 200 duty-free menthol cigarettes that I'd bought on a cross-channel ferry in the summer and successfully hidden from my parents in my luggage and opened the first pack. I took a long drag of minty-flavoured freedom.

4
Clouds and silver linings

Initial impressions of Cambridge had been a disappointment to all of us apart from Nan, who marvelled at Dad's resourcefulness in obtaining enough petrol coupons to get us there. Dad moaned about the paucity of adequate parking facilities and Mum the lack of a large-windowed suite of rooms with a view of the river like the ones she'd seen on TV.

My worries were more to do with my contemporaries. The brutalist block seemed to be full of homely sorts of girls, who put postcards of cute kittens up on their walls rather than fully grown cats with blood and political messages dripping from their fangs. They had milky drinks before bed and it wasn't long before they had made a rota for nightly cocoa preparation. I wasn't on it.

There were some nice students on my corridor, and I made a few friends, but as term progressed, I realised that this crowd were not the ones I wanted to be with. I speedily ditched any sham ideas I had about intellectual discussion and serious political debate. The cat poster remained but I'd spotted that there was a kitten-free side of student life and I wanted to be part of it.

In the college bar there was a loud group of boys. Confident and noisy, they gave the impression they were in charge. They were the rugby crowd, the footballers and rowers, the actors – the big players in college life. They had floppy, unruly hair, which Mum would have been aching to brush, and wore old men's overcoats which they'd bought from charity shops to keep out the chilly autumnal evening air. I heard their posh voices, felt their superiority, and I wanted to be part of their entitled world.

But it was hard to break into their set if you hadn't been to school with them or known them before. They played a connections game to see if you were suitable for the clique. "Do you know the Whyteleafes? They're from Essex." If you couldn't find a distant cousin in common, your dad hadn't served in the regiment with which they had an association or your uncle hadn't courted one of the family, the conversation went no further.

"Mum says Uncle Pat has been out with half the women in Essex," might have worked, but I doubted that even my father's brother and partner at the bookies, whose girlfriends changed more frequently than the lights on the Mile End Road outside his flat, had permeated their set.

Like Pat and the rest of us, Mum would have failed to score highly enough on the posh-o-meter but she would have approved of Monroe Cholmondeley (though I doubt she'd have pronounced his name correctly) because he looked like an extra from *Brideshead*.

Many of the names of the upper classes (and those who aspire to be thought of as such) are not written as they are said. It's a device to sort the patrician sheep from the plebeian goat. He was Munro Chumlee, if you were in the know, Chummers to his mates, and he was the Captain of Boats.

She would have thought the name thing stupid. "Just like your Gran," she'd say, never missing a chance to get a dig in at her mother-in-law. "Only the Irish could get Ev-een out of AOIBHEANN." The 'Seven Deadly Sins', as Dad called his mother and her six sisters back in Cork, all had names that had confusing spelling defying English phonetics.

Despite being guaranteed to fall into the pronunciation trap, Mum would have thought this 6'3" floppy-haired Old Etonian was definitely on the syllabus for 'getting on'. I thought so too the minute I set eyes on him, lounging seductively with his feet up on a table in the college bar. He looked like Rupert Brooke, whose picture was on the cover of my book of his poems. I can't vouch for Chummers' ability with verse, but, like Brooke, he was admired by many and generously shared his affections with a selection of conquests not only at our college but throughout the University. Shoving a pair of knickers up the boathouse flagpole was how he identified his success.

No one in Barking looked like him and I wanted to be in his crowd. Chummers did not belong in the world of the thirties semi. I knew instinctively that he didn't live in a house with a sunburst gate, coloured leaded fanlights and painted 'beams' on the facade. There was no pebbledash on the walls of his ancestral pile, his mother certainly wasn't called Shirley nor did she sit in a lounge or pass plates through a serving hatch. How was I going to infiltrate this clique and in particular secure the attention of Chummers?

The mixed blessing of Simeon Goldblatt potentially provided me with my answer. He was the nerdy older brother of a girl I'd been friendly with when we both started secondary school. I'd barely spoken to him then and wasn't even aware he was at Cambridge now let alone at the same college. He'd spotted me though.

I wouldn't say he followed me around, but he often appeared round a corner in the college in sensible clothes and a cagoule even when it wasn't raining. If a garment was made in Gore-Tex, you could bet Simeon would have one in his wardrobe.

It was several weeks into the first term when he first approached me and used my full unabbreviated name at quarters close enough that it was impossible to pretend I hadn't heard.

"Veronica?" He was coming up the stairs as I was going down. "You don't remember me, do you?" I didn't say anything. "I'm Miriam's brother. Miriam Goldblatt."

"Simon?" I suggested, not wishing him to think I'd given him a second thought over the eight years since Miriam and I had met.

"Simeon," he corrected. "Like Joseph's brother."

"Joseph?"

"Yes. The one with the coat of many colours and eleven brothers." He was very precise. "And he actually had a sister too, though she is often forgotten about."

There was an awkward silence. I got the feeling that being an expert on the Old Testament wasn't quite how Simeon had wanted to come across and he was wishing he could re-wind.

Mum was keen to encourage the friendship between Miriam and me. The Goldblatts, after all, lived in Upney Lane, which had been the pinnacle of desirable housing stock in Barking when my mother was a girl.

Nan had picked up on this. "Did you know, Vera Lynn lived in Upney Lane during the war?" I and everyone else knew this fact because Nan pointed it out if anyone mentioned her or the road. Hidden behind *The Racing Post*, Dad would mouth along with this Pavlovian response made if even there was a merest mention of the white cliffs of Dover, or the tiniest excerpt of *"We'll Meet Again"* was broadcast.

Miriam and I remained friends but were less close as we went up the school. Our social circles expanded in different directions. She was a scientist, and I liked the arts. Mum was disappointed not to maintain the connection, one of her objectives being to get inside the Goldblatt property to have a good nose.

I made my excuses to Simeon and his treasure trove of theological knowledge. Mum would have been horrified. Giving Dr Goldblatt's son the cold shoulder? Insane! He was probably going to inherit the Upney Lane mansion.

He worked in the bar some evenings. "Not got your nose in a book then?" he always asked when I walked in. This habit was something he constantly referred to. I was anxious not to get a reputation as a super swot, particularly in front of the group I was trying to impress.

They gave each other mysterious nicknames. Why were 'The Wobster', 'Bomber' and 'Ripper' so named? Smallcox is what they called Simeon. I quickly got the message that this was not an affectionate nickname. He was 5'4" so it was based on his height and not, I hoped, a public appraisal of a specific part of his anatomy. I knew little enough about rowing but I'd learned what a cox was – the little one who faces the other way and shouts at the big, sweaty, muscled ones holding the oars, then gets chucked in the water at the end of the race, whether the team has won or not. I realised with a sudden sense of delight that Simeon Goldblatt was the college first boat cox and had direct access to Chummers.

The short term sped by, just eight teaching weeks. As the vacation approached, I received a Christmas gift. A drippy looking girl I'd barely bothered to speak to on the floor above decided to take a bath before going to bed at 8:30 just as I was going out. When she realised that she was that evening's cocoa maker and rushed to fulfil her obligations with the milk saucepan and Bourneville, she forgot to turn off the tap filling the bath.

I was in pursuit of an entrée to the chosen clique so I couldn't sound the alarm as the water came cascading through my ceiling. Nor was I underneath when the plaster gave way and crashed down into my room.

Initially, Mary, whom my mother had considered ideal for a bubble perm, allowed me to sleep on the floor in her room. She was a good sort who was also studying English. We went to tutorials and lectures together, but frankly she was a bit dull. She was the first person I'd ever met who read more than me. An emergency mattress and blankets were found and the college was apologetic.

I was unfazed. I was not fond of my featureless cell with its breeze block walls and functional furniture. I longed for an escape to a more picturesque setting where vines and creepers covered the walls, stone steps dipped and wooden staircases were scuffed, worn by centuries of scholarly feet.

Despite Mary's offer to share more permanently as there were no spare rooms in the block, I did a good job of convincing the college that I did not want to remain there in the circumstances. Lack of confidence in the structure of the building, trauma caused by having most of my notes saturated and useless – I came up with some pretty good reasons why I should be moved into a more traditional setting.

There was one other room vacant, sharing with a third year in a set. It had a marvellous view of the river, two small bedrooms joined by a shared study, and beautiful eighteenth-century windows. Brideshead to perfection. I said yes immediately.

But, as they say, you should be careful what you wish for.

'... senses, affections, passions?'

My cohabitee turned out to be Binka, a girl I'd seen hanging out with the elite round college. Everything about her was impressive. Her long hair was voluminous, with a level of backcombing my mother would have been impressed by. It was sometimes casually piled up on her head, twisted round and held up with a pencil instead of pins or a slide. She'd remove the pencil and the whole lot would come tumbling down. This wasn't an easy feat. I'd tried it. Not only was a mere pencil insufficient for my weight of hair but my curls prevented the pencil coming out with anything like the speed Binka could manage. More often than not I'd have to cut the pencil out because it had become so entangled.

Binka had a large Indian cotton scarf twined round her neck and wore workmen's type dungarees. One strap was always hanging off her shoulder in a deliberate kind of way. If Mum had seen me with that look she'd have said, "You want to tighten that strap on those dungarees. It keeps falling down," so frequently that I'd have stopped wearing them.

Binka's mother probably didn't even notice; she may even have worn that kind of thing herself when she wasn't in a ball gown or hunting clothes. She certainly wouldn't have got her hair done at anywhere like The Mayfair Salon.

And the name! Binca was a type of fabric we'd had at primary school. It was unlikely she'd been called after a brightly coloured, holed canvas that was used to practise embroidery stitches, I thought.

Despite the similarity to the embroidery weave, I thought the name said much classier things about Binka than Roni with one n and an i did about me. None of the cool gang was called Alison, Rachael, or Susan (my best friends at school) or even Veronica. They were mostly known by names like Muffy, Dodo or Wiglet.

To emphasise her upper crust credentials, Binka also had a surname which you said differently to the way it was spelled.

"You're Binka Coke," I stated rather obviously when she opened the door.

She didn't smile. She looked me up and down and continued rolling up a cigarette with one hand. "That's really cool to be able to do that," I gushed.

"It's said Cook," she offered eventually. There was a pause in which I wondered if anyone had told her I was arriving.

"I'm …"

"Yeah, I know. Fucking inconvenient." There was a longer, more painful pause. "I don't know where you're going to put all that stuff." She hadn't yet looked along the landing to see an unwieldy tower of more of my belongings with Mary's legs buckling beneath it.

"Christ," she said when we were eventually allowed through the door. Her voice was deep and she spoke with the elongated and tortured vowels of the upper classes. "At least you haven't got any books." It was true. Many of my books and files had been ruined in the flood and I'd yet to replace them. "You know that the last person left about a week into the year, don't you?" I didn't but I reckoned keeping quiet might be the appropriate response. "Anyway. You'll have to get on with Bomber if you're going to stay. I'm going out. You'll have to move all the stuff off the bed in that room if you want to sleep on it." She indicated one door and picked up her coat. "Don't go into my room or mess with my things, OK?"

"Are you sure?" asked Mary when she'd gone. "I really don't mind you sharing the floor in my room."

Mary was calm and helpful and what she lacked in excitement she made up for in practicality. I realise now that she was mature beyond her years. She helped me clear up the empty wine and vodka bottles, overflowing ash trays and general rubbish that was covering every surface in 'my' room in Binka's bunker. For some reason the curtains had been tied in knots, so Mary undid them and, not without some difficulty, opened the window to let some air in.

"It's not really fair of her to take over both bedrooms…" Mary began.

"It's fine," I replied, trying not to retch at the mould-covered half-drunk cup of coffee or tea lurking on the windowsill. Two milk bottles were making cheese near the bed. Mary removed them. She had a point, but I tried not to be fussed about it. I didn't suppose Binka had to do much housework when she was at home. She probably didn't know how.

"You know where I am," Mary said, "if Bomber gets too much." But I had no intention of going back to the 1970's horror building and the cutesy kitten loving girls with Lady Di haircuts and Laura Ashley piecrust collars.

We both knew who Bomber was. You couldn't miss him. He was very large and very loud with a voice which could summon a taxi half a mile away. He was often laughing in the bar, frequently, you suspected, at you. I hadn't realised that Binka and Bomber were a couple. Or perhaps they weren't. Couples were so suburban.

The origin of his name was revealed the next day when I returned from lectures. There were loud noises coming from Binka's room: whoops and the sound of someone pretending to fire a machine gun, explosions and aircraft engine sounds. I edged closer to the open door.

"Come in, red leader, bandits at four o'clock. Release bomb doors, GO!" It was Bomber's voice unquestionably. Through the door I could see Binka lying on her bed, stark naked. Bomber, trouserless but still wearing a shirt and a sheepskin-lined leather flying jacket, was astride her. Her bra was draped over his head, its cups forming the earpieces of a make-believe flying helmet.

"Tally HO!" shouted Bomber when he saw me, bouncing up and down like he was in the 2:30 at Towcester. My father might well have accepted a bet on him.

"Shut the fucking door!" ordered Binka. "And your mouth. It's wide open." I did as I was told.

The reason for Bomber's nickname was now apparent. It was quite a lot for a girl from Barking to take in. I was surprised how shocked and bourgeois I felt.

Not having a boyfriend whilst I was at school had prevented me joining in with the Monday morning catch up. My classmates eagerly discussed who'd been chucked and who had got off with whom at the weekend at the various parties I never attended. I was envious of them.

"I really wish I was clever like you," one of the party-going types in my class had once said to me. "You could be a doctor or something." She was unintentionally patronising, but I reckoned she probably knew that I'd prefer to be hanging about after school near the railings with a long-haired dish from the boys' school than swotting towards the possibility of examining someone's varicose veins for a living.

"And you're funny." I was also aware that the ability to mimic the Head of Chemistry talking about acids and alkalis did not get you prime position in front of the school railings with the hunk of your choice.

The railings were the scenic background in front of which couples could perform to an auditorium of other pupils passing by on their way home. This one scene play, the gist of which was a demonstration of how far and for how long they could hang their tongues down each other's throats, was presented to the unloved and unrequited. If you missed this very public display, then there were opportunities to catch encores at the school bus stop and in shop doorways along the main thoroughfares home.

I doubted there was such a raw display of rampant hormones at Mary's grammar school, which no doubt had a huge wormery of book consumers. Whereas I read anything, she was selective and stretched herself. She read beyond the set texts and around the subject. There was a noticeable difference. There is no doubt that in Mum's eye the amount of time Mary spent with print would preclude her from ever finding true love.

One consequence of my move to the older and more attractive accommodation in college was that Simeon Goldblatt was quite close at hand. As a third year, he too had an older-style room, though I imagine the action within was confined to writing up experiments and doing complex calculations rather than piloting missions on a human Halifax.

He'd taken to hanging about at the foot of our staircase or in the court just outside. Whilst this was irritating, I realised that now our paths crossed frequently I would be able to ask for regular updates on the boat's performance and increase my access to the captain himself. In addition, it was clear that Bomber was right in the heart of the rowing set. Despite having the height and strength required for pulling an oar, he would not have been able to fit into the narrow boat. However, his land-based support for the team in the college bar was unquestionable. Things were looking up.

I assumed Bomber did have his own room somewhere. I wasn't sure where, as he never seemed to be in it. I wondered why he hadn't taken up residence in the spare room in the set. Perhaps mixed sharing wasn't officially allowed. He wasn't there all the time, so he did go to other places. Something told me that they were unlikely to include the library and whichever department had him as a student.

Even Bomber, whose poor powers of observation in real life

would have prevented him fulfilling any of the key roles in a wartime RAF Wellington, noticed Simeon Goldblatt lurking near the entrance to our staircase. His constant coming and going to fulfil his assignations with Binka now involved passing the cox lingering downstairs.

"That little Smallcox chap, Silverblob, spends a lot of time hanging about outside. Do you know him?" he asked.

"I knew his sister. A long time ago," I replied, trying to sound casual.

"Hmm." Bomber was trying to process this information. "Was she ever so tiny?" He sounded intrigued.

"Not particularly. I can't really remember."

Perhaps he was wondering what it would be like to have a miniature girlfriend. Bomber was a very big man. He would be able to pick up Simeon Goldblatt in one hand and hold him like King Kong grasped Fay Wray beside the Empire State Building. Maybe Simeon would have to promise to fix him up with his sister in order for Bomber not to grab him and crush him with a slight squeeze of his hand.

He was a good model for King Kong, despite lacking fur. The only suggestion of hair on his pale skin was a fair, unkempt tangle on top of his head. It put me in mind of a doll I'd had as a child which I'd given a hairdo by washing and backcombing her nylon tresses. The poor thing was stuck with a frizzy mop like a blonde Brillo pad which, brush it as I might, never returned to its original lustre. None the less, Bomber's body shape was a good match for an outsized gorilla's.

He never seemed to have any books or even a piece of paper. I don't think he owned a pen. He wasn't in the hall for meals, preferring to exist on a liquid diet of subsidised college beer. He varied this with occasional forays into spirits when the drinking games he got involved with meant lining up drinks with a smaller volume but higher percentage of alcohol.

His lack of intellect meant even the simplest of games was a trial to him and his forfeits were frequent and inevitable. The group who hung about with him banged the bar tables with a frightening and overbearing command of the entire room. When they were at large, other groups huddled together whispering, as far from this dominant core as they could get.

Simeon Goldblatt was employed as a barman some evenings. I wondered why he did this job. Surely someone who was a doctor's son and lived in Upney Lane didn't need to supplement his grant by putting up with the constant abuse they hurled at him.

"Hooray it's Goldie!" they'd cheer when they entered and found he was doing a shift of pint pulling. "He's only a Smallcox!" I'd hang about the bar when they were at large, pathetically hoping to be noticed and included.

One evening they were particularly boisterous. Simeon ignored them. He was, however, keen to remind me of our shared past in a voice easily overheard by the rest of the drinkers. "Do you remember coming to my Bar Mitzvah?" he asked at peak volume one evening. Of course I remembered. It was my first year of secondary school and I had been invited as Miriam's guest. The event was memorable as it was my first introduction to smoked salmon – a delicacy far superior to the flavourless pale pink fish we called salmon and got out of a tin for Sunday tea.

Mum had been beside herself with excitement. Despite having an inkling that there was a vague connection to religion, this was the kind of event she thought I should be attending. "Ron's been invited to a bar-mizzle where the food is being prepared by caterers," she told the neighbours, her customers and most of Greater Barking. "The function is taking place in a marquee because the family have a very large garden in Upney Lane." Mum had yet to survey the Goldblatts' plot and she'd made the tent part up. Lack of precise information wasn't going to get in the way of embellishment. "Apparently," she continued, "they're having real music, not records." This too was speculation, but Nan was excited about the prospect of Vera Lynn being there and serenading us whilst we celebrated.

"It was a long time ago," I replied.

"Goldstein's Bar Mitzvah! There's a sought-after invitation," sneered a rowing acolyte named Torquil Powell who insisted his surname was pronounced Pole. For people who were so pernickety about their own names, they were disrespectfully casual about remembering the cox's correctly. I had to admit that Simeon Goldblatt, or whatever he was being called at that moment, wasn't cowed by these people. The rest of us, weaker and unwilling to stand up for the bullied, would laugh sycophantically along with them.

A rowdy game of Cardinal Puff was in full flow. As far as I could make out, this involved reciting a precise script whilst tapping the table, underneath and on top, tapping glasses and then drinking a hearty glug. If you messed up there was a forfeit (more booze). If you got through round one then you had to double everything up, then triple and so on. It would have been a challenge with water. For Bomber it was like asking him to recite the Gettysburg Address whilst playing a complicated Bach fugue on the chapel organ – impossible for most mortals, beyond impossible for King Kong.

"Oi, Goldfinger!" he shouted when his glass had inevitably been emptied. "Get us another, there's a good fellow."

"You've got my name wrong." Simeon was forceful. "If I'm getting you a drink, you can call me by the right name." Now it was clear; he felt in command when working behind the bar.

"Sorry," said Bomber belching. He was obviously drunk but not incoherent. "Simone, please would you pour me a glass of your best vodka? If you'd be so kind."

"It's Simeon," he persisted. I had to admit, he had some neck. Bomber got up. He really was huge. It was like David and Goliath.

"I apolo…apolo…gise, my little chum Silverberg," he managed before sliding down the wall onto the floor. "Give Smallcox a round of applause," he continued for no reason at all and then passed out.

"Veronica…" Simeon began.

"Ooo, get you, Goldman. Ver –on –i –ca!" imitated one of the few who could still speak.

"She's Binka's new roommate, poor cow. She won't be interested in you, Gold-what-ever-it-is," shouted Sholto Fanshaw (or Featherstonehaugh if you were writing it down).

"You know my name is Goldblatt," he insisted. Personally, I would have quit whilst I was ahead.

"Get the unfortunate lady a large drink, shortarse, whatever your fucking name is. She's going to need it."

I said nothing. I felt very uncomfortable, but I stayed silent. Simeon made no attempt to pour any drinks. He had no intention of serving them any more alcohol. What was going to happen now?

"Roni, love, see what you can do to cheer up his Smallcox," smirked a ginger-haired beanpole with the improbable name of Barnaby ffoulkes-ffarryingdon.

"Get him some pork scratchings," suggested another, "or perhaps he'd prefer smoky bacon crisps?" They all laughed raucously. The sound was deafening, reverberating off the walls. The room pulsated with this unpleasant cacophony; there was an atmosphere I had never experienced before.

Simeon stood firm. He was dignified but he said nothing. Shamefully, neither did I. I was a coward and I left.

This was the moment when everything I needed to know about Bomber, the boaty gang and the braying mob that I considered the 'in crowd' should have been confirmed.

I was as bad as them in some ways, complicit by my silence. What happened to Simeon later in the year was my fault. I didn't speak up then just as I didn't stick up for him that night. I should have looked more closely around me and not been tempted by the preposterous fantasy that I desired and wanted to be part of this objectional group. It took other events and other people to make me see sense. I suppose it's called growing up. This was the beginning, but it wasn't the last time I kept quiet.

6
Living in the Mess, avoiding the flak

The overall impression I might erroneously give of Cambridge in that time is that it was full of public-school boys and deb-like girls. In fact, many of the students, I later came to realise, were nothing of the sort. Many came from grammar schools and comprehensives like me – though that didn't prevent them feeling the need to pass themselves off as privately educated posh kids.

Sloane Rangers, of whom the new Princess of Wales was the figurehead, were at full gallop. Many a socially unsure student used the jokey satirical *Sloane Rangers' Handbook* as the instruction manual for what they should say and how they should dress. A certain type of suburban girl with Lady Diana-style pearls hoped a boy from a 1960s new town wearing a Barbour coat might think she lived off the Kings Road, whereas his only experience of country pursuits was a pub lunch with his parents on holiday in Devon. The place was full of re-invention.

I felt socially insecure, but that wasn't new. School had been the same. I'd have loved to have been hanging about after school by the railings with a David Cassidy lookalike shoving his tongue deep into my throat. Or slow dancing at the end of a party on a Saturday night. A boy with the lank blond hair (but probably not the serve) of Bjorn Borg who came from Ilford rather than Sweden, would have done. But it was not to be. I was the girl who got full marks in tests and had her nose in a book. Not unpopular but different.

Encouraged by Evelyn Waugh and the Granada TV adaptation of his novel, my initial attempt at fitting in at Cambridge – trying to mix with the toffs – was naïve. I didn't speak or think like them, and our worlds had never overlapped in any way. Serving hatches and leaded lights might be features of grand country houses but their interpretation in an interwar semi with fitted carpets and night storage heaters was unlikely to compare. I wonder if things might have been different if I had come across Ferris any earlier but it's a pointless speculation.

Life in Binka's shadow mostly involved trying not to get in the way of her energetic sexual sorties with Bomber. This wasn't easy but, although prolific, they followed, at least, a predictable routine: after lunch, teatime and after supper (but before he held counsel with his mates in the college bar) were peak flying times. Weekends were less active. An over-indulgent Friday night often prevented Bomber from going on operations for most of Saturday and much of Sunday too.

Despite being an idiot and a fairly despicable human being, he was quite nice to me, always grinning and cheerful. His social circle encompassed many of the college characters I considered worth trying to know better.

Styling myself Roni was an advantage for Bomber, who could manage to call me Ron. Veronica McNamara and its eight syllables was way beyond his memory and verbal dexterity. He frequently amused himself by singing at me "Doo de, doo de, Ron Ron!" I assumed this tuneless chant was derived from the song Da Doo Ron Ron by the Crystals. The lyrics remained incomplete, retrieved from the small part of his brain which constituted his memory. He would then guffaw with laughter for quite some time.

Even eighteen years after my birth my name continued to be the subject of friction at home. Dad used the un-shortened version at every available opportunity, mostly to irritate Mum. He said he liked it because of the blue flowers of the same name and because

Veronica in the Bible was a compassionate and kind person who wiped away Christ's tears and ended up with an image of him on her hankie. Having been brought up a Catholic, the instruction he'd received was seared into his consciousness.

Mum would raise an incredulous eyebrow when this reason for his choice of name was trotted out. This was because she considered it hypocritical for, in the tradition of many Roman Catholics, he was truly lapsed.

"Isn't it just a lovely reminder of the sixth station of the cross and our Lord's final journey?" Gran would state if Dad was describing the origin of my name. His bogus explanation served a double purpose – annoying my mother and currying favour with his own.

The reality was that my father liked the name because Veronica Lake, a sultry 1940s film star with long silky hair, was someone he had fantasised about since he was a boy. It was an irritation to Mum that he had got his way, because she suspected the real reason for his choice. "She was an alcoholic with a string of husbands. Her real name wasn't even Veronica." Dad would remain silent. This piqued Mum, who was after a confession that he had chosen it because of the film star and not the hankie and flower nonsense, but he never took the bait.

It didn't really matter. Any comparison between me and the poor woman ended with the name. A curly-haired dark redhead, I have never managed to recreate the buttery-blonde cascade of hair that flopped alluringly over one of her eyes. She was barely five feet tall and I am nearly ten inches taller. If I worried that this might be a disappointment to my father, I only had to remember that if the coin had landed the other way I would have gone through life as Brenda. Thank God no-one at college knew that.

Bomber, whose real name, I discovered, was Ralph StJohn, loved nothing better than to belittle some poor serf who didn't know that he really ought to call him Raife Sinjin. Luckily for most of us, ignorant of the ways of the pretentious snob, he was almost always known by his nickname.

Names were important in Bomber and Binka's club. If nothing else, I realised, my names would be a bar to entry, particularly the middle one. Of course, they would have come across a Brenda, but she would be someone who cleaned Mummy and Daddy's silver or came up from the village to help in the kitchen. She was only ever going to be ancillary staff.

Binka, as a girl, was only an honorary member of the collection of Peregrines, Cosmos, Tarquins and Caspians that Bomber hung about with. The Grahams, Steves, Geoffs and Martins from the boys' school in Barking, would have been wasting their time even to hope for election to Bomber's crew; they'd have been blackballed immediately for having such dull names.

It did occur to me that Binka and her female chums, Widget, Pinkie, Nic-nac and Dizzie, who fringed the male core of the hip set, may well have adopted such nicknames to disguise a normal sounding Jacqueline, Denise or Susan. I had no proof, just the slight whiff of a cover up. Binka's own given name remained a mystery I never solved.

I couldn't ask what her first name was and there was no label on the door. There was no need; everyone knew it was her room. And it remained very much her room. I was an inconvenience that she had to accept to avoid being charged double for the space, but she left no doubt that I was unwelcome.

My access to the elite was made easier by Bomber's undeniable affability. He certainly didn't give me the cold shoulder or the impression he thought I was anything other than someone who might appear desirable to the merry band.

"What are you reading?" I asked him once bravely, hoping to discover which faculty of the University had the pleasure of the hearty chuckle on a regular basis. He was hanging about in our room, waiting for Binka to arrive. I picked my moment. I wouldn't have dared to talk to him if she was there. I wasn't sure what the reaction might be.

"Reading?" he replied. "Hmm, nothing just at the minute. Not a big fan of books. Not like you. You've got absolutely loads of them." He paused as if he had observed something quite unique within the confines of the college. He racked his tiny brain for a connection with print. "I look at page three in The Sun!" I think this was supposed to shock or unnerve me, which it did, although it was likely to be true. Undoubtedly the rest of the paper would be too taxing, but he certainly could have given the impression of keeping up to date with world news by gawping at a woman with no top on.

We were often awkwardly together in the room, both awaiting Binka's arrival. He there for his after-lunch appointment, taxiing about the room prior to take-off, and me on alert for the cue to piss off for the next half hour or so.

"Bonking anyone?" he asked out of the blue one day. It was a casual enquiry, as if he was politely asking about the weather or my health. He must have known the answer, unless he thought my sorties took place elsewhere.

"You're a choice bit of totty," he leered. But instead of being offended, I took the compliment, despite sensing the possibility of the hint of an invitation. Going on operations with Bomber was not something I or anyone in her right mind would consider. Quite apart from the issues of repulsion, who would be willing to take on the repercussions when Binka found out?

She spoke to me rarely and only ever about my making myself scarce from the room or mistakenly waking her up before lunch. She was always rude and unpleasant. At least she was consistent. Not only was she never nice to me, she was bad-tempered and foul-mouthed to everyone, including Bomber, who presumably didn't mind. Possibly he was too stupid to notice.

I foolishly considered I'd made some headway in getting in

with the right crowd. They'd all join in with Bomber in a chorus of tuneless da-dooing ending with a triumphant 'Ron Ron' when I appeared. This made me feel a preposterous glow of pride when I was with other less cool people who would be totally ignored.

I had supervisions with my year group and I went to lectures with Mary and we ended up eating in the hall together with the other girls from the brutalist block. None of them could see why I was happy to live in the room I did or consort with the crowd who hung about there.

"I met her on a Monday…" bellowed a patrician voice across the dining hall. Then he was joined by a chant of "Ron Ron!"

A girl called Penny, who had the dubious pleasure of being in charge of the cocoa rota, looked concerned. I barely spoke to her, but she was a friend of Mary and frequently in her wake. She often wore a corduroy pinafore dress and corralled her hair with hairclips, ensuring that there was never a moment when she might look remotely attractive. She was very efficient, often first to the library to get hold of the limited copies of the week's recommended books. I loathed her precise perfection and neatness. This was a girl who wrote the date and title (underlined twice) on the top of her page before she got to the lecture in order not to waste time doing so whilst she was there. Want to borrow a pen or find a piece of blotting paper? Look no further. She'd lend you anything, but only with a withering sigh at your lack of preparation and long entreaty to ensure you returned it at the end of the session. I'd rather have written notes in my own blood than give Penny the satisfaction of lending me an ink cartridge for my empty pen.

"Roni," she began, "I think you're very good how you never react to those dreadful boys teasing you. That's absolutely the right thing to do. Ignore it and hold your head up high. Well done," she added patronisingly.

Silly Penny couldn't see it was a sign of acceptance. At least I thought it was. Who did she know in the third year? Did anyone call out to her when she walked around college? Did anyone even notice her? I was incensed. But she had planted a seed.

Unlike Bomber, whose features were over-large and whose physique looked like someone's first attempt to make a man out of plasticine, most of his group were attractive in a rather predictable kind of way. Perhaps it was the air of superiority and entitlement which hung about them like an expensive perfume that added to their allure and seduced me into having what Gran would call 'wicked thoughts'.

I began to realise that success with the inner clique was not only unlikely but probably undesirable. It was doubtful I'd be bringing a Lysander or an Ambrose back to Barking. An aloof toff called Atticus, whose nose stuck in the air as if a particularly pungent kipper well past its sell-by-date was permanently beneath it, had put me firmly in my place when I'd told him where I was from. "Barking? Where on earth is that? I thought that was something dogs did." He snorted with laughter as he turned towards someone who came from a more desirable page of the A – Z.

I still held a vain hope that the Captain of Boats might notice me. Despite spending a good deal of time on the river, he was much freer in his associations. Romance as a notion was not in the sphere of these young men, who, I was beginning to realise, viewed women in a far baser way. But Chummers's conquests were so frequent and legendary that presumably you just had to get within pulling distance at the right time and you'd be another notch on his oar.

Predictably, with such a huge pot of potential partners, and despite a non-existent sense of commitment to the feelings of any of them, he was spoiled for choice. This guy could afford to be fussy and left a trail of broken hearts and disappointed suitors in the wake of the college first boat as he rowed away from his latest win yet again.

I made no progress. University terms were short and busy. We were actually at home far more than we were at Cambridge. The eight weeks of term flew past at incredible speed. The end of the year, exams and May Week came surprisingly quickly.

Binka was unconcerned about her finals. She was, however, obsessed with 'stiffies'. Surprisingly, this turned out not to be something Bomber could provide whilst on yet another airborne mission. They were invitations on thick card which she displayed on the mantelpiece above the fireplace in our communal room. She was determined to collect not only as many as possible but all of those allowing access to what she considered the essential drinks or garden parties of the two weeks in June that were confusingly known as May Week.

I was looking at them one day whilst she and Bomber were dropping 1000 pounders over some unfortunate enemy. It was impossible not to tune in to Bomber's constant stream of radio contact with whichever Lincolnshire aerodrome he was keeping abreast of his mission.

Payload gone, they appeared at her door. Binka was wrapped in her dressing gown. "If you have any stiffies do put them up," she invited bitchily, expecting that no-one would have invited me anywhere.

"I have got one," I admitted gingerly. "For the Drama Soc. drinks on the Fellows' Lawn."

"Ha! Won't get a shag there," shouted Bomber, who was still wearing his brassiere flying helmet. "You're wasting your time, love."

It was difficult to see why Binka remained loyal to Bomber. Perhaps she just didn't have time for anyone else, such were the demands he placed upon her. As far as I was aware she was boringly faithful to the idiot. He was an enigma. How did he even end up at the university? He can't have had any A-levels.

"If you've only got one invite, you're going to be at a loose end for most of the week. Shame." Her hair was standing straight up on end. She looked like she'd been wired in to a high-voltage electricity supply to demonstrate static for an O-level Physics class.

Her unbrushed mop was in the fashion of the counter-Sloanes of the early 80s, voluminous 'big hair' which often added several inches to your height. Sometimes she stuck things in it: some glitter, a flower from the college herbaceous border or even fag ends or shards of boiled sweets – which I assumed had got there unintentionally.

Occasionally, Binka rambled on about 'art and the expressive medium', whatever that was. Bomber would pull a face and mince round the room in response. Binka ignored him. Sticking a statement Rizla paper amongst the high-piled crown could easily have been a comment on homophobia or existentialism. Either way, it was lost on Flying Officer Stupido and frankly on me. I don't think she expected either of us to have any valuable opinions and certainly not to discuss them with her if we did.

In fact, I also had some other invites. My tutor was having a party on one of the college lawns. Together with the promise of the tedium of his earnest conversation was the knowledge that he was a zealous tee-totaller. Not only was he fabled for his surprisingly brightly coloured non-alcoholic concoctions but also for his parsimony with any crisps or titbits to accompany them. Not much hilarity or sophistication there, I feared.

The brutalist block was having a joint tea party for a group of girls who had birthdays in June. Different types of tea were to be on offer and a selection of cakes. I had been introduced to a Chinese tea called Lapsang Souchong and to Earl Grey as the daytime tipples of the Cocoa Club. Neither was what Nan, myself and certainly not my father would call a proper cup of tea. You wouldn't find that kind of dishwater in his Thermos. The former tasted like the remains of a garden bonfire and the latter like watered-down perfume. Neither was served with milk which, I have to admit, for teatime with Binka, who always had pints of yoghurty cheese or fully separated curds and whey festering somewhere in our room, would have been an advantage. Despite the lack of Sainsbury's Red Label, there were likely to be huge chunks of homemade cake. So, I had decided to turn up, grab a slice of butter-creamed Victoria sponge and push off before they could make me drink the evil brew on offer.

Elizabethans, a rather pompous English Literature society which had very few members, were having a 'Novels and Nibbles' party. It wasn't clear whether any drinking would accompany the nibbling. They invited anyone who was reading English, in fact anyone who could read. Even Bomber might qualify under that criterion, if the standardised reading age required wasn't too high.

None of those invitations was going on the mantelpiece. It would be like swinging a matador's red cloak at a raging bull.

Binka lit a roll-up. She hadn't made one for Bomber. She examined her collection of stiffies. You needed a strong constitution to cope with these endless events if you were lucky enough to be invited to several on the same day. One caught my eye – the college Boat Club. Punch in the boathouse at noon. I knew who would be there, his eye roving for a new conquest. This was my last chance realistically. He was graduating in the summer and moving on to an even larger river in which to stick his oar. Binka must have seen the look in my eye.

"I don't think so," she admonished, and for a minute I worried that she could read my thoughts. "It's very small. And select. You have to be invited by one of the crews."

A relief: she had no idea about my lust for the captain. She was merely reiterating her importance in the college in case I hadn't taken on board her high social position relative to my non-existent one. Why she felt the need to emphasise it was unclear. The last two-and-a-bit terms living within earshot of her every movement told me everything I needed to know.

She didn't know about my plan either. A small gathering? Who was small and unlikely to have a guaranteed guest for his invite? Simeon Goldblatt's lucky day had arrived.

Pole position

7

Ma y Week – the fortnight in June when students had completed exams but were ignorant of the results and were in pursuit of vast quantities of alcohol. There were college balls in the evenings and club and society parties in the afternoons and often in the mornings as well. It's hard to remember precisely.

On the morning of the Boat Club party, I woke late. As Bomber had predicted, I had returned from the Drama Soc. drinks with only the promise, now fulfilled, of a lingering and persistent hangover. I felt nauseous as I struggled to get dressed and be out of the room in time to get to the boathouse before Simeon Goldblatt. If he survived to the day of the party without being dismembered as part of a forfeit doled out in one of Bomber's drinking games, I had decided that, despite being the kind donor of my ticket, I did not want to arrive with him.

"I'll be able to fill you in on the PhD I've been accepted for. It's about how macromolecules form part of polymer chains," he promised. I couldn't wait.

It was the end of term; trips to the launderette weren't high on my agenda. I was down to the final clean pair of pants. Old, large and baggy, I'd worn them at school for PE and they were all that was lurking at the bottom of my drawer.

Bloomers is what Nan called pants. "No, people say 'smalls' these days," Mum would correct her, not entirely sure, as ever, that this was in fact what the right kind of person called them. In this case, smalls would definitely have been a misnomer.

Naturally, not only were they regulation school uniform style, huge and made from indestructible fabric, but they had a large nametape on the outside. Big red letters announced my name in capitals. Mum had insisted on having it all. "There's no extra cost and it'll be useful in case there is anyone else with a similar name." Fat chance. How many people in Barking in the late 1970s, let alone at my school, would have had a name even similar to VERONICA B. McNAMARA? They didn't do tapes long enough to include my whole middle name. For that at least I was thankful.

I'd never actually spoken to the Brooke-like Chummers, or read any poems written by him for that matter. He did smile at me once when our paths crossed leaving the library. That was enough. I didn't care if he wrote the worst doggerel; we would have a passionate affair possibly ending in him dying of sepsis like the poet. I wasn't sure about that bit. Brooke's end was decidedly unromantic and not as heroic as my imagination would prefer. But nobody's perfect.

Chummers's personality was irrelevant in this fantasy. If I'd thought about it long enough, I could have probably worked out more than I wished to know about how he operated in relation to other people. Like the idealism of Rupert, I ignored it.

It was a hot day and I'd had nothing to eat, not an ideal combination however appealing the Cam looked as I approached the boathouse. If she'd seen what I was wearing, Gran would have been round her rosary at least three times by the time I arrived ready for action.

There were several of these buildings on the banks of the river. They had gables, fake wooden beams on the outside and garage-like doors on the ground floor. Ours had an outside spiral staircase leading to a balcony giving views onto the river. Downstairs, behind the doors, were stacks of ridiculously long and thin craft for eight rowers on racks, one above the other. There were also smaller boats for four, two or just a single rower. A faint air of damp hung about the place.

I showed my invitation to the two Boat Club members acting as bouncers outside and climbed the spiral staircase to the balcony. Beyond it was an indoor room with oars mounted on the walls and shields and cups displayed in cabinets. A huge punch bowl and glasses had been placed temptingly on a table by the side of the entrance.

One advantage of being early was that you got a full glass of punch with very little of the fruit salad lurking at the bottom of the bowl. It tasted potent but sweet, just what you need if you've got a touch of low blood sugar on a hot day. The first one went down very quickly and I got myself a second, not only to quench my thirst but because there was no-one in the room I recognised. I pretended to be fascinated by the trophy cabinet so I didn't look too awkward. There was no sign of Chummers.

After drink number three, I decided to go onto the balcony and pretend to be looking out at the river. That's what someone with an abiding interest in rowing might do, I reasoned. The punch now tasted a little sickly so I asked for some of the fruit to be put in my glass as well, reasoning that that might soak it up a bit.

A saving grace from staring at the water outside came in the form of someone I vaguely knew from the English faculty. "Hello, Roni, didn't know you were a rower," he said.

"I'm not. I've never been in a boat in my life. Well…that's not factually correct, actually. Last summer I went in a Cross Channel Ferry across the sea to France. And back." I laughed hysterically. "And I've also been on the lake in Barking Park in a boat, but I wasn't in charge of the oars." I was aware I was rambling.

"How many of those have you had? It tastes quite potent to me."

"Not enough!" I protested, "Get me another will you?"

He obliged but wisely made his excuses when he delivered it.

"You've got a mint leaf between your teeth," was his parting, confidence-boosting comment.

Chummers was still nowhere to be seen. I made do with another couple of lads in stripy college blazers. I didn't know who they were. They didn't mind my nonsense because, like me, they were on punch number four or five. It may even have been more.

The glasses of early arrivals were adorned with a paper umbrella in Cambridge blue. Latecomers, I noticed, did not get one because they had run out. No trophy to take back to your room to show that you'd really been there. I was very proud of my umbrella and determined to hang on to it to show Binka.

Several top-ups later, whilst trying to illustrate a particularly animated story, I knocked the umbrella out of the glass and it flew a considerable way before landing under a table. I should have left it.

I recognised that stooping anywhere near the floor was risky given the heels I was wearing and the potency and speed of intoxication that the drink was providing. But I wanted it back. As I bent down, performing a sliding manoeuvre which might be described as a cross between a one-legged version of the splits and part of a Cossack dance, there was an unmistakeable ping and a certain loosening of fabric around what Nan used to refer to as 'the nether regions'.

I'm too fat now for elastic to serve much of a purpose in my knicker world. It might leave a bit of a red line if I wear some of the smaller pairs in my collection, but generally it is not essential. As in the magician's trick, where a cloth is drawn from the table but the crockery remains, my pants stay up regardless, caught by the folds of middle-aged spread.

In those days, when postpartum sag and menopausal thickening were just a promise of the life to come, it served a vital purpose. Unfortunately, as the underwear in question was past its prime, inevitably a certain fatigue was showing in the stretch department.

After the ping, my first objective was to get up. This was not easy given my balance was suffering and kneeling with one leg outstretched in front is not an easy starting position, even before you have sloped to one side. Having reached as far as I could under the table for my umbrella, I was beached like an inebriated whale on the boathouse floor. Several people, including the boys I'd been chatting to, were laughing. I refused their offer of help, knowing that if I didn't clench my legs on the way up there would be knickers round my ankles to add to the amusement.

It was at this moment that Simeon Goldblatt arrived.

"Veronica, are you OK?"

"Yes, thank you very much. I am fine. Just looking for my umbrella."

"Umbrella? You won't need that. The forecast doesn't predict rain at all. I checked." No-one could accuse Simeon of being unprepared for any eventuality, though the one presenting itself just at that moment was undeniably challenging.

"It's a little, tiny umbrella. A weeny one on a titchy stick and it was in the top of my glass until very recently." I realised I was slurring and was acutely aware that I kept using words like little, tiny and weeny. "Small," I spluttered unintentionally. "Not you, but the umbrella. You're actually quite big. Relatively. The umbrella would be too miniature even for you." I managed to stop myself saying any more.

"Have you been drinking the punch, Veronica?"

"Of course. That's how I got the umbrella. Can you see it? It's under the table."

Simeon, who hadn't had anything to drink, bent down and easily retrieved the rather crushed-looking umbrella. He gave it to me and I stuck it behind my ear for safe keeping, a sort of homage to Binka-like hair decoration. I only had use of one hand because the other was holding up the pants through my skirt.

"Dear me," he began, "They've just realised that the Secretary of the Boat Club has mis-read the instructions for mixing the cocktail. He confused metric and imperial units. It's easily done if you don't check first. The recipe was in pints and fluid ounces and the drink is sold in litres. Today Pimm's is sold as a 70cl bottle, that's just over a pint, and lemonade, a large bottle that is, which is two litres, about three and a half pints." I burped loudly in response. "Ideally the ratio is 3:1, a large bottle of lemonade to a bottle of Pimm's. Quite simple, really. However, the problem occurred where he tried to convert the units, metric to pints or vice versa, quite unnecessarily."

"Really, how absolutely uninteresting," I said by mistake. Fortunately, I was slurring so badly that it came out as one long word ending in 'interesting'.

"I'm afraid you have been drinking a concoction of seven pints of Pimm's to two pints lemonade. 3 and a half to one and the wrong way round!" he chortled, oblivious to the chaos around him caused by this monstrous mistake.

Speech eluded me. I smiled inanely.

"Better get her up," someone suggested. Thankfully, this was not left entirely to Simeon. Several people, most of them suffering from the calculation error themselves, joined in to heave me from the floor. All the time I was clinging to the knickers with one hand. Eventually, once I was reasonably upright, someone slung my other hand and arm over Simeon's shoulder. Surprisingly he was the perfect size to enable me to use him as a kind of crutch and we stumbled out onto the balcony and towards the spiral staircase.

"Going down!" I shouted with a flourish as my finale to the assembled crowd. I wasn't sure where we were going, or why, and didn't particularly care.

I couldn't hold on to the banister because one hand was holding up the elastic-free pants and the other was grabbing onto Simeon. He was one step ahead, to prevent me tumbling down. It seemed a long journey to the bottom.

"Here's hoping the Secretary isn't going on to a career where quantities matter. Oncology, say, or chemical weapons production," Simeon snorted from somewhere just in front of me. All I could manage now were hiccoughs.

When we got to within sight of the river, I was unable to stand unaided. The world was spinning.

"Sime-e-nun," I said, "I need to do a very large wee. Very soon."

Fortuitously, because he was the cox, he knew the layout of the downstairs part of the boathouse where the boats were kept and where there was a basic lavatory, the type where people say, "You'd be better off going elsewhere. That's a boys' loo."

What they mean is: there are plenty of spiders but no paper; the seat, if it is present at all, is permanently up; the floor is covered in poorly aimed urine. There's also probably a window through which outsiders can look (or at least pretend they are going to). Inevitably, the flush only works one pull in four; if you're there after three previous visits all sorts of joy awaits in the pan. Once wedged into this cabin, holding your nose, on top of everything else there is no lock.

Once inside I could use my other hand and let the knickers descend as they had been trying to do for the last half hour. I dropped onto the cold pan, not centrally but fortunately far enough across to prevent other mishaps. Getting up again was a challenge. My feet were caught up in the pants and I could only get one out. There was nothing to grab hold of to heave myself upwards. I was shaking the other leg trying to free it from the clinging knicker whilst grabbing for the chain dangling above me. It sounded like I was kicking on the door.

"I'm opening the door to help, but I'm not looking," announced Simeon. He was speaking in a loud, clear voice, separating the words from each other. It was like he was evacuating a building or explaining he was about to try to defuse an unexploded bomb.

As he opened the door with one hand, he was looking pointedly in the other direction and shielding his eyes with the other hand.

At last, the pant was free of my foot. I was underwear free and could feel the breeze now blowing off the river. "I'm feeling a bit better, and I'd like to go in a boat and read poems with Rupertchummers," I announced.

"I'm not sure you would," replied Simeon, steadying me with his door opening, non-shielding hand. "Are you decent?" I belched. Simeon took his shield away and looked relieved to see I was fully clothed. "The Captain of Boats has just been violently sick into the first eight's new shell. I won't be going out on the river in that tomorrow," he reported.

In the dark corner of the space was the unmistakable, fine figure of Monroe Cholmondeley. But it was bent in half and he was groaning.

"Piss right off, Goldblatt." He spoke in a weak voice quite unlike his usual smooth, confident burr. The pungent odour of vomit wafted towards us with the breeze.

Once outside the boathouse and all along the towpath, Simeon had to support me. I could put one leg in front of the other but in a random and unsure way which made locomotion unpredictable. I was like a newly born foal trying to stand for the first time.

We crossed some grass as a shortcut back to college. My heels sank into the moist earth, which meant I had to pull up each foot with incredible force to dislodge it before I could take the next step. I was like a moonwalker wading through quicksand. Simeon kept up a commentary on how he should have realised this was going to happen.

"The surface area to weight ratio is the problem with that kind of footwear on this kind of ground," he began, before calculating the pounds to square inch ratio of me to my slim but tall heels. "I'm not entirely sure how much you weigh of course but I'm taking a probable guess based on looking at you." I remained silent but would have kept the vital information quiet, even if I had been able to speak.

After an indeterminate period of floundering about, lurching uncontrollably nearer to Simeon Goldblatt than I really wanted, we were back in college at the staircase to my room. I couldn't climb it alone. That was quite clear. So up he came.

"Cleared for take-off!" shouted an unmistakeable voice as we opened the door. Fortunately, this announcement referred to the imminent departure of Binka and Bomber, presumably to the boathouse for a post-coital cocktail. "Hey, look at Goldman! You're stronger than I thought, old chum!"

I would have hit Bomber, hard, if I could have co-ordinated my arm and found enough strength to do so. He held open the door to my bedroom as Simeon guided me through and I managed to project myself face first onto the bed.

"Whoopee!" Bomber exclaimed, "She hasn't got any undercrackers on!"

My short skirt had flipped up as I lunged, revealing my lack of underwear. Bomber was snorting with excitement; his propellers were rotating, ready for action.

"Nice arse, eh, Golding? Hey, Binka, fancy going commando at the boathouse?" But Binka had left and Bomber followed.

My hand floundered behind my prostrate back, trying to pull down my dress. I couldn't do it and I couldn't get up. Out of the corner of my eye I saw Simeon's face colour red. He delicately used two fingers as if he was touching some ancient, fragile manuscript to place the skirt back over my bare bottom. "Smimenon," I said, "I think I'm going to be sick."

He picked up my waste bin from under the desk and managed to get it in the correct position just as I threw up. I remember thinking it was lucky that it contained some notes on the romantic poets that I'd thrown away, because they slowed the drip of vomit through the holes of the wicker basket.

When I woke up, it was obvious some hours had passed. The light was different. My curtains were partly closed and there was an extremely unpleasant smell in the room. It reminded me of the secretary's office at junior school. There was always some puking child in there holding a bucket whilst waiting for its mum to come and take it home. I sat up. God, I felt rough. Then I saw Simeon sitting on the floor in the corner. He'd been reading one of my books.

"You're still here?" I said rather obviously. I noticed that the wastepaper basket had been replaced by the bowl from the sink in the communal kitchen. Thankfully it was empty, apart from a couple of tannin-stained cups which Simeon had omitted to remove.

"I thought I ought to make sure you had finished vomiting," Simeon stated matter of factly. "There have been a number of incidences when people have inhaled their own vomit because they are inebriated. It causes aspiration pneumonia. I suppose you could say you drown in your own sick whilst you are asleep." I felt nauseous again immediately. He laughed. How could anyone be amused by being put in the situation I'd created?

"It smells in here." This was the beginning of my apology.

"I took the precaution of opening the window. I hope you don't mind."

"I'm sorry." There, I'd said it. "You've had to sit in here all this time. It must have been very unpleasant." My voice rasped. I was thirstier than I'd ever been.

"I anticipated dehydration." He indicated a glass of water placed by the side of my bed. "And I passed the time reading about Dylan Thomas." He tapped the book. "Very interesting. I've discovered he wrote much of his work in a boathouse." He chortled at the co-incidence. "Famously, he was a great drinker, of course, as was his wife. Did you know she was a McNamara? Ironic."

I drank the water in one. Was Simeon Goldblatt being pointed and arch? I decided he was incapable of being nasty; he was just matter of fact.

"They met in a pub," I added, though I expect he already knew this. Simeon was bound to have read the biography thoroughly. No skimming through and reading the last chapter first like I did.

"Do you think you'll be sick again?" he asked. I shook my head. "Well, I'd better take this back then." He picked up the bowl and opened my door.

Just then Bomber and Binka arrived back. "Who-hoo!" Bomber was grinning. "Still here? Good one!" He thrust his fist in the air as he said this. "Had a cup of tea to celebrate? Good on you," he exclaimed, indicating the bowl. "Don't suppose you want any more booze. You bastards drank the lot! Goldthingummy, he's the man with the golden knob!" he sang, making a pistol with two of his fingers and posing like James Bond. "Got there at last, eh?" His musical 007 theme continued tunelessly with the few words he could recall of *Nobody Does It Better*, "The cox who loved me… Do de do de do de do de do de doooo."

"Shut the fuck up, Bomber," said Binka. You could tell she was cross. "I'm bloody pissed off. Not a drink in sight and we went all the way there! Chummers could barely speak and most people had gone on somewhere else. Who bloody organised a party without enough drink?"

"As a matter of fact, there was an error…" began Simeon, who was about to explain the intricacies of the imperial to metric miscalculation. Binka clearly did not require a response to her question.

"Oh, it was worth going to see your panties up the flagpole!" guffawed Bomber, who was poor at knowing when he ought to shut up. "Congrats, old girl. That's the best laugh I've had all day. Flappy flappy, flying in the breeze." His non-pistol hand pretended to be a pennant in the wind. Then the other's pistol imitated shooting it down. "007 at your service, Madam."

"You have no proof that they are Veronica's undergarments," Simeon protested.

Bomber grinned. "Oh yes we do! They've got her name on. Bloody great letters. The whole of Cambridge knows." His tone lowered in admiration. "Chummers must have hoist them up there. You got your shag at last. Pissed as a fart and still able to give her one. You've got to admire him." Binka scowled but Bomber carried on, "Two in one afternoon. And you're in good company, Goldenknob! Put the kettle on, mate, will you?"

I still felt sick and my head was thumping. Simeon left with the bowl. He didn't return.

8
Brief Encounter

I had returned to bed having drunk several pints of water and taken more than the recommended dose of paracetamol to try and kill the gremlins with pickaxes who were trying to burrow their way through my skull.

I woke up with a start. In Binka's bedroom, Bomber was carrying out a raid over enemy territory complete with the sound effects of the explosion of large ordnance. It was dark.

"Hello, Red leader, over. We've passed the flak over the coast. Whisky Tango coming in for landing. Bomb doors up, wheels down. Landing commencing. Roger and out."

There was a long groan which I guessed was his undercarriage hitting the tarmac. Operations over, I decided to make a bid for the lavatory at the end of the corridor, hoping they wouldn't see.

When I returned, they were both standing by the window of the communal room looking out. "What the fuck is that?" Binka asked. She was wrapped in a sheet and looked like a classical statue. "It's kind of red."

"Dunno." I wasn't surprised that Bomber didn't know the answer to a question. "Ron Ron, what do you think?" He beckoned me to the window. I was conscious that I probably didn't smell too fresh and tried not to get too close.

Even from where I was standing there was an obvious red glow in the sky. It was coming from the direction of the river. "Looks like a fire."

"Oh great, a bonfire! I wonder if there'll be fireworks."

Bomber was excited and began putting his flying jacket on. On cue we heard the sound of an emergency vehicle siren from the same direction.

"It could be a boathouse," Binka suggested.

"A proper fire with engines! Let's go and have a look!" Bomber was like a small child, jumping up and down as he pulled on his enormous boots. He had the biggest feet I'd ever seen and even in the height of summer wore leather boots with thick soles which made his feet sweat. The only thing disguising the stench emanating from my room was the overpowering odour of Bomber's socks.

Neither Binka nor I were tempted. "I'll go on my own, then."

We continued to watch from the window. You couldn't see flames but you could hear people outside and see their outlines against the glowing sky. We could make out Bomber moving at quite a pace in the direction of the river.

Binka opened the window further and called out, "Hey, Muffy, you fucker, what's going on?" This was the endearing way in which Binka spoke to her best friends.

It was a boathouse, we learned from Muffy, who seemed to be very well informed. It was fully alight and there were two engines down there trying to put it out.

Even Binka looked slightly animated at the news. "Want a roll-up?" In the two terms we had been roommates she had never once offered me anything. No tea, no coffee and certainly not one of her tobacco creations.

You had to hand it to her. She was a master at the roll-up, a skill I'd never mastered. She licked the Rizla provocatively and sealed the perfectly formed fag. She looked at me quizzically as she offered me a light as well. Things were looking up; we were getting all cosy and chummy.

"You're a dark horse," she commented eventually. "I'd got you wrong. Tell me, how did you get Chummers in the sack? I've been trying to do that for over a year."

"Not in the sack," I started. My head was spinning. A non-filtered cigarette was not the best hangover cure. This was the moment when I could explain about the elastic and the descending pants, how they'd been left in the boathouse by mistake. A bit of tobacco was loose from the end of the roll-up. I had to pull it out of my mouth before I could speak.

"Ok, yeah, I know not literally, but you know what I mean. I heard he likes to do it in the double sculls: cosier, fewer rowlocks." She grinned; I assumed in case there was a double entendre to be had as well as some factual information.

Binka left me no time to explain further. "Has he got a huge dong?" she asked. Her uncouth frankness disarmed me. I was used to her foul language and base conversation but usually I was an eavesdropper. Here I was, the only person other than her in the room, a participant in a duologue. I couldn't reply. "You know – dick," she continued. Before I was required to reply she'd moved on to my assumed second encounter. "And then that little coxy chap. Two in one bloody afternoon. It must have been interesting one after the other." She looked thoughtful. "Just because you're knee high to a grasshopper doesn't mean you've got a tiny dick. Quite the contrary sometimes. Perhaps he's better hung than Chummers. What a thought? How do they compare?" This was an earnest enquiry and she seemed genuinely interested.

"I wouldn't like to say," was the best I could manage without committing myself to assessments. The truth was that comparative dicks hadn't formed part of my A-level studies and didn't seem to be on the syllabus for part one of the English Literature Tripos at the university. Indeed, where 'dongs' were concerned I was a novice.

I'd once burst into the bathroom when my dad hadn't locked the door and was drying himself after a bath. This had been a shocking yet not particularly informative experience. We were a very female household and family. There were no standards by which to assess my father's equipment and, I thought after the quick glimpse I got before he wrapped the towel round the offending area, it was pretty unappealing anyway. I had no brothers or male cousins, just Uncle Pat, who, when he came to see us, only presented his face and clothed body for comparative purposes. He looked quite like my dad but spruced up a bit. I assumed the rest of him was pretty similar.

Despite lusting after Chummers, my infatuation with Rupert Brooke and my constant close proximity to the coupling of Binka and Bomber, I hadn't really thought about the reality of a physical relationship. I hadn't had a boyfriend and the naive notion of romantic love that I had cherished all this time suddenly, in that moment, seemed pathetic. I realised that I hadn't really moved on from discussing which of the Osmonds I preferred with my schoolmates and kissing Donny's picture on my bedroom wall before I went to sleep.

"You're being too polite. How sweet." Binka was being nice to me. This too was a revelation. "Us girls have got to stick together."

I was surprised by her friendship and smiled at her. She smiled back warmly. "You can ask me anything you want," she confided in a grown-up-sister kind of way.

"There is one thing I'd like to know."

"Go on…"

"You know Bomber…" I realised that this was a ludicrous way to begin. Of course she did. They went on missions over enemy territory at least three times a day on weekdays. He practically lived in our rooms. Binka braced herself for what was coming next.

"What subject is he reading?"

There was a silence. I thought I had blown it. She was expecting to offer some experienced rogering advice and I was more concerned with his academic profile.

"Christ, he's not at the bloody university!" She buckled up in hysterics at the thought. "He can barely write his sodding name.

I had to teach him to tell the time. He still gets the big hand and the little hand confused."

"So what's he doing here?" I didn't understand. I knew he was stupid but, contrary to popular belief outside the university, within it I had discovered some very stupid people.

"He lives with the chaplain, his uncle. He was just hanging about at home getting in the way, so his mother sent him to live with her brother. She thought he might learn something. I might have taught him some things," she added cheekily.

Somehow, I managed to ask Binka the next question by facial expression alone. I guess it was a question on a lot of people's minds: what on earth do you see in him?

"He's heir to a castle and a massive estate in Scotland. His dad's a duke. Bloody loaded they are. They've got a town house in Cheyne Walk and a villa at Cap Ferrat. Really nice place. The chaplain is a dopey git. He's got no idea what Bomber is up to. Bomber just has to show his face in Chapel on a Sunday and the rest of the week they plough their own furrows. Works rather well for both of them, really. Oh, and he's a great shag." She tacked this on to the end, as if it made her acquisitive pursuit of money and status slightly less brazen. "He's got incredible energy." With this I had to agree.

It explained why Bomber never ate in Hall, his lack of even the most basic stationery and his inability to understand relatively simple words. It even explained why I thought I'd seen his massive bulk disappearing into the chapel one Sunday morning when I'd got up early by mistake, thinking it was a Monday.

I slept fitfully that night, thirsty, nursing a bad head and convinced that in future I would never again touch any alcohol. In the morning, when I could stay in bed no longer, I decided to go out for some fresh air.

There were few people about, unsurprisingly as the previous day had been what was known as Suicide Sunday. This was the name given to the Sunday which separated the two weeks of May Week, the day with the most parties and maximum drinking opportunities. I walked down to the river and along the path to see what had happened the previous night.

As well as the unmistakable smell of burning which hung in the air, a police cordon blocked the tow path. I realised with some horror that it was our boathouse that had caught fire. 'DANGER: No Entry' read a large sign. Parts of the building were still smouldering and the doors of the part where the boats were kept were charred and hanging off their hinges. The fire had burned parts of the balcony, including the spiral staircase from which I had made my final gracious exit from the party only the day before. The flagpole at the other end of the balcony had survived and from it, slightly sooty, drooping in a lacklustre way, hung my pants. The feeble breeze meant they were almost immobile and the name was now not as visible as Bomber had described. Only selected letters were on show.

Had I been able to, would I have got them down? This conundrum occupied me as I walked back to college. How had they got there? Bomber and Binka had assumed Chummers had relieved me of them as some kind of trophy. Would other people know that the singed VnaMNr that you could make out on the label was me and draw the same conclusion? At least the unattractive nature of the garment could be attributed to fire damage. The whitest knickers in M&S would look grey and tired if they'd been in close proximity to a blazing building.

I felt grey and tired myself as I reached the college. I really wasn't feeling well. Mary ran across the court towards me. "There you are, come on," she called. "I came to find you. You're late for the June birthdays party."

"Oh no! I can't. I just want coffee and sleep." The prospect of the Cocoa Club en masse swapping postcards of puppies with bows and embroidery tips was the last thing I needed.

"Then it's perfect. Lots of tea and coffee on offer. And some cake to soak up your hangover."

"How do you know I've got one?"

"Roni, everyone knows. You were quite the talk of the block last night."

Word had got round, then. I followed her. A large slice of sugary cake was probably what I needed.

A collection of dreary looking girls in their best flowery summer frocks were chatting excitedly on the grass outside the brutalist block beside a trestle table laid out with cakes and an urn. It had a pink tablecloth and some flowers in a jam jar. There was no alcohol visible, which in the circumstances was a relief. I got some odd looks as I arrived. There was a bit of whispering.

"Roni," said Perfect Penny with a concerned look on her face and a patronising tone in her voice. "How are you?" I was very glad I wasn't having to ask her to lend me a pencil or ruler.

There was a silence. "We're all really sorry." As person in charge of the cocoa making rota, she had obviously been appointed spokesperson. "I hope you're OK." She passed me a slice of cake on a plate. It was decorated with vanilla butter icing, piped rosettes and large chocolate buttons. One of the birthday girls' mums had brought it down from Lincolnshire in a cake tin. I was unsure whether eating it would be wise, but I was certainly hungry. Other cakes on offer were a chocolate refrigerator cake, the ingredients of which I knew would send me in search of the nearest available vomit receptacle, and a flat, burned sponge which everyone was trying to avoid whilst saying how delicious it looked. Someone had donated a packet of custard creams which was not what was expected of a June Birthday girl. Nobody said anything but there were disapproving looks.

"Can I have a cup of tea to go with it?"

"Of course you can." The atmosphere was tense, as if someone I knew very well had died. There were some sympathetic noises.

"Your friend from the Boat Club is probably in big trouble," said a girl who I didn't even know the name of but had seen around. She wore her hair in ringlets, as if she was an extra in a Jane Austen serial on TV, and had a reputation for speaking frankly.

"Lizzie!" Several of the others admonished her. I supposed the news of my knickers flying from the pole horrified and fascinated them at the same time. Maybe they had made the same assumption as Bomber. I expected they might be jealous; even they couldn't have failed to notice Chummers's charms. Naughtily, I decided to egg them on.

"I doubt it," I replied.

"Really?" there was a horrified intake of breath.

"Has he done it before?"

"Of course. He just did it to amuse everyone!"

"People can't go around behaving like that, I don't think it's funny." Lizzie was on her high horse, disregarding the pointed looks of the others imploring her to show some sensitivity. "Well, the police are involved, anyway. I saw him being taken away in a panda car."

I was confused. How had this happened? Surely no-one had called the police about Chummers's behaviour. I'd already worked out that he'd probably found my pants on the floor of the boathouse and shoved them up the pole. Not everyone might share the joke but that wasn't an offence. "Police?" I queried.

"Arson is a crime. He's been arrested." There was no holding Lizzie back when she was in pursuit of the dissemination of unverified facts.

I must have looked shocked. "Oh Lord, she doesn't know. Poor Roni." Penny's arm went round my shoulders and her faced simpered close to mine. The other girls had gathered round to make sure they didn't miss anything. Chummers set light to the boat house? Why?

"There was thousands of pounds worth of rowing equipment

in there. Some of those boats are really expensive." Lizzie was cramming a large slice of butter-creamed cake into her mouth, presumably having taken advantage of the stupor which had overcome the rest of us in order to grab the last slice. "Apparently the Master was apoplectic," she continued, cake crumbs spouting from her mouth as she emphasised the syllables in this last word.

"But why?" I asked eventually. Chummers would never jeopardise the boat club and its equipment. It didn't make sense.

"He's going to be ok," chimed in another, her needle reaching maximum on her sympathy-o-meter. "They gave him first aid at the scene. He'd inhaled some smoke unfortunately."

"Apparently the firemen rescued him, from the balcony," explained another as if she was auditioning for some creaky melodrama. "He was clinging to the flagpole because the stairs were burning so furiously and there was no other way down." She was warming to the theme.

So Chummers was hoisting the pants when the flames had got out of control. I was flabbergasted.

"Still waters run deep," said a girl called Sue, who spoke rarely but only in aphorisms as far as I could tell. Not an appropriate example in this case anyhow, I thought.

"I've heard," continued Gill, whose careless monitoring of her running bath had provided my escape from the brutal concrete prison of these bores, "some people say it was because he was bullied by them. They're horrid those rowing thugs. Especially to their coxes. They weren't very nice to him." She paused to let everyone consider this statement. "He probably just snapped. He'd had enough. Even small people have feelings." She spoke with the conviction of the small and bullied and those who may have snapped in the past.

I could feel my temperature rising. I was hot and breathless. I thought I might pass out.

"I don't blame him. I hope the police take the abuse he put

up with into account," someone was saying as the world began to spin and I found myself falling to the floor.

"It's been a terrible shock for you." Penny was bending over me as I came to. "I'm so sorry; we thought everyone knew about poor Simon. It's been the talk of the college all day. Mary will take you back to your room if you like. Best have a lie down."

I didn't know which was worse. The simpering kindness of Penny, whose face I wanted to slap, or the appalling and unbelievable news which I had just heard.

Not Chummers but Simeon Goldblatt? It hardly seemed possible. I knew they treated him badly but arson was going a bit far. It was so irrational, and he was so sensible and oblivious to their comments, or so I thought. I picked myself up. At least I hadn't landed on my plate of cake, although I had sprayed the tablecloth with tea on the way down.

Lizzie hadn't finished her broadcast. "If he wasn't leaving anyway, I expect he would have been sent down. Can he still be awarded his degree if he is charged?" There was some quiet discussion about this.

"Come on," said Mary. "Let's go back to your room."

"Of course, his PhD is looking a bit unlikely now!" Lizzie was nothing if not persistent. "They won't have him back in this college. Nor in any other, I shouldn't think." She paused for effect. There was some tutting and sighing from her audience. "If you're not going to eat it, can I have your cake?" she asked me. "It only got a bit of grass on it when you collapsed."

The Liberty Bell does not ring for me

9

There's one Cambridge event which, certainly in my time, was worth going to – at least once. Despite the expensive ticket, a college May Ball was an experience not to miss. The cost meant that for many the main objective was to eat and drink as much as possible. Our ball was held on the Tuesday, unfortunately not long enough after the Boat Club fiasco for the effects of my hangover to have worn off.

In the 1980s, the dress code was formal. This made the university sport of trying to gate-crash more difficult. If you appeared at a ball in combat gear and a balaclava you were likely to get rumbled for having made a ticket-free entry.

For the colleges on the backs, gate-crashing usually meant arriving by water. Swimming across the Cam or even arriving by punt was a risky business when dressed like the fairy on the Christmas tree.

I certainly was dressed unusually. I could have been an extra in a Hollywood movie, perhaps doing a dance routine behind Judy Garland whilst she belted out a song about St Louis. I looked like a chorus girl, draped in yards of Technicolor fabric for the 'box social' in *Oklahoma!* or an antebellum Southern Belle swooning over Rhett or Ashley in *Gone with The Wind*. My ball gown was vast and luminous lilac. To be fair, it would have been a useful parachute if only I'd had a light aircraft, glider or even a hot air balloon to jump from. I could have crashed every ball in Cambridge in that dress with the right airborne transport and the nerve to jump out of a moving object into the night sky.

Imagine the fuss at The Mayfair Salon when I mentioned to Mum, in our weekly phone call, that I was going to a ball. The nearest she'd got to a ball was dancing at the Ilford Palais, where she'd first met my dad, one Saturday night when he'd been 'lucky on the gee-gees'. This had put him in an unusually good mood, and he'd wooed her with his sharp suit, narrow tie and ability to dance the jitterbug. Dad had hung his dancing shoes up a long time ago, so Mum danced alone in our through-lounge to records playing on the radiogram.

I used dream about dancing at a ball as a child, most of this reverie based on the Ladybird book *Cinderella*. In this version Cinders went to not one but three balls, presumably to pad out the story enough to fill the statutory size for a Ladybird book. Each time she wore a better dress than the last. She had a pink one the first night, a pretty blue one with lacy side panels on night two and finally a white sparkly one. I read this book and studied the pictures intently so often as a child, that I knew all the words by heart and can remember the images to this day.

Mum knew this and I think she thought she was doing me a favour when she asked Gran to make me a ball dress as a surprise. She was a dressmaker and had private clients as well as working in a West End department store doing alterations and adaptations for women who bought off-the-peg clothes and got Gran to make them look like couture. "I'm good with a needle," she'd tell me, "but I can't make a silk purse out of a sow's ear. The woman did not have the hips for a pencil skirt."

Mum and Gran admired Princess Diana's 1981 wedding dress. Gran was unusually complimentary. "It's a beautiful gown; sure, it's every bride's dream to be married in a frock like that." It wasn't my dream, but I understood why Gran, who'd been married during the depression, and Mum, who was married in a dress sewn out of an old pair of curtains, might think so.

Creating a lilac conflation of Cinderella's second night wonder and Diana's silk meringue was a triumph of imagination over style. Gran's re-incarnation as the fairy godmother meant that she waved her wand to produce an amalgamation of the two. It arrived at the Porters' Lodge by post in a large box a week before the ball and I'd had to hang it behind the door in my room because it wouldn't fit in the wardrobe. Gran had instructed I should hang it up to let any creases drop. Its vast bulk, with several underskirts and layers of net, was in the way of both opening and closing the door and it frequently got trapped around the frame and hinges.

"Christ, what's that?" asked Binka when she first caught sight of it seeping round the door like a lilac bubble bath that had got out of control. Now we were very much on speaking terms, she gave me a quizzical look and asked, "Where on earth did you buy it?"

"I didn't. It was made," I explained, completely truthfully. This was acceptable to Binka, who, although she didn't own or wear such things herself, was at least familiar with the concept of having a dressmaker run things up for you.

"Something of your mother's?" she asked with a knowing look. Binka's mother probably had a 'little woman', someone like my Gran, who copied couture frocks for her to pass off as the real thing.

I wasn't sure if Binka had noticed a patch on the dress, where I'd had to rub off the faint smears of sick that had been seeping through the wicker wastepaper basket when Simeon Goldblatt had carried it past on his way to dispose of it. But there again, Binka, in a sort of post punk way, might have considered this a positive addition.

Tickets to the May Ball were only sold in pairs. Mary had devised a plan to get round the awkward process of issuing (or waiting for) an invitation for those without partners. She'd gathered a group of eight people and we were attending as one party. No misunderstandings there, I hoped. I won't disguise the fact I would have rather been on the arm of Chummers but was realistic enough to know that this was unlikely.

Fortunately, Perfect Penny, Lizzie Tell-it-like-it-is and most of the other ghastly bedtime drink gang were not part of the group. If they were attending, they were paired up with drippy boyfriends from home. If opting out, they were sticking to the usual cocoa routine, turning in before the main events got going. Mary had got together some of the English group we shared supervisions and seminars with. They were not wildly exciting. This is not how I'd hoped the year would end.

I felt indifferent about the whole evening as I was putting on the lilac wonder. There was no fairy godmother to wave her wand and grant me a good time. No pumpkin transformed into a coach or mice morphed into white chargers to pull it. I'm sure Mum was hoping I'd lose one of my shoes and that a handsome prince, perhaps from a house even bigger than those in Upney Lane, would find it and be round at my room in the morning getting me to slip my foot inside. It didn't look much like this was going to happen.

We gathered in a boy called Tom's room before the Ball. Despite my dress and me taking up more than our fair share of the space available for so many people in such a small area, everyone was very interested to see if I had an insight into the boathouse affair. It was the most dramatic thing that had happened in college since a former Master had absconded in the 1930s with a good proportion of the college silver, some rare and valuable books and the wife of one of the porters.

"Weren't you at the Boat Club drinks party with Goldbloom the pyromaniac?" asked a particularly annoying boy called Julian Sousa. His main claim to fame was supposed kinship with John Philip Sousa, the American composer of marching band music. Consequently, he played records of these tunes very loudly in his room and kept his windows open. Undergraduates and dons alike were, however much they tried, unable to resist keeping in step as they passed by.

In addition, he played the sousaphone, a huge brass instrument named after his relative. It was so large that it had to be worn like a life belt slung around his neck and shoulder. Once he was inside it, his head poked up through the coils of tubing, making him look as if he'd been rescued after slipping on a canal towpath. Julian's enthusiasm for the low notes produced by the yards of pipe and massive brass bell was not matched by his ability with the instrument. You could be forgiven for thinking a large ship was coming into dock when he managed one of the two or three flatulent notes in his repertoire. He was not popular with his neighbours.

Neither was he popular with some students who shared Shakespeare seminars with him. He was always first to chip in with insightful comments on passages about which we were all supposed to have opinions. Irritating though his self-confident, know-all, floor-hogging approach was, it did at least allow others of us to sit back and abstain from making foolish and inept remarks of our own.

Sousa was keen to get to the bottom of what had gone on before the Goldblatt arson affair and quizzed me like a youthful Sherlock Holmes. "Did you not sense a certain irritation on his part with the way he was treated, a frisson of discomfort with the way he was regarded by the crew? Might it be viewed as the culmination of an unspoken desire for retribution? There is, is there not, a dichotomy between being the one who tells every crew member, stroke to bow, to work harder whilst remaining inert oneself. The glory of being part of a team that wins, but not really part of the engine of that vehicle, is subtly combined with the blame apportioned when things don't go well. Yet the cox is not responsible for the execution of the strokes he orchestrates. Or is he?"

There was silence. Either the others were trying to work

out what the hell he was on about or they were stupefied by his pompous delivery.

"I didn't spend much time with him," I said eventually.

"The police have let him go," said Sally, who fortunately spoke simply so you could understand what she meant. "I saw him returning to his room." This provoked some interest from the assembled company. "He got into a taxi outside the Porter's Lodge later. It looked like he was going home as he had a pile of stuff with him."

Simeon was on his way back to Barking then – an early return on the train and shameful premature slog along the District Line with his belongings. What if I ran into him during the holidays? What would I say? Given that, until this year, our paths had not crossed since I was 11 or 12, I thought it unlikely that we would meet – but then again, he did live only about half a mile from us.

Some sweet supermarket sherry was produced, and I was invited to sit down. Finding space for me to do so wasn't easy. Gran had gone to town on the Princess Di puffed sleeves, which widened my shoulders by about a foot each side. It was like wearing a balloon at the top of each arm. When I sat on the bed between two other girls much shorter than me, each had one cheek squashed as if by a giant boxing glove.

"Lilac is a nice spring colour," announced Mary, who always tried to put a brave face on things. It might well have been if I had been draped in the finest of silks, so that the accompanying sheen and tricks of light upon the fabric would have made it less glaring. Unfortunately, although Gran was a good needlewoman, her budget was meagre. The yardage required meant she'd used a polyester from the market which, although not entirely unattractive and which didn't crease much, had a certain 'keep away from naked flames' feel and look about it. The colour was verging on the neon – high visibility and an excellent choice for highway or railway workers.

We moved on as group from Tom's room, but it soon became apparent that long-winded, brassy Julian's main objective was hanging around me. This came as a shock and a surprise. When he said, "I must say you are looking very lovely, a picture in pink, in a most exquisite gown," my suspicions were further aroused. Either he was colour blind or he was completely blind. Perhaps he had memorised the sentence from a book entitled *Phrases for a Gentleman to Use When Courting a Lady* that he'd picked up from a second-hand shop.

My realisation was confirmed by some encouraging looks and nods from Mary, who had clearly been complicit in allowing Julian to join the group, enabling him to engage in a courtship ritual of excruciating embarrassment. I should have been flattered, but his bombastic, self-satisfied pronouncements irritated me. And, with the exception of the Monty Python theme tune, I wasn't that keen on military brass band music either.

I managed to avoid standing next to him when we listened to the main music act of the evening, a well-known band of what Julian referred to as 'popular artistes'. None was playing a sousaphone. The rest of our group seemed to melt away. When I made an unsuccessful bid to escape unnoticed to the hog roast, he followed hotly on my heels.

His party piece was finding lines of poetry to suit any occasion. Whilst we were in the queue, he sought to entertain others in the line by reciting, in a loud and sonorous voice, some porcine verses drawn from the cornucopia of poems he knew by heart.

"*And there in a wood, a piggy wig stood, With a ring at the end of his nose,*" he chuckled, as we stood waiting for our pork roll. "*And they bought a pig and some green jackdaws, And a lovely monkey with lollipop paws.* Lear is very good for pig references, don't you think?" I nodded despite it being something I'd not really considered before.

"Ah! *The pig-tailed quidding pirates and the pretty pranks we played,*" he continued after a while. "Masefield. *The Ballad of John Silver*. Cheating a bit. I'm not sure that really counts." People were staring at us. I tried to look as if I was queuing with someone else.

He tapped his head frantically with his hand, like someone bashing a vending machine that has swallowed his coin. "Ah! I know. What about this?" He was so pleased with himself that he jumped up and down and his voice rose several decibels. *"That was the winter that my mother died, half mad on morphine, blown up at last, like a pregnant pig."* He looked about, as if for applause. Someone ahead of us in the queue sniggered. "Anne Sexton. American. You probably haven't heard of her," he said directly to me. I hadn't, so said nothing. "Perhaps not entirely appropriate for this occasion, I dare say."

Once we had had our food, the dance floor beckoned. Even though it would have been almost impossible for any close contact to occur, on account of the copious pleats and folds of lilac polyester which would have come between us, I wasn't going to risk it. Good old Gran. She could have patented her chastity frock, a godsend to girls in situations like mine. Father O'Connor could have endorsed it.

I declined; I thought politely in the circumstances.

"To be truthful," he confided, "I agree. Not my kind of music either. We could go to my room and listen to Sousa's *The Thunderer*. I have it on an LP. It has a marvellous counter melodic section. I'm learning the sousaphone part."

Enough! I pulled the old 'going to the cloakroom' stunt. This enabled me to put some distance and time between us and effect an escape.

10
Behind the arras

I was looking for a quiet place where no-one would find me. There was an entrance from the Fellows' Garden which led up to some rooms which I was confident wouldn't be being used on the night of the ball. I climbed up the old stairs and wedged myself and my huge skirt round the first turn of the narrow staircase. It seemed a good place to hide. How had it come to this? Cinderella didn't have to do any hiding, not until the clock struck midnight anyhow. The huge, puffy, pumpkin-like arms of my dress made a comfy rest to lean against at least.

Presently, I heard two male voices at the bottom of the staircase. I stayed very still, hoping they weren't going to want to climb up a level. I was shocked to recognise the unmistakable patrician drawl of Chummers. Was he, too, fed up with everything, just waiting for me to come into his life and make it all OK?

"Where the hell have you been, mate?" It was the voice of another of the boaty gang, known for indiscernible reasons as The Wobster.

"I've just been keeping out the way. Fuck. It's a disaster." Chummers replied. The smell of what my mother called 'funny tobacco' began to waft towards me. "The regatta is off. No boat, no cox. Ripper can't sit down."

"Is his arse OK?"

"It was looking a bit manky, so he turned up at Addenbrooke's A&E just in case. He's got some cream for it."

"I thought we decided he wasn't going to do that?"

"He worried it was going septic or something. He's such a wanker. I don't think anyone there will make a connection. I'd love to know what he told them when they asked how he did it!" They both laughed. I was intrigued and repelled at the same time. What had Ripper been up to?

"Bloody bit of luck the dwarf turned up. We couldn't even have blamed Ferris this time." There was that name. I kept hearing it.

"Why did Smallcox come back?"

"Christ knows. I think it's all to do with that stupid girl he trails around after. They were in the bog downstairs earlier on." My ears pricked up, my face reddened.

"Was he giving her one in there? I can't believe it. I can think of better places." The following silence, I assume, was due to them both imagining not only the cox 'in action' but also the unpleasant venue he'd chosen.

Eventually Chummers continued. "Hard to believe, isn't it? Macca's cocktail had stonking effects. It was lethal. I must have passed out in the boat shed for a few hours and when I came to, I found the tart's pants on the floor." There was a pause whilst they both inhaled deeply and passed the joint between them. "I ran them up the pole as a joke. I thought everyone would assume Smallcox had done it!" They both laughed rather more than I would have liked at this revelation. "Bloody hell you should have seen them! They even had a sodding name tape on them." There was more hilarity. It was the joint having an effect. I hoped.

"We were bloody lucky to get out of there."

"No thanks to you, Wobster, mate. It's your fault, this whole thing."

"No it's not. It was that moron Macca and his bloody cocktail recipe. Everyone was so pissed, something was bound to happen."

"Any fucking idiot knows if you're near a flame you shouldn't spray an aerosol," Chummers snorted. I didn't know if he was really angry or subduing a laugh.

"Ripper's farts are so rank. I don't know anyone else who can let one out with such a stench. A bit of air freshener was just what was needed."

"Not when I'm setting fire to one of them with a candle!" There was a pause before they both collapsed in fits of hysteria.

"Why were you doing it right by the curtains? Trust you to drop the fucking candle so the whole lot went up. You're as big a dickhead."

"Not such a dickhead," continued Chummers smugly. "Who told the police that Snow White's mate had done it because he didn't feel he 'fitted in'?"

"Yeah. That was a masterstroke. The sight of that Fireman rescuing him from the flagpole was hysterical. We'd be in big shit otherwise."

"Bigger shit," corrected Chummers.

They went, leaving me with the burden of information I had just heard. So, Simeon Goldblatt must have returned to the boathouse to get my knickers off the pole. And, as far as I could tell only Chummers, The Wobster and Ripper (nursing a burnt bum) knew the whole truth. And now me.

Simeon knew he hadn't started the fire and presumably had told the police so. Did they believe him? Even if the fire brigade investigated the cause of the conflagration and concluded it had been started by a candle causing the curtains to catch light, what proof was there that it wasn't Simeon who had deliberately done so? There was plenty of evidence that he had been teased and bullied by people in the Boat Club. Although it was out of character for him to fight back, who would tell the police that?

It was probable that Simeon didn't know how the fire started. The least likely person to set light to the boathouse would be the Captain of Boats and his committee, particularly with a regatta coming up in a few weeks.

I sat wedged on the stair for a while processing what I had just heard. The obvious person to tell the police was me. I would have to go to the station in the morning and do so.

They say you should always sleep on things. I managed to get back to my room without being lassoed by a sousaphone and forced to march around the dance tent. I spent a fretful night tossing and turning, sleep prevented by the noise of other people enjoying the ball and having fun, mixed with a constant replay of what I had overheard.

When morning came, I did not feel enthusiastic about meeting PC Plod. Nor did I feel encouraged by the alternative, going to the college authorities. How popular would I be if I did either? It didn't bear thinking about.

Perhaps the secret would slip out some other way? Surely a blabbermouth like The Wobster would be unable to keep his trap shut? What about Ripper and his singed arse? Could he avoid a fart-flame anecdote in the bar? Surely not.

A couple of days later, Mum and Dad were due to pick me up for the summer vacation. I began transferring my luggage in good time down to the Porters' Lodge, hoping to avoid them having to come to my room. I couldn't get the lilac cloud back into the box it had come in. It seemed to have grown. I left it on top of the pile outside the Lodge whilst I went back for the last bags. At my staircase I was horrified to run into Mum coming the other way.

"You're early!"

"Oh, you know what your dad's like. He's parking the car," she said with a knowing look. "I've just taken Nan to your room." I was speechless. Binka and Bomber would be there re-arming for their afternoon mission. "She needed the lav, so we went to find you and a nice young man showed her where it was and said he'd look after her whilst I went to find your dad."

I hurried up to the room. Nan was sitting in the armchair in our communal room. There was no sign of Binka, but Bomber, in full flying gear, was sitting on the arm next to her. She had two

Thermos flasks and some Tupperware containing the inevitable sandwiches on her lap.

"Tally ho!" cried Bomber when he saw me, stuffing a wodge of ham and cheese into his mouth. Nan was laughing and animated.

"Fortunately," she said, "I've run into this chappie from the Air Force. He's going on operations this afternoon so we're having a farewell tipple." She held the Thermos cup aloft and Bomber took out a hip flask and poured a considerable amount of what I assumed was neat spirit into it. "Bottoms UP!" laughed Nan, downing the entire contents in one large gulp. "Roni," she said in a loud stage whisper, "I'm giving him all the sandwiches because he's finished his rations and," she mouthed the last few words, "he may not be coming back." Bomber crammed two egg and cress triangles into his mouth and winked at me. I hadn't heard Nan string together so many words in a coherent way for a long time.

"Nan, are you drunk?" I asked.

"I might be a little tipsy," she giggled. "He got some whisky from an American at the base. If we are pie-eyed, who cares? We could be dead tomorrow!"

"Come along," said Bomber, helping Nan to her feet. "We've got a dance to get to."

"Apparently Glenn Miller is playing with his Big Band!" Nan confided, flirtatiously linking arms with Bomber. He guided her towards the door and down the stairs. I was dumbfounded. I picked up my last bags and followed them.

"Porters' Lodge?" asked Bomber, posting the last of the sandwiches into his grinning maw, before sticking the empty Tupperware under his arm like a swagger stick.

Dad was pacing up and down just outside the gate. He was looking anxious about having had to leave the Cortina so close to a 'Strictly No Parking' sign when he arrived. Bomber gently led Nan out of the college and settled her into the back seat of the car.

Mum and Dad had found my pile of belongings beside the Lodge and stuffed them into the boot and fixed them to the roof rack. The ball gown was inside the car in middle of the back seat. It had taken on a life of its own, sitting there like an extra passenger. It made a barrier between Nan and me. Bomber saluted and shut Nan's door like a liveried doorman at a posh hotel.

"Good luck! Let the Jerries have it!" she called to him, blowing a kiss, and promptly fell asleep against the big lilac pillow.

"Chocs away!" Bomber shouted back to Dad as the car, heavy with my belongings, accelerated very slowly away from the college.

Nan dozed peacefully as we left the city behind. It was a relief to get away. I felt a pang of guilt because I hadn't spoken to anyone about what I'd heard on the stairs. I was hoping that someone else would break the story. That was bound to happen, wasn't it? No one could accuse me of not speaking up if they didn't know I had anything to say. Would I ever see Simeon Goldblatt again anyway?

"Ooo, Ron," said Mum excitedly, turning round from the front seat, "I meant to tell you. Guess who has started coming to the Salon?" Nan let out a long, low, slow snore in her sleep.

"Who?"

"Only Miriam's mother, Mrs Goldblatt!"

11
Home and Away

Nan seemed to have forgotten about Bomber by the time we got home. She went straight up to bed without even asking if we thought she should sleep in the shelter.

I was intrigued by the way Bomber had dealt with her – on the one hand completely irresponsibly but on the other very successfully. If you cast filling her with considerable amounts of neat whisky to one side, humouring her in every other way was harmless and made her very happy.

Every night, Mum tried to explain why she shouldn't worry about the tiny gap in her bedroom curtains. "Do you remember? We don't need to bother with the blackout any longer."

Why not pretend the war was still on? Just play along and fix the curtain gap. Tell her you'd heard the All Clear, that Mrs Barnes's son had returned from the Far East none the worse for wear and that her knitted socks for PoWs would be well received. Why not?

By the time we were back in Barking, she'd forgotten about their encounter and the promised date with Glenn and his Big Band. No recollection of any of it remained. The war lingered on even so, central to her daily life, curiously fused with our modern-day comings and goings almost forty years after it was over.

So much for distancing myself from Simeon Goldblatt and his wrongful arrest – or perhaps he'd been charged, bailed and was awaiting a court hearing? We'd soon find out – the next time Mrs Goldblatt was in getting her roots done.

The Mayfair Salon, located on the 1930's built Faircross Parade close to our house, and not in the affluent district of London of the same name, was looking a little shabby and old-fashioned by the time I went to university.

Younger women, not wanting a shampoo and set, were having what my mother referred to as 'wash and wear' haircuts. Although Mum had embraced the blow-dry, they began to frequent trendier salons where no-one wore a housecoat and you might find male stylists. They had names like *Kutz* or *Strands* or *Up in the Hair*. Nonetheless, Mum retained a loyal, hard core of ageing clients who favoured the helmeted Mrs Thatcher look and had a weekly appointment as much for the chat as the grooming.

Mum was an entertaining raconteur and the stories her clients received at their weekly appointment were an assurance of repeat business. It was a two-way process; Mum was receptive to all their gossip and was happy, without filter, to pass it on to me. Half an hour doing my homework at the kitchen table when she was in full flow told me things about people in our locality I didn't always want to know: the Haymans at 43 were getting a divorce but Mr Hayman didn't know yet; Valerie Walker (who had been in my Junior School class) had an older brother who had 'got someone in trouble' on a school trip to Le Touquet; Mr Jones had warts on his bladder and it was affecting his 'waterworks'; a man we called Uncle Sid, who wasn't an uncle but ran a newsagent and sweetshop, was no longer able to 'have relations'. She proffered no explanation of what this meant other than a look on her face which suggested it wasn't to do with family being invited over.

All this news was a burden to me when out and about and likely to come across the characters involved. It put me right off going a couple of doors up from The Mayfair Salon to Uncle Sid's for a quarter of sherbet lemons.

Mum was clever. She knew better than to disseminate this gossip back to other clients and ensured her offerings were family based: Gran's family to be precise. Most of Mum's tales began with, "My mother-in-law's sister…" As there were six of them, this was a fertile seam of tittle-tattle and the customers loved it. If you saw a woman in Barking with a rigid shampoo and set, you could assume that, if she'd come from The Mayfair Salon, she'd be up to date with the goings-on of the extended Sullivan family.

I don't think Gran ever made the connection between her conversations with my father when she saw him on Sundays and the ever-present ear of my mother, gathering material to relay to her clients the following week. Gran's monologues, delivered to *The Sporting Life* behind which Dad sat, mostly consisted of a transfer of information about what was going on with her sisters, their enormous families and complicated lives back home. They may have been visited by plague or infidelity, but Gran's sisters wrote to her weekly.

Their misfortunes gave my mother endless news to pass on as she snipped, curled, and backcombed her captive audience. Medical problems and faltering relationships, births, deaths and disease, misfortune and miracles on a grand scale formed the plot of a real-life soap opera whose protagonists were unable to complain. Mum's entertaining narrative kept her customers loyal.

"My father'd say, 'I've a girl for every day of the week'," Gran would reminisce and she'd run through their names in order, something I could repeat but not spell. I found it impossible to work out who was who; you'd need diagrams, complex family trees and biographies to make any sense of the information or to put it into any kind of context. If any of them ever came to England, we never saw them. Their lives were so eventful it's no wonder they never left the confines of Cork.

Gran sped from sentence to sentence at high speed. "Siobhan's husband put a nail through his thumb when he was fixing the roof the other week. Well, he's been trying to work with just the one hand but it's proving very difficult. The pain was excruciating, apparently. It makes you think what our Lord had to go through on the cross. It makes you grateful for His sacrifice. Does it not, Mick?"

My father had learnt the trick of making appropriate hmms and aahhs with the occasional yes or no thrown in for good measure as an indication he was listening when he was not. It usually sufficed but every so often he took a punt on the wrong reaction.

"Hmm. No, not really."

"Oh, how can you joke about such a thing, you naughty boy? I'm glad Father O'Connor can't hear you now."

As Mum regularly pointed out, despite having a direct line to the Almighty, Father O'Connor only received carefully filtered sins at confession from Gran – lest he thought badly of her. Perhaps she didn't want to overburden him with too much information. God obviously had a divine memory, but Father O'Connor would have been stuck with a human one like the rest of us, no matter how devout he was.

"Father Bloomin' O'Connor!" Mum would mutter under her breath. "As if any of us would be telling that man anything." I must admit I was into my teens before I realised Father O'Connor's first name was not Bloomin, but from an early age I knew Mum didn't have much time for Our Lord, and in particular, Catholicism. Mum raised one eyebrow for Protestants and non-conformists but two for the Roman church. When Gran was about, Mum's face was very mobile, eyebrows rising and lowering like a department store lift.

There was an uneasy truce between them by the time I was old enough to be aware of such things. Early disapproval then animosity had given way to a kind of tolerance. Mum had a grudging respect for her, despite the obsession with religion. Dad's father had been killed during the war when he and Uncle Pat were very young, and she had brought them up alone. She didn't speak of her husband's demise. I didn't enquire; conversation about him was always discouraged. Neither did I ask Dad, who had been barely more than a baby when he died and knew very little about him. The flat that they lived in had a direct hit and was destroyed along with most of the others in the building. All their possessions had been lost, but this was only referred to obliquely.

"There was not a scrap of anything left," she'd respond to any requests for old photographs or things about my grandfather. "We'd to start again, completely from scratch." That was the final word on the matter.

A very well-dressed woman, I never saw Gran look a mess or caught her anything less than groomed for the outside world. She was lean and sharp-featured and smiled infrequently. A headscarf covered her hair when out and about, hiding a rarely revealed French pleat.

Mum could hardly refuse to do her mother-in-law's hair, but appointments didn't happen that regularly. This wasn't because, like a Holy sister, few people ever saw her hair.

Mum always suggested she should come at the end of the day. Gran took offence at this, thinking it signified a lack of importance about her coiffure. "It's so you can see Ron," Mum explained. "She can drop in on her way back from school." Neither was the truth. Mum was wary of having the other clients and Gran there at the same time.

Once I witnessed why she had good reason to be so. Gran arrived early and we met outside. Slim, with hard bony knees and elbows, her face was gaunt with a sharp nose. I'd spotted her weaving in and out of slowcoaches getting in her way. Unlike Nan, who ambled about unsure of exactly where she was going or why she was going there, Gran moved at high speed.

That particular afternoon, Mum would have had to be looking out of the window at just the right time to see her approaching. Rather like the V2 rockets that Nan was so frightened of, she often arrived before you had any inkling she was coming.

A particularly chatty lady, the last paying customer of the day, was seated in the chair waiting for her final immobilising shower of lacquer. Mum was on the phone taking a booking and hadn't noticed Gran had arrived early. We went in together whilst Mum was still mid-call.

"Ah! You must be Shirley's mother-in-law. She's has been telling me all about your sister," squealed this lady who was now glad her appointment had overrun. It was obvious she had been furnished with a description of Gran previously and was delighted finally to meet the star of some of Mum's juicier gossip.

"She has, has she?" Gran replied coldly.

"Which one is it, Shirl?" the lady called, "The one with the prolapsed womb or the one whose son is good at tap dancing and dropped out of the seminary?"

"That'll be Caoimhe, who has had thirteen children, God bless her, or Sinead, who anyways has another son who is already a priest," explained Gran with a stony face. "What has she to say exactly?"

Mum paused her call. "Deal with this Ron, will you?" she said, thrusting the receiver into my hand. "No, that story was about someone else, you've got mixed up," she explained to the customer. Mum wasn't convincing.

"I thought you said it was one of the Irish sisterhood." The woman was oblivious to the panic ensuing. "There's so many of them and I can never remember their names." Mum drowned her out, her finger pushing hard on the button of the can of lacquer so it made a dreadful noise. That woman's hair could have withstood a force 10 gale by the time she left the salon.

What would entertain Mrs Goldblatt when she was in next in the salon? The saga of Grainne's appendix, grumbling away for months, mistaken for constipation then finally removed in the nick of time? Mum enjoyed the punchline. "She asked to bring it home because without it she didn't feel 'whole' anymore. It's in a jar on the mantelpiece. In her dining room, if you please!"

And what would Mrs Goldblatt trade in reply? An eyewitness report of how drunk I had been? My pants up the pole and the sorry tale of Simeon's gallant gesture?

I was anxious not to encounter any of the Goldblatt family, but around every corner lurked a Simeon look-alike. My heart was constantly missing a beat when I thought I'd spied him, Miriam or their parents out shopping and approaching me on every street in Barking. I steered well clear of Upney Lane.

The phone rang one day. It was Mary, coming to my rescue. "Whatever happened to you?" she asked. "We were all wondering. You just disappeared. I rang four other McNamaras in the telephone book before I got the right one."

Good old Mary: how thoughtful she was. I willingly accepted her invitation to go and stay at her home in Muswell Hill for a few days. With luck it would not be the holiday destination of the Goldblatts or the location of any relatives they had suddenly found themselves compelled to visit.

Mary's house turned out to be a version of ours on steroids. Same period, – interwar 'tudorbethan' pastiche – but bigger. It had a touch of the Upney Lanes about it. Mum would be interested.

The sound of an oboe greeted my arrival. Someone was practising a classical piece. This immediately suggested that an atmosphere of worthy endeavour pervaded the house.

Mrs Featherstone opened the door. "Hello, Veronica. How lovely to see you. Do excuse Richard. His largo is really more of a larghissimo – as I expect you've noticed." Mary's mother indicated the room from where this appalling musical travesty was coming.

Musicians, rather those who consider themselves musically superior, lay traps for the uninformed. Just like the surnames that are not said as they are spelled, if you're not part of the club, you won't know what a larghissimo is, let alone if it is inappropriately applied. I suspected that she didn't really think I was troubled by what, to me, sounded like a record being played. "I know that tune," I wanted to say. "It's the one off the Hovis advert. Sounds alright to me." But I didn't dare show my true ignorant colours. My weak smile and silent response were all she needed to confirm my cultural inadequacies.

I suspected that Mrs Featherstone didn't put on Frank Ifield LPs when her husband was out like Mum did. Wagner, maybe, or some Russian composer I'd never heard of. Instead of singing along, as she swept her duster along the mantelpiece in time with the music, Mary's mother would have to sit down in a chair to absorb the discordant notes. Jarring and unexpected chords would bar her from either remembering the non-existent melody or being able to concentrate on anything else. Surely no-one really enjoyed that kind of music. But who wants to be the first to stick their fingers in their ears and shout, "Turn that row off!" That might mark you as a philistine, the bête noire of the educated middle class.

She had Mary's hair but wore it as a forty-something-year-old woman might have done twenty years earlier. It was tightly done and pinned into obedience, rather as I suspected Mary and her brothers were at home. I was glad Mum wasn't there to recommend a bubble perm.

During the evening meal that night, Mary's parents were almost in competition with each other as to who could outsmart the other with ridiculous questions about my parents' cultural activities. "Have your parents seen *Glengarry Glen Ross* at the Cottesloe?" asked Mr Featherstone out of the blue.

"It sounds like something my dad drinks on the rocks." I chanced a gag but it fell flat.

"That's Glenfiddich, I think," he replied without a flicker of a smile.

Mary's mum broke the somewhat awkward silence which ensued. "We went to ENO for *The Gambler*. I can't help thinking it's better in Russian." I had no comment to make. Any gags popping into my head connecting my dad's business and the title of the opera remained unspoken after the reception my last effort had received. Anyway, they had misheard when I described his occupation as turf accountant, convincing themselves he spent the day up to his eyes in audits and tax returns. It would be too difficult to explain.

"I don't see why Prokofiev is better in Russian – just because he was one. *The Love for Three Oranges* is much more enjoyable in French," replied Mary's father grumpily.

Mary's parents weren't being deliberately superior, I decided. They were naturally so.

Chez Featherstone, all meals were eaten in the dining room instead of round the kitchen table. I wondered if this was for my benefit. At home, on the very rare occasion that someone outside the four of us was invited for a meal, or at Christmas time, we ate in the back part of our 'through lounge'.

"You'll have to put the leaf in, Mick," Mum would say roughly two weeks before the appointed day with daily reminders afterwards. The teak G Plan table that my parents had bought when they first got married (but rarely used) was pulled into the centre of the room with its upholstered chairs supplemented by chairs brought in from the kitchen. "Make sure you sit on a kitchen chair," Dad, Nan and I were told. "So people don't notice they're not matching." Quite how this furnishing faux pas was disguised from our guests by these hard seats momentarily being covered by our bottoms, I failed to see.

Mum had noticed that tablecloths did not feature in pictures of modern dining that she saw in magazines at the salon. However, the table's teak top had lightened through exposure to daylight over the years. Because it was rarely removed from underneath, the leaf was still its original colour and a cloth would disguise this mismatch. Were Sherlock Holmes to be invited round for Christmas, he would easily deduce from a cloth-less table that the leaf was an infrequent addition and conclude that my parents were not regular dinner party hosts. This was not the impression she wanted to give.

Mum suspected throwing a dinner party was the key to social advancement but Nan put the kibosh on fine dining with company. Her incessant worries about not hearing the siren going off, about using up all the rations at once and about missing Mr Churchill on the radio would have interrupted any interesting conversations that Mum might have thought would be taking place. In truth, the only other bottoms sitting on a G plan upholstered dining chair belonged to Gran and very occasionally my Uncle Pat.

There were other differences in the Featherstone dining room. There was no sign of an ashtray, and there was neither a teapot nor teacups and saucers to fill from it. My parents, and Nan in particular, would find this most peculiar, I thought. Earnest conversation was encouraged, usually involving discussion about politics and current affairs. There was no tittle-tattle or sharing of gossip Mary's mother had heard at work, and the goings-on four houses down the road didn't feature in sensational news. Perhaps the inhabitants of their street were very dull. There were no laughs around the table.

"Tell us about saving that man from the burning building," Mrs Featherstone asked, in an uncharacteristically gossipy way at the last meal before I was due to go home.

"Mum, that's not right," Mary insisted. It was clear that the narrative surrounding the burning boat house had a life of its own. Mary and the rest of the first-year brutalist block were fanning the flames of its creation. They were all sorry I'd had to share with Binka and, by default, Bomber. Gill, whose bath had overflowed, was consumed with guilt. It was her fault, they maintained, that I had had to fend off the upper-class twit elements of the college body. As for Simeon Goldblatt, they were all devastated that he had turned out to be an arsonist.

It amazed me how lack of information didn't prevent the invention of elaborate scenarios to fill the gaps, which were then absorbed into the narrative as truth. I was the chief topic of their chatter, the discussion that went on whilst they were supping their cocoa. Even Mary's mother had a version.

Mary seemed ashamed that she had related this story to her mother, who in turn had added her own embellishments. She looked at me for forgiveness, unaware that I had the key to the truth and was keeping it to myself. It wouldn't have been too late to tell it and admit that I hadn't put the record straight with the College authorities. Not informing them earlier painted a less than admirable picture of me, I recognised that. Yet doing so once the holidays had begun meant there would have been few repercussions for me. Chummers and the rest of the boaty horror show were gone, cast into the outside world with their degrees and reputations intact. Poor Simeon was home, potentially in disgrace.

A narrative was being created which cast me in a better light than that of a supergrass. Gran would have said God knew the truth, but she would also have admitted that it was better that Father O'Connor did not. Did it matter if others did not either?

12
The Generation Game

Barking was looking quite attractive in the summer sun when I arrived back. I was pleased to return home to a place where everything was familiar and unchanging. I was surprised by my new-found admiration for my birthplace. I'd got my usual summer job lined up, working at the open-air swimming pool in Barking Park. Dull though that might have been, sitting in a kiosk issuing the odd ticket to a hardy swimmer, I was paid to do it and I could read at the same time.

When it opened in the 1930s, this outdoor pool was referred to grandly as The Lido. By the early eighties it was a shadow of its former self. Its memorable tiered fountain, presumably constructed to give it a Riviera feel, lingered on, but the pool remained freezing cold on all but the hottest of days and swimmers with open mouths got a gob full of leaves (or worse) if they weren't alert. Mum and Dad were rude about it and its murky water. The glamour and excitement of the fifties, when photos showed them lounging around its edge, posing as if they were in the South of France on a smart holiday rather than a random day off, were long gone.

On the bus from the station, the sight of it and the park gave me a comforting feeling. I was confident about the next year at Cambridge. I was going to work a bit harder, try and do some acting and make some decent friends and put silly first year mistakes behind me. I would be living in a better room than those in the brutalist concrete bastille and I would be in it on my own.

When Dad answered the door, he had his useless look on. He had a way of looking uneasy in his own house sometimes, usually when something was going on that was a bit outside his normal routine. "Not at the shop?" I asked, "Are you ill?"

"Your mum's in the kitchen." He didn't move. He just stood there with his hand outstretched on the open door.

Mum was sitting at the kitchen table with a cup of tea. Mrs Green, the neighbour, was there too. When she saw me, she got up, even though she clearly had a full cup still to drink.

"Roni, don't hesitate to come and get me if your mum needs anything." She left. I heard her saying the same to Dad as she went. "I mean it, Mick, anything at all."

"Are you ill, Mum? You look dreadful. Have you seen the doctor?" Mum tried to smile, but she couldn't look me in the eye.

"It's your Nan. When I took her up her cup of tea this morning, she'd gone." For a split second I thought she meant Nan had absconded, gone AWOL, fled from the advancing Germans like a refugee with a hand cart. Mum's face told me the truth. Pale and trembly, she was uncharacteristically wordless.

Dad was lurking in the doorway, still looking like a spare part. "It's a nice way to go. In your sleep."

"I dropped the cup," Mum's voice faltered. "The tea went all over the eiderdown. It'll have to go to the cleaners. When the doctor came it was all wet. I had to explain. I didn't like to take it off the bed."

"Is she upstairs?" I asked, half-horrified myself that the tea might be seeping through and, as it was now about four o'clock, Nan might be getting a bit of a soaking herself.

"The undertaker's been," Dad explained. "You're alright." He obviously thought I might feel obliged to go and view the body. "Though you can go to the chapel of rest to see her if you want to say goodbye."

This was too much for Mum, who began to cry. I joined in,

which made it worse. Dad put the kettle on. Something I think he'd been doing rather a lot all day.

I remember that day when Nan died very clearly. It was the day when my childhood ended, when the status quo which I had accepted without question changed. It was the beginning of the transfer of responsibility and authority which happens between all children and their parents at some point.

I was probably a parent myself before I could view my own close relatives as people. They emerged as individuals, not just an extension of myself – an entourage existing purely for my benefit – once I had responsibilities towards others. Perhaps that realisation comes earlier for some, but I remained inconsiderate of the effects life-experience and circumstance had had on my parents and grandparents until I was well into my twenties. Their past exploits were just a series of anecdotes and facts which I didn't consider had any bearing on their personalities. This was particularly true of Nan, who died whilst I retained the mindset of an adolescent.

I never viewed Nan as a whole person whilst she was alive. She had looked after me since I was a baby whilst Mum worked, a character in the great show that was ME! Initially, she had been part of a double act of indulgence called Nanandgrandad, whose every treat confirmed that I was indeed the centre of the universe. My grandfather died when I was eight, and she was left alone, like Wise without Morecambe or Laurel without Hardy, and she began the long slow slide back into the war, where she remained.

As I got older and she became battier and more demented, I found her an embarrassment and an irritation. I think it was because I found it uncomfortable that she was no longer the person she used to be and was too immature to cope with it.

Granddad was fifteen years older than Nan and enjoyed telling me that he had been born when Queen Victoria was on the throne. He seemed to spend all his time in the front room of their house, dressed in a shirt and tie as if he was going somewhere important, sitting in his armchair engulfed by a huge cloud of pipe smoke.

As a small child I thought Granddad lived only in that front room; he never seemed to leave it or the chair. When I used to be sent in to see him, he was frequently reading a pink newspaper and writing tiny pencil notes in a notebook. He had a globe, a massive, coloured football spinning on a pole. "We're here," he'd say, placing my finger on the small pink shape which he told me was England. "Hold on tight…" then I was allowed to spin the world round and try and name the country nearest my finger when it came to a halt. "Where are you going to end up my girl?" he'd ask wistfully.

My grandfather had been a regular soldier and fought in the first war. His arthritic finger with its yellowing nail used to point on the globe to places I'd never heard of elsewhere, but to which he claimed to have been: Flanders, Salonika, Dardanelles, Mesopotamia and somewhere called the Wipers Salient, which I imagined to be a place which was so rainy that you had to have the windscreen wipers on in the car the whole time.

It was only after Nan died and I noticed some medals amongst her things that I learned that he had been decorated for bravery in the field. Mum told me that he had been invalided out with shell shock and suffered from alarming flashbacks in his sleep for the rest of his life. Mum and Nan didn't mention the first war in front of Granddad in case it set him off. But it was never far from his mind, its spinning locations something he wanted to share with me.

Lighting his pipe involved performing a complicated series of short and long puffs. Success came when vast clouds of smoke indicated that the tobacco was successfully lit. When Gran told me about how it was known when a new pope had been elected, I imagined the cardinals all puffing their pipes like mad up the papal chimney to give the sign. Granddad smelt a bit; all that puffing had an undesirable effect. Getting close to him was not so pleasant but I was prepared to put up with that and his whiskery, cold-lipped, slow-motion kiss because this was the prelude to being given a piece of the chocolate he kept near the globe.

Granddad and his world have vanished like the old currency that went with them. It's a long time since he died, so long that I remember him only in vignettes, like short snatches of cine film. I have no real memory of his voice.

Nan's descent into senility, which started when Granddad died, was based in experiences which had never really left her. When I was little and we were out and about, she'd point out houses where people had either had lucky escapes or tragic ends. "A whole family went there in a direct hit on the shelter," she'd indicate as we passed a corner house on Longbridge Road. She'd point to the rockery in the front garden, which I assumed was what remained of this shelter, as we went past. The idea of being eternally entombed under the alpines and succulents amongst which someone had more recently placed a garden gnome made quite a big impression on me. So much so that if I hear the words 'direct hit' a vision of this little chap with the red cap and fishing rod pops into my head.

Other houses were homes to husbands who never returned, sons who hadn't grown into proper adults and children who never finished school. This, too, was alarming to a sensitive girl like me. The lady who served in the greengrocer's and always made a fuss of me had no children, I was told. "Her husband was a prisoner of the Japs," Nan stated without further explanation, leaving my puzzled mind to figure out the connections.

"Mrs Atkinson popped out to take the dog to do his business and when she got back the whole place was gone. Doodlebug." Before I could ask about the huge house-eating insect and whether it had finally been swatted and enquire as to what line of work her dog was engaged in, she'd be on to the next near miss or annihilation. Her final recollection was always as we turned the corner into her road. "That's where the unexploded bomb fell," she'd say, with what I considered a certain lack of immediacy to move on elsewhere. I was always relieved when we returned from a shopping expedition intact.

Latterly, what had been a remaining anxiety from a traumatic time became a daily confusion which, when Dad and I weren't finding it amusing, drove us almost as demented.

Nan's obsession with the war was matched by Gran's obstinate refusal to discuss anything about it. They were not often together, but once Nan was living with us, Gran's weekly Sunday visits meant there was an unavoidable conflict between them.

"You're a war widow like Mrs Kirby," Nan would begin. "She keeps all his letters in a Peek Freans biscuit tin. The other day she thought she was offering me a lemon puff, but it turned out to be a letter from Tobruk."

Gran would remain silent at such revelations. Occasionally, if Nan was on her favourite topic of direct hits, Gran might acknowledge that she had been in receipt of one. "They say you don't hear the one that has your name on it. There's something to be thankful for," Nan would pronounce. "Aoibheann, did you hear the one that got your flat?"

"I did not. The Good Lord be thanked we had gone to the shelter." Gran would cross herself. "I can't for the life of me fathom how the dead can tell you they didn't hear the bomb that killed them," she would add, logically.

As Nan got worse, she forgot that Gran had war experiences too. Her comments concerned only her own perceived situation. "I won't have another cup of tea, Shirley. I don't like to drink too much when I'm sleeping in the shelter." Gran would catch my father's eye and they would share a moment of solidarity.

Nan was gone and with her the end of my childhood. It was a

jolt back into the real world, to the place and the people to whom I belonged. Yet I had seen beyond and outside, where life was different though not necessarily better. It was unsettling.

13
Tea and urns

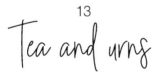

Nan had been a regular attender at the ugly, brick-built church near our house even before she lived with us. She would take me along on a Sunday morning and I would get a biscuit and colour in a picture of Jesus doing some miracles whilst Nan went to the service. Mum didn't like this but couldn't do much about it. Gran was horrified, which naturally stopped Mum forbidding it. Dad hid behind *The Racing Post*.

When Nan really started losing the plot, she thought the church bells on Sunday morning were the signal that the invasion had begun. A horde of Nazi paratroopers were about to land in the garden before the SS in panzers bulldozed their way up Upney Lane. Mum had to stop her going to the service. Her constant and voluble worry about whether the Germans had arrived yet and why the vicar hadn't barricaded the door to prevent access when they did took the attention off the worship. The grumpy vicar complained that he could not focus on communion when one of his parishioners was shouting, "They're here. I can hear their jackboots on the pavement outside," as he shared the Blessed Sacrament. It added fuel to Mum's anti-church fire to witness, as she termed it, the lack of Christian charity and forgiveness on display on Sunday mornings.

When Nan died and the tricky prospect of arranging her funeral was on the agenda, Miserable Vicar had been replaced by Modern Vicar. This man, for whom a liking for the 70s fashion for long hair was not matched by a generous enough application of shampoo, was all huge glasses, teeth and bombastic enthusiasm. He was understanding and keen to perform the funeral service even though he had never met Nan. He kept saying "Splendid!" when Mum and Dad went to see him about it. Dad was already keeping a book about how often this word would feature in the service. This was a secret between me and him and Uncle Patrick. Ungodly though she was, Mum would have thought this insensitive.

The congregation was a curious collection of mourners: the three of us, Gran with her missal (just so that God wouldn't be confused as to her true allegiance), an assortment of Nan's former neighbours, including Mrs Kirby, and some parishioners none of us knew. Several of Mum's best perms were on show, modelled by ladies who knew Nan from the last few years when she had been a fixture in the salon along with the hairdryers. Uncle Patrick (under instruction from his mother to be there) had brought his latest paramour. She had a massive bouffant hairstyle, a low-cut jacket in fuchsia pink with padded shoulders, a tight black skirt and enormously high heels. It was obvious she thought that they were going on a date 'up west' not a funeral in a 1950s church, because her scowl told us so.

"Will you look at that?" Gran asked no-one in particular in a stage whisper that reverberated amongst the congregation. "Chewing like a ruminant cow. May the Lord forgive her."

"I'm Tamsin," she told us when an introduction from Patrick was not forthcoming. She was indeed half-way through her second pack of Juicy Fruit before the Vicar had begun.

"Splendid to welcome you all here today."

Tamsin couldn't go five minutes without taking out her emery board to check her nails or her powder compact, lipstick and mirror to refresh her makeup. Even when the vicar was doing his best to sound as if he had any idea who Nan was – "Marjorie was a splendid member of the community…" – she was checking in a small pocket mirror that her mascara hadn't smudged.

The vicar had racked up twenty splendids and was onto his twenty first, using the adjective to describe how Marjorie had been the lynchpin of the Bible and a Bourbon discussion group, when Mum could contain herself no longer. Mid-eulogy she called out loudly, "Her name was Margaret but she was called Madge by everyone. I don't know who Marjorie is, but my mother never went to a Bible discussion group and she couldn't stand Bourbon biscuits."

The mouthful of teeth, permanently in a rictus grin, was useful in this type of situation. The vicar continued smiling despite this unusual interruption. "Isn't Madge short for Marjorie?" he asked.

"I don't know. What's it matter? My mother was called Margaret." Mum was fuming. The whole funeral business was difficult for her and this, combined with her dislike for the church, for religion and what she considered the hypocrisies that accompanied it, had bubbled over into this tsunami of an intervention.

"Splendid," said the vicar unsurprisingly. Through the massive lenses of his glasses, you could see his magnified eyes, wide with alarm.

Gran was bristling with indignation, partly with the ineptitude of the cleric and the casual nature of the Protestant service, but mostly for the irreverence my mother had shown in God's house.

Uncle Patrick was trying to stop himself laughing. Tamsin didn't see the funny side and was chewing furiously, anxious to begin the date she still thought she was going on.

Once outside the church, whilst the hearse was being loaded for the trip to the crematorium, there was much gossiping about the Vicar and his inability to get basic facts right. To the handful of parishioners who attended the church this was familiar territory.

"He does the same eulogy for everyone. I've noticed," commented a lady called Mrs Nugent who was a funeral regular.

There was barely one she missed. "Of course, it's difficult when the deceased hasn't been a recent regular attender. He has to say something."

There was a consensus from these old dears that this was indeed a problem. They should know, Mum pointed out to me sotto voce. Not only were they part of a rent-a-mourner group, but they never missed out on an opportunity to wolf down a fistful of sandwiches and cake at the 'afterwards'. She'd even heard a hint of disappointment when they realised that Nan's afterwards was to be at our house. We hadn't booked a hotel function room, nor even the back room at The Royal Oak, where they might have also been able to get a sweet sherry or port and lemon out of Dad by way of a thank-you for their concern.

Mum got into the car accompanying the hearse. "Come on, Mick," she called. Mrs Kirby got in too. Gran and Uncle Patrick sat on little dickie seats facing the wrong way. The funeral regulars realised that they now had to hang about for a bit before the principal mourners returned to hand round the food.

"Ain't you going?" asked Tamsin. Her face was pale orange, thick with foundation, I noticed out in the daylight. "Didn't ya get on with your Nan?"

"Yes, but there's only five seats in the car." Only then did it strike me as strange that of the five accompanying Nan on her final journey, only one was a blood relative.

"You could have had Pat's seat," Tamsin pointed out with barely disguised irritation.

"Mum doesn't think children should go to the crem," I explained, yet in the back of my mind I also remembered a conversation about the cost of the cars and how they didn't want to pay for two. "I've got to go back to the house to put the kettle on and look after the other guests."

"How old are you?" she asked incredulous. I told her I was twenty and she seemed relieved. "Well, that's not what I call a child. You can share a ciggie with me then." She got a pack of menthol cigarettes out of her bag. Long, with white tips, they were exactly what I would have guessed she'd smoke.

There were no gravestones in the grounds of the church. Burials were all at Barking cemetery at the far end of Upney Lane and we needed to screen ourselves from the censorious view of the mourners and so Gran couldn't see us as she slowly disappeared off down the street backwards. Fortunately, a huge bush provided the cover we required.

I wasn't quite sure how to make conversation with Tamsin. I felt a bit sorry for her, abandoned by Uncle Patrick and presumably tricked into attending in the first place. It didn't matter; she barely drew breath to enable me to join in her monologue.

In the ten minutes it took to puff our way through a luxury length St Moritz I learned all about her. She'd grown up in a prefab in Ilford. She had two ex-husbands. One was a bankrupt, the other was in HMP Wandsworth doing what she referred to as a 'long stretch'. She had no children and had never wanted any. She'd met Patrick in a bar but wasn't looking for another spouse. Just as well, I thought. My uncle was unlikely to be the answer to a girl who dreamed of weddings and confetti. She'd worked as a croupier in a club. She didn't say which one but implied it was where a protection racket was in operation. The world of the gambler was not unfamiliar to her. Up close she looked older than I'd thought initially. Uncle Patrick, although he took care with his appearance and was in good shape, was, after all, nearly fifty. Despite inheriting the Irish gift of the gab, he could no longer attract women in their twenties or thirties. The more I listened to her, the more I thought I'd been hasty in my judgement and that she was a good person for him to go out with.

We walked back to the house together, the old dears from the congregation and other mourners following behind at what they considered to be a respectful distance. They were keen not to lose sight of us and thus their access to the buffet Mum had prepared, even though the venue was not entirely to their liking.

I could see that Tamsin had been completely stitched up by Patrick, but she wasn't afraid to get stuck in helping to get some pots of tea going and taking foil off plates of sandwiches and sausage rolls. These were placed on the table which had been left ready (leaf in, cloth on – after much deliberation) in the middle of the back part of the through-lounge.

The ladies from the church remained gathered on the pavement, at least for a while. It was easy for them to check buffet-readiness from outside as Mum had recently removed the net curtains. Now you could see right into our through-lounge, almost from the other side of the road, without having to squint up close through the front window as before. Mum was acutely aware that there were disadvantages to this easy access but *Woman's Own* had decreed that the net curtain was dead. After a good deal of conversation and angst, which had occupied the hiatus between Nan's death and the funeral, she had taken the plunge. Mum knew her lounge would be under scrutiny after the service.

"If you don't like it, put them back up," suggested Dad, who was fed up with the endless and, to his mind, pointless debate. Net-free access did the trick for the hungry mourners, however, for as soon as the foil was off and a teapot had been passed through the hatch the doorbell rang.

The parishioners and neighbours piled in. Despite it being midsummer, they were all wearing coats and there was a fuss about where they would be leaving them and how they might be going to retrieve them when they eventually left. I took them upstairs to put on Nan's bed but there was some consternation that climbing the stairs to get them back might combine a physical challenge with a lack of respect by entering the deceased's bedroom.

The bell rang again. It was Mr and Mrs Green from next door, closely followed by the vicar. Both were full of apologies, the former for not being able to attend the service and the latter for his faux pas with the name. The vicar was relieved that Mum wasn't back yet. You could sense he wasn't looking forward to that encounter.

Everyone stood around awkwardly wanting to start the buffet but conscious that they shouldn't really before Mum and Dad got back. "They'll not be long," Mrs Nugent promised. After all, she was an expert at all types of funeral. "The crematorium part is very quick if you're not having the service there." She did little to disguise the fact that a mini pork pie had taken her fancy and positioned herself near a plate of them at the table. She'd obviously calculated there weren't enough for one each, so speed was essential.

Mum had put some chairs around the room, up against the walls. We'd had to borrow some from next door. Mrs Nugent wasn't going to be caught out being last to the table because she'd settled herself in a chair. She remained standing. Others had nabbed what they thought looked like the comfiest seat and now had a conundrum to work through before the green light for food was lit. Dare they surrender their berth in a rush to secure the best sandwich or should they remain still until the seat they had chosen could not really be nabbed by anyone else? This risked the possibility of just being left with the less popular snacks or potentially nothing at all.

In the event, the vicar solved the problem of when it was seemly to begin by diving in uninvited. "What a splendid spread!" he announced, taking a plate and cramming a mountain of pork pies, sandwiches and vol-au-vents onto it. He had filled the plate with so many treats that when he noticed a bridge roll bursting with ham and Primula he was unable to add it to the mound. He just shoved it straight into his huge mouth all in one go. The impossible number of teeth which occupied this cavern acted like a threshing machine, macerating the entire roll into digestible parts. Fascinating and repulsive at the same time. "I'm afraid I can't stay long," he explained, particles of bread and globules of cheese spread flying from his mouth. "It's communion class this evening."

No-one seemed that bothered, preoccupied as they all now were with loading their own plates. Handbags, ever-useful props, solved the issue of chair ownership. One placed on the Dralon seat of a vacated G plan would mean another person would have to have a great deal of neck to remove it and plonk herself down in its place. This was now an issue the veteran but chairless Mrs Nugent had to solve, once the desired mini pork pie and a good deal else besides had been secured.

Tamsin and I retreated to the kitchen to make more tea. "I don't even know your name," Tamsin admitted. "Pat probably said but I've forgotten."

"It's Roni."

"You ain't got a twin called Reggie 'ave ya?" she laughed. A certain type of person of her age from East London liked to suggest they might have known the notorious Kray brothers, Uncle Patrick included. Mum said it was all rubbish. Pat was trying to make himself more interesting. I wasn't sure how association with convicted murderers and thugs might do that.

"My real name is Veronica. Not many people call me that." I had a quick flashback to Simeon Goldblatt and his insistence on using my full first name.

"Don't you like it? I don't like my name either," Tamsin confided. "It's Eileen. A bit old-fashioned so I changed it. Tamsin is a bit more classy and up-to-date. Don't tell Pat. Mind you, quite often he can't remember what my bloomin' name is anyhow!" She didn't seem upset or disappointed by this, which was strange, I thought. She wasn't needy, Tamsin. She was tough and accepting. She just got on with it.

The vicar had timed it wrong. Just as he was making his exit apologetically from the house, the Daimler turned up outside, back from the crematorium. He managed to avoid Mum by continuing his apologies as he walked swiftly from the house. His long legs were making good ground in one direction, his head swivelled round like an owl's in the other. His perma-grin was on maximum wattage as he disappeared like a clerical Cheshire cat down the road.

"I'm glad I missed him," Mum said, but you could tell she felt it was another insult to add to the others he'd distributed during the afternoon.

"Well, what do you expect?" asked Gran, leaving the reason for low expectation unspoken but hanging in the air. "It's probably for the best. I'd a mind to tell him what I thought about his service and all. And, may the Good Lord forgive me, I would not have held back," she promised.

Dad heaved a sigh of relief and made for the kitchen. He fetched a bottle of whisky from the cupboard and poured one for him and Patrick. "Mick, Tansy would like one, I'm sure. She likes a drink," suggested Pat, whose apology to Tamsin had begun with a lascivious squeeze and arm round her waist.

Gran appeared. "Now what are you boys up to? I'll have a bit of that in my tea, if you will, Mick."

Gran eyed Tamsin up and down. She was assessing her clothes in the same way as Mum had assessed her hair when we were waiting for the service to begin. "That lot have made inroads into the tea, I see. How about waiting for the bereaved to return from burying their dead?" Gran was on full power.

"We couldn't stop them once the vicar had helped himself. Tamsin and I did our best."

"Ah, you'd be powerless in the face of that man and his manners, that's for sure." There was a short pause whilst we all wondered if his poor behaviour should exonerate the others from their greed and lack of etiquette. "I thought Pat said your name was Tansy." Gran looked suspiciously at Tamsin. She didn't miss much.

"It's Tamsin, actually," she replied, casting me a look which begged me not to reveal the Eileen secret.

"Right letter. Give me that," twinkled Pat. Even he realised that the success of the evening ahead was not assured. He needed to do something. "We ought to be moving." Tamsin had just lit up another St Moritz but stubbed it out enthusiastically when the possibility of release presented itself.

"Nice to meet you," she said to Gran, who remained unresponsive. "I'm sorry for your loss, Shirley," Tamsin shouted through the hatch to Mum, who was mid anecdote with a client from the salon in the other room.

Once they'd gone, Gran was conflicted. Her lips were pursed. Pat hadn't covered himself with glory but she never criticised him. We were all wondering if we'd ever see Tamsin again. Past experience suggested the odds were slim.

"She was really helpful," I said in her defence. Gran moved into the other room without comment. She'd no interest in the buffet, which was just as well as there was barely any left. The parishioners, having demolished the greater part of it, were trying to decide if any cakes and biscuits would be brought out to round off their meal.

I could tell Mum was uneasy. Her clients and her mother-in-law were in the same space. These perms on legs, proud examples of my mother's talent with curlers and strong chemical solutions, were, of course, regularly entertained by 'stories from the Emerald Isle'. Her collection of slanderous and adulterated gossip, such a popular feature of their appointments, which, although based on genuine news had been embellished and exaggerated in the telling, was in danger of being exposed. Fortunately, the nature of the occasion prevented even the most curious shampoo-and-set from approaching Gran direct for elucidation. They just looked at her surreptitiously across the room, as you might a film star you had spotted in a restaurant.

The doorbell rang. I went to answer it.

"Roni, good to see you after so long, despite the circumstances. I was sorry to hear about your grandmother. I just wanted to pop in to share my condolences with your mother."

It was Mrs Goldblatt. She looked knowingly at me. I think. I wasn't quite sure. Had Simeon told her what really happened at the boathouse? Had he even told her that we had been to the party together and that he'd been trying to help me? Had he been sent down?

Mum was all over Mrs Goldblatt, her star guest. She thanked her for coming to the wake. "Mrs Goldblatt, let me get you something to eat. I'm afraid there's not much left on the table," she apologised.

"Call me Ruth, please."

Mum presented her with a plate and a smarmy smile. "It's not much, Ruth, but there are some cocktail sausages left." The plate of non-Kosher food was thrust towards her, but Mrs Goldblatt politely refused. Mum, who, despite her strong dislike for religions, was startlingly uninformed about any of them, remained oblivious to her faux pas.

Permission to use Mrs Goldblatt's first name had gone to her head. She couldn't stop using it. Just when I thought it couldn't get any more embarrassing, Mum asked, "What is your son doing now, Ruth? You did tell me at your last appointment. He's left The University of Cambridge has he not? We both have children at The University of Cambridge."

This was a general announcement for the assembled company, to ensure that none of them was in any doubt as to the fact that my mother was equal in some way to Mrs Goldblatt, who lived in Upney Lane and chose The Mayfair Salon as her hairdressers. Mum's voice had taken on a strange affectation.

"His plans have changed," Mrs Goldblatt admitted quietly. I was sure she was looking at me, despite my own eyes being fixed intently on the carpet. She went on to explain that Simeon had changed his mind and decided to accept an offer he had previously rejected from Harvard and not to pursue his PhD at Cambridge. "It was all a bit last minute, but he decided he could do with a change of scene," she added. She didn't explain why.

It was a relief. Simeon would be peering down microscopes and stirring chemicals in test tubes on the other side of the Atlantic. Looking back on it, I probably did him a favour; or favor in his present circumstances. Don't think that I haven't checked up on him since. Today, all these years later, thanks to the internet I can now keep abreast of Simeon Goldblatt's every move. He is still in the US at the forefront of research into some kind of polymer chain which is helping with clean fuel. His wife is careless on Facebook and has security settings low enough for me to spy on them and their five children without being discovered as a stalker. They had a cat called Veronica for a bit – until it was run over. I had it coming I suppose.

I still feel guilty about not speaking up, but Simeon doesn't know that I know he didn't set fire to the boathouse. If I met him at some college event, would I own up?

14
Envy meets Anger

The name Webster Ferris was familiar to me before I had even set eyes on the man himself. When I arrived for my second year in the autumn of 1983, it was the big news; he was returning to college after a year 'out'. He was now in the second year with us whilst his cohort had naturally progressed to the third year. This was something they collectively deemed to be a relief.

Despite his name sounding like an American crime writer of one of the yellowing 1960s paperbacks we had on the bookshelf at home, I doubted that he had the easy charm of a transatlantic student. Webster Ferris was more likely the name of an estate agent or accountancy firm. It wasn't that unusual for the poshest members of the college to bear corporate type names. Monroe Cholmondeley could easily have been an upmarket dealer in real estate in the Home Counties. Aubyn Scrope, the mention of whose name reminded me of a nasty and contagious Victorian skin problem, could also have been an old-fashioned firm of solicitors. Torquil Powell? Surely a Savile Row tailor.

Much hilarity ensued when I suggested, "I suppose Webster Ferris is an Etonian?"

"I wouldn't say that to his face," advised a third year. The look on his own suggested that, having unwisely made a derogatory comment when they were both first years, he was now keeping conversation between them to a minimum and avoiding eye contact.

Webster Ferris, it turned out, was not a department store or a company of bailiffs but an angry, short-tempered morass of seething bile and invective from Rotherham. He was a big Yorkshire socialist fish-out-of-water who had mysteriously disappeared for a year but had now returned.

Everyone assumed he'd been sent down, given his track record of getting into fights and verbally abusing those members of college who had the misfortune to irritate him. Apparently, he'd had several 'meetings' with the Master (a man who rarely involved himself with undergraduates) and a warning from the Proctors, the university's 800-year-old private police force, who were in charge of the behaviour of its junior members. His card was so well marked that it was a wonder he had lasted a whole year.

His unruly behaviour, I had to admit, did not sound all that different from some of the worst excesses of the braying Hooray Henrys I'd tried to ingratiate myself with. Perhaps if you swore and shouted obscenities in a Northern accent it was considered more offensive. I made a note to ensure any trace of my own East London origins were kept under wraps next time I spoke to someone in less than polite terms.

He was a man from proper working-class roots, the son of a miner (so it was said). He wasn't a privately educated weekend socialist whose commitment to the cause peaked at being returned as a Labour MP in a school election. He wasn't friendless, they said, having been the lynchpin of the Cambridge Organisation of Labour Students (at that time probably ten years after the peak of its strength and power) and spent his time with a group of activists and left wingers from more aggressive colleges. It was generally felt that he'd have been better off at one of them rather than our gentle little scenic college with its picture-perfect buildings (brutalist annexe aside).

Ferris, apparently, knew what he was talking about, and his anger and commitment were terrifying. Why was he back?

Rumours abounded. He'd been the defendant in a court case and got off or, worse, been convicted and had been serving time at a low-security prison. He'd absconded with the subs from the Cambridge Labour Party but no-one had been able to prove it was him – despite the fact that he had spent the past year travelling Eastern Europe. He'd been in a clinic, drying out from his excessive alcohol dependency or receiving therapy for his violent personality. He'd abandoned his studies to take up professional boxing but hadn't made it because, although he could punch you very hard indeed (and there was documented evidence of that), he couldn't abide by Queensbury Rules.

Kinder rumours suggested that his year out had been approved by the college as he had been helping with the Labour campaign of 1983. Secretly, perhaps, they were hoping that he would never return. The fact that in June the Tory victory was the most decisive since 1945 went some way to explain the volcanic fury that accompanied Webster's return to East Anglia.

No one knew why he had left and certainly no one knew why the most terrifying student in Cambridge had returned. He was frighteningly clever, but he also scared the shit out of anyone who had to engage with him. And absolutely for certain, everyone had it on very good authority that his mother was an alcoholic and his sister was on the game in Rotherham.

The former was confirmed because Mrs Ferris, dressed in a completely inappropriate apricot lace ensemble with matching hat, had been seen with him when she visited towards the end of his first year. He had had to support her as she walked because she was so off her face she could barely stand up.

Close contact with the putative upper classes hadn't been a rewarding experience and it was not one I intended to repeat in my second year. The Brideshead world belonged in the book, in which, I realised, people of my social background were small parts, pilloried for amusement.

Even so, this man whose name was on everyone's lips seemed equally repellent. There were so many stories about Webster Ferris that I knew it was him instantly when our paths eventually crossed at a supervision with Dr Bennett.

He was sitting in an armchair, one leg jiggling involuntarily with impatience, an unsmiling, high-cheekboned face, black brows scowling above equally dark eyes and a mop of curly, unbrushed black hair. He managed to suggest there was an exclusion zone around him without saying anything. No one would dare to go within two yards of this leather-jacketed, coiled serpent. Long, spindly, tight-clad spider legs looked ready to strike out and sting you if you came within range. His Doc Marten boots looked like they had squashed a thousand Tory maggots beneath his feet. He fixed me with his gaze as I entered the room, following me until I sat down.

Another student, whom I recognised but also didn't know, was sitting waiting, silently. Both she and Dr Bennett had chosen chairs as far as possible from Ferris. I was left with the last one, dangerously within range.

"You're late." This was from Ferris, a gruff northern statement with which I couldn't argue but a comment which one might more reasonably have expected to have come from Dr Bennett.

"Ah, this must be Veronica McNamara." Dr Bennett's voice was reedy and insecure. He shuffled some papers as if to check that he'd got my name correct. Perhaps he was looking for an official confirmation in case Ferris was going to challenge him. "Are you indeed the leader of the band?" Bennett chuckled to himself. I defy anyone of a certain age not to refer to the song about McNamara being the leader of the band when they hear my surname. It's a tedious Pavlovian response.

I smiled weakly. The other girl looked nonplussed, and Ferris's face remained immobile. "Irish?" the scary one accused eventually.

"I'm from County Barking in Essex," I stated, with a lilt in my voice. Not the best joke in the world but perhaps deserving of a slight smile in the breaking-the-ice kind of situation we were in. Nothing was forthcoming. There was an awkward silence.

"Surely the county is Essex itself, I might suggest," Dr Bennett queried, looking confused.

Things were not looking good. I was stuck in a small room with a mute, a psychopath and someone who was very literal indeed and unlikely to be an inspiring interpreter of English literature. A shaft of October sunlight suddenly shone blindingly through the window like a laser beam fired by a malevolent invader. My hastily written essay on D H Lawrence was probably not going to go down well.

Unsurprisingly, Ferris had plenty to say on Lawrence. Indeed, it became obvious that there was something to be grateful to him for. He stole the air waves with his opinions and carefully thought-out comments and arguments. No need to have to contribute all that much. Dr Bennett certainly wasn't going to rock the boat by asking either of us girls to venture our feeble opinions, not when forceful Ferris might spring up and eat him as a light snack at any moment.

"Indeed, an excellent point," Dr Bennett enthused, snuggling down into his armchair, a potential nap only prevented by the need to keep his eye on Ferris in case he decided to lob a hand grenade in his direction to liven up the supervision.

The realisation that this was the pattern for the term, if not the year, was only marginally improved by hoping that, against logic, Ferris would manage not to get sent down again. Whilst he was there, the necessity for me ever to have to read out an essay in a supervision again was minimal.

Webster Ferris did not linger once the session was over. Neither did he heed any bourgeois crap about ladies first or saying goodbye. He pushed past all three of us and sped down the narrow stairs and into the court.

"Ah, a man with a mission," sighed Dr Bennett, possibly

with a hint of regret that his own missions were now confined to a singular intent. Securing a glass of sherry and a chair by the fire in the Senior Common room before correctly timing his arrival at high table was the only item on his agenda. Avoiding having to sit with the Chaplain or any dull scientists who lacked esoteric conversation about lesser-known seventeenth-century metaphysical poets was a necessary part of his dining experience. He was blissfully unaware that many of the rest of the SCR were equally intent on not sitting next to Dr Bennett, who was considered dreary and dull by almost all of them. Similarly, the undergraduate body at our college were united in their desire to sit as far as possible from Ferris at mealtimes.

I hoped my encounters with him would be confined to a once-a-week hour of listening to his opinions on whichever author we were asked to study. A bonus was that he was incisive and original, and I quickly realised that if I took notes about what he said they would be more useful than any thoughts Dr Bennett could cobble together in the brief moments when Ferris was drawing breath.

My mission for the term and possibly the year was to enlarge my participation in drama, potentially outside the confines of the college. I had joined the college drama society, but I yearned for the pretensions of the university groups who performed little known works in small spaces to tiny audiences or classic works adapted with a contemporary take in larger venues. Why? I was in pursuit of contemporary experimental theatre, the kind of claptrap which I would avoid at all costs these days.

There were plenty of students in Cambridge devising that type of production and I sought them out. It wasn't long before I was giving my interpretation of Envy in a lunchtime performance of an abridged version of *Dr Faustus* set in a parallel universe at an unspecified point in the future. The cast outnumbered the audience even though two of the Deadly Sins had withdrawn at late notice due to illness.

I was wearing bright green tights, stripy shorts and a large, spherical, green paper Chinese lampshade. These lampshades were popular at the time. This one was enormous and the fitting for the bulb at the top had been removed and the hole enlarged. Same at the bottom. The paper on the sphere was supported by rings of wire. The person whose job it was to make the costumes thought that putting the shade over my head and pulling it down over my body, then cutting holes into it for my arms to stick through, was a suitable way to represent Envy. My face was painted bright green and my hair was packed tight under a woollen hat (also green) the size of a small suitcase. I looked like a pea which had sprouted limbs.

One afternoon, after a lunchtime performance, I was hurrying back to my room, not without some difficulty, to remove all of this stuff because there were no dressing rooms at or near the cupboard where we had been performing.

"Fook me. What the hell are you dressed like that for?" I was stopped near the entrance to Dr Bennett's staircase by an accusatory Northern bellow. "Get a move on, we've a supervision in two minutes." I had forgotten all about it but I couldn't not attend now I had been discovered in time. Webster Ferris would tell Dr Bennett or set fire to me as an example to other students who threatened to interrupt the progress of his studies.

I had to go up the stairs, Webster Ferris following in my wake. For an hour I sat there, arms at an awkward angle, green stage make-up, like a fast-growing mould, migrating from my face to my fingertips and therefore onto my armchair, whilst Webster Ferris enlightened us all on realism and idealism in Arnold Bennett's *Five Towns* series.

Dr Bennett's contribution was to insist several times that the author was not a relation, suggesting that the only fact which he had extrapolated from the text was that he shared a name with the writer. He shot me sideways glances from his armchair, but he didn't ask me why I was wearing a large paper ball.

The other girl, continuing her vow of silence for the duration of the supervision, wore a slightly greater look of confusion than usual, which I attributed to my appearance.

Ferris's gruff face did not give much away. He was the only one of us to have been to Stoke-on-Trent and therefore was uniquely qualified to give a genuine appraisal of the potteries as presented in the novels. In a brief aside he ventured his opinion that Stoke-on-Trent wasn't really 'up North' at all. No-one argued. Bennett clearly never left Cambridge and possibly never went beyond the college walls. The silent one kept her origins and adventures to herself. I'd been on a factory tour at Bourneville once, but it didn't seem relevant.

My contribution to the session was nil. Dr Bennett didn't even bother to ask where my essay was. I did not provide any of them with the answer to the question they were so obviously wishing to ask. How characteristically British, I thought. Despite the brief exclamation outside, three people were sitting in a room with a green-faced, green-legged giant vegetable with its arms shoved through two holes in a huge paper lampshade and an enormous hat on its head. And none of them could muster the perceived impudence to ask why. I looked absurd but no-one liked to mention it.

I thought I caught the twitch of a suppressed smile on Ferris's face as he pushed past on his way out but decided this was an involuntary movement or indigestion after lunch. He didn't go in for small talk or any kind of social talk, really. He didn't go in for smiling or laughing. I'd never seen him do either.

Why should I care what he thought of me? I was busy, like everyone else, trying to keep well out of his orbit.

15
Pared-Down friends

s the term progressed, Mary and I spent time with each other cycling off to lectures at the Sidgwick site. This was the post-war-built, white-faced, mean-windowed, flat-roofed cluster of unattractiveness where the English faculty was located. The buildings surrounded a large Victorian villa and perched on concrete stilts, as if they were afraid of treading on the toes of their previous, more attractive incarnation.

I'd made some new friends from other colleges too, none of whom appeared to be involved in rotas to prepare cocoa in the evening. I realised I'd settled down a bit now and felt part of the place.

At our college, Webster Ferris continued to be the topic of the day. It was said there were black eyes and sore ribs to attest to the friction he'd caused with others. Those who thought it good sport to wind him up paid for their temerity. If anyone had a bit of a bruise or cut or began walking with a limp, these injuries were attributed to Ferris rather than a more likely brawl on the rugby pitch or mistimed step when leaving the bar. I'd never seen him hit anyone, but there was ample evidence of his quick and nasty temper.

I made it to Christmas avoiding conflict with the dreaded Webster. I arrived at the day to go home for the holidays without being minced up to form the stuffing for his seasonal turkey or roasted with some chestnuts by his fiery temperament for a Yuletide snack. He had tutted a few times in supervisions as I read my essays out, but I hadn't seen the reported fracas that he supposedly caused around the college.

Mum and Dad came to pick me up at the end of the short term. I'd moved my bags to the Porters' Lodge to wait for the car to arrive as instructed. Suddenly, across the road, Mum's head appeared, flustered and gesticulating wildly from the window of a car I didn't recognise.

She dashed out of this unfamiliar vehicle and opened the boot. "Get your case in quick. He thinks he saw a warden," she advised, hurling in some of the smaller bags I had with me. It seemed I was part of a getaway from a jewellery heist.

"What's this? Where's the Cortina?"

"Get in and I'll tell you!" Dad's foot was already on the accelerator, just like the getaway driver in an episode of *The Sweeney.*

Not only had they bought a new car but, Mum informed me, we were going on holiday. Over Christmas and overseas.

This sounded ominous. Dad had become a bank robber? A rainbow's end had landed on our crazy paving? He was printing his own bank notes in the shed at the bottom of the garden?

How they had afforded to pay for all this was revealed by a simple explanation about where the money had come from. There were no hold-ups, protection rackets or Premium Bond winnings. Nan's will had been proved and it turned out she had left a large amount of money. She hadn't known she had it, of course; it was another of the details of her life which she had abandoned. In fact, Mum wasn't sure she ever knew. When he died, my grandfather had left everything to her apart from the knowledge about what he was doing drawing all those tiny figures all over the pink newspaper which I liked looking at. His investments had paid off handsomely over the years.

I was speechless. As a family we never went abroad on holiday and we always spent Christmas at home. Dad had been overseas during his National Service, but Mum and I hadn't even been in a plane.

This wasn't the response Mum had expected. Her voice broke a little. "The thing is, I don't think I want Christmas at home without your Nan. It won't be the same."

So we flew to Tenerife, leaving Uncle Pat the only audience for Gran's run-down of Father O'Connor's Christmas message and the veiled criticism of lack of attendance at a place of worship by the rest of us that would accompany it.

On return, having a suntan in January was a talking point for the Cocoa Club as 1984 began. It didn't go down well with Webster Ferris. At our first tutorial, he took one look at my fast-fading Tenerife souvenir, something I was keenly promoting by wearing clothes far too brief for the chilly temperatures, and couldn't hold back.

"You didn't get that colour sticking about at home. I know it's warmer in the south but that's ridiculous. Is it make-up?"

Rude – but three sentences with no expletives and all in a row? This rarely happened outside the discussion of English Literature, where Webster Ferris did not draw breath. He didn't do small talk or chitchat. 'How are you?', 'Nice to see you!', 'Have a good holiday?'. A seasonal 'Happy New Year.'

"I've been on holiday," I said and then immediately wished I hadn't bothered to continue the discourse.

"I can see that. Fook me. You've not been to Bridlington I take it? Alright for some."

"No." Why did I carry on the conversation?

"Oh! It were Scarborough then, were it?" He wasn't going to let it rest.

"Where did you go?" Dr Bennett had woken up and seized an opportunity to delay having to discuss *Far From the Madding Crowd* with Ferris, who would undoubtedly know more about it than him.

This was not what I had in mind. "Do tell!" Even the silent one had broken her vow and demonstrated that she did have a voice after all.

"Oh, just away." I opened my book hoping that the tutorial would commence.

"It must have been by aeroplane," Dr Bennett mused, showing that even if he hadn't been outside Cambridge since the time of Bathsheba, he did at least know that beyond the city lay far-away lands where the temperature exceeded a mild 60 degrees in high summer. "I went to Italy by aeroplane once," he admitted. "A long time ago now. I'm afraid I found the turbulence a problem and was violently unwell. A charming hostess lady came and handed me a brown paper bag, but I fear she was a little tardy."

There was a brief hiatus while we all ran this charming image through our minds. Ferris ignored him but he wasn't done with me.

"Been to Mummy and Daddy's villa, then?" Ferris rebounded, aiming at the jugular.

"No," I replied defensively. "It was a hotel actually."

"Ooh, by heck, that's posh for you. A ho-tel." He took a long time over the word, as if it was precious and unusual. I wanted to kick him, very hard, but I was worried he might kick me back, even harder.

"I'm not a fan of hotels per se," Bennett continued. "I prefer a small pensione, out of the way, in a remote location. One gets to know the staff and the clientele so much better."

Even Webster Ferris must have been running through his mind the scenario of spending two weeks in close contact with Dr Bennett and a select few other fossils, off the beaten track in a foreign country with no means of escape.

The Doctor was caught up in a reverie of times past. "What a pity we are not discussing Forster's *Room with A View*." Bennett lay his head back on the armchair and was soon asleep – presumably dreaming of Italy. Webster Ferris told us about Hardy's Bathsheba and her three suitors, whilst Bennett mouthed, "Ahh, Miss Honeychurch," every so often in his slumbers.

I felt lucky that I rarely came across Ferris beyond Dr Bennett's study. Occasionally he'd be in earnest conversation with one of his political allies in the dining hall or I'd see him holding a placard or banner on King's Parade as I cycled past. He never acknowledged me.

My social life in Cambridge during that second year revolved around the people I'd met through the small drama society which had produced *Doctor Faustus* the previous term.

Roland was the lynchpin of the Pared-Down Players; it was his baby. He was intense and purposeful with an unchallengeable belief that his interpretations of playwrights' works were an improvement on the originals. If only Christopher Marlowe could have seen how much his *Doctor Faustus* was enlivened by stripping away the majority of the plot (too long for a lunchtime show), many of the characters (as much through lack of willing participants as from pruning) and dressing me in a spherical green lampshade, painting my face green and calling me Envy. As deadly sins go, I was certainly unappealing – though not repellent enough to prevent Faustus from making his pact with the devil. Like me, he was blinded by Roland's bullshit.

Faustus's flaws – folly of ambition and a confusion of true with illusive power – were shared by Roland, though none of us acknowledged it at the time. They dogged his every decision. Roland was the embodiment of pretension.

He didn't perform in his own adaptations; he felt he was above that and his intentions were focused on a career directing his kind of tosh in the real world. I was taken in by his mesmeric pontificating. Anyone who could talk that much, with so many elaborate hand gestures to accompany the obscure vocabulary he used, had to be saying something worthwhile. His inner circle got to call him Roly. This was an honour not yet bestowed on me – we were very much on Roland terms for the time being.

Roland took himself very seriously indeed. His hair appeared to be randomly wayward although his backcombed eighties shaggy mullet was carefully gelled into place. His look was hours in the making. You can't appear so artfully tousled without a good deal of time looking in the mirror using several types of hairbrush.

"Looks like he's been pushed through a hedge backwards," was Mum's unsurprising verdict on the mane when she met him after a half-hour re-working of Aeschylus's *Oresteia*. It was staged in a small, panelled room in a college rather than an open-air Greek amphitheatre. The greatest triumph of Roland's production was making this three-part tragedy, which takes at least five hours to perform in the original version, an excruciating thirty minutes that seemed to last five hours.

I was cast as Clytemnestra, a husband poisoner who got her comeuppance only twelve minutes into the thirty minutes worth of tedium; I was off stage for nearly two thirds of the time.

This freed up Mum, who like the rest of the audience found it hard to keep up with the plot, to study Roland sitting in the front row, intensely making notes to give us after the show. His highlights and slick of eyeliner were not features my mother was accustomed to finding on men. Though that didn't stop her tapping him on the shoulder afterwards to suggest that the use of foil rather than a hook piercing a rubber cap might give better results to his streaks.

"What did you think of the performance, Mrs McNamara?" Roland was not used to such personal comments about his appearance and was sensitive to criticism.

"I thought it was too short. I don't know why you had to kill her off so soon. Ron's dad is still parking the car; he's missed it." Mum didn't hold back. "It was hardly worth the journey."

For Roland, used to the sycophancy of his acolytes and still smarting from the professional advice he had received about his coiffeur, this was the final straw. He flounced off taking any remaining hope I had of getting to call him Roly with him.

The founder members of the Pared-Down Players became my closest friends. Roland's productions may have been brief but the rehearsals were long. We spent a lot of time together.

Lucy and Steve were a couple who had a tempestuous relationship at the best of times. Their on-off partnership was the subject of many nights' weeping and wailing on Lucy's part and as much sympathy as I could muster hearing about his lack of empathy all over again.

"I just know he doesn't care," she'd complain. What he was supposed to care about was never specified but generally related to any number of causes Lucy was in the process of supporting at that particular moment. It also referred generally to Lucy herself. I wasn't convinced he didn't care about her. He just failed to tell her that he did often enough.

"Roni, I should break up with him, shouldn't I?"

"Yes. Probably."

"Oh, you don't really think that do you?"

"If it would make you happy."

"Oh no. I'd be so miserable. So wretched. I'm not sure I could carry on."

"Stay with him, then."

"How can I when he doesn't care?"

My tactic was to tell her what I thought she wanted to hear. Given that she didn't really know herself it was difficult to be consistent.

When protesting against Barclay's Bank's alleged support of Apartheid, she accidentally superglued her fingers to the cashpoint. She made the machine useless (as intended), but Lucy's obvious culpability because she could not run away had hilarious consequences. She had no alternative but to stand there receiving abuse from irate and cashless students and members of the public. Steve found it amusing – a poor move which, to Lucy, showed how much he didn't care.

Everyone was talking about it. Even the *Cambridge Evening News* showed up and took a picture of the rain-sodden Lucy and some fist shakers who had come in from outside villages to get some cash. It was, in the end, good publicity for her cause.

Steve was a nice lad who had found himself in deeper than he intended after an ill-judged lunge at a cast party. Lucy could be fun, but she was intense and emotional. Steve was from Croydon and, like me, from a 'normal' home. His mother didn't waft about crying over the beauty of a rose, throw a tantrum about the impossibility of world peace or rant about the destruction of the rainforests. Like my own, Steve's mum would have been more concerned about getting to Sainsbury's after work before it shut and worrying about whether she should put the washing out if it looked like rain. Lucy was a mystery, both fascinating and terrifying to him. He hadn't met a woman like her before and her intensity frightened him. Trouble was, he was too nice to dump her.

Lucy came from somewhere near Guildford and her concern for 'the working man' was, whilst genuine, not matched by acquaintance with them at any level. She hadn't had a holiday job in a shop or factory, and she didn't really travel by public transport.

When I was invited to her house for her 21st birthday, I knew it was posh before I saw it. It had a name and not a number. Sure enough, it was vast and surrounded by a garden about the size of Barking Park.

It had two sets of stairs. I'd never seen this before – a grand staircase and another more basic utility one with direct access to the kitchen. Chasing around playing sardines was a whole lot more enjoyable than it would have been in our house. A three-bed semi with a through-lounge lacked the hiding opportunities of an Edwardian pile where they had arguments about how many bedrooms there actually were. Our airing cupboard might have provided a hiding place. I'd never tried to get a group of people inside, but common sense told me it was unlikely to hold any more than two and they'd have to breathe in to get the door shut.

Going up the back stairs led me to the attic. Once there, I spent rather too long in a wardrobe with some old furs, a moth-eaten army greatcoat and a boy Lucy had been to school with who had drunk too much and was desperate for the lavatory.

Lucy's mother wore kaftans and her mind occupied another universe. In conversation she said, 'Marvellicious, Darlingo', 'Kookie', 'Super Dupes' and other things that weren't proper words. I'm not sure she really listened to or cared about what you were saying.

"I'm sorry, Mrs. Cuthbert-Smith, but Giles has pissed in the wardrobe because the others were so long looking for us that he couldn't hold it in any longer. We tried to mop it up with the fur."

Her reply would be something like, "Tutti Frutti!" or in translation, "I don't give a shit." No wonder Lucy was so obsessed with people caring about her, or anything for that matter.

The antagonism between Lucy and Steve could have been useful for method acting if Roland had decided to adapt a play where the major roles were a couple who are completely unsuited. Yet Steve the appeaser, forever in search of the quiet life, always gave way. He didn't want to hurt her feelings, so he hid his own desire to turn on his heels and run. Lucy was always at the point of quitting a production because of the latest way in which Steve had failed to show his lack of empathy, so the poor boy had to continue the charade for the good of the company.

"You'll just have to tell her somehow. You can't live a lie," Danny would suggest. This had little currency because Danny, who was from Manchester and had a domineering mother and an Asian girlfriend, lacked the ability to own up to his own narrative.

Not only did Mrs Burgess believe that Danny was single because a girl from what she considered to be the right calibre hadn't taken his eye but she also was duped by the lie that he spent all his spare time in the library working towards a first. He dreaded the holidays, when he would be paraded around Didsbury, the hard working and eligible son waiting to be match-made with a suitable girl. Mrs B loved to explain to prospective brides how he had given up his love of the theatre to concentrate on his future.

"He doesn't mix with those showbiz friends anymore. His sights are set on the legal profession, where he will be earning a very good salary."

If only Mrs Burgess had known that Danny had found love in *Doctor Faustus* and rarely went to lectures or the library, preferring to spend whole afternoons lying on Ameerah's bed whilst she worked at her desk. He got up when they went to rehearsals together. She had not been unkindly cast as Pride for she was rightly proud of her achievements. He was an excellent Sloth, a part to which he brought the rich experience of his student life. He was nailed on for a third and had no interest in the law, which was probably just as well.

They may have been drawn together because they came from the same city. She came from Longsight, which was geographically handy for secret assignations in the holidays, but its proximity to Didsbury had a drawback too. Ameerah's father was a pillar of the Pakistani community. If their secret had got out, it is not impossible that Mrs Burgess and Mr Shah could have been immediately rushed to the same mixed cardiac ward at the Manchester Royal Infirmary. This nightmare scenario kept Danny awake at night.

He wasn't the only anxious member of the players. Neil had plenty of neuroses but didn't have genuine relationship problems because he'd never had a relationship. Not that he wouldn't have liked one or didn't spend a lot of his time trying to fathom out how he was going to go about getting one. I suppose that might be a relationship problem in itself. He asked me for my advice, which was pointless. I knew barely more than him.

There weren't any other gay pupils at his grammar school in North Norfolk. At least that's what Neil had assumed. When he got away as far as Cambridge and discovered that there were others just like him and they were openly celebrating being out, he realised he had probably been wrong. Neil came out in our second year – but only to me. I was forbidden to spread the news. You couldn't say he came out of the closet. Rather he invited me in there with him, a bit like Giles in the wardrobe. We were in there together just like in sardines, waiting for love to discover us.

He was not effeminate in any way. When he wasn't decked out head to toe as Anger in a one-piece, red fun-fur animal suit Roland had found on sale in a fancy dress shop, he could get pretty aggressive in the second row of his college rugby team. He was very masculine. No-one could have guessed. Lack of honesty was a crucial flaw in Neil's crusade to find a partner. The list of people he didn't want to know featured his parents and family, the rugby team, everyone in his college, anyone from his school, the population of Cromer – or more accurately in East Anglia. Rather than shortening, it grew longer and longer.

He would sit in my room long into the night plotting how to catch the eye of a boy he'd seen somewhere. Nothing ever came of it. Neil's nerve always failed him, and he had an unfortunate predilection for fancying straight men. That didn't help.

We were a tight and happy 'band of brothers'. I had found my place.

"... from pig to man"

e all agreed that, at least in theory, the arrival of 1984 gave Roland an obvious book to pare down. How could he resist the opportunity to condense and improve the famous novel by George Orwell with a cast of six? A gift for this re-worker of well-loved literature.

However, a plot as complex as *Nineteen Eighty-Four* was a challenge even for Roland, who had managed to cut the twelve-hour running time of Shakespeare's longest and most convoluted trilogy, *Henry VI*, down to a very respectable 45 minutes. Surely Roland should have been able to attempt a pruned version of the complexities of life on Airstrip One and the shenanigans of The Ministry of Truth?

As a prelude to a future Orwellian production, Roland began with *Animal Farm*. He decided that those of us playing animals should wear huge animal heads, which, though potentially realistic, were so close fitting that not only did they impede breathing, but they also made delivering the lines almost impossible. If the piece had been any longer there would have been fatalities.

"Roni, you're going to play Clover," he announced. Initially I was just glad not to be cast as a pig, until I remembered that this carthorse is a sturdy beast whose characteristic is that she is slightly stupid and unable to think for herself. Roland's smiling face revealed that he was highly amused at his own casting.

Danny was the cynical donkey Benjamin, bad-tempered and lacking inspiration about the rebellion and not up for change. Boxer the carthorse, strong, loyal and dedicated yet slow-witted, was ably portrayed by Steve. No apple carts upset by this reliable beast.

Roland differentiated the other girls. Ameerah was the intelligent, passionate and eloquent Snowball, a most loyal pig, and Lucy was Mollie, a vain and flighty mare who loved being groomed and pampered. The very embodiment of the bourgeoisie, the role was ideal for her.

As Roland's productions went, this could have been one of the better ones – if anyone could have heard his abridged lines clearly. The whole thing was inaccessible to those who relied on the words to convey the meaning of the piece. This was an advantage to us, the performers, we realised, once we had received our costumes. Learning the lines was unnecessary.

Fortunately, audience numbers were low, not helped by a snowfall which lingered for the entire run. Our venue, or 'space' as Roland termed it, a lecture theatre, was cramped – or would have been if there had been an audience in double figures. It certainly didn't extend to a backstage or dressing-room area. At the end of the performance, I had to return to college dressed like a pantomime horse escaping from Dick Whittington.

Not only did I have a huge horse's head to contend with, I had coconut shells tied to my wrists and ankles which I was obliged to clack together when I moved to make the clip-cloppety sound of hooves. The wrist ones were easy to operate, the ankles less so. Fortunately, the head was removable, and I could carry it under my arm like the ghost of an equine Anne Boleyn. The snow didn't help, icy pavements and cobbles making walking about hazardous even if you were dressed normally.

Neil, who remained in his Old Major costume, needed help removing the boar's head, which was a tight and suffocating fit. We went back to his room after the show in order to take it off. I was carrying my horse's head under one arm whilst linking the other with Neil's so that we remained upright. Navigating a passage down King's Parade in a fun-fur one-piece whilst wearing thin plimsolls was not easy in the wintry weather.

The tiny, piggy eye slits of his headdress made seeing properly difficult and Neil spent a good deal of the show careering between a crudely made sign saying 'Animal Farm' which gave you splinters if you got too close, and a giant cartwheel made of heavy metal propped up against a lightweight straw bale. Every time someone collided with it whilst sightlessly moving about the stage like a crazed participant in blind man's bluff, it wobbled and threatened to fall. Every member of the cast then fled from it as it slipped and teetered. No-one wanted half a ton of rusting iron and solid wood flattening their thinly covered toes.

We made it through the Porters' Lodge of Neil's college. The porter on duty called out, "Evening, Mr Carrington," recognising Neil immediately and completely unfazed by the fact that his human head had been replaced by a giant, round boar's one complete with tusks. We crossed the first court, where it became apparent that Neil was walking in a zigzag.

"Roni, get it off!" he pleaded. Actually, he said, "Nerni, brt bt ruff," but I worked out what he meant. Freeing him from the monstrosity, which had a disconcerting number of fangs protruding from its mouth as well as the pointy tusks, was not easy. It was the size of an astronaut's helmet, and I needed a good amount of purchase to yank it from his head. We had reached the doorway of Neil's staircase. He bent over so I could pull it off, but this time it refused to budge. I put my foot against the stone architrave of the doorway and involuntarily made grunting noises as I began to tug. Neil was nearly bent at right angles as I pulled violently, letting out a primeval scream as I did so.

His own head was suddenly released, like a cork from a bottle, and Neil ricocheted through the opening and fell back against the bottom of the staircase as he did so. He yelled out in pain. His face was red and rivulets of sweat coursed down his face. His hair was flat and matted against his head. He looked as if he had been trapped in a sauna or got lost in a tropical jungle.

Suddenly the door to one of the downstairs rooms opened.

"You guys should do that in the privacy of your own room." It was an angry American voice and its owner had obviously just got out of bed. "Do you know what time I get up in the morning? It's like in about half an hour." The voice belonged to an athletic body, finely toned. Its muscles were highly defined and numerous. Pyjamas were obviously not part of this gentleman's wardrobe, even at this freezing time of year. A tiny towel protected his modesty. Both Neil and I stared at him, mouths agape. Could he be real? He looked like a statue from the antiquities section of the British Museum but waxy, as if he had escaped from Madame Tussaud's.

It turned out he was real and called Dale. He was an American post-grad Neil had been contriving to bump into in and around college. His powerful athletic build spent most of the time in very tight rowing shorts as he was hoping for a place in the Cambridge boat for the Boat Race.

Neil was distraught. He'd been setting his alarm to get up at a ridiculously early time in the mornings to try and skip down the stairs at the same time as Dale left for his early-morning training. After they had made eye contact and said good morning, Neil pretended to be going somewhere and then, when Dale was out of view, turned round and returned to bed for another four hours. Neil's romantic plan had not progressed further than this.

Dale slammed his door with a forceful 'Don't mess with me' gesture. If there were any other early-to-bed rowers on the staircase, this would have woken them up.

"Does my hair look ok?" wailed Neil. I watched a drip of salty sweat run down from his forehead until it formed a hanging drop big enough that it finally fell from his nose. "Have I blown it?"

"You look fine," I lied, noticing his face had become even

redder now he was blushing as well as overheating. He was as appealing as the bulging, bright pink saveloys the chip shop near The Mayfair Salon used to sell. Only to be taken if you couldn't afford fish and just a bag of chips wasn't filling enough.

"But he thinks I'm shagging you!" He realised he'd spoken with more repulsion than necessary. "No offence."

I decided to leave. I didn't feel up to an hour or more of Neil's trials and tribulations in the land of love. You had to be in the right mood for that.

It was a Saturday night, the last night of this particular production. The sight of a headless horse slipping and sliding though the market square caused a good deal of hilarity and loud abuse from people who had come in from the surrounding villages for their Saturday night's entertainment.

The pubs had shut and there were groups of airmen, in from the local bases, hanging about looking for trouble. They usually targeted students who had overdone it in the college bars and who tried to take them on verbally. Experience showed that physical aggression does indeed hurt more for those prepared to test the hypothesis that words are not as wounding as blows.

"Give us a ride, love," shouted a young man clinging to a lamppost. "You can pull my cart any day." A police car pulled up. Its arrival silenced him momentarily until he let out a massive belch which prefaced an impressive fountain of vomit ejected into a nearby drain. It was a neat manoeuvre and one I felt he had perfected over several years of excessive Saturday nights.

I was able to escape as there had obviously been some kind of incident at which the police had arrived, characteristically after events had ceased.

I became aware of a trail in the snow. Like the line of breadcrumbs left by Hansel and Gretel to show their path into the forest, it was leading to my college. Under a streetlight I realised that what looked like a trail of bright red pebbles was pools of blood.

Not only was I trying to avoid the slippery snow, but I also now had to step gingerly round the drops of blood. When I got to the college gates, they were shut. I would have to ring the night bell and risk the wrath of the porter.

There was a pile of bikes by the entrance. They had been leaning against the wall, but it looked as if someone had thought it would be great fun to pull them all over. They were all padlocked and had fallen inconveniently for anyone wishing to pass by. They made an obstacle course which was particularly tricky for people avoiding icy snow or pools of fresh blood or for those wearing animal suits with coconut shells dangling from them.

In the dim light, whilst looking for the night bell, I realised that the bicycles had fallen over because someone had fallen into them and that person was still there, collapsed amongst them.

"Are you ok?" I asked, completely pointlessly. It was clear this person was definitely not alright. It wriggled, struggling to get up. "Can I help you?" Limbs were moving but to no effect.

"Why don't you just fook off?" Oh Lord. It was Webster Ferris, the last person I wanted to see. A dilemma. Do as he asked (it was tempting) or do the right thing?

It was clear, in the dark recess of the ancient college doorway that Webster Ferris was not going to disentangle himself from the bicycle pile-up without a hand from me or someone else. I looked down the lane. The snow glistened in the moonlight but there was no-one else there.

"I'll help you up," I said unenthusiastically.

"You're all right. I've no need of it," he replied churlishly. No word of thanks, I noted.

"Go on then!" I challenged.

The limbs moved again, long legs thrashing at the spokes of some unfortunate bike, but he was too entangled to extricate himself without help. I reached for his hand to pull him up.

"That's not the way to do it," he explained uncharitably. "You should grab my arm at the elbow, and I'll do t'same to you." I was relieved not to have to hold hands with him and did as he said. I pulled and by pushing down with his other hand on a nearby bike saddle he was able to get his feet flat on the pavement. Another pull and he staggered upright and teetered about like a new-born giraffe. He lurched uncoordinated towards me, and I suddenly realised that the drops of blood I'd been following were coming from him. It was coursing down his nose and from a huge gash above his eyebrow. The eye below it was swelling up and had narrowed to a slit. I steadied him with my hand and the blood began to drip on me.

The little door which was cut into one of the great big doors to the college and through which pedestrians entered when the gate was closed, suddenly opened. The night porter emerged looking displeased.

"What's going on?" Neither of us replied. "Oh, it's you, Ferris. There's a surprise. Drunk again? Don't think you're coming in here in that kind of state." The porter retreated behind the small door. He knew better than to try and remonstrate with Ferris without a shield or barrier in front of him. His head alone stuck out beyond the defences. "And may I ask, Miss, why is you dressed as an 'orse?"

"That's rich coming from someone wearing a bowler hat in this day and age." Webster Ferris had a quick retort even when appearing to be half dead. The door slammed shut.

"Sod you!" he shouted, I assumed at the porter. "Come on, you can climb in round t'back. I've done it loads of times." He then slipped on the ice and fell over, landing on his hand and showering the white ground with a spray of new blood from his head.

"Oh, my fooking hand." I could see it was already raw and swollen, I guessed from hitting some poor bloke very recently.

"You're not going to be climbing up anything," I said, keeping well out of the way in case he wanted to try the sore hand out to see if it was still in punching condition. "You probably need a stitch in that gash above your eye."

"Good at needlework are you?"

"I thought you should go to A & E perhaps…" I waited for the abuse to follow.

"I can't," he said. He sounded surprisingly pathetic. "I tried getting a taxi earlier, but they wouldn't take me. Didn't want blood on his seats. Fook me if I'm going in an ambulance." I didn't take this as an invitation. He said it as if the emergency services were for wimps and whoopsie southerners, not proper Yorkshiremen like him.

I had an idea.

Ferris and I stumbled back up the lane towards the taxi rank in the Market Square. I had to support him and for a while we had to grab the railings by the Senate House in order to make progress along the passage, which had now frozen solid. It felt like dragging yourself by a rope up a mountain pass in a blizzard, or what I imagined that might be like, not having been up any mountains or in any blizzards. Snow had begun to fall again.

When we were near the rank, I detached the tail from my costume and quickly mopped up as much blood as I could with it before disposing of it in a nearby bin. I was hoping the flow would stop until we were ensconced inside the taxi.

"Can you take us to Addenbrooke's?" I asked the last remaining vehicle in the rank, obscuring Ferris crowning himself with the head whilst I did so. "My friend has got this horse's head stuck on and he can't get it off."

"You're lucky. The weather's worsening. I was about to go home." The driver eyed us suspiciously as we got into his cab. He surveyed his passengers in the rear-view mirror. Horse Head Ferris was silent; anything he might have said would have been muffled by the head anyway. We both sat very still, hoping that the driver wouldn't notice the river of blood which was starting to run down Webster's neck and seep into his T shirt.

"Why did he put the horse's head on? Or shouldn't I ask?" the driver chuckled, "Honestly, why you lot can't just do it the normal way like me and the wife, I don't understand."

Outside A&E, when the taxi had gone, Webster removed the head. It was soaked in blood.

"I can't see a thing," he admitted. Both eyes were now swollen, and his eyelashes were caked in blood; he looked like something from a graphic war movie or one of those disturbing adverts imploring people to 'clunk click, every trip' that were shown before wearing seatbelts was made compulsory.

We got through triage quickly – it was clear that, despite years of experience with the inexplicable in A&E, the nurse didn't want to spend too much time in the company of a man whose face had been replaced by a blood bath and a woman who looked like a headless horse escaped from the knacker's yard.

"You don't seem to be drunk," I said to Webster as we sat down for a promised three to four hour wait, "but I'm worried you might bleed to death." He squinted at me through the slits behind which I assumed his eyes were still functioning.

"I'm not. More's the pity. But you really are dressed as a horse, aren't you?" I clapped my coconut hooves. Webster Ferris very nearly laughed.

The next thing I remember was someone shaking me awake. "Come on, you old nag, he's done." A grinning male nurse was standing beside me. Even in the small hours, he was jolly and laughing. "Look at you," he said, "taking up four chairs…" I was indeed stretched out over several of the waiting-room chairs, where I had fallen asleep. There remained a small gaggle of walking wounded still waiting to be seen, none of whom found it possible to share the camp humour of Mr Irrepressibly Cheerful. "Ooo, look at that thing," he continued, pointing at my horse head, which had rolled on to the floor, its eyeless sockets staring up through the blood-caked fur. "It's like the Godfather!" No-one laughed. "Well, we've done some embroidery on your boyfriend and dressed him up for Hallowe'en. Don't let him ride you home!"

Webster Ferris was standing to his side. His hand was bandaged as well as his head. He looked like a mummy or spook from an episode of *Scooby-Doo*. Perhaps this was part of the nurse's fun way to spend a long night shift, see just how many bandages he could get away with winding round one head. Or perhaps he was new to the job and hadn't made a very good stab at it. I hoped there was no one else with wounds in need of bandaging; supplies in the stock cupboard would have run dangerously low.

I sat up and grabbed the horse head just as a policeman and a policewoman came from a side room with a nurse pushing a wheelchair containing a woman patient.

"Been to a fancy dress party?" the policeman asked me accusingly.

"I was in a play. I was playing a mare." Although it was true, it sounded like a lie and I felt shifty. It reminded me of how I felt in Miss Carroway's assemblies at school.

"A member of the public has reported that a girl in our school uniform was behaving inappropriately at a bus stop in Ilford. You know who you are and I know who you are. I expect you in my office at break-time for a full explanation."

I would blush profusely, consumed by guilt even though I walked home and lived in Barking. I almost felt obliged to turn up at the office just in case I had inadvertently hopped on a bus, larked about at a stop on Ilford High Road and then gone home and forgotten all about it.

"What's that?" the PC said indicating the head. It was obvious his immediate assumption about people was that they had done something wrong, and it was his quest to find out what.

"It's a horse's head. It's not real. Look it's made of fun-fur."

"I can see that," he said sarcastically. "Why is it caked in blood then? Was being decapitated part of the plot?" He grinned, pleased not only to have used such a long word as decapitated but also in the right context and in a humorous way. "Bit of a night MARE, I'd say." He was on a roll.

"That's him!" interjected the patient in the wheelchair. "Under all them bandages. I'm sure of it."

Everyone turned towards Webster Ferris.

"Ooo, fancy," squealed the nurse. "Have you been a naughty boy, then?"

17
Bandmaster

I'd slept very badly in what little remained of the night. I had returned to the college alone. I'd managed to remove most of the horse suit, down to the waist at least, whilst I was outside and had pleaded with the night porter to let me in. Luckily there were two on the shift and the other one had answered the bell, just as grumpily but without the knowledge that I had been part of the previous visit.

Next morning, after I'd had a shower and cleaned myself up, I suddenly felt hungry. So, unusually, I went to breakfast. The college buildings looked very beautiful in the early morning sun. The roofs and the grass in the centre of the courts, iced with a thick, sparkly cloak of freshly laid snow, were lit by weak rays of sun against a background of a bright blue sky. It was a scene to remember. When you live somewhere that is very attractive you often forget to look at it – you just pass through it. It was almost worth getting up early to appreciate such a sight, I thought. I came to my senses quite quickly when a fog of tiredness descended around me, but it was a nice idea whilst it lasted.

It appeared that the Cocoa Club had been up since shortly after dawn and had been early into the queue for breakfast. This meal attracted people I had never seen before: the larks who rowed (already back from the river) and those to whom a 9 o'clock lecture was considered mid-way through the morning. They inhabited a different time-zone despite living within the confines of the same place. It was a Sunday too – no need to get up at all if you didn't fancy it.

Last year's inhabitants of the brutalist block were all there. They were magnetically attracted to each other as if tied by a piece of college elastic which prevented them straying too far from the place. Such a vast combination of the Laura Ashley winter range – tweedy wools and corduroys, piecrust collars with home knits – was enough to put you off poached egg and tomato.

"Oh gosh, it's Roni!" announced Perfect Penny as if I had appeared suddenly from a magician's hat or in a puff of smoke. "To what do we owe this great honour?" She bowed down before me dramatically. I ignored her, sarcastic cow. She may as well have said, "You are generally not organised enough to get up for breakfast because you are a pathetically immature human being, unlike myself." If there had been kippers for breakfast, I would have slapped her about the face with one. I've always had a desire to assault people who annoy me with flat fish. Getting up early was not good for me, I decided.

Lizzie had a mouth full of toast but that didn't prevent her cutting to the quick with the news of the moment. "Have you heard about the pool of blood? It's like a murder scene at the Porters' Lodge. I went and had a look. It's frozen into the snow. Turned it bright red." As if to illustrate her point, a piece of bread splattered with raspberry jam shot from her mouth onto the table.

"It's disgraceful. And I expect you can guess who's responsible." Penny gave a little sniff and smoothed down her blouse, which had slipped a millimetre out of her skirt.

"He stabbed someone just outside the Porters' Lodge. The night porter was a witness!" enthused Gill, whose passion for the dramatic never got in the way of verifying the truth.

"Personally," Penny began, though strictly speaking this word was redundant because she believed her opinion was also that of everyone else, "I think if he hasn't gone already, he should be sent back up north immediately. There's no place in this college for such behaviour." There was a note of suggestion in her voice that poor behaviour might be more acceptable or commonplace 'up north'.

I chose not to engage in the conversation. Whilst buttering some toast I noticed that there was still dried blood under my fingernails. I wondered if Gill or any of the rest of the chattering cocoa drinkers would notice. That would give them something to discuss over a milky drink that night.

Mary appeared. "Don't usually see you at breakfast, Roni."

"Really?" I snapped unreasonably. She was stating the truth after all.

She sipped her tea conspiratorially. "I think Ferris has had it this time. The porter has reported him, apparently; he was blind drunk and had been fighting outside the college with some sort of weirdo dressed in an animal costume. There were others but they ran off when the porter went out into the street to see what was going on. Brave of him, eh?" I said nothing. "He took a swing at the porter, but he dodged it and managed to get back inside. They were all full of it at the Lodge this morning when I came back from my run."

My heart sank. Running before breakfast? Who were these alien creatures? "Has the animal borne witness to this?" I asked.

"Goodness knows. It's all a bit odd. It vanished, apparently. There's a huge puddle of blood in the snow. Why would anyone be going round dressed as an animal in this weather? Perhaps it was a mystical being sent to do battle with him. Do you think Ferris was fighting his way through a whole menagerie of mythical creatures?" Mary giggled. She was getting carried away and needed to stop reading *Lord of the Rings* late at night.

The porter was obviously bragging about his heroism, exaggerating his version of events to show himself in a better, braver light. I had escaped being identified as the animal. I went back to my room and fell asleep.

Later I went down to the pigeonholes to see if I had any mail. This was a scenario I followed at least once a day, often more. There was always the vain hope that my little wooden slot would be filled with interesting correspondence.

Occasionally I got a letter from Gran, usually containing some wise words passed on from Father O'Connor or a little leaflet with a sentimental picture of the Virgin Mary and a verse to look up in the Bible.

Mum would regularly send me a brief note on light blue Basildon Bond. Although she had plenty to say face to face, she found the written word more difficult, the opposite to me. Considering the treasure chest of personal information she collected at work, her letters were banal to say the least. Perhaps she was wary of committing such calumnies to paper.

There was no chance of having a proper letter on a Sunday when there was no delivery. But there was an internal mail system where you could get messages from people in other colleges. Roland used this to summon us for rehearsals or auditions. Tutors and supervisors in other colleges used it too. My pigeonhole was predictably empty.

Ferris's was not, I noticed. A large white envelope was sticking out of it. No one else was in the pigeonhole area. I pulled it out furtively. 'W. Ferris' it said, unsurprisingly, then printed at the bottom 'from the Master's Office'.

What had happened to Ferris? Had he made it back to college? Was he still at the police station? Last time I saw him he was gingerly getting into a panda car, his huge, bandaged head like a beacon in the night. Perhaps this letter was the outcome of the porter's report about the alleged battle of the beasts outside the Lodge. I took it out of the pigeonhole and put it in my pocket.

It was lunchtime so I called into the buttery and picked up

some egg mayonnaise sandwiches, a couple of cartons of juice and some bananas, all things you could eat if your jaw was stiff or if someone had thrown a punch at your chin.

Ferris's room wasn't hard to find. Everyone knew where it was. It was well known, and greatly resented by people in the college who cared about these things, that Webster Ferris had got a better room than he should have. Quite why was the subject of endless conjecture. He lived in an old and attractive part of the college on a staircase without other undergraduates. His neighbours were foreign PhD students (for whom the language barrier would provide some cushion from his foul invective) and a couple of young dons who had clearly drawn the short straw on account of their youth.

The most sought-after rooms were allocated to students who had performed best in end-of-year exams. No one could quite remember, because Ferris had been away for a year, how well he had done at the end of his first year. Although he was clearly one of the most able students in the university, it suited the narrative to ignore the possibility that this room was awarded on merit and suggest that it was a form of containment away from the main student body.

The ground floor room had windows opening onto a pretty court. Very similar, I realised, to the one through which Sebastian Flyte throws up in *Brideshead Revisited* and thereby meets Charles Ryder. No-one, however much they had drunk or how nauseous they were feeling, would contemplate the consequences of chundering through an open pane into a room occupied by Webster Ferris.

Knocking on his door was a scary proposition itself when it came to it. I tapped gently to start with. There was no response. If he was still mummified by the bandages there was no way he was going to hear anything but a twenty-one-gun salute through so many layers of crepe and cotton wool pads. I knocked again, more forcefully.

"Hello!" I didn't feel comfortable shouting his name. I'd never called him by it before. What should I say? "Webster"? Far too familiar, "Ferris?" Potentially rude. "Mr Ferris?" Preposterous.

"Are you there?" I called, rapping loudly on the door.

The door opposite opened slightly. "He's in there. I heard him come back when I was going to chapel this morning. He was groaning and making a terrible din." A small nervous man was sticking his considerably large nose through the tiny aperture he had created, like a mouse sniffing from his mousehole to see if the coast was clear of cats before he ventured out. "Are you sure you want to go in?"

"I've brought him some lunch," I explained.

"Good luck," he replied quickly, closing the door before he could be pelted with egg sandwiches or sprayed with juice.

I knocked again. No answer. I tried the handle and it turned. It occurred to me that Webster Ferris might be dead or unconscious on the other side. I couldn't not go in. I opened the door enough to peer inside. It was gloomy, the curtains still closed, but there seemed to be a body on the bed.

"Hello?" I tried again. The body groaned. "It's me."

"Who's me?" Ferris sounded as if he had performed a tonsillectomy on himself and then trekked through the desert for a week without water.

"Roni. I brought you some lunch."

"What the fook for?" He was obviously not at death's door, his charming personal skills well and truly on display.

"I thought you might eat it," I said sarcastically. "You can write an essay on it, or wear it, or model it into a figurine of Lenin if you'd prefer." Perhaps I'd gone too far. I waited for the response.

"I can't see anything. Open the curtains would you?"

I pulled back the curtains and, trying to avoid a large and spiky cactus, knocked over a dead houseplant and a pile of books as I did so. "Shit!" I said, under my breath. Fortunately, Ferris couldn't see me kick the plant under his desk.

"Has Ironside got you?" he asked. What was he on about? "Roy Ironside, my cactus."

I was taken by surprise. Who, least of all Webster Ferris, would call a cactus Roy Ironside? I could imagine him having such a plant – vicious, capable of surviving in adverse circumstances, prickly towards unwanted visitors but giving it a human name was surprising. He grinned and I noticed dried blood was caked on his lips. "I've got Rod Fern too." This was unusual behaviour in more ways than one. He'd obviously not noticed the demise of Rod, now unceremoniously booted under the desk.

The room was large but spartan. Rod and Roy were obviously paying lip service to interior design. There were no posters on the walls, but every surface was covered in books or piles of pamphlets or leaflets. A yellowing copy of *Socialist Worker* was plugging a gap in the window frame. Balanced open on the windowsill next to Ironside was a large book, *The Reader's Digest Book of Garden Birds*. This was an illustrated guide for people wishing to identify feathered friends at their bird tables. Through the window, close by, I could see a birdfeeder full of seeds hanging from the branch of a tree. There was a tick by goldfinch on the open page. Webster Ferris was a twitcher? This was even harder to understand than the anthropomorphised pot plants. Perhaps he had an air rifle and picked them off whilst they were innocently nibbling at his seeds and fat balls, cataloguing the species he'd murdered like a train spotter collects diesel engine numbers.

He had obviously slept on top of the bed not in it. He sat up and I could see that the full bandage arrangement was still in place and he hadn't changed his clothes.

"I got you egg mayonnaise and bananas. I thought they would be easy to eat." I put them on the desk with the juice. He took the carton, but his bandaged hand couldn't get the little straw to pierce the hole. I did it for him and he sucked at it noisily. "I noticed this letter in your pigeonhole too. I think it's from the

Master". Given it said so on the front of the envelope, this was a disingenuous statement.

"I can't see to read that." He thrust it back at me. "Go on. Why don't you open it? You obviously want to."

"Oh, I didn't mean that. I thought I'd bring it because I just noticed it when I was getting my own mail," I lied. Fortunately, I couldn't see the expression on his face. One eye was covered completely by a large, round, white, padded dressing and the other, which peeped out beneath the bandage which encircled his head, had swollen to monstrous proportions. His jaw was developing a nice range of coloured bruises where there had just been red marks the night before.

"Asking me to tea is he? The man's an idiot."

I opened the letter. It contained one side of thick paper with 'From the Master' embossed on the top. The message was curt and formal, written in fountain pen. "He wants to see you at 11 tomorrow morning 'to discuss the events of Saturday night'," I summarised.

"Didn't take him long."

"You'll need to explain to him," I said.

"What's the point? He can ask the police," he snapped. "Haven't you got any work to be doing?"

He started to get up off the bed. He was either heading for the egg mayonnaise or about to sling a left hook at me with his good hand. I didn't wait to find out.

On Monday morning, I was up early again. The snow had turned to slush and the winter wonderland was over – like breakfast, which had stopped being served as soon as I appeared in the dining hall. Perfect Penny, speeding out the other way in case she failed to get to her lecture 15 minutes early, gave me a look which combined an insincere 'Poor you!' with 'What do you expect if you turn up at this time?' I turned and made my way through the Fellows' Garden to a door labelled 'Master's Lodge'.

I knocked on the door brazenly and presently a lady answered.

She had the haughty grandeur of one who imagined her rightful place was bossing menials about in far flung corners of the Empire. She was obviously the Master's wife and not who I was expecting.

"Yes?" she said, looking through her bifocals at me, preparing to tell me that deliveries should go to another door.

"I'd like to see the Master," I announced.

"Wouldn't we all? He'll be in his office, no doubt, hiding."

Perhaps that explained why no-one ever saw the Master; he spent a lot of his time hiding. He only appeared with a retinue of other ancient academics trudging into the Hall in voluminous robes when there was a formal meal. They sat on a raised platform at what was known as High Table, well away from the noisy pool of inferior intellect which comprised the student morass beneath them. Each in his turn tripped, or narrowly avoided doing so, on the step up to the dais as he processed from the door to the table, and this developed into a kind of drinking game for the spectators in the cheap seats. Place your bet (trip or not) on the antique presently making his way to his seat and forfeit a whole glass of wine if you are wrong.

"The staircase in the corner takes you to his study. And good luck to you." She slammed the door.

Through this unimportant looking opening, I found a small, well-trodden wooden staircase which I climbed to the top. There was an ornate carved banister and wood-panelled walls. It was obviously a very old part of the college. The smell of beeswax polish hung in the air. There was only one door, so I knocked on it. There was no answer, but I could hear shuffling inside. I knocked again.

"Hello?" I called.

"Who is it?"

"Roni McNamara."

The door opened. "Thank God. Do come in." He shut the door quickly behind me. "How lovely to see you. I'm sorry, I thought you might be someone else. Are we supposed to be having an appointment?" I shook my head. "Excellent, just how I like it. I'm always happy to see a pretty member of the college." He paused slightly. "You are a member of the college, I take it?" The Master had a permanently surprised look. I reckoned he spent much of his time not quite sure what would happen next.

"I'm Veronica McNamara. I'm in the second year."

"Oh, how lovely. Charming. McNamara! Are you the leader of the band?" How ever many hundred times this gag had been mentioned in the past, I still hadn't worked out a response to it. Despite the predictability I must have looked perplexed.

"You know, the song, McNamara's Band." He sang the familiar first line. "And you're a lovely girl from Ireland. A colleen! You haven't got much of an accent."

"I'm from Barking. In Essex. Well, it's in Greater London now."

"Ah, Essex is a much-maligned county, such a pity they moved you. Still, it all must be much of a muchness after the green fields of the Emerald Isle." He was lost in thought for a moment. "Who is it that plays the flute? Don't tell me, I'll remember…"

He hummed the tune quietly sounding the occasional word, then dancing a little jig as he recalled more of the lyrics. "Drums… cymbals… Da-da-di, da-di old bassoon, and blah the pipes da da / Oh! Somebody, somebody, something the flute…" He slapped his forehead with his palm. "Ah! Dash it! Who is it plays the flute?"

"Hennessey Tennessee."

"Of course!" He was conducting himself with one hand. This was a surreal experience and not what I was expecting.

"I need to talk to you about Webster Ferris."

"No need to worry yourself about him, my dear." He whistled the tune and began marching round the room in a spectacularly uninhibited kind of way, banging an imaginary drum. "It's coming back to me now."

I noticed *The Racing Post* was open on the desk. He noticed that I had noticed and on his next circuit quickly covered it up with a large, folio-sized book, which was obviously kept close precisely for that purpose.

"Research," he explained, running his hands through his thick white hair lest I thought he spent all day picking out potential winners instead of studying ancient texts and running the college. His mouth opened wide in preparation for a deafening final rendition, "Oh, my name…"

"My father is a bookie." This interrupted the singing.

"Really?" He eyed me curiously. I was hoping it might put him in a sweeter frame of mind. "How interesting." He sidled towards me, "Does he get any, how shall I say, tips? Does he have contact with the trainers or jockeys?" He lowered his voice. "They have information you know." It was as if I had just admitted to him that I was a KGB spy and I was making contact with his sleeper cell.

"Inevitably there is some 'inside track' if you are involved in the industry." I did not know this for sure so tried to sound oblique. He looked pleased with his putative new contact as he pulled the racing paper back out from under the camouflaging book.

"Webster Ferris…" I began.

"My dear, you have no worries on that count. That particular gentleman has been walking on very thin ice and I think he fell through a large crack in it on Saturday night. You won't be seeing him for much longer." Pleased with his metaphors, he adjusted his glasses and began running his finger down the list of runners in the racing paper, still humming the tune of McNamara's Band. "There's a horse I fancy in the 11:00. I usually study the form. For statistical purposes you understand."

"I must explain, Webster Ferris saved a girl from being raped on Saturday night. He intervened when some lads in the Market Square were attacking her and other witnesses decided to look the other way."

He looked up and removed his glasses. "Really? That sounds improbable. Are you sure? Though there is no doubt he is what I believe in some circles is known as 'handy' with his fists."

"I went to the hospital with him, and the girl was there too. She recognised him. He's given a statement to the police and is going to be called as a witness. By the way, the porter wouldn't let us into the college."

"I believe he was alarmed by the quantities of blood. And apparently Ferris was trying to bring a horse onto the premises. That's against college statutes you know."

"He's got an appointment with you at 11."

"Ah yes. The Bursar and the Head Porter are coming for, shall we say, back-up purposes. Do you know Mr Boulderstone? He was a champion boxer when he was in the Army, a useful attribute in a Head Porter. The Bursar is skilled in a martial art which I believe is known as Taekwondo." He lowered his voice. "I'm told it can be lethal."

There was a brief pause whilst I assume he was either contemplating the legal consequences of the Bursar killing Webster Ferris or alternatively wondering if this skill could be used to encourage reluctant students to settle their college bills.

"The Chaplain offered to come along but I think he would be of little use and is far too conciliatory to my mind. The captain of the first XV has offered to pop in. He has a very powerful physique."

This last I did know; I had noticed it myself.

Although the Master had no idea who the majority of students in the college were, he was clearly familiar with the name and reputation of Webster Ferris. He had obviously spent Sunday lining up a team of mercenaries for self-protection at the meeting.

"He might get a citizen's bravery award." I made this up but it wasn't an impossibility.

I knew Ferris would never have told the Master that he was the hero not the villain of this piece. He'd be reprimanded at the least, possibly sent down and then, when the truth came out, probably not re-instated. Whatever the outcome, his intransigence would cause more problems. Ferris seemed to have a self-destruct button which he was constantly on the point of pushing. The spectre of Simeon Goldblatt hung over me – forced to another continent by my reluctance to tell the truth.

The Master considered this new intelligence for a moment.

"Naturally, my invitation is to congratulate him for his valour and honour promoting the good name of the College. Will there be press coverage do you think?"

"Not immediately if there is to be a trial. Maybe afterwards."

The Master was clearly looking for a page of reflected glory in the *Cambridge Evening News*, with luck in the national press.

"Might I ask," his tone was avuncular, "would you consult your father about Sir Badsworth?" For a brief moment I thought this was his pet name for Ferris. "Its name jumped out at me – too much of a co-incidence. It has no form but the odds are good for a win. An opinion from someone 'in the know' would be useful. 11:00 Bangor. You are welcome to use my telephone."

His own 11 o'clock appointment had been playing on his mind, obviously. I couldn't really say no. I picked up the heavy black Bakelite receiver and dialled the number of the shop, hoping it would be Dad not Uncle Patrick who'd answer. I could hear the Master humming *McNamara's Band* as the phone began to ring.

Uncle Patrick said Sir Badsworth was unlikely to win and therefore McNamara Bros were offering 20:1 on it. I passed this information on with the caveat that this was the advice of my uncle and not my father.

"Considering the nature of the incident after all, I will take it that on this occasion Sir Badsworth is Sir Goodsworth and choose another." He seemed relieved. "And an uncle 'in the know' too, most opportune. I look forward to our next little chat."

I escaped in the direction of the birdfeeder and Roy Ironside standing menacingly in the window. Eventually, and somewhat reluctantly, after some knocking, Ferris let me in. The bandages had been removed but what was underneath was not pretty. I tried not to look. He was obviously busy collating leaflets for the university Labour party. His red and black face matched the colouring of the flyers.

"What do you want?" he asked gruffly.

"I'm well, thank you for asking," I replied sarcastically. "I've seen the Master."

Ferris stopped fiddling with his leaflets. "Why did you do that?"

"Because I didn't think he would know the full story. And he didn't."

"Don't you think I have a tongue in my head?"

"Well yes…"

Ferris hadn't looked up from his leaflet pile, but he had stopped sorting.

"Oh. I see. Happen it's better coming out of your posh, southern mouth."

"No, I… I thought that because I was there, I could verify what you'd say."

"You didn't think he'd believe me without your confirmation?"

"No, not at all, I…" He was clearly quite angry. "I'm not posh, anyway."

"Really?"

He turned round and looked straight at me, through the little slit between the swollen upper and lower lids of his right eye. "You came back with a suntan in January! Aren't fancy holidays posh? Do you know what's going on in Yorkshire? In Rotherham?

Where I come from?" He thrust a leaflet at me. It had a picture of a miner on the front.

"Do one of your fooking stupid plays about that."

Not for the first time, I wanted to hit him very, very hard indeed but I calculated that even in the state in which he found himself, he would be quite capable of flooring me with a flick of his little finger. Being punched looked painful.

I hated him more at that moment than I had ever hated anyone. It was a frightening emotion. Before I did something I regretted, or, more correctly, something the consequence of which would be detrimental to myself, I left. I slammed his door as a futile but harm-free display of my anger. Big nose across the hall had heard raised voices and was peering out of his only very slightly ajar door. "Piss off, Beaky!" I screamed as an unnecessarily unkind departing gesture.

I cried for about half an hour afterwards.

That evening, I lined up at the call box and rang home. Dad answered. "Veronica! You rang yesterday," he said, stating something I already knew, "and it's only Monday today. Pat said you rang the shop this morning. Are you alright?"

"Yes," I lied.

"Did you get a tip?" he asked. "That horse, Sir Badsworth, it won! How much did you put on it? I won't tell your mother…"

18
Sir Badsworth rides again

The year 1984 was memorable for a number of reasons.

That spring in Cambridge, Roland was fretting about his adaptation of *Nineteen Eighty-Four*. He knew it was an opportunity he couldn't miss but condensing down the novel into a Roly-sized 'gist of it' snippet which enabled the audience to be back in the bar within three quarters of an hour of the first line was proving challenging.

But things were looking up for the Pared-Down Players. Roland had acquired a reputation amongst the student body and suddenly his productions were the hot ticket in town. It may seem unkind of me to suggest that there was a certain attraction in their awfulness, but who cares if you're selling tickets?

Roland didn't intend his shows to be awful, but it didn't escape the Pared-Down Players themselves that there was a touch of schadenfreude amongst the audience of their suddenly popular shows. Whilst outwardly the players themselves maintained a loyalty to our own director, we sincerely hoped that if there was anything amusing or of low quality in the show it was the ideas and the script itself and not our performances.

The prelude to the fiasco that was Roland's *Nineteen Eighty-Four* is how I came to be wearing a Liverpool strip in March of that year. The changing reputation of the company allowed us to perform in a more prestigious venue – or at least on a bigger stage.

His version of *Romeo and Juliet* was a triumph of ambition over ability for both Roland's vision and his cast's talent. He was vaguely aware of the tribal differences and rivalries between Everton and Liverpool and somehow had become aware of the cup challenge that was playing out between them that year. The prospect of a love affair between two male players in rival teams, thwarted at the last moment by some misunderstood event which would end in tragedy, filled Roland with an enthusiasm which he was never going to realise.

Lucy was Juliet, in this production Graeme Souness, the Liverpool captain. I was cast in a comedy part as usual, the nurse, here Bruce Grobbelaar, the goalkeeper. We both had stick-on moustaches. Steve, who, despite coming from Croydon, supported Liverpool, was cruelly cast as Everton captain Kevin Ratcliffe, the Romeo with whom Souness had fallen in love. We even had a proper set for this production because it was in the student theatre. A large painting of the Liver Building took pride of place on the central scenery flat, whilst a goal at either side of the stage indicated Anfield and Goodison Park.

And with the student theatre came the techs. Techs need the actors to give purpose to all the messing about with wires and fiddling about with heavy lamps high above the stage that they do, and actors cannot put on a decent show without them. An uneasy truce exists between the two camps.

Trying to keep everyone in order was Phil, a smiley, unflappable post-grad engineering student. He mediated between Roland, frequently asking the impossible of the crew, and the lighting and sound posse, who produced endless reasons why Roland's requests were unfeasible. The first thing I noticed about him was how calm and reasonable he seemed in the face of so many people wanting their own way.

The Pared-Down Players' efforts were usually received by a blanket silence punctuated with the occasional coughing fit, but this production inspired a good deal of reaction from the audience. At one point a rendition of *You'll Never Walk Alone* from the one side of the auditorium drowned out the jeering coming from the other. Unintentionally, *Graeme and Kevin: Star Crossed Lovers on Merseyside* had become not only a comedy with a serious message but an immersive theatrical experience where the audience took sides in full participation. We thought Roland was a genius.

For once, people I knew came to watch and were complimentary about Roland's ability to mix serious topics like tribalism and acceptance of same-sex love with a deft comic hand. And it was all over in less than fifty minutes. Ideal! At one performance, I even caught sight of Webster Ferris sitting in the front row in a red and white scarf. I tried not to be cynical about our success, though I knew he was.

I hadn't spoken to him since the violent incident in the Market Square and my encounter with the Master. Although we shared a supervision where, as usual, he taught me and the silent one the salient points about whichever text or author we were supposed to be studying whilst Dr Bennett snoozed in his armchair, I avoided him. It was easy. He was always on time, tutting when I turned up late, and he always left first. It wasn't hard to dodge him elsewhere. If I saw him at all, he was with his equally threatening mates on King's Parade handing out information about the miners' strike under a banner made from an old sheet. It read; "Coal not Dole. Support the Miners." The group of co-demonstrators shouted, "Thatcher out!" every so often.

The Master, on the other hand, was my new best friend. Often the only content of my pigeonhole was a little note in his handwriting asking, 'Any tips for Cheltenham?' or 'Ask Papa about Burrough Hill Lad in the Gold Cup'.

"It's a possible, can't guarantee. They'll give you 7/2," I scrawled on the paper and sent it back. I was trying to fob him off, having consulted the newspaper and not 'Papa' about it. Unfortunately, this horse won by three lengths, which encouraged the Master, despite earlier poor information about Sir Badsworth, to consider me a direct link to inside information.

A message at the end of term read, 'Greasepaint or Hallo Dandy in the National? Please ask advice.' I didn't, of course. I didn't want a winner. My parting shot before going home for the holiday was to reply, 'Hallo Dandy.' It was 33:1 and bound to lose, or so I thought. Naturally it won – I should have put some money on it myself.

1984 was a year of strikes and demonstrations. Ferris and his Cambridge Miners' Support Group chums were not the only ones highlighting the cessation of mining and closure of collieries. Arthur Scargill and a man called MacGregor were frequently in the news.

A couple of girls went to Greenham Common to demonstrate about cruise missiles but came back swiftly when the lavatory facilities proved too primitive. The Cocoa Club looked on disapprovingly over a milky drink.

Unlike the long-haired, Afghan-wearing sit-in demonstrators of the late 60s and 70s, the students of the early 80s were mostly apolitical. The truth was the majority of undergraduates were just busy listening to Duran Duran or Spandau Ballet and having essay crises.

There was a lovely hot summer to take your mind off what was going on elsewhere. It wasn't as good as '76, but even in Cambridge, where the wind blows across the Fens direct from Siberia, May and June were hot and sunny.

Despite the runaway success of *Graeme and Kevin*, I couldn't commit to *Nineteen Eighty-Four*. Exams were coming up and I was seriously behind on my work. The cult the Pared-Down Players now attracted meant that part of Roland's problem with Orwell's novel was solved. He had found it very difficult to trim down the complex plot and numerous characters of *Nineteen Eighty-Four* without his potted version making no sense at all. Students were queuing up to audition, which meant that Roland could work with a bigger cast on the stage at the same time. It also meant that I was able to ask for a very small part. Roland obliged and I was a receptionist in the Ministry of Love whose only line was 'Mr O' Brien will see you in Room 101 now, Mr Smith,' and then file my nails for the rest of the scene.

At least it allowed me to take a book along to the theatre each night and do some revision. Roland had hit the big time – a whole week of shows in the student theatre with proper lighting and sound. I got to know Phil better whilst he was being useful testing sound effects and bossing the other techs about backstage. He was easy going and amenable; nothing was ever a problem for him. Webster Ferris could have done with a few lessons in 'getting on with people' from him, I thought.

I spent most of the production in the wings, in everyone's way, with my book, kidding myself I was revising whilst waiting to go on. I couldn't do this back in the dressing room because this production was all over in thirty minutes. If I'd gone anywhere, I would have missed my big moment.

"Excuse me, Roni," Phil would say politely when I was leaning against the sign saying 'Ministry of Truth' or perching on the box of homemade rats about to be needed on stage. I was trying to cram in some quotations in the half-light of the wings whilst he lugged a filing cabinet with 'ALTERNATIVE FACTS' painted on it on and off stage. He never lost his temper with the techs, who were as highly strung as the actors. He alone could calm the waters if someone moved a lamp slightly or mucked about with their gaffer tape.

It proved too difficult to condense the nuances of *Nineteen Eighty-Four* into a short timeframe. Like Winston Smith, Roland had taken on a bigger entity than he'd assumed.

I was unmoved. I had got myself into a very strict routine: getting up early, exercising to wake myself up and then doing long shifts in the Seeley Library, a modern building which had big windows and comfy seats. It was just right for dozing off in the afternoon sun when Dickens got a bit lengthy.

I had also found paradise. This was an outdoor swimming pool no-one else seemed to know about a short cycle ride out of the main part of the city. It was right by the river and had an old-fashioned feel about it which reminded me of the pool at Barking Park. Early in the morning it was deserted apart from the old guy selling the entrance ticket. I imagined he'd arrived with the pool pre-war and never left. Why would you when you had discovered heaven on Earth?

Unusually the deep 'end' was in the middle of the pool so it had two shallow ends. It was very long but quite narrow. Even though in the early morning the heat had not really come into the day, a dip into its clear cool water was refreshing and woke me up.

I devised a little challenge for myself. I dived into the middle part, turned when under water either left or right and then tried to swim submerged until I reached the far end of the pool. It was impossible to do, unless you were a pearl fisher who could hold your breath for an unlikely amount of time.

One morning I thought I had broken my own 'record' when I surfaced – still well short of the end of the pool. "Fooking hell!" exclaimed a familiar voice. "Where did you come from? Frightened the bloody life out of me. Like a U-boat surfacing."

The unexpected and unwelcome sight of Webster Ferris greeted my breathless emergence from the water. He had a float under each arm and looked uneasy. I had frightened Ferris? This was an unusual situation. I got the feeling water was more my milieu than his; it was a liberating experience.

"You look right different with your hair wet. What are you doing here?"

"I'm conducting a survey of people asking stupid questions. Thanks for taking part." I reckoned if he went for me, I could kick my feet and splash him in the face, giving me time to swim away. The floats indicated that despite a well-formed torso he wasn't Mark Spitz.

Feeling confident, I carried on. "Your hair isn't wet at all. Don't you like putting your head in the water?" His black curls were their usual uncombed free-style.

"I can't swim," he replied simply. I should have guessed. He was standing on the bottom of the pool with the water about up to his waist. I felt a bit ashamed of my comment. "I expect you had swimming lessons and all that type of thing when you were a kid," he continued accusingly.

I should have expected that comment. I had of course, but not quite in the way he envisioned. When I was about six, I'd been taught to swim by a brusque PE teacher appropriately called Miss Towel, who was a client of Mum's. "She could just go to the barber to be honest," was Mum's verdict on her hairstyle, a short back and sides with no rollers, perming or colour. She didn't even go under the hair dryer. Mum disapproved of very short hair for business reasons but was cute enough to keep her opinions quiet if there was some trade in it. In fact, I suspect a quick trim of the practical hairdo was probably in exchange for my lessons.

We went to Barking Baths, in an old-fashioned building near the Town Hall. Like the pool itself, Miss Towel's methods were Victorian. You started in the shallow end, tantalisingly close to the edge but not quite in reach of it. Miss Towel had a long wooden pole which she dangled ahead of you in the water, again just out of reach. Just when I thought I was near enough to the pole to grab hold of it and prevent myself coming to a watery end, she would move it further away. By a process of intimidation and sheer fear I learned to swim quite quickly, and it has been something which has given me a huge amount of joy ever since.

I wasn't going to let Webster Ferris and his implied spoilt, middle-class kid swimming lesson jibe spoil that. "Why does everything you say have to be so unpleasant?" I turned and swam back to the other end of the pool very quickly. Just in case.

I didn't want him curtailing my morning's activity, so I swam back again, my best front crawl, making sure I gave him a wide berth when I got back to his end.

"Show off!" he shouted, but he was laughing and his face had softened. I had been showing off and I'd overdone it. I was out of breath and had to stop to catch up with myself. I tried not to let Ferris see.

He waded through the water towards me. "Roni." It seemed odd to hear him refer to me by my name. I wasn't sure he'd ever done so before. "About the post card…" I could hardly believe it. Was this going to be an apology or another insult or criticism?

He was referring to a confrontation we'd had in the pigeonhole area a week earlier. Mum and Dad were on another holiday; Nan's money seemed to be burning a large, indulgent hole in Mum's bank account. Either that or Dad had cleaned up on some punters placing less successful bets than the Master's. This time it was a cruise of the West Indies and Mum sent me a postcard from every port. I'd turned up at a supervision with a colourful card saying BARBADOS on the front in letters so large you would have to have a strong prescription from the optician and have mislaid your glasses not to be able to read them. I tried to keep it concealed in my book but maddeningly it slipped out and onto the floor in full view of Ferris and the silent one. Dr Bennett dozed on.

If only it had fallen the other way up and they could have read Mum's message on the other side. 'The beach is much nicer than at Southend but the tide doesn't go out as far. Your Dad saw Desmond Haynes in the sea but he didn't reply when Dad said, 'Hello Desmond.' I expect he tries to keep private.'

In my pigeonhole next day, was another. Dad's enthusiasm for rum was providing more West Indian cricketers for him to run in to. This time it was Garry Sobers in a bar in Antigua. 'At first he wasn't very friendly and said his name was Mark,' wrote Mum, 'but Dad bought him a rum and he admitted it. Garry was charming and told lots of cricketing stories.'

Ferris saw me giggling. "More postcards from Mummy and Daddy's holiday? Alright for some, eh? Christmas in the sun and now a cruise," he sneered.

I'd had enough of him. "Get lost, Ferris. It's only the second time they've ever been overseas. They never had proper holidays because they couldn't leave their work and until Nan died they didn't have the money. Get your facts right before you judge other people." He looked taken aback, surprised, shocked even, by my outburst. I felt bold because I was angry, but I still made sure that I maintained more than an arm's length between him and me as I stormed out. Webster Ferris made me more worked up than anyone I had ever met.

Ferris waded closer to me. He looked ridiculous with the floats under his arms, but he hung on to them as if he knew that if he let go, he would slip under the water forever. "When I say things, happen they come out wrong sometimes." I found this hard to believe. His fluency when he was discussing literature was astounding. He had a facility for making what he said, which was often quite complex, easily understandable.

"I've not really thanked you for helping me when I got beaten up have I?"

"No, you haven't mentioned it. And you should have done." I was as truthfully blunt as he was; perhaps he'd understand that.

He was quiet. I noticed his eyes. They looked sad. I wondered if he might cry. Lordy, what was I going to do if he did? Perhaps it was a reaction to the chlorine. "Go on then! I'm listening."

"Thank you. I should have… you know," his voice trailed off.

"Yes?" I was going to get an apology out of him if it meant taking his floats and kicking my feet to splash him with water until he did.

He couldn't look me in the eye. "I'm very appreciative and I should have told you so before." It was very formal and sounded like something his mum might have rehearsed him saying.

I accepted his apology. Quit whilst you're ahead, especially when you're dealing with a volatile temperament, that's what I say. I started to resume swimming a length. I thought I'd showcase my breaststroke this time.

"You're a bloody mermaid you," he called after me. "Could you teach me to swim?"

I was about to say, "Not on your Nelly, chum. I'd rather see you drown." But when I turned to look at him, 6'4" standing in the shallow end, looking useless, and involuntarily one of the floats popped out from under his arm making a squeaky fart noise as it did so, that seemed unnecessarily harsh and I couldn't help but laugh. He laughed too and it was such a surprise that I found myself agreeing.

So, every morning until our exams began we met at the pool. We left college separately and we returned separately. I thought up little exercises for him to do in the shallow end whilst I completed a couple of lengths. Then we moved on to something else. I didn't really know what I was doing; I made it up as I went along. I didn't have a pole like Miss Towel and the idea of putting the fear of God into Webster Ferris to make him swim seemed unwise. By the end of term he could do a width doggy paddle without the floats. If he fell in the Cam he would survive, which would be a huge disappointment to a great many people.

Exams over, he vanished. No word about when or where he was going, no thanks as usual. I felt curiously upset about this, although there was no reason other than politeness to expect otherwise. I tried to put him out of my mind.

The day after I got home for the holiday, I was watching the news on TV. The headline story showed rows of helmeted policemen, some on horses, at a coking plant called Orgreave.

There were violent clashes with some unarmed pickets. The police charged towards them with huge plastic shields and the pickets began to throw stones. The police started beating them with batons, heavy blows raining down, and in turn some of the constables got a battering themselves.

It looked unreal, as if a re-enactment society was doing Agincourt or the Battle of Hastings. It could almost have been one of Roland's re-imagined plays. *Henry Vth* with the modern-day South Yorkshire Police playing the English and the French in jeans and T shirts without any weapons, just pea shooters. I wondered if Roland was watching too and whipping up a quick script for the Pared-Down Players. A twenty-minute adaptation was tempting.

Cry 'God for Arthur, Orgreave and South Yorks.'

There was an image of a police helmet hanging on a piece of fencing. The final shot was of two policemen leading away a demonstrator. His hands were behind his back in handcuffs and a heavy stream of blood was flowing down his head. He turned his face to the camera, and I wasn't surprised to see it was Webster Ferris.

19

Things are never what they seem

It was as if an extended period of good weather, the sight of Webster Ferris first in a pair of swimming trunks then in handcuffs combined with the news that he had yet again achieved the highest exam score in English Literature at the university wasn't enough to make 1984 a memorable year. There was something far more shocking in store that summer.

The splendid weather meant that the pool in the park was busier than usual. Sometimes there was even a queue at my kiosk and more than once a strange bolt of nervous energy ran through me when I thought I'd spotted Webster Ferris with a rolled-up towel standing in line to pay the 80p entrance.

Unsurprisingly, it wasn't him on a day out from Rotherham, but someone more local who greeted me one day. "Hello, Veronica." It was Miriam Goldblatt. I hadn't seen her for a long time, certainly not since her brother had left Cambridge early the year before. "Fancy seeing you here! I'm surprised we haven't bumped into each other before," she said cheerfully.

I wasn't sure what to say. I opened my mouth, but nothing came out.

"I've heard all about what you're up to because Mum hears from your mum when she gets her hair done."

Oh Lord. Had Simeon mentioned the knickers or how appallingly drunk I had been? Had Mrs G and Mum discussed it? A year had passed but Simeon's spectre still haunted me. If I saw short, dark-haired men or students in cagoules, he was the first person I thought about.

"How's things?" I managed eventually, trying to be non-specific.

"I'm off on holiday next week, to see Simeon in Boston," she grinned.

Instead of saying something, I made a noise like a cat makes when someone treads on its tail.

"He'll be interested to know that I've seen you. He's told me all about what you two got up to at Cambridge."

"Is he there for good?" I asked, immediately regretting it. I thought that this question might sound harsh, or worse, as if I was hoping he might return soon.

"His PhD is going well, and his chest is much better."

"Chest?"

"The effects of the smoke inhalation were quite severe. As you know he has asthma anyhow." I didn't but I nodded and copied the sympathetic face Perfect Penny always made at me. "He was in Barking Hospital for a week. Mum and Dad were grateful the college insisted he went home early. Otherwise, it might have been a different story."

I could do nothing but make another cat noise. Miriam looked perplexed. "I'm sorry things didn't work out between you," she said quietly. Had Simeon told her how badly I'd treated him? Did he know I'd just used him to get an invite to the Boat Club? "He just felt that the US was too good an opportunity to miss and that he needed to go despite everything."

"Everything?" I asked.

"Well, you know, the college were keen for him to go back. He's been very modest about it all. And I know he was sorry to break it off with you." I couldn't help but look incredulous, but I still couldn't speak. "He didn't want the college authorities to make a big deal over his attempts to save the boathouse. But he should have told you in person, he said that to me," Miriam explained sheepishly.

Not sent down then, but the hero of the hour! Simeon Goldblatt was entitled to his own version of the truth. Why not? I gave Miriam a ticket for her swim. A queue had started to form behind her.

"I'll tell Simeon I've seen you," she promised with a faint suggestion that this might bring him to his senses about rekindling our 'relationship'.

This had been a strange encounter, but there were more surprises.

As I approached our front door at the end of the day, I could see through the net-free windows that Mum, Dad and Uncle Patrick were in the lounge. Dad was sitting in his armchair, Uncle Patrick was leaning against the mantelpiece and Mum was standing with her arms crossed. They stopped talking when they heard me come in.

"What's going on?" I asked. It looked serious.

"Your Dad's had a bit of a shock," Mum explained. "Your grandmother…" She had her 'I told you so' face on.

Not Gran? Surely there couldn't be a replay of twelve months ago when I'd come home to discover Nan had died. Dad looked pale and confused.

"Shirl, don't," Dad replied. "It's nothing, Veronica."

"It's not nothing, Mick. It's about time there was a bit of honest truth in this family. Ron's an adult now and she should know." Mum was loving this, whatever it was, I could tell. Gran wasn't dead, that was clear, but she was in the doghouse. Perhaps Father O'Connor had been over familiar with some of the choir boys – or Gran even. There was a thought.

"I've just come back from holiday." Pat spoke but explained nothing. There was silence again. "I've been over to Cork." I was still none the wiser. "Tamsin came too. You remember her, Ron?"

This was news. Uncle Patrick had had a girlfriend for over a year. It was a record as far as I could remember. I was kept well away from the week-to-week details about who he was taking out. A plausible reason for this may have been because, generally, it was difficult to keep up with the changes. Perhaps they'd got married and Gran didn't approve because Tamsin wasn't a Catholic.

"Get to the point." Mum was firm. "Or I will." This was very dramatic.

It was like being in a cliff-hanging, series-ending episode of *Dallas*. Instead of 'Who shot JR?' it was 'What did Uncle Patrick do in Ireland with Tamsin?' Our house wasn't much like Southfork, the Ewings' vast ranch. You'd need to use your imagination, apply some creative licence and suspend disbelief to enable the full experience, but that was something *Dallas* viewers were used to doing.

"Tammy suggested I should go to Ireland after all these years and all the Guinness and whiskey I've enjoyed." Pat was a storyteller; he always had a yarn to spin. Mum pulled a face suggesting these were irrelevant details to the main narrative.

"We found a lovely little pub in a village called Ballyclough." So far, so predictable. "Tamsin got chatting to a couple of old blokes, you know, as she does."

"It's not just the old ones, is it?" Mum couldn't resist a dig if the opportunity presented itself.

"She just happened to mention my name and it turned out that they'd just buried a man of the same name." Coincidence though this was, it didn't seem earth-shattering. There weren't too many Patrick McNamaras in Barking but presumably Ireland had more than its fair share.

"I'm the spitting image of him apparently. They called the family down to the pub to meet me and they couldn't believe it. They brought photos and everything."

"That sounds a bit unlikely. What are the chances?" I asked.

"They're saying he's some kind of relative? Too much of a coincidence. You go into a pub by chance…? Does he owe money or something?" In truth I was a bit disappointed – 'Man in pub in Ireland turns out to be related to a bloke with Irish parents from the same area.' Not really a front-page headline unless you're really hard up for local news, when it might scrape in alongside the dog show results and a mention of hot weather or persistent rain.

"He's not just any old relative, he's your grandfather." Mum felt compelled to cut to the quick. "Or he was, until he died last month."

"Well, that can't be the case," I replied. "Dad's dad was killed in the war. Wasn't he?"

There was a moment of silence.

"That turns out not to have been exactly what happened," Dad said simply.

"What proof did they have? Sounds unlikely to me. It's just too far-fetched." Uncle Pat liked a good story, but he'd gone a bit far this time.

"I found Mam and Dad's wedding certificate in a drawer once. It had the name of his father, our grandfather." Pat explained. "It was one of the few documents that Mam said had survived the bomb. I didn't volunteer the information to the geezers in the pub but it matched up with what they told me. I met Paddy's wife, and she told me he'd come back to Ballyclough from England at the beginning of the war."

"Wife?" I cried. Dad and Pat looked shifty. "But Gran was his wife."

"Yes. She was," said Mum firmly.

"Have you asked her? Have you told her he may have survived after all?" Poor Gran, this would severely test her faith in the Lord. I could imagine her with her rosary asking God for some explanation.

Dad and Pat remained silent. As usual Mum filled in the details.

"She already knew. It wasn't a surprise to her. She knew he was alive and in Ireland and she didn't tell those boys. All these years they thought they didn't have a father and they did – and they could have met him too."

We had strayed into a *Dallas* plotline. Any minute there would be a knock at the door and a host of women waving marriage certificates would be there demanding to know who was the real Mrs McNamara. Or perhaps Paddy McNamara senior would have risen from the grave and have come back to haunt us or not turn out to be dead after all.

"Bigamist," stated Mum slowly, savouring the word which all of us were thinking about.

"I can't believe Gran would lie to you. Are you sure it's true?" It didn't seem to add up for me.

"I know. It didn't seem entirely kosher. So we went to see Mam's family in Cork…" Patrick explained.

In my head, I ran through the roll call of Gran's all-girl family, those names that she'd taught me which I could recite but not write down: Caoimhe, Sinead, Aoibheann, Gráinne, Siobhan, Saoirse, Dearbhla. You could have one of those American spelling bees based around the names of Gran, her six sisters and their extended families.

"They all knew. All of them," Mum emphasised in case any of us hadn't taken on the enormity of the deception the first time. It seemed that this incredible piece of information had been confirmed by all and sundry.

"Didn't you have any inkling?" I asked Patrick and Dad.

"Your Uncle Patrick had suspicions, didn't you?" Mum had missed her vocation as a prosecuting barrister, wheedling the truth out of some silent felon. "But you didn't think to pass them on to your younger brother."

Patrick looked uncomfortable. He was usually so self-assured and cocky. It dawned on me that this was not some fictitious invention he'd concocted, leaning against the mantelpiece as if it was the bar in a pub, but the truth.

"We weren't the only boys without a dad after the war; we all made up stories about what had happened to them. Mam wouldn't be drawn on details. We made up all sorts of tales to tell people at school."

"You did," snapped Dad.

Pat took a long draw at the cigarette he'd been holding but not smoking.

"We had no details, so I used to imagine he was still alive somewhere. Maybe with a dodgy memory, in a jungle not knowing the war had finished. I wanted it to be true, that he was alive and had had some miraculous escape and one day he'd come back."

"You always told me those things were stories," insisted Dad.

"They were. I knew no more about him than you. There weren't even a photograph. The bomb saw to that, or so she told me. She wouldn't talk about it. I had to make it up. I just had a bit of an inkling."

"You never said. Not once in all those years." Dad looked shell-shocked but still not entirely convinced. Perhaps Pat, as the older brother, had heard things as a very small boy which he couldn't process at the time. He would have been four when the war started.

"You did know Ballyclough was his birthplace, though," Mum persisted. "It wasn't entirely a coincidence that you showed up at the pub in this small place." She wasn't going to let Pat get away with the 'just showed up at a random pub in Ireland and the regulars thought I looked just like someone who used to live there' scenario.

Pat stubbed out the cigarette in an ashtray on the mantelpiece. Perhaps it was Tamsin who had smelled a rat and fuelled the gnawing inconsistencies that had been bothering him for the last forty-five years.

"Well…the good news is that we have a number of half siblings. Five in total," explained Patrick, trying to lighten the mood but with predictably unsuccessful results.

"Five! And they don't all share the same mother, if you please." This was enough for Mum, who went off into the kitchen – to make me a cup of tea, I hoped.

"Where is Gran?" I asked.

Pat looked shamefaced. "She's been in the church every day since I got back and told her what I'd found out."

"Has she told Father O'Connor?"

"Lord, no!" exclaimed Dad and Uncle Pat in unison. Father O'Connor, unlike most of the inhabitants of County Cork and potentially many of the residents of Barking, Essex, was not going to be in on God and Gran's secret.

Was Mum working out how she would pass on this gem of gossip to her clients next week and disseminate Gran's shame even further? Or was this just a little bit too close and personal to her to be shared? Was there any lawbreaking involved before he became a bigamist? Or perhaps he'd never married the other woman. Pat hadn't explained why his father had suddenly left. I became convinced that Mum wasn't going to share the revelation even though she had made it quite plain what she thought about her husband being kept in the dark all those years.

The news on TV showed York Minster ablaze. The cathedral had been struck by lightning and a huge amount of damage had been done. Massive flames leapt into the sky from the transept. It was dramatic and spectacular, more unbelievable plot lines for our July 9th episode of *Dallas*. I half expected to see Webster Ferris sneaking away in the back of the shot with a box of matches and a Coal Not Dole banner.

"There you are. That'll be God getting his revenge on your mother," Mum stated forcefully in a totally inappropriate way. Dad ignored her. For a confirmed atheist with only a basic understanding of theology, this was either a tasteless joke or an insensitive jibe at her mother-in-law in her absence. The only person affected by this comment was Dad, who'd probably had quite enough for one day anyhow.

I lay in bed that night thinking about it. Certain facts, or lack of them, that I'd picked up over the years now fitted in to place.

Despite a bomb destroying the flat, it was odd not to have a single photograph of your husband, the father of your children. Gran had nothing of my grandfather to show me, not even anything from his home in Ireland. No-one from his family had ever visited and if any of Gran's sisters came to England to see her, they never met us. I knew lots and lots about them and Gran's family (apart from how to spell their names) but I'd never met any of them. "It costs an awful lot to visit home," Gran would explain if I asked to go when I was little. It seemed to me as a small child that Ireland was the far side of the Earth or even perhaps on another planet. She went to this place of fable and mystery far, far away sporadically and alone. Even Dad and Uncle Patrick stayed behind in London.

I'd heard no anecdotes about Paddy McNamara senior, only his name and that he was dead. But that last fact was now disproved. Had Dad never asked Gran about him? How could he not have been more curious? He seemed crushed now, betrayed. There had to be a reason. Gran, who spent her time commenting on other people's morals, wouldn't have done it out of spite. There was only one person who could provide me with the answer.

20
Dimitte nobis debita nostra

The pool was quiet the next day, which gave me time to think about what I had learned. After work, instead of walking home, I got on the tube to Mile End. I bought a packet of biscuits at the kiosk in the station.

I knocked on the door of Gran's flat. I knew she was in; I could hear rustling.

"Gran, it's me, Veronica." The door opened just enough for her to check this was the case.

"Have you your father with you?" she asked. I was let in, somewhat reluctantly, when she'd checked I was alone. Gran looked like she had been awake for a very long time and, although her hair was as neat and wisp-free as usual, she looked diminished and cowed.

Her flat was spartan and meticulously clean. There wasn't much decoration. The Virgin Mary looked down on us from a rather sentimental painting on one wall. The mantelpiece had a crucifix at one end and a school picture of me at the other. Soon it would be replaced by a graduation portrait, I assumed. Gran never had lots of photos about, I realised. Not surprising then that there was never a wedding photo or family group.

The television was on for the news. Gran turned the sound down. "You'll have heard about the damage to the Minster in York. Sure it's a terrible thing." What kind of furore would I have created if I had told her that Mum said it was God's retribution for what she had done? How easily you can upset the apple cart by being completely truthful and frank. I gave her the biscuits and she disappeared into her small kitchen to make a cup of tea.

When she returned, she brought just two of the biscuits back on a plate, with the teapot, strainer, milk jug and sugar on a small tray. Gran knew I didn't take sugar, but she liked to do things properly.

"I'll not be having a biscuit myself but you're welcome to help yourself if you'd like." Gran was always restrained. It was permanently self-denial week for her.

"Uncle Patrick told me about his holiday," I said, choosing my words carefully, keen to air the subject.

"He did, did he?"

"Dad's OK. He was just a bit …surprised."

Gran put the strainer in the cup and poured the tea. She said nothing. I bit into a Maryland cookie and the crumbs shot onto the table. "That's what the plate is for." Gran was particularly tetchy, not surprising I supposed. She got up and went to get a cloth. Gran never stayed in one place for very long. She would have been a difficult target for a sharpshooter.

"I'm sure you had a reason, Gran." She didn't make eye contact with me as she swept the table.

"I did," she said taking the cloth back into the kitchen.

"Then you should tell them." I raised my voice so she could hear me. I couldn't be sure she was going to return.

"It's been too long. Where would I start?" she replied from the kitchen.

"Start at the very beginning, Gran." I had to stop myself breaking into that song from *The Sound of Music*.

Eventually she re-appeared. She poured herself a cup of tea and sat in the upright chair she had stationed by the window. This is where she sat when she was finishing off some garment by hand. It had the best light.

"I did not see you coming today," she began, "usually I'll know if I've callers." The chair was also Gran's viewpoint. She sat there like a grande dame in a box at the opera surveying the audience below – in her case the goings-on in the street. There wasn't much that happened in her road without her knowing about it.

"Do you know how long I've sat in this window watching what goes on? It's over forty years since we got this flat. Your dad was just five when we were given it. He doesn't remember any of the other places we had after we were bombed out." She was momentarily distracted by something outside. "I've been watching to see if his father was coming round the corner and down the street all that time. To see if he'd found out where we were and decided to come home."

"I'm sorry he never came," I said.

"Well, I'm not." She spoke firmly. "He was the last person on the Earth that I wanted to see, that I would have wanted my boys to meet. Now I don't have to look out anymore."

This surprised me. Whilst I was at the pool, I'd invented a narrative about what had happened, reasons why Gran hadn't told her sons the truth about their father. She was a woman abandoned by her husband, hoping that one day he would return. Then, even when at some point she discovered he was in Ireland all along with another 'wife' and five more children, she'd still prayed that he would come back.

But this was wrong. He wasn't welcome. Even the plaster relief of St Francis that hung on the wall above the table seemed to have a surprised look on his face.

"I'm not sorry the man is dead. That's the truth of it, God forgive me." Gran was known for being forthright but her feelings here were unequivocal.

I didn't really know what to say apart from, "Why?"

Gran got up and opened a drawer. For a moment I thought she was going to show me a photograph or a document, a newspaper cutting even. She brought out some sewing and sat back in the chair.

"I had my reasons right enough and since you have bothered to come and see me you may as well know the truth." She didn't look at me as she threaded her needle and began.

"My father was a strict man, but he doted on us seven girls. He'd one for every day of the week, he'd say, but we were all crammed into a tiny house. These days you'd not believe the state of the place. No running water, an outside privy, no electricity." I'd heard all this before, usually when I was complaining about something trivial. It was part of a 'you don't know you're born' monologue that got trotted out periodically.

"My father loved us but he really wanted a son. Poor Mam had one baby after another, but we were all girls. She died having Dearbhla." I'd heard that bit before too. I always complained about the injustice of a boy having more value and the fact that the desperation for a male child had deprived all the girls of their mother. "Oh, you're one of them women's lib sorts, aren't you?" Gran would reply, only half joking. "The modern world is a different place. I started with a dressmaker when I left school, and I was only fourteen." I could never tell whether Gran entirely approved of my being at university and not earning a living.

"Paddy McNamara had all the charm in the world. Your Uncle has some of it, but not your father." I was unsure if Dad's lack of inherited charm was considered a good or a bad thing. "He drank in a pub next to the workshop where I worked and he'd take the bets for the racing at Mallow. Gambling wasn't legal in those days so they used to have runners to take the bets from the punters to the bookies. I used to see him, and he noticed me and started calling in when he was around. He was a good-looking man, when he was younger." Any compliment Gran gave had a caveat.

"Da worked in the distillery and he didn't want his daughter mixing with someone who drank so much of its products. He warned me, but I didn't listen. When I was 17, yer man said he wanted us to get married and move to London but my father wouldn't have it. Paddy was in some kind of trouble, though I was too naive to work that out. We ran away, across the sea to England, and ended up here in Mile End where he had a mucker from Ireland." Gran eloping? This was an eventful story for sure.

"The priest agreed to marry us and right enough I was pregnant with your uncle. Yer man worked as a runner here, collecting the bets for the horses in the pubs, and drinking, of course. He'd got involved with the bare-knuckle fighting too. All illegal but he sometimes won money – not that I saw any of it. Sometimes we had money and sometimes we had not." She was matter of fact, with no emotion in her voice. "By the time I had fallen pregnant with your dad he was using his bare knuckles on me. He'd spend all the money and have no housekeeping to give me. It was my fault, he said. I made him angry. I was the reason he couldn't get a drink." She spoke as if she was uninvolved in this tale.

"That's awful," I said rather obviously.

"Ah well, I could make money on the side by sewing clothes, but I hid it from him. We'd have had little to eat without it and the rent would have stayed unpaid."

"Why didn't you leave? Go home?"

"It wasn't so easy then. My father said he'd have no more to do with me after I'd run away. I'd no one to help me and a small boy and a baby. The war was coming and Paddy was worried that he'd get called up. Anyways, the man had started using the punters' money to place bets himself and he didn't always win. It wasn't long before they were after him." Unexpectedly, Gran started to laugh. "The fighter, the great angry fighter, turned out to be a coward! Running away from everything." She cut a piece of thread decisively with her scissors as if to illustrate the end of their union.

"One day he didn't come back and the day turned into weeks and then months. I thought he'd been got at by the people whose money he'd stolen. I hoped he wouldn't return, God forgive me.

The war started and when the Blitz came our building had a direct hit and all we had was lost. To everyone else he'd just vanished. Presumed killed. It wasn't uncommon. No-one asked about him. They were glad he was gone too, I shouldn't wonder. We were rehoused and it was a chance to start again without him."

"But didn't Patrick at least ask about his dad?"

"He was four when he went, and your dad was a baby. They didn't remember anything about him. When they were older it was easier to say he had died than tell them what a dreadful man he was. Who'd want a dishonest drunk for a father, who hit his wife and had probably been beaten up and thrown in the Thames by some men no better than himself?" There was no question on Gran's part that this part of her story was not justified.

"So how did you find out what happened to him?"

Gran stopped her sewing. This part of the tale was obviously harder. "They say the truth catches up with you, don't they? My father died before I ever saw him again, before the war was over. Some time after it finished, my sister Siobhan came to London to find a job. She lived with us for a short while, but decided to go home. I thought about going with her but one day she let it slip. She told me that Paddy McNamara had been seen in and around Cork and it was said that he was living back in Ballyclough, where he came from. I knew we couldn't go back. That's when I started looking for him out of the window, coming back to tell me that it was all my fault and to get his sons."

It was obviously necessary for me to say something at this point. "I understand, Gran. You did the right thing." I wasn't entirely convinced. It was a complex situation.

"I should have told them when they were old enough to understand. I know that. I didn't want them to get mixed up with him, to look for him and be disappointed when they found him. And I didn't want him to find me. It was easier to make him, and us, victims of the war."

I understood now. "You were very brave, Gran, and it must have been hard for you with two children all on your own. They'll understand if you tell them why, and God will know why you did it."

I felt a bit of a fraud saying this because I didn't actually believe God, if he existed, could possibly know why people did things. Gran did; she thought he knew everything. 'The eyes of the Lord are in every place.' He is omniscient, as she was always telling me, a supernatural know-all you can't hide things from.

I should have told Gran that I loved her at that moment, but I didn't. Later, it was the wrong time. It's something I have regretted ever since.

The revelation of that history affected me although it made no real difference to my life in the way it altered those of Dad and Uncle Patrick. My perception of Gran had changed, as well as that of people in general. I wondered whether I could really trust anything I'd been told. Who would have thought that Gran of all people would invent a truth to cover up the real one? Was it the right thing to do? Did it matter? In some circumstances, is fiction better than reality? Was it better for the boys to grow up thinking their father was a casualty of war with a potentially heroic story or a wife-beating drunkard who didn't care about his children?

I was different, anyhow. Further from childhood and nearer to the cynical adult I have become.

21
"Season of mists and mellow fruitfulness"

When I returned in the autumn of 1984, I felt different. Gran's exposure as the biggest secret-keeper yet had changed the dynamic of our family. Outwardly, things went on as normal. Dad, Uncle Patrick and Gran made peace with each other and there was a degree of understanding about why she had behaved as she had. Gran kept out of Mum's way and she in turn, with great and uncharacteristic restraint, tried very hard not to mention the revelation when the opportunity presented itself. It felt different, though. The spectre of Paddy McNamara senior hung heavily in the air, where previously he had been entirely absent.

I had to think about the future too. The real world where you had to go to work and earn money was looming. I had no idea what I wanted to do.

I wasn't much excited about the year ahead which, after all, amounted to a third of my time at the college. Finals loomed, their results the price you pay for indolence or otherwise during your time at university.

Despite the fact that it must have been obvious to everyone that I was feeling down, only one person said anything to me. It wasn't Mary, as you might have expected but, surprisingly, Webster Ferris.

I wasn't the only person to have spotted his cameo on the Nine O'clock News. Not only had he made the BBC but a photograph of his bloodied head and sour expression was featured in several newspapers of conflicting political persuasions. It was interesting how the same photograph with a different caption could be said to be illustrating a different version of the truth. Whichever newspaper you read or side you supported, no-one could believe that, like the proverbial bad penny, he had returned to college yet again. It was fortunate that the Master only read the Racing Post and that Ferris had not made his demonstration suffragette-style and interrupted the races.

I'd done well in the room ballot and finally had the old-style room that I'd been after all along. It had an open fire, which I was not allowed to use, and poorly fitting windows which rattled and were a clear conduit for cold air during even the mildest of winds. Its carpet was threadbare, its curtains thin and it had not been rewired since three pin plugs had appeared on the scene. Using my hairdryer with a two-pin adapter blew the fuse every time. Worst of all, the bathroom was a walk away across the court. The college had been mixed for a few years, but its facilities had been poorly thought out when it finally admitted female students.

It wasn't long before I saw the distinctive body shape and fast-paced walk of Webster Ferris striding across the same court. His legs were so long he took giant steps at a terrific pace. Others who saw him coming scattered, like mediaeval peasants making way for the monarch. He caught up with me as I was crossing the court to my staircase. I had been too slow to avoid him.

"All right?" he asked. I was so surprised at this friendly overture I was unable to respond. "What's up with you? You seem to have lost your sparkle." The South Yorkshire Police had obviously put Ferris into some kind of charm programme when they had decided not to charge him with any offence after Orgreave.

"Since when have you been the sodding sparkle monitor?" I asked. He looked surprised. I don't think he was expecting that kind of reply.

We stopped. Ferris indicated the staircase next to mine. "I'm in this one. Not a bad room." So, we were not only sharing a court but neighbours. It was a good sign in that it showed I had earned myself what was considered a good room in the general area of 'top rooms'. However, the close proximity was a bit worrying. There was silence for a moment.

"Do you ever wonder what you're doing here?" I asked him. It seemed not only unlikely that he managed to cling on to his place at the university but strange that he wanted to.

There was a curious paradox about him. He was sincerely a man with a mission about current politics and a genuine participant in the manifestations of it, yet also someone with a passion for literature and poetry of all periods. One minute he was getting into fights with men he didn't know who were seeking to take advantage of women in the Market Square, the next he was fighting for the mining communities of the North of England when he wasn't even employed there. He frightened the shit out of most of the other members of the university. But he wasn't rent-a-thug; he spent whole afternoons analysing the poetry of Wordsworth, he had charmingly tried to teach himself to swim in an open-air pool, he gave his pot plants names and was keen on ornithology.

He laughed. "All the bloody time. Where's that come from? Do you mean on Earth or at Cambridge?"

"Here. At university. I've only just thought about it really," I told him. "I just came here because my parents were so pleased that I'd been offered it. I didn't even think about it."

Ferris had obviously expected a 'did you have a good vacation?' type of conversation. He looked surprised. A creeper growing attractively up the walls of the court was starting to turn an autumnal shade; it really did look most attractive. He fixed his eyes on it in order not to look at me.

"My teacher was the one who suggested I apply to university," I confided. "No-one but my mum really thought I'd get offered a place at Cambridge. And she knew nothing about it. She just fancied me marrying Sebastian Flyte because she'd watched *Brideshead Revisited* on the telly."

"That's Oxford. And Sebastian is a homosexual."

"Mum's not too sure about the difference with either, really, to be honest," I said. "I think it was the large house that made him a good prospect."

Webster Ferris gave a rare smile. "Have you met him then? There are a few types here with big homes. How's a council house in Rotherham take you?" My God! He was making a joke. It started to rain lightly. "Come on, then. We'd better have a brew." He began to walk in the direction of his staircase and turned round to see if I was following. "Speed up. You'll get wet else."

Against all expectations and with a slight sense of misgiving, I ended up in Webster Ferris's room having a cup of tea. It wasn't in a delicate china cup and, unlike Gran, he hadn't used a milk jug or produced a sugar bowl. I had a chipped mug with NUM on the side and I tried not to think about how carefully it might have been washed. He did at least sniff the milk bottle before pouring some of its contents into the extraordinarily strong tea. At least I could be assured that I wasn't in for a sour or yoghurty surprise at the first sip.

Despite having the best room in college (presumably the result of a protection racket if not because of spectacular exam results) it was as barely decorated as the last. And there were two parts. It was called a set. There was a bedroom through a door off the study similar to the rooms Binka had had to share with me in her last year. Though hers had two bedrooms and came with the inconvenience of a roommate. For entirely understandable reasons, this set was for single occupancy. The furnishings were as tired as mine, except he qualified for a worn-out sofa and an armchair whilst I only got an armchair and an upright chair at my desk. Bigger brains obviously need more seating. Roy Ironside, the cactus, had survived the summer holidays during which it was unlikely that he had been watered. In fact, his prickly spines seemed to have benefitted from six months of poor husbandry and drought by growing longer and more vicious-looking than last time I'd seen him close to. He was in place on this new windowsill, standing guard as a warning to those outside merely considering entering the staircase. He had grown so much he was almost too big for his pot, a triumph of benign neglect.

There was no sign of Rod Fern, who had already been barely clinging to life before I'd accidentally kicked him under the desk. I expect he had lingered there, brown and thirsty, before giving up and wilting entirely. In one corner of the sizeable study stood the bird feeder. It was yet to be positioned outside within view of the window as a magnet for unsuspecting birds. There were no signs of a slingshot or air gun.

"Why did you call your cactus Roy Ironside?" I asked.

"He was our goalie. 220 appearances." This didn't explain much. "It were difficult to get past that bugger, just like it's hard to avoid not getting spiked by that one there." He poked at the cactus, teasing it to prick him. "He were in the team in both games when we were in the final of the League Cup."

"Was Rod Fern in it too?" Webster viewed me suspiciously.

"I used to have a fern called Rod. He died. Rod the player were far too young to be in that cup side. He only retired last year. I didn't know you followed football."

What should I have said? I don't. But I'm a weirdo who remembered, even though you only told me once, some time ago, that you had a plant called Rod Fern and I am partly responsible for his demise? I decided to say nothing.

"Name me one of the scorers of the two goals in the first leg of the final then," he asked. It was like an initiation test. Unless he had a superhuman kick it was unlikely to be Ironside the goalie. It wasn't Fern, he'd told me that. I didn't even know what team or year we were talking about.

"Here's a clue," he continued, warming to the theme. "It happened on the day I were born."

I chanced my arm. "Webster?" I'd always wondered why he had such an unusual name. It was a punt.

"Absolutely right. Barry Webster! Good girl. I'm right impressed!"

"Blimey, you could have been called Barry." I said this without considering that we both probably did know a Barry even though very few boys with that name managed to get past the admissions team at our college.

"Or Kirkman." He chuckled. I realised he seriously thought I knew these names for myself. "Me dad chose the name. He didn't tell Mam until he got back from the Register Office and she couldn't change it. There's not many others. Or Ver-on-i-cas. Not up north anyhow." He spoke my name as if he were an upper-class twit.

"My parents aren't posh. I keep telling you that." He gave me an unbelieving look. "I'm either called after a film star my dad fancied or a character in the Bible. Take your pick. I would have been called Brenda if Mum had won the toss." This was all suitably bizarre and un-classy to satisfy Webster's posh-o-meter. Had the needle gone too far along the scale I would presumably have been booted out with an Ironside-like goal kick or the cactus version embedded in my derrière.

We sat in silence for a while. I was building up the courage to make my excuses and leave without it looking too obvious that I was desperate to go.

Webster spoke, but he was looking at his shoes, not me. "The only reason I'm still here is because of my Mam too."

This was rather too personal information. I felt uncomfortable but unable to leave. His mother, the alcoholic who couldn't stand upright when she visited the college? Had she promised to go to AA if he completed the course?

"Before she died, I promised her I'd get my degree."

Lordy, she was dead! This was getting worse. Webster Ferris had gone into confession overdrive, and I was in the role of confidante.

"I'm sorry to hear she passed away," I managed, but failed to get, "but I really must be going now," tacked on to the end.

"I'd be long gone if it weren't for that."

"But why? You're so talented, you run rings around the rest of us in supervisions, you're always top in exams, and you're better and wider read than most of the teaching staff. You're going to get a double first, I bet you. And I bet your mum knew that too."

"She knew fuck all about anything," he said bluntly. It seemed a bit unkind. I didn't know how to respond. "That's the point really. She'd had no education and no-one expected anything of her. It didn't matter that she were intelligent; she'd no way of using it. She were trapped, just like me dad. She brought me up single-handed and she wanted better for me. I don't fit in here, but she didn't understand that."

"And what's your dad say?"

"He died when I was four. In an accident down t'pit."

This was getting ridiculous. I was trapped in a black and white *Play for Today* set in a post-industrial early 1960s northern town with Rita Tushingham and Albert Finney. Any moment Hylda Baker would appear and tell him not to be such a big girl's blouse and get back t'library before the factory hooter went.

"What about your sister?" I asked and immediately wished I hadn't. I remembered that she was on the game, probably because she had to earn enough to supplement his grant and pay her rent. Webster Ferris shot me a glance to emphasise that this was a bloody stupid question.

"I've not got a sister. Why do you ask about a sister?"

"Must have got you mixed up with someone else. Sorry."

"There's just me so I had to look after my Mam in her last year. They let me take a year out to do it."

So here was the reason Webster Ferris had disappeared for a year. Nothing to do with crime or correction. Just compassion.

"Liver failure, was it?" I just couldn't help opening my great big nosey trap. The dipsomaniac's final hurrah: a liver that refused to play anymore.

"She had MS. It doesn't affect your liver."

I felt awful. What had I got to complain about? A grandmother who had got carried away with an adapted version of the truth, created with the best of intentions. We'd made up things about Webster Ferris because we didn't know the truth; Gran made things up because she did.

He'd opened up to me in a way I couldn't have foreseen. When I made my excuses and finally left, I almost felt that he was sorry to see me go.

As winter approached, although the High Court had ruled that the miners' strike was illegal, and the NUM's assets were frozen, it continued. But the fight was limping to a slow but predictable end. Mrs T. was the victor, Scargill the vanquished. This affected Webster, who had taken to lending me books and then asking me to discuss what I thought of them. I didn't know if this was to take his mind off external things or if it was a way of being in control of something – me! It was terrifying, like a proper supervision where the supervisor is awake and probing what you say, criticising you when you waffle or talk nonsense. Striking miners were starting to go back to work, and Ferris, like the union, was crushed.

I didn't tell anyone about the grilling Ferris was giving me on the wide range of books he found to foist on to me. I think he was grateful to find another bookworm, somebody who was happy to spend all afternoon reading. I should have been reading the set texts for my course, but Ferris's reading list was more interesting and more unusual than that of the university department. Why did I keep quiet? It was a perfectly ordinary, if nerdy, thing to do. I suppose I didn't want people to know I was associating with him.

I started going to Webster's room for another reason too, not only for my extra 'supervisions'. The weather was getting colder and my room was becoming uncomfortably chilly. A huge draught whistled down the chimney and on the top floor, in the eaves, there was no insulation. I was given a two-bar electric fire. It had a revolting smell when it was turned on, dust and particles burning off the element. Ten minutes or so after switching it on, having given out this appalling stench but very little heat, the fire would go bang and switch off. The electrics would have given up again and everything would fuse. My neighbours on the staircase did not find this acceptable so I contrived to be out as often as I could.

Ferris's two-room set was relatively cosy. The best room in college had an attractive fireplace and surround, crowned by a stone mantelpiece. Sadly, the days of having a 'man' to come in and lay a fire then stoke it until it was roaring for when 'Sir' was back from whatever pursuits had taken up his afternoon were gone.

By 1984 it had a big gas fire set in the aperture of the fireplace with a sturdy but ugly pipe and a lever to turn on the supply. This had probably been installed in the 1940s and was looking dangerously obsolete. It had to be lit by a match or, if you had one, a long taper, and doing so was a frightening experience. First you turned the gas tap until the gas was hissing and then you hoped that it would light first time when you gingerly poked the match or taper towards it. If this failed, gas escaped into the room and the eventual lighting was accompanied by a flash which would burn your eyelashes or eyebrows if you got too close. Dangling bits of fringe were particularly vulnerable. If I smell singed hair today it reminds me of that fire. Once it was lit it was superb. Flames licked all along its burner and copious amounts of heat filled the room. After a while the oxygen was sucked out of the air so a soporific fug overcame us. It was a calming narcotic which made me sleepy and mellow and very glad to be indoors when it was chilly outside. That fire even managed to take the edge off Ferris's quick temper and acerbic personality. What a treat, as winter approached, to toast crumpets or muffins on a long poker as afternoon autumnal mists curled silently around the stately architecture outside.

I've always thought autumn the most attractive season in Cambridge. From October onwards the Backs have beautifully coloured displays of falling foliage. How wonderful to walk in the low sun through the crispy browns, oranges and yellows of the leaves, crossing the Cam into the grounds of the colleges, looking down mid-span of a bridge onto the tourists making a hash out of punting on the waters beneath.

It was getting near the holidays. With only eight weeks of teaching allocated to each term, you're never more than four weeks away from a holiday. One Saturday, I was returning from the Sidgwick site, the ghastly concrete-on-poles, mid-century blocks which were the face of post-war Cambridge architecture and the home of the English Department. It was starting to get dark, although it was still late afternoon. Like a school kid, I thoughtlessly kicked my way through the leaves which had been piled up for removal. I crossed the river and made my way towards my college. I'd found a book I thought Ferris would be interested in, so I decided to drop it off. I entered his staircase and knocked on the door to his room.

He looked glum but his face brightened when he saw me. He had taken the prospect of the miners' defeat very personally and often sat soulfully in his armchair. If anyone was counting sparkles, they'd have had trouble finding any on Webster Ferris.

He was listening to the football results. Perhaps Rotherham had lost and that was the reason for his miserable face. He turned the radio off decisively. "I'm glad you're here," he said unusually.

He didn't talk about his emotions much. He didn't need to; you could identify how he was feeling by his demeanour.

Angry, furious, apoplectic – all easily spotted. Irritated, cross, perplexed – again fairly easy answers to the 'I spy with my little eye, Webster Ferris is feeling …' game. Softer emotions were harder. I sometimes wondered if he had them. They certainly weren't on show in public. He did smile sometimes, even laughed occasionally, and could give the impression that he was tolerating your company, but he had never actually said so until then.

"I've got two crumpets left," he announced, handing me a poker. "There's a bit of butter on the window-sill outside that's still this side of rancid." He'd missed his vocation as a waiter tempting diners in a Michelin-starred restaurant.

Crumpets toasted, butter brought in from the makeshift fridge, sniff checked and applied, we shared his one plate on the sofa. I gave him the book. He did find it interesting and began reading immediately.

"Hang on! Don't get your buttery fingers on it," I warned, "or I'll get a fine for that when I take it back."

"Sorry," he grinned. He held the book in one hand and wiped the other offending hand on the sofa. It didn't seem too disgusting at the time. Years of student hand-wiping and probably worse had seeped into its threadbare fabric and the semi-exposed stuffing beneath. His hand stayed on the seat and his long spindly fingers moved towards mine, gradually interlinking with my much shorter ones. He didn't look at me but carried on reading the book. Encouraged that I hadn't withdrawn my hand on contact, he gradually manoeuvred it so that we were holding hands. We stayed like that for a while until eventually he put his arm round me, and I lay my head on his shoulder whilst he continued to read.

So, quietly and furtively and just between us, that was the beginning of my relationship with Webster Ferris. The official beginning, that is.

I can hear the protests. "You silly cow, who are you kidding? It began a long while before."

We had developed a closeness and affinity that was new to both of us. Like Roy Ironside the cactus, without any nurturing it had grown, slowly and imperceptibly, without either of us noticing.

22

"Youth's a stuff will not endure"

ow long is not that long ago? To me, the 'hot summer of 1984' not only retains its adjective but also its proximity. That prolonged period of continental weather and Gran's exposure as a manipulator of truth are inexorably entwined for me. I can't think of one without the other and neither feels that long ago. The autumn which followed, sweetened by the honeyed scent of first love, seems tantalisingly close yet impossibly far away.

This paradox was exposed as soon as Mary got hold of my number and started pestering me to come along to the forty-year reunion. It couldn't be that many years ago, surely. When she first asked me, the date seemed so far off that I thought I could come up with a reason to pull out nearer the time. For, in truth, the idea filled me with a creeping anxiety.

My closest friends at university were undoubtedly the Pared-Down Players. None of them was at my college so they wouldn't be at the reunion. After graduating we kept in touch. They came to our wedding and Roland was invited, my last attempt to get onto Roly terms. It didn't work. Only his hair underwent a shortening. He'd dropped the highlights but gave Mum a very wide berth – just in case she had views on his new pretty-boy crop with swept-over fringe.

Roland had got himself a job at the BBC, he announced, and the rest of us were jealous but pretended to be delighted. He then disappeared from our orbit, although we were all expecting to see his name appearing on a screen sometime soon. If it came, I missed it.

Inevitably, in time, we lost each other in the business of daily life. It took a worldwide pandemic to prompt us to seek each other out: a lockdown from normal existence which made us aware of our own mortality and perhaps gave us a yearning for earlier, more settled times.

First we made a WhatsApp group and tentatively dipped out toes back in the waters of friendship. After a while, looking through the gaps between the fingers of the hands shielding our eyes as if we were back behind the sofa hiding from the Daleks in *Doctor Who?*, we saw each other on Zoom.

It wasn't too awful – there's a certain art to positioning the laptop so that it doesn't focus on your double chin and getting the light in the right place so that your complexion doesn't look like papyrus from an ancient Egyptian tomb. We recognised each other immediately. It was a relief that we clearly looked like ourselves. Although we were distorted and far less appetising than thirty odd years earlier, like a Golden Delicious which has sat in the fruit bowl a bit too long, we were still identifiably apples. Golden but not as delicious.

Other than me, only Ameerah and Neil were married – but not to each other. Lucy and Steve managed to appear on the same screen and let bygones be bygones. Both were divorced and Lucy had had several partners, none of them Steve. Miraculously he had avoided ending up marrying her just because he couldn't bear to hurt her feelings. He had married two other women, though, both of whom had decided to leave him. In a predictably saintly way he had brought up a selection of offspring single-handed. Danny was single and had only escaped the matchmaking of his mum when she passed away. This proves that inertia can get you what you want in the end.

What stories there were to tell, slowly and carefully. There were revelations to be made no doubt. I think we were all reticent to come clean immediately. Better to talk about the university past, our communal history, the stories we could verify and check for over-elaboration. Tentatively, we talked about meeting up, face to face, but that would mean we couldn't blame the yellowing papyrus on poor lighting and would have to 'out' the beer belly and menopausal spread which a judiciously placed desk can hide on Zoom.

We had a good old laugh about Roland and his preposterous adaptations and how we were taken in by his pretentious nonsense.

"What a pseud he was! He's probably got an Arts Council grant for a collective theatre group which does underwater performances. *Anthony and Cleopatra* with a cast of five and the audience in scuba gear. How could we have thought such a pillock was worth listening to?" I was warming to the theme, chipping in with rather more enthusiasm than was strictly necessary.

"I know what happened to Roly," Neil explained.

Roly? Since when had Neil been on Roly terms? We waited in anticipation. "He died." Momentarily there was silence. Neil's voice faltered, "Of AIDS in 1989. We were an item for a while. He was my first love. We sort of got together at your wedding, Roni. He was a lovely man really."

There followed a lot of backtracking about what a lovely man Roland actually was and the raking up of examples of his loveliness. Being dead earned Roland the kind of respect he thought he had whilst he was alive.

"But you never told us." Ameerah was surprised. "Weren't we your friends?"

"I couldn't," Neil explained. "I kept thinking I was going to and then time went on and it got too long. I had to keep it from my parents and anyone who knew them, and it just seemed easier not to."

I'd seen Neil during this time, and I hadn't known. I'd been so bound up in my own world I hadn't been able to share his. "I'm sorry I was rude about him."

"It's OK," Neil said. "He helped me a lot, but being honest with myself was always my problem. I was terrified afterwards that I would have it too, but I was lucky. I feel better now I've told you, even all these years later."

I wondered what secrets the others had which were lurking, waiting for an outing just before the Zoom meeting timed out, like a cliff-hanger at the end of a soap. Face to face and my own revelation would have to wait.

So it remained. I was going to a reunion of people I didn't particularly want to see, where there might be encounters I'd prefer to avoid. I must have had an angry look on my face when my husband saw me. "Just don't go if you don't want to. It's not compulsory," he suggested with the irritating conviction of one stating the bleeding obvious. "Personally, I can't see why you wouldn't want to. I've really enjoyed the ones I've been to." I knew this and he knew that I knew. Reiterating the fact wouldn't help persuade me.

The idea that rekindling a connection with some of my college contemporaries might turn out not to be a good idea did not occur to him. I could think of an infinite number of scenarios (one in particular) where reacquaintance might be inadvisable.

"You think too hard about things," he continued. "Just enjoy yourself. If you find you're hating it, leave early." It must be hard being so sensible, but he's had years of practice. He'd been to several reunions, or gaudies as they are known in some circles, with all his sensible friends with whom he's kept in touch since leaving university. There isn't really much point in them going back to college; reliving the good old days is something they do on a regular basis much closer to home.

I'm jealous. It's not hard to work that out. I envy the neatness and practicality of his university group: a core number of friends who continue to see each other once a year, who often bump into each other in workplace scenarios and at sports fixtures. That's what you get if you are a sensible engineer who went to a modern, functional college and stayed there to do a Masters because there isn't really anywhere else better to do it. They enjoyed their studies and had a good time. I was rude about them then, but I am jealous of them now.

"It's nice Mary rang you," continued the calm and ever practical one, "and I'm glad you were able to say yes and forgive her for not coming to our wedding." There was a smile on his face; this was well-worn ground. The idea that I was bearing a grudge about it all these years later was always mentioned if Mary cropped up in conversation, which she did very occasionally. I should have ignored it, but he got me every time.

Mary was invited to our wedding, but she did not attend. I was upset at the time because we invited only a very few guests and she offered no explanation. I was puzzled why she turned down the invitation. We didn't see each other again but it wasn't because I was cross with her. Ever since then, this had been the suggestion – in jest I might add. Never hilarious the first time, the joke was decidedly thin thirty plus years later.

Persistently and obviously, Mary now wanted to see me. She was determined that I should be there. How strange, I thought, after all these years. It was almost as if she too couldn't face it without me. Something about her perseverance made me suspect there was more to it and that intrigued me enough to ensure that after almost forty years I was headed back to Cambridge.

23
Familiar places

Surely someone's come up with a theory about time speeding up towards things you don't really want to happen? Root-canal treatment, serious operations, lunch with your batty senior relations – they arrive in no time. Just like the college alumni gathering (as they were insisting on calling it).

It is a particular kind of horror. It's easy to see through the flimsy attempts to get you to contribute to the new dining room or leave 'a lasting legacy' to aid another student. If you were minded to do either of those, you wouldn't need a combination of mediocre wine, chicken in unidentifiable sauce and the disappointment of what time has done to the twenty-year-old bodies and minds of your contemporaries.

At best an opportunity to say hello to someone who you barely spoke to forty years ago and probably will never see again, it's more likely an encounter filled with neurosis and insecurity. Unless you are resoundingly successful, have retained or enhanced whatever physical attractions you had as a young person or have a certain kind of generous personality, it's going to be an afternoon or evening of envy and disappointment.

A few will be able to enjoy rubbing their school friends' or university buddies' noses in the sickly treacle of their undoubted good fortune. The rest will have to deal with this life-story one-upmanship, a verbal CV delivered by someone to whom you barely gave the time of day and whose looks have been improved by clever hair transplanting and expensive dentistry. It's a real-life Top Trumps of who has done best.

Although I didn't really want to be at the reunion in person, I had to admit I had an inexplicable and probably unkind fascination with what had become of everyone. Judicious stalking on Linked-In had given me much of the information I needed about many of the people I could remember from college. Googling and finding appearances in the columns of the gutter press had indicated the progress of some of the others.

The most likely scenario would involve bragging by generation hop. Boasting is more acceptable when it's about one's offspring. I would have to be prepared for fiercely intelligent, focused children and the cost of their extra-curricular activities. For how it had all been worth it because they managed to have extra lessons in greasy pole climbing from a marvellous private tutor and triumph in higher education at Russell Group universities or be awarded full scholarships to Ivy League colleges. Afterwards they'd have found full and fruitful employment, successful relationships and would now be vigorously commencing the latest must have: the production of any number of cute baby grandchildren.

Returning somewhere which, a long time in the past, has been very familiar is an odd experience. No one expects a place to be the same, yet you still feel wrong-footed when things aren't where you thought they should be. The memory can play tricks but more likely planners and 'improvements' put a spanner in collective memories and spatial awareness.

Try going to Barking if you haven't been there for thirty-five years. There are moments of familiarity, fleeting references to the past – your house painted an unexpected colour and sporting an extension on the side or roof like some kind of tumour, bits of your school looking familiar but as if they have been dropped by an alien space grabber amongst another lot of buildings altogether. Well-trodden roads suddenly merge into new bypasses, corners disappearing only for a recognisable building to wink at you from an unusual location. I expect this of my hometown. It's a busy place which has changed in many ways since I was living there.

I had been back to Cambridge only a few times over the years, not as often as I might have – given that being there felt like coming home. I always come away unsettled. Is it the same for everyone? I remember fun and joy but also sadness. This place where for just a short time my heightened emotions made it the vital and all-enveloping nucleus of my life. You leave it as a graduate with a tempting menu of possibilities in front of you and you return knowing the reality of how it all worked out.

Forty years on everything was recognisable. But it was an illusion. Walking about those familiar streets was unnerving. Like recently bereaved people who think they have glimpsed their departed, I was haunted by improbable sightings of my contemporaries, their ghosts – one in particular – leaving an imprint on the present.

Today's students have to work very much harder than we did and there's much less time for enjoying yourself and extracurricular messing about. Roland's adaptations, all over in fifty minutes at the most, would be very well received – the man was ahead of his time. Cambridge seems to have a lot more clothes shops now but there are fewer bookstores. I guess the students just sit in their rooms, book-free, directly wired into their computers but dressed so much better than we were.

I was regretting giving in to Mary's powers of persuasion. I had very few friends in my own college and, Mary aside, I doubted any of the rest of them would be there. There had been something desperate in her voice which had made me relent but now I was annoyed by this.

Occasionally, when Dad and the Cortina were unavailable, I had walked to and from the station when arriving or leaving. I was clearly fitter and quicker then. The same walk that September afternoon made me hot and bothered, confused and feeling elderly before I'd even set eyes on the college. By the time I arrived at the Porters' Lodge I was scowling and cussing. It was warm and I could feel a trickle of sweat running down my back. The porter had his hair shaved at the sides and a slick of bottle-blonde flop on top. A tattoo of a colourful lizard wound round his neck. He wore no bowler hat but had an earring and a badge saying, "DEAN. Happy to Help." I sincerely hoped this wasn't the Dean of the college.

"Hey there, Veronica," he grinned when I told him who I was. Even as a miserable low-status undergrad I was called Miss McNamara. I considered a more appropriate badge for him: "DEAN. Happy to call you by your first name even though we haven't been introduced and you are at least thirty-five years older than me."

"You guys are in the Techno-Cam IT building." Guys? The what building? Swiftly he produced a coloured map and proceeded to draw large circles round huge parts of it with a biro.

"You're here." He circled a building clearly labelled as 'Porters' Lodge'. "And we've made the accommodations for the '82 gang in this facility." He drew another circle covering about half of the college and encompassing a grey rectangle obscuring what had been a lovely garden last time I was there. "Like, you're really lucky. It's the newest lot of student accommo we have. Wet rooms, ultra-fast broadband, digital hotspots."

I was speechless: Guys, '82 gang, the unnecessary and inappropriate use of like. Which was worse, accommodations or accommo? Does no one have a room anymore? Luck? I wanted to die. All my bêtes noires in one speech.

"What is Techno-Cam IT?" I asked eventually, trying not to stare at the lizard, whose tail slid down beneath his collar.

"It's kinda like the sponsor of the building. They're really cool. Here's your digital fob. Any probs then give us a tweet."

He scribbled '#collegeportersRus' on to the map. "We're here 24/7."

Christ. It was a terrifying all-day nightmare. Where was the bowler-wearing human rottweiler Mr Boulderstone, who frightened the life out of you and had the power to admit you or not to the building, even though you were paying to live there?

Dean passed me the fob. It was about the size of a 5p coin and joined to a very small tab with the number of the room on it (I presumed – it was too minute to read without glasses). "Neat eh?" he said, expecting me to be impressed by this tiny token, which I was highly likely to lose between the lodge and the unidentified room. "It's impressive. It's all you need to do anything," he added rather improbably. I hoped he was right – summoning Paul Newman (alive and as he looked in *Butch Cassidy and The Sundance Kid*) piloting a helicopter to get me out of here would be good. I considered telling Dean this but thought I might be opening up a can of explanation worms.

The first court looked familiar and I managed to find my way to the Techno-Cam IT building. I didn't doubt that the massive letters spelling out its name could be seen from space, a useful talisman for astronauts missing Earth as well as reminding them of the largesse of the donors.

Having kept a sweaty palm clutching the fob without losing it, I managed to use it to get me into the building. Silently, a door slid back automatically and allowed me access to an entrance foyer. I shouldn't have been surprised to see a lift, but I was. Stairs were clearly the option for the claustrophobic and obsessively energetic and not considered an alternative for a gym advertised on a poster nearby. I remembered Dad struggling and cursing up several flights of stairs in the brutalist block carrying my belongings on the day I arrived.

Stairs were also for fob losers, I realised, because entry to the lift was dependent on the fob. Another girl jumped in just as the doors were closing. I say girl – in reality she was an elderly-looking woman with a wheelie flight case just like mine. I wondered if she was a fob loser and had been lurking round the corner waiting for someone carrying the techno version of 'open sesame' to appear.

"Hello!" she chirped. "Great to see you."

"Likewise." I had no idea who she was, and it was obvious she either didn't recognise me or, having recognised me, had nothing whatsoever she wanted to say to me. I debated asking whether she'd mislaid the fob but decided I couldn't be bothered to engage in conversation either. We rode in silence up to the second floor, where I was staying. "See you later," I said to her, rather hoping I wouldn't.

I fobbed myself into the room and fobbed on the lights. I could fob the curtains shut and then fob them open again. I could open the window from the opposite side of the room with it, though the pane halted at a certain distance. I assumed this was a safety feature. Even the slimmest person would have trouble falling out or committing fobicide through the tiny aperture created. You would burn to death in a fire and swelter in a heatwave – but maybe there was a fob emergency service on hand to rescue you, if only you could find the right sensor pad to call it.

Having fobbed myself into the ensuite wetroom, I discovered that the shower was also activated by fob. Some ill-advised fob fumbling exploration whilst trying to fob the flush had resulted in an unexpected spray of cold water which not only flattened my hair and soaked my clothes but made the tiled floor treacherous underfoot. A hard towel about the size of a piece of A3 had been provided and I had to sacrifice this in a mopping up operation so that I didn't slip and break my neck. Perhaps there was a drying blast of air one could fob into action after a shower. If there was, I couldn't find it.

Back in the main room, I caught sight of myself in the mirror as I fobbed on the mini kettle to make myself a cup of tea with the one tea bag and pod of long-life milk provided. I looked a mess.

If the evening turned out to be excruciating, I decided, I could come back to the room and spend a happy couple of hours activating things with my fob, provided of course that I hadn't lost it. Fobbing would potentially be a lot more exciting than standing about with a drink pretending I cared what the last 37 years had involved for a person who I couldn't even be bothered to speak to between 1982 and 1985.

Losing the fob once in the room would prohibit you doing anything in it. Life depended on the fob in the way it never had with a key.

I sat on the hard bed, part of a selection of immoveable pieces of furniture in the bland room, amazed by the huge number of bookshelves provided and the length of the desk stretching down one side of the room. No bookshops, everything on laptop but lots of bookshelves? I decided they were just shelves. Modern students must have objects to display, feng shui rules to adhere to and obsessions with shelf-based Hygge or whatever the latest craze is. There was no disguising the fact that the desk, about ten times longer than the one that had been provided for me, was designed for some serious IT provision and lengthy essay production.

My phone rang. The screen told me it was Mary. My first thought was that she was telling me that she would not be able to come. I'd gone through this scenario in my head; without Mary would I carry on with the evening? She lived in Cambridge because she taught at the university. If she didn't come, if she used some excuse like Covid or Brexit or the Suez Canal being blocked by a tanker, I could go round to her house and make her. Or go home.

"Are you here?" she asked when I answered.

"I'm in the Techno-Cam IT building," I announced. "I've had a shower fully clothed and used up my teabag allowance.

If I find the right thing to fob, I ought to be able to teleport to wherever you are. You're somewhere, I assume. Everyone has to be somewhere."

There was a pause. "Are you OK, Roni?"

"I've just found a note saying 'no hairdryers provided' and I can't sign into the wi-fi because it's too complicated. I can't re-arrange the furniture because it's all bolted to the floor, and the bathroom is like a skating rink. Other than that, I'm fine."

Mary was hesitant. She sensed reluctance. "Everyone is in the Cruddas Room having welcome drinks. You are coming aren't you?"

24

Forty years on

The Cruddas Room, a wood-panelled chamber probably designed by Wren or someone who would have called in an exorcist if he'd experienced the Techno-Cam nightmare, was familiar territory. I knew where I was going. I made myself look as presentable as I could in the circumstances and tentatively headed over in that direction.

The room was surprisingly full, crammed with lined and wrinkled people. It was a University of the Third Age convention and Saga cruise reception rolled into one. I recognised no-one. I was given a badge with Victoria MacNamara in letters slightly too small to be read with the naked eye by nearly sixty-year-olds with age-related long sight.

"Welcome back, Victoria," gushed a college representative with 'Amanda. Alumnus Relations. Ask away!' on a badge.

"I'm Veronica McNamara," I said pointedly.

"Sorry, I must have misheard you. No worries at all. You've got the wrong badge, you've got Victoria's. Are you twins?" she looked at the badges left on the desk. There weren't many remaining. "I can't see a Veronica. Perhaps I gave your twin your badge. Has she already checked in?"

"I haven't got a twin."

"Really?" she looked unconvinced, "Oh, no problem, your sister then."

"I'm an only child."

"What a coincidence! Two people with very similar names!"

She surveyed the few badges left to be claimed. "Doesn't look like Veronica is coming."

"Yes she is, she's here," I insisted.

"Perfect. Maybe you could just swap badges with her then, Victoria?"

Why do people say 'perfect' when things quite clearly aren't? Why do absolute morons get well paid jobs that are obviously beyond their abilities?

"Roni! Still late thirty-seven years on!" It was unmistakably the voice of Perfect Penny but coming out of a caricature of a stalwart of the WI living in a commuter village somewhere outside Guildford. She was surrounded by a gaggle of similarly dressed, middle-aged clones.

"Is it raining?" a woman with blonde hair asked. She was filling her mouth with several canapés whilst she spoke. This had to be Lizzie. Student Lizzie had brown hair but I quickly realised few of these women had brown hair any more. As the daughter of a hairdresser, I was acutely aware of the grey cover-up. "You're soaked and your hair is all plastered down. The forecast didn't say rain." This was all true.

"Roni!" Mary, like a knight on a white charger swept me away and towards the drinks table. "There's an awful row going on," she warned.

The re-formed Cocoa Club had been out to lunch earlier in the day and Penny had produced a spread sheet to work out the bill for the pre-ordered food. There had been some disagreement as to who had ordered what, how the bill should be paid, the amount of tip given and, most contentiously, what had been served as against what was ordered. The implication was that Perfect Penny was no longer fully entitled to be regarded as perfection. Indeed, she had messed up royally. Her spreadsheet was woefully inadequate and downright inaccurate.

It says something about my inability to mature sufficiently

over the previous thirty-seven years that this caused me an inappropriate amount of pleasure. I could see her trying to remain aloof whilst being assaulted on all sides by a bevy of dissatisfied lunchers.

"I deliberately didn't drink in order not to have other people's alcohol costs added to my bill," one complainer in a floral dress a size too small for her was proclaiming.

"I didn't have a starter," another chipped in, "but I seem to have ended up supplementing the lunches of those who did. And some had a pudding as well."

"Some people chose the most expensive things on the menu expecting us to subsidise them. I ordered pesce spade alla griglia and I got paccheri spade melanzane e mentuccia," huffed a pointy-nosed individual. Although most people had no idea of the difference, there was a general tutting and shaking of heads. "I can't eat anything with gluten," she grumbled by way of an incomplete explanation.

Penny was trying to rise above it but her face was flushed and she looked uncomfortable. "Perhaps someone else would like to organise it next time," she suggested.

Mary and I looked on with pleasure and for one moment we were twenty-one again, laughing in synergy.

"I didn't know your real name was Victoria." Having finished the last of the savoury choux, Lizzie was drawing breath before tucking in to some gravlax on rye bread.

"It's not."

"So why did you ask for your badge to say it?" she persisted.

"For a laugh," I replied. Despite having retained her appetite and ability to read the name badges from a comfortable distance without glasses, it was obvious that Lizzie had neither acquired a sense of humour nor deviated from her early commitment to take everything at face value.

Mary indicated her badge, which showed she had now

morphed into Marie for the purposes of obscuring identification. I was all for remaining incognito and regretted that I hadn't asked for the badge saying Susannah Jones or, more controversially, Lawrence Farnsworth. Neither of these names was familiar to me. They were lingering on the table with Victoria when I arrived. Either they were not coming, or the badges had been produced for Susan Jones or Laura Fernsworth, who, quite rightly, had refused to wear them.

"He's not here," Mary explained sotto voce. "I've looked at the list."

"Who?" I asked, trying to give the impression I didn't know who she meant.

"Webster Ferris."

"Perhaps he's on the list as Fester Worries?" I tried to make light of my huge relief. Mary smiled weakly. Why was she so concerned about Ferris turning up? Why did she think I'd care forty years on? Everyone has history.

The clink of a spoon on a glass indicated we should fall silent, and the ever-cheerful Amanda Alumnus Relations welcomed us all back to college. We were ushered into the dining hall where a seating plan was posted on an easel.

Had I not seen that the name of the man next to me was Julian Sousa I would not have recognised him. An intense monologue about marching band music or obscure poetry might have given the game away after a minute or so, but physically he was completely changed.

The days of playing the sousaphone, the instrument which coiled round him like a boa constrictor, were clearly over. There was no brass instrument on Earth which could encircle him now without having to be dismantled piece by piece to remove it. Like Henry VIII in full armour being lowered onto his horse by a crane, getting it over his head would require electrically powered machinery. He was vast.

He squinted at my name badge once we were at the table.

"Victoria?" he queried, "I'm afraid I don't recall. Have we met? You've obviously been caught in a downpour. I should have brought my umbrella."

I wanted to point out how, as Veronica, I had spent a whole May Ball trying to avoid him and his boring instruction about military marching bands and his musical relation. I couldn't do so, however, because he turned away to converse with his neighbour on the other side. The only time he addressed me thereafter, having invaded my space with his overflowing bulk, was to ask if he could have my bread roll as it appeared that I was not going to eat it.

The Great Hall was more magnificent than I remembered. I hadn't appreciated its panelled walls and grandeur when I had sat at its long tables as an undergraduate. It certainly wasn't something I had been used to, coming from a school built in the 1930s. I was surprised that I hadn't been more impressed with it at the time.

Portraits of previous masters lined the walls, above them large windows with panes of coloured glass showing heraldic shields. To one end, High Table, running perpendicular to those seating the riffraff below, had a panel of intricately carved woodwork behind it and a portrait of a Tudor man, stockinged legs planted sturdily apart, arms aggressively on hips. No need to ask if he was in charge.

By contrast I spotted a later addition to the collection of masters, the one from my time. He'd been painted in a modern style, his face misshapen and grey, his eyes twitchy and anxious. He held a large book, which I imagined was disguising the Racing Post underneath. He looked ill at ease, certainly not in the process of singing a little Irish ditty to himself. Maybe he'd had an unsuccessful punt on the day of the sitting.

A door opened and a small procession of gowned academics entered. All in pursuit of a free meal, I thought. Once in place, the

Master addressed us. "Kia Ora," she began. I hoped this wasn't the announcement of a substitution of wines from the college's renowned cellars with the sickly orange beverage I had drunk a lot of in the 1970s.

Grace was then said in Māori. This was a surprise to those of us who hadn't realised that the Master, although not a Māori herself, was from New Zealand but it explained her first greeting.

"Good evening. I am the Master of the College. My name is Jan and my pronouns are ze zir."

There was a sharp intake of breath from several areas of the room. Certain sections of the assembled company were having to process the fact that not only was the Master a Kiwi but that ze was potentially, but not necessarily, a Mistress as well.

"Today's college is a very different place from the one you knew," ze began. Zir accent was thick and zir tone challenging. "Academic standards are up; we are high in the Tompkins Table." There was low-level booing from a section of the room who deemed that improvement in the annual table of academic excellence which ranks colleges according to their undergraduates' performance was not necessarily something to be praised.

"We are innovative and inclusive, and our students are now hard-working and inquisitive, forward-thinking and caring."

It gradually dawned on all the diners that implicit in these statements was the idea that the Master considered, intentionally or otherwise, that none of us was or ever had been any of these things. The gathering momentum of disquiet building from the floor was only silenced by zir next revelation. Ze cleared zir throat and in thickly accented kiwi continued.

"At a recent college poetry slam, I performed a spoken word poem which I created myself and which I feel encapsulates the importance of the college to its students and its relations with its alumni."

There was a brief hiatus whilst some of the audience tried to work out what a poetry slam was and those who knew wondered what was coming next.

"*Our College.*" Zir voice was loud, zir face expressive. Ze waved zir arms expressively, like an air-steward indicating emergency exits.

"*Birth giver of our nexts / Nurturer of our dreams / Provider of our future.*"

The arms were gesticulating, indicating the future ahead of us: comforting for those of us approaching our seventh decade. Zir voice rose, bouncing off the antique walls.

"*We live within your womb / Before we emerge into the planisphere of life / Through your welcoming vagina.*"

Mistakenly, sforzando fortissimo, Julian Sousa exclaimed, "Goody goody!" I feared he had misunderstood what might be the after-dinner entertainments.

Momentarily, all eyes turned to him, but zir hands whooshed and pushed, demonstrating giving birth – albeit at a faster pace than (certainly in my case) had been any lived experience.

"*You are the you we made / The life you have lived is because of us / Cocooned in our college uterus / You were nourished by the placenta of our walls.*"

Ze hung zir head. The room fell silent. The accompanying academics nodded their appreciation. I could see Penny and the Cocoa Club; their faces suggested that mention of birthing parts had clearly put them off their anticipated dinner. Some of the men were smirking. Others, who retained the vestiges of critical faculty, were striving to critique the work. I caught Mary's eye and had to look away.

Amanda Alumnus Relations then stood up. Lacking the performance skills of the Master, she needed a microphone.

"I think we'll agree," she started, though a long blast of very high-pitched feedback drowned out the main part of what she was saying, "…and if you'd like a form to indicate the level of your bequest and of course a Gift Aid slip as well, I'll be here all evening to help. Ask away."

Dinner passed quickly, most guests eager to leave the room before Amanda's charm offensive could catch those with an unprepared excuse or judgement-clouding belly full of wine. The sight of her bearing down on an unsuspecting possible donor waving a Gift Aid form was enough to persuade the hungriest of alumni to skip the cheese.

We set off to discover the bar. I half imagined Simeon Goldblatt would be there resiliently ignoring the anti-Semitic jibes of Bomber's chums. It seemed hardly possible that all that had happened nearly forty years ago. The bar was located in the same place but now, like everything else, it looked different. The interior reminded me of a corporate hotel where people in office wear carrying laptop bags get inappropriately drunk because they are on expenses and off the leash.

"I thought it was you." A pleasant-looking man with a full head of hair tapped me on the shoulder. "I recognised you from behind. We used to have seminars together. Tom Percy."

Greatly encouraged that the back of me at least still looked twenty, I offered to buy him a drink. I did remember him; his front had weathered as well as his hair. This was clearly the Tom whose room we had gathered in for the May Ball when I wore the lilac Cinderella and Sousa fancied his chances.

"Have you seen this?" He shoved a stiff card saying 'cocktail menu' at me. "Well, Victoria, what are we having?" I had noticed him surreptitiously checking out my name badge and looking confused. I couldn't be bothered to explain.

There was a professional barman who made a great show of agitating his cocktail shaker just a little too much when he was preparing our drinks. I had a 'PhD', which had a gin base, elderflower cordial mix and ribbons of cucumber and mint. Tom went for the 'MSc', which comprised rum, coke and brown sugar cubes decorated with a number of orange slices. Both came in huge glasses with ice and a paper umbrella in the college colours.

The umbrella brought it all back. The party at the Boat Club, the knickers up the pole, the lethal cocktail and Simeon Goldblatt's unfair dismissal. I suddenly felt sick.

Outside there was some expensive garden furniture on a decked area and we went to get some air.

By feigning sudden deafness and applying a telepathic unity of purpose surprising after such a long time apart, we managed to avoid having to join the table where Penny, Lizzie and Sue were discussing which type of HRT they were taking.

Tom was enjoyable company if a tad dull. He quickly established several facts which told me all I needed to know about his past 37 years. He had a barn conversion in the Yorkshire Dales, he had married Sally the plain speaker, who was unable to come because she was caring for her mother, who had dementia, they had no children but kept a herd of goats and made their own cheese. He didn't say 'instead' but that was the implication. Now it was my turn; he waited expectantly.

"Do you remember Simeon Goldblatt?" I asked. I'd decided it was time to tell the truth. It had been gnawing away at me all these years and the cocktail umbrella had rekindled the guilt.

"Wasn't he the guy who set fire to the boathouse in our first year? Small. Clever." There was a silence. I was finding it hard to speak the words. In the lull, Penny could be heard bemoaning the fact that the rooms we were staying in had no soap provided.

"You didn't marry him, did you?"

Mary appeared. "Hey, Mary, Victoria here married Simon Goldfinger, that little pyromaniac cox!" Tom was grinning manically at this so-called discovery. Other nearby conversations stalled and tuned in.

Mary looked at me. "How many of those cocktails have you had? You're a naughty girl. Victoria!"

"Did someone say Roni married that titchy bloke who got sent down?" Lizzie, munching her way through the fruit garnish of abandoned cocktail glasses, true to form, was showing she had missed her vocation as a town crier. "You must have looked an odd couple in the wedding photos; you're about twice as tall as him."

I wanted to point out that had I converted to Judaism, married Simeon Goldblatt and had photographs of the occasion taken outside the synagogue, this would not have been the only set of photos in which I would have towered over him. I couldn't say this because the PhD was having an effect not only on my speech but also on my ability to turn up my pedant factor to warp one.

"I'm going home," said Mary quietly. "Come and have breakfast with me tomorrow. Please. There are things I'd like to discuss. I thought we might be able to talk tonight but…" her voice trailed off.

"OK," I agreed. The idea of having breakfast with the Cocoa Club and the reprimands I'd get for not being there before sunrise was not appealing.

"I'll pick you up if you like. I don't trust you to get to Gwydir Street without incident. Don't have any more cocktails," she implored.

"I'll take a crab," I slurred.

Tom hadn't heard any of that. He'd been back to the bar.

"Victoria, you are studying for a DPhil and I'm trying my hand at an MLitt." He handed me another huge balloon glass, full of bright pink liquid, glace cherries bouncing on the surface, and, on top – another umbrella.

25

The morning after the night before

I was disorientated. I couldn't work out where our bedroom had gone. I heard the siren of an ambulance coming closer. Sun was pouring through the window and the curtains had not been drawn.

I sat up and realised I wasn't at home. I was still fully dressed. There were certain advantages to this, I concluded, given I was feeling a bit shaky and I seemed a bit too dizzy to be dealing with putting on or taking off complicated garments. Far better to be in them already. My mouth and throat were parched dry.

After a short while, I remembered that I was in a college room and miraculously it did seem to be the one I had been allocated to stay in. On the whole, things could have been worse. The biggest drawback was that I had used my teabag and milk. I went into the bathroom to rinse the cup and fill it with water, only to remember that nothing worked without the fob. There was a commotion going on in the corridor outside so I gingerly opened my door to see what was occurring. Perhaps someone could lend me a teabag?

An officious man was striding down the corridor. "We're evacuating just in case," he ordered. "I'd be obliged if you'd vacate the premises."

"What's going on? Was there an alarm?" I asked.

"Technical error on the alarm front," he admitted. "It's a water-related incident which may have affected efficiency fobwise."

I went back for my suitcase. Apart from the hairbrush, which I had used to try and deal with the unexpected drenching I had received the night before, it was still packed. Going to bed without undressing was looking more and more of a good idea.

The lift was out of order due to the mysterious incident. Just as well, because I hadn't found my fob. I went down the stairs, dragging my bag behind me. The noise it made as it dropped down each step in turn sent a shock wave through my head. I had no recollection of returning to my room, only that I could, if so minded, add PhD, MSc, MSt, MPhil and possibly several other letters to the BA that I had previously earned through academic endeavour. I had drawn the line at the MEd, I recalled, leaving its purple gloop, which reminded me of the kind of cheap bubble bath my daughters used to soak in when they were teenagers, in the glass.

An ambulance was parked outside, its back doors were open and a gaggle of people were standing around with concerned looks on their faces.

"What's going on?" I asked. Penny and the Cocoa Club were looking shifty.

"It's Gill," explained Penny with a patronisingly insincere look of concern on her face.

Sue spoke, finally, it seemed, having found an aphorism that was vaguely appropriate. "A friend in need is a friend indeed. We didn't realise she had arrived. She was in her room all along."

Lizzie was obviously aggrieved and less sympathetic. "We had to pay her share of the lunch because she wasn't there. And she'd ordered all the most expensive items on the menu. Three courses."

"Strictly speaking, given that you ate it all, it should have been you paying the extra alone." Penny spoke sharply. Mention of the lunch and spreadsheet mismanagement was a sore topic.

"Is she OK?" I considered the possibilities. She couldn't have chucked herself out of the window at the prospect of the evening to come, they didn't open wide enough. Had she ended it all in some other way? It was understandable but a bit extreme.

"She got into a bit of trouble with her fob, we think," a mousey little woman I'd never clapped eyes on before explained. "She got stuck in the wet room with the shower on. She'd been there since midday yesterday. Couldn't get out or turn the water off. We rang her phone, but obviously she couldn't answer it. She'd left it in the bedroom."

"She's traumatised, naturally. No one heard her shouting. We only realised when the water started dripping through the ceiling of the room below. The paramedics are doing what they can." Penny's voice was soft as if she was explaining to a five-year old that their bunny had gone to live in heaven with the Big Wabbit in the sky.

"It took all night for the drips to start coming through. They must use some pretty efficient sealant." Lizzie was warming to the theme. "The amount of water going down the plug hole was marginally less than the incoming amount flowing from the shower. Very slowly, the water just rose and rose. If she'd been there any longer, she'd have been doing lengths of the bathroom and she's not much of a swimmer."

I'd forgotten Lizzie had read science. She sounded like the sort of problem I'd had to do in my O level. People in maths questions were always filling up tanks with small holes in them or had taps dripping into sinks with blocked up overflows. "If there had been a bigger differential she'd have drowned." She seemed to take a certain satisfaction in this alarming scenario.

Gill, of course, had been the one to leave the bath running and provide my escape from the brutalist block. How ironic and appropriate. I wondered if anyone else remembered this.

"Someone should have checked her room earlier," stated mousey woman, quite enlivened by a potential tragedy. There was an embarrassed silence. Collective responsibility had been assumed. Tactfully, no-one was naming names.

Amusing though this all was, I couldn't disguise my hangover much longer and knew I couldn't be responsible for my actions if Penny were to make a comment about it. "I'm afraid I have to go. I can't stay for breakfast."

"Oh, we've all had breakfast already," she laughed. "You haven't changed, Roni."

"Neither have you, Penny."

"See you at the fiftieth. If we're still alive," said Lizzie cheerily. "By the way, Ron, it looks like a bird has made a nest in the back of your hair."

Fortunately, given I couldn't locate my fob, the emergency evacuation of the building meant I wasn't expected to hand it back at the Porters' Lodge. A large sign I'm convinced wasn't there the day before told me there was a £50 fine for mislaying it.

"Cheers. Have a nice day. Laters," grinned the twelve-year old behind the desk. No tattoos on this one but wild hair and a selection of piercings. The most revolting and unavoidable of these was a large ring through his septum which made him resemble a bull about to charge. Mr Boulderstone must have been turning in his grave.

I thought I'd walk to Mary's house to try and get rid of the fuggy feeling, but by the time I'd got to the taxi rank in the Market Square I'd given up on that as a good idea. I remembered Webster Ferris sitting in the back of a taxi there with my horse's head covering his bloody face. Thank God he hadn't turned up at the reunion. I was pretty sure he wouldn't have done but I couldn't be certain.

It was the right decision. Mary's house in Gwydir Street was further than I thought it was. It was a small 'two up, two down' terraced house where the front door gave directly on to the street, a workman's home which these days would sell for a fortune.

There was a front room accessed straight from the street and a staircase running across the house at the top of which you turned right into the front bedroom and left in to the back one. The bathroom was downstairs, under the stairs, and the back room, now a kitchen-diner, had been extended with a glass roof. Outside was a cute courtyard garden with hanging baskets and planters. Mary had a vast collection of books; they lined every wall and were meticulously sorted according to author and content. It was perfect, really, all one or possibly two people could need. She had some coffee brewing and there was a delicious smell of home-baked bread. After I had brushed my teeth, combed my hair, washed my face and slathered on a ridiculous amount of make-up in the unlikely hope that it would make me look bright and breezy, I told her about the events of the morning.

"Do you remember the Shelley Winters character in *The Poseidon Adventure?*" I asked her. "Swimming like mad against incoming water on the sinking ship?" We laughed until our stomachs ached – not wise in my delicate condition.

"It's so good to see you!" she said. "Why has it taken us so long?" There was a silence. I knew I had a reason.

"It's funny how things turn out," she commented cryptically. "I may have made some errors in the past. Not with things I have done, necessarily, though in retrospect there are things I might have done differently. It's more to do with how I reacted to them."

This was getting a bit heavy and personal. I hadn't even had a slice of the delicious bread yet. She saw me eyeing it.

"Want some? I'm a sourdough bore, I'm afraid. A lockdown convert. Aren't they the worst sort?"

Fast infusion of carbohydrate was what I needed to soak up the cocktail menu and its aftermath. She cut me a thick slice and produced a big slab of artisanal looking butter. Did she make that herself too, milking a cow in the shed outside? A sleek black cat jumped on the table and wound itself around Mary, rubbing its fur against her upper body. "Silas, you are not supposed to do that."

Had Mary turned into a caricature of a together, at-peace-with-herself, independent woman, entirely able to function as a separate being without E numbers or last-minute dashes to the corner shop for emergency milk? Here I was, 59 years old with the biggest hangover I'd had since the millennium, unable to remember much about the end of the night before. I'd learned nothing about self-control or self-preservation. Where was Tom? How did I get to my room? Why hadn't I got undressed before passing out on the bed?

"Did you stay long in the bar after I left?" Mary looked as if she already knew the answer to that one.

"No. Not really. Just a couple of drinks." A couple of drinks *was* all I could remember clearly. There had certainly been more.

"You were up to your tricks, naughty!" she chastised. "Fancy letting everyone think that you'd ended up with Goldblatt."

"I didn't. People make assumptions. They believe what they want to believe, what's interesting, or surprising. The truth is boring."

"And how is your lovely hubby?" she asked, then blushed, immediately realising, I supposed, that I might think she had equated boring with my spouse. Easily done.

"He has his dull moments," I laughed, "but he is very reliable and supportive and he has been a good husband. What makes a good husband is not necessarily the same as what makes an exciting boyfriend." There was a moment of reflection.

"I've never been married," she said simply. "I wouldn't know. There have been a couple of partners but no-one who has completely shared my life. It's difficult when you have a child."

Oh God! An alarm bell started ringing in my head. This was getting close to a life story. Not something I was hoping to share. We could be getting into 'All men are bastards, the heartless sod left me with a child to bring up on my own' country.

I knew she had a son; she'd told me when we'd first reconnected. There were no photographs or other signs of him or any other men about the house. I'd noticed there were no male things in the bathroom, no tell-tale products or shaving equipment. There was no scum or bits of stubble lurking round the basin and the seat was down on the loo. I'm quite the Miss Marple when I want to be. Mind you, if Mary had been coming to our house, I'd have been round with the Dettol and rubber gloves, putting seats and even lids down as if it was their default position.

"And you've got three children. Lucky you."

"Yes – but you have had a very successful career as well, Dr Featherstone. I hadn't realised how much you'd been published. It's quite an achievement. And this house is absolutely charming."

"I've been here since I left college," she sighed. "Dull, but I don't know if I could leave it now. My grandmother died just after we graduated, and I inherited some money. I rented it at first and then the landlord was looking to sell and it seemed like a good idea."

"A sound financial decision." I heard myself saying this pointlessly obvious comment and regretted it. What had happened to the light atmosphere of my arrival, the bit where my stomach hurt from laughing so much and I momentarily thought I might have to bring up the remaining vestiges of the MLitt in Mary's pristinely clean bathroom?

"How are your parents? Still in Muswell Hill?"

"They both passed away some years ago, I'm afraid. We had a bit of a parting for a time, but things were better just before they died."

Oh Lord, I should have known not to go there. Odds on, at our age, if at least one parent or both hadn't died, the remaining portion would be demented, disabled or in a nursing home working through any inheritance you might have hopes of.

I tried moving things along by talking about my parents.

"Mum and Dad retired and moved to a bungalow in Clacton a year or so after we graduated. When the regulations changed for betting shops, Dad and Uncle Patrick sold up to Coral's. The days of the old 'shutters down and no windows' were over."

"I thought your father was an accountant..?" You had to be up early to get one past Mary. It was too hard to explain the turf accountant/chartered accountant confusion after all this time. I decided to ignore it.

"Mum fancied a place by the sea. It wasn't a success really. They missed Barking. By the time they'd decided to move back, they'd got too old and the town had changed too much. They had to stay in Clacton. They're dead too." I added this to try and empathise, but it came out as rather flippant and disrespectful.

"You've been happy though, haven't you?" I'd told her so but she seemed to want it confirmed. "He's a kind man and it was obvious that he was always very keen on you."

"Was it?"

"Oh yes. A lot of people were, you know." I didn't. This was news to me. They could have been a bit more obvious at the time, I thought. "I'm sorry I didn't come to your wedding. At the time I felt I couldn't come, for personal reasons."

What should I have replied to that? 'I've been carrying a grudge all these years'? 'Oh, don't worry. We hardly noticed you weren't there'? 'I thought you were my friend, you bitch'? – 'Personal reasons? Ooo please do elaborate in minute detail…'?

Actually, not that last one. I wasn't sure I wanted to hear – though it seemed obvious things were heading in that direction.

"Got any more coffee?" It was a pointless diversion. She kept talking as she fired up her Italian stove-top coffeemaker. Her back was to me.

"I've wanted to tell you something for a very long time. For over thirty years, in fact." She paused. "The longer it became, the harder it was to start the conversation. I know it will hurt you, but you must believe I didn't mean it to. It was a moment of madness on my part. I'm really so glad you came here today. I'd planned to tell you last night, but it was obvious when it came to it that that wasn't the right moment."

My stomach clenched. I thought this was in anticipation of some awful confession, but it could have been another after effect of the cocktail binge. What could saintly Mary have to tell me that would be so awful that she'd been building up to it for over thirty years and needed a special moment for the announcement? I was crap in *Two Gentleman of Verona,* another Roland special? This was not news to me. I already knew I hadn't made a good Shakespearian heroine dressed as a cowboy.

Mary turned towards me and poured the coffee, concentrating hard. "It was right at the end of our time at Cambridge," she gulped, "that I got pregnant."

This was unexpected information, I had to agree. I spent a long time stirring milk into my coffee to give the impression that I didn't think this was in any way not what I was expecting. Saintly Mary with child? Yes, I could cope with that, but a conception which took place when, to my knowledge, Mary was not having a relationship with anyone? A closet coupling? A one-night stand? An Immaculate Conception? All ridiculous.

"I didn't realise at first. I thought it was stress stopping my periods. Before your wedding I'd done a test and found out. I was in a terrible state. I just couldn't come."

"I'm sorry to hear that," I said, despite thinking it was a tad over dramatic.

"My parents were difficult about it, about me continuing with the pregnancy. They were worried about my PhD. It was all set up and they thought I was throwing away my career," she explained. "I insisted I wouldn't get rid of the baby, so they left me to my own devices for a long time."

"How long?"

"About ten years. If it hadn't been for Grandma's money, I would have been almost destitute."

I remembered Mary's parents, her mother's pretentious one-upmanship and her father's complete lack of humour. Who'd have thought they'd behave in such a cold and heartless way? I'd have imagined Mrs Featherstone would have liked nothing better than boasting about a grandchild. Obviously boasting about a daughter with a PhD was preferable. As it happened, she ended up with both. It just took her ten years to realise.

"That's why this house means so much to me. It's where Luke and I found refuge. It nurtured us." I felt a spoken poem coming on.

"Where is he now?"

Oh Lord, why did I ask that? Why couldn't I stop myself being such a nosey parker? She had been cagey about him when we had spoken previously. He obviously didn't live in the house; there were no signs of him anywhere. Perhaps he was dead, or had been dead for ages – a cot death she'd never come to terms with? Or had he been in a long-term coma in hospital for the last twenty years and she had to visit him and sit with his unresponsive body in the bleak hope that he would one day give her a sign of recognition? Perhaps he was in a high-security prison having committed a terrible crime which she found impossible to talk about – until now.

"He's a university professor." Of course, the Featherstone genes! "He was the youngest professor of English Literature they ever appointed," Mary explained, confirming my thoughts.

"Thank God for that," I said out loud by mistake. Mary looked puzzled.

"He's at Oxford, funnily enough." It was odd Mary hadn't mentioned this before given that we lived so near the city. Did she visit him? Why hadn't she suggested meeting up before the reunion? She seemed flustered, embarrassed almost.

"You could google him, if you wanted. He is currently exploring the conundrum of the Wakefield Master and the Towneley Mystery Cycles." She softened and looked proud.

I certainly would be googling him. I'd also be checking out what the Wakefield Master had to do with the Towneley Mystery Cycle, whatever the bloody hell that was. I didn't want to seem stupid by asking her. I considered a gag about secret bikes but decided removing myself to the bathroom with my phone in order to look it up might be better.

"Wow, amazing!" I exclaimed with an inappropriate amount of faux enthusiasm.

Was the Wakefield Master a mediaeval version of Roland? The Pared-Down Players had performed the York Mystery Cycle once. Roland reduced the customary 48 stories from the Bible to a fifteen-minute skip through selected excerpts in various locations around the university. The fast-paced sprint left several of the audience with asthma attacks and an admission to Addenbrookes after a cardiac 'incident'.

Good old Roland. He had also decided to interpret the word 'mystery' in the modern sense. The finale had a Hercule Poirot type character (strangely missing from the Bible most of us were familiar with) assembling the disciples in one room and exposing Judas as the traitor.

"Remember Roland's York Cycle?" I chuckled, hoping to lighten the atmosphere. "Yes, I have known all along zat it was you, Monsieur Iscariot, who betrayed ze Seigneur." I thought my Belgian sleuth impression was rather good.

"It was the first and only time I have slept with a man. And we conceived. Subsequently I've had relationships with women."

The only time she had been with a man? How many more confessions was a single invitation to breakfast going to provide? "I was complicit," she continued. "He didn't force me. In fact, I should admit I encouraged him. It was the day of our graduation, my parents had left early and I was on my way to the Master's sherry party when I met him. I think he was probably looking for you. He looked despondent. He told me he thought he'd never see you again." Mary couldn't look at me. "Everything was coming to an end. We went to my room and got carried away. For me it was an experiment. I'd had three years at university without a boyfriend and I wanted to see what it was like."

"That's OK," I replied. She looked sheepish.

"I want to say, I'm sorry…" her voice trailed off, further words were plainly difficult. It suddenly dawned on me. The interest in my husband and marriage, her refusal to come to the ceremony – was she telling me this was his child? Had he slept with Mary? They knew each other and we were not together at the time obviously so it shouldn't have been an issue – except there was a child. I wasn't expecting this.

I wondered if Luke had ever asked about his father, but I didn't want to dwell on that. A chill shot through me. "Does he know about Luke?" I wasn't sure I wanted to hear the reply.

"No…" But there was a hint in her voice that she thought the time had come to let us know and I was first in the queue. I felt hot. My throat was dry. A menopausal flush? The stonking great hangover? Or the realisation that our lives had just become even more complicated than I had ever envisaged.

Mary was distracted. She was looking for something. "I can show you a photograph." She moved towards a drawer and opened it. Why was the photo hidden? You don't keep a photo in a frame in a drawer. It had obviously been exiled there. Had she done so because I was coming?

Mary's hand was shaking as she passed it to me. I felt myself redden as I looked at the image of the young man in academic dress. "It was taken a few years ago," she breathed heavily. I was speechless.

"I'm sorry, Ron. It must be a shock to you, but I've wanted

to tell you all these years and if we are going to resume our friendship, which I hope we will, then you need to know." I gazed at the picture. "Please say something. I can explain," she pleaded.

Eventually I was able to make a comment. "This young man certainly looks like his father."

"I knew you'd be upset." She sighed.

"It's a long time ago. Things happen." I tried to appear calm, as if I wasn't at all bothered.

"I knew once you saw him you'd work it out just by looking at him." I was transfixed by the photograph. "Regardless, I wanted to tell you before you meet Luke."

The shock and the unwelcome burden of recognition prevented me from saying more. Even a mortar board and long academic gown could not disguise the familiar face and body shape of this graduate. He looked nothing like my husband. I should have felt happier about that than I did.

A big, coal-grimy, northern stork had delivered a baby under Mary's gooseberry bush and he'd grown into the spitting image of Webster Ferris.

26

Angry Young Men

found it hard to process the extraordinary news I had learned. There was no question that Luke was Webster's child, Mary had no reason to lie and supporting photographic evidence had been provided. I thought my relationship with Webster Ferris was our secret. Looking back, although it began furtively, I had been naïve to think we had hidden it from everyone else.

When 1985 began, snow followed. Roland showed up too. He'd graduated the previous summer but was back with a plan for a final Pared-Down Players production. We probably should have worked out that this was the consequence of the real-life theatre being harder to break into than he'd anticipated. Instead, we assumed that, buoyed by the runaway success of his Liverpudlian Romeo and Juliet, *Graham and Kevin, Star-Crossed lovers of Merseyside*, he was revisiting Shakespeare as a sure-fire ingredient for success.

Roland was dreaming big. Not only would we perform at the student theatre (now willing to give him a week of shows before Easter because of the guaranteed takings at the box office) but he had booked a date at the professional theatre in Cambridge for after exams in the summer term which would be followed by a run at the Edinburgh Festival Fringe. Roland was aiming high.

The fact that *The Two Gentleman of Verona* is generally not considered to be one of Shakespeare's more accomplished works and that it is rarely performed in the professional theatre didn't put Roland off. He'd discovered that not only is there Verona, Italy, but there are several others. At least four are in the USA – one of which is in Texas. Setting his version in The Lone Star State and pointlessly dressing the characters in Stetsons and cowboy boots with spurs whilst they waved lassoes, was too tempting for Roland. I practised my 'Ye Ha!' in anticipation.

Gran had come round for Christmas dinner, but relations were strained. Uncle Patrick and Dad were trying to pretend nothing had happened whilst Mum was making it quite clear she hadn't forgotten what had. I got stuck into some serious revision to make sure I was out of the way.

I'd vaguely thought about asking Webster to Barking for Christmas because otherwise he would have been on his own but decided definitively that it would be a bad idea. Ferris himself made it plain he would be returning to Yorkshire and that I wasn't included in any of his holiday plans and I was relieved but also annoyed. He had that effect on me; it was infuriating.

The farce of Mum getting out the best plates, the leaf in the table debate and seat choreography to make sure that our guest didn't sit on one of the kitchen chairs by mistake was a Bourgeois firecracker waiting to be lit. Besides, I couldn't be sure what Ferris would come out with. He didn't do small talk and his vocabulary frequently featured words for which, after confession, Father O'Connor would be giving you ten Hail Marys, an Our Father and a Glory Be. Gran's rosary would be going into overdrive.

On top of everything, the slightest sniff of a relationship or romance would have Mum and Gran looking for Mother of the Bride ensembles and patterns for meringue-type wedding dresses. Potentially it could have been a post 'Paddy McNamara revelation' bonding experience for them but one I was unwilling to instigate.

A cold snap after Christmas meant that I was spending more time with Ferris and his gas fire, away from my own room.

Webster encouraged me to stay there, although we strove to keep our closeness quiet and undiscovered by the gossips in the college. I never really questioned the reason for this and it gave another frisson of excitement to the relationship, which was highly charged anyway. It wasn't hard to do because we were only ever together in his room – never around college or out in the town. We lived in a quiet, out of the way court and his were the only rooms on the ground floor of his particular staircase. My own was right next door which made it easy to be discreet. Or so I thought.

Webster Ferris craved time on his own but was increasingly happy to have me present whilst he got on with solitary pursuits. For the most part this was reading. He devoured books of all sorts, cross referencing information as he proceeded through them. His room, though spartan, wasn't tidy. A conurbation of tower blocks made of books covered every surface, one balanced precariously on top of another at angles defying gravity. Despite this, he knew where everything was. Reaching for one mid-stack was like playing a game of giant Jenga.

Without a doubt I had never met anyone like him before. He was still terrifying and unpredictable, but I had to admit that this excitement was part of the attraction.

Gradually, always without looking at me, he began to talk about his past. I found myself back in the plot of a gritty 'It's grim up north' kitchen-sink drama, one of those late 1950s and early 1960s black and white movies. Everyone has a hard life, and the women always end up getting pregnant with the wrong man. Accidents, illness and death are rife and the inequalities of the sexes and classes in the period are demonstrably clear. There are no happy endings.

Not that Webster Ferris told me his family went in for infidelity or accidental pregnancy, but their life had been remorselessly difficult. He was the 'angry young man' and I could see why.

It occurred to me that he could have invented all these things he told me about. But one certainty of which I had become aware was that Webster was pathologically honest and truthful, almost to the point of rudeness. I wondered how he would cope with the carefully curated truths I had discovered at home and occasionally pedalled myself.

He described his sadnesses and misfortunes without comment or judgement. Only his eyes, if I managed to catch sight of them, betrayed the pain that these memories may have caused him.

Webster's opening-up required just an ear to listen. I was not expected to contribute my own recollections or experiences. As I listened, I got carried away imagining films whose monochrome gritty realism described each episode he was telling me about.

The accident that killed his father, some kind of underground rail incident deep in the pit, had happened when he was only four and a half. "He took me to my first game at Millmoor. Less than three weeks later he were dead. I don't remember anything about it, but we beat Crystal Palace 3-0."

"Good job you won then, given it was his last game," I replied in my best Thora Hird. In my head, of course. I had to bite my lip to avoid saying it out loud. That's the trouble with being a vivid daydreamer – sometimes your imagination gets mixed up with the facts.

"The worst part is, I can't remember his voice. However hard I try, I can't hear him."

Webster confessed that he never really felt he fitted in, particularly when he went to school. People never understood him, which made him angry and easily taunted. His reputation as a fighter and puncher was established over the milk crate in the infant school classroom. Only books had saved him from getting into real trouble, along with the support of his mother.

One day he confided that I was the only person he had ever been able to talk to. This put an end to my silly fantasies about kitchen-sink dramas. He was serious and I should have been more responsible. I was immature, unsympathetic even, but I found it difficult to know how to be helpful. It was a relief that I wasn't expected to comment or advise. Instead, I immersed myself in the Pared-Down Players as usual.

Roland's rehearsals began in earnest and we were soon engulfed by the Texan cowboy accents and swagger which we were supposed to assume when approaching the parts. There was new blood, too, in our group. Word had got round that Roland's 'comedies' were hilarious and were he to take a show to the Fringe it was bound to be a hit. Who wouldn't want to be part of that? As far as I'm aware, word had not reached Roland, who would have been deeply wounded to think that an audience was going to watch his work to laugh at it.

I was playing Julia, a woman in love with Proteus (one of the eponymous two gentlemen) and who, in true Shakespearian style, dresses as a boy for a large portion of the play. I rode about the stage galloping on a hobby horse, dressed in massive chaps and a pair of cowboy boots which were a size too small but the only ones available.

Lucy was the other main female part, Silvia, the daughter of a duke and dressed in a pretty gingham frock with a large skirt in which she flirted attractively with the other characters on stage. I tried not to feel jealous.

For once, Roland's abbreviated version made no difference to the understanding of the tortuous plot. However, the addition of lassoes to the props list was both unnecessary and dangerous. The twirling loops of rope caught in the lights and parts of the scenery with predictably disastrous results. Several cardboard horses were decapitated unintentionally as they grazed at the back of the stage, and Valentine (the other gentleman) was almost hanged when he became entwined in a rope which couldn't be dislodged from the rigging above the stage. We were all wearing huge Stetsons (Lucy apart) which were routinely knocked off by flying lassoes, leaving their owners scrabbling for the correct hat to put back on.

Inexplicably, Roland, for once, was keen not to stray too far from the Shakespeare original and decided to include the most expendable character, a dog called Crab, in his Pared-Down version. Although it was irrelevant to what was left of the plot, only a real-life hound would do. Roland couldn't believe his luck when the landlady of the digs he was staying in produced a large, brutish mongrel belonging to her daughter, and Frank was duly incorporated into the cast.

He was a short-tempered and excitable mutt with a matted, inky, curly coat and a frightening bark. Someone joked that he was a canine version of Webster Ferris and, hurtful though this was in some ways, I had to agree there was a similarity. Frank had a long, pink tongue and drooled constantly. I hadn't seen Ferris do that, nor did he leave a slippery trail of dog slobber on the floor to show the path he had taken when moving from A to B. The soles of cowboy boots are curiously grip-free and the stage became a slippery ice rink after Frank had made his entrance.

Frank's sudden emergence from the wings, his unpredictability and uncontrollable lurching completely dominated the short time he was actually on stage. The highlight of the first night was when he cocked his leg on some picket fencing near the front of the set and an interminable flow of strong-smelling dog piss fused all the footlights. The audience loved it and the run sold out every night of the week.

Webster complained that he'd only been able to get a ticket for one night. I'm not sure why he'd have wanted to see it more often, as he was moaning quite a bit about my involvement in the production generally. He'd looked upset when I went to rehearsals and resented the time I was at performances. We were both out during the day at lectures and seminars but he no longer spent time with his Cambridge Socialist mates. I was beginning to feel smothered. He stayed in Cambridge over Easter and I went home.

In honesty, I missed him, but I felt a sense of freedom away from him, which surprised me. Mum didn't seek not to be with Dad; they just co-existed with each other. I wondered if that's what happens when you have been married for a long time. I felt confused. The intensity of emotion I felt around Ferris frightened me. It was like a live wire travelling through my body. I couldn't decide if I liked it or not. Was it love or just lust? Maybe I wasn't supposed to be part of a couple.

When I returned after the holiday, it was clear that Webster was delighted to see me. The cold weather had long gone and my own room was habitable, as it had been at the end of the previous term. Even so, he clearly wanted me to continue sharing his bed and his living space. I decided I should put a few ground rules in place. I wouldn't stay every night, I would do some revision apart from him, with Mary perhaps, and I would spend time with the couple of friends I had in college and those I had from other colleges.

He was confused by this. It wasn't what he wanted and he found it difficult to see this as anything but me rejecting him completely. I tried to explain how I found the whole experience too intense and needed to get away from it a little, so that I appreciated the times we spent together more. I told him I found him frightening, which was, in retrospect, not a sensible thing to do. That's when he told me that he loved me. Not only that, but I was also the only person apart from his mother that he had ever loved.

I tried to make him understand that the intensity of the relationship was what I found scary, not that I wanted to end it, but I just needed to stop it dominating everything I did. I thought he would share this concern, but he found it difficult to see why I would seek not to be near him.

I stuck to my guns and Mary and I spent time together revising in the run-up to finals. She and I were never with Webster together. As far as I knew, Mary was never with Webster when I wasn't there either. Thinking back to that time, I had to conclude Mary must have been telling the truth about their last-minute coupling.

One day he told me what he had been doing over the Easter holiday. Various American universities had offered him a postgraduate place and representatives had been in Cambridge meeting candidates. If you are prodigiously clever and not a slacker by nature, these people come looking for you.

"I think the Harvard offer is the best I've had," he explained. "It's near Boston, which would be a nice city to live in."

I was surprised but felt I couldn't really complain given that I had put some distance between us emotionally, or so I believed. It wouldn't mean the end of our relationship. Cambridge, England and Cambridge, Massachusetts they weren't so far away, were they?

As usual I had thought no further than the next few weeks. My target was to survive my finals and then enjoy the last hurrah of the Pared-Down Players. Webster was invaluable guiding me through those final exams. I had left everything to the last minute so his advice about what to concentrate on and how to make the most of the little time I had before they began was crucial. Without him I doubt I would have got a degree, let alone done as well as I did.

Soon it was over. It was drizzling when we came out of the room where we'd been sitting our last paper. Whereas I had imagined high spirited celebration, there was just a feeling of numbness and exhaustion reflected by the grey sky. I sat on his sofa staring into space. The final exam had seemed particularly long, and I was feeling drained.

"You have to get a visa in your passport," he announced casually. I knew about this extra requirement for travel to the US. There didn't seem to be any urgency. "I think you'll have to get on a course because you'll need a student visa. You can't stay long on a tourist one."

"What do you mean?"

"They've told me they can get you on something, once we know you have passed your degree. They might even be able to get you some kind of scholarship. I've had a letter from them." He waved a piece of paper at me.

"Who's they?"

"Harvard."

"Why would I want to be on a course?"

"Because," he explained in a tone reminiscent of someone telling a child to be careful with the scissors, "you're not allowed to stay in the country without the proper visa. They will chuck you out."

The post-exam stupor that had descended over me lifted. I felt butterflies in my stomach. "It'll only be a holiday. Surely that's what a tourist visa is for?"

"You're coming with me, aren't you?" Webster eyed me curiously. He was weighing up whether this was a joke or not.

"When did I ever say I was coming with you?"

"You didn't say you weren't."

"I don't say I'm not going to do lots of things but that doesn't mean I'm going to do them." This was a bit of a convoluted sentence. I tried to work out if it said what I had intended. "I can't come with you."

"Why not?"

"What about Mum and Dad? And Gran and Uncle Patrick?"

"They will still be here."

"I can't leave them. Not just like that."

"Why not?"

I was flabbergasted that he had even thought I had any intention of going to the US with him. We hadn't discussed it at all. I hadn't told him that I wanted to go with him. I thought we had been avoiding the subject. Unwise, perhaps, I realised. Where there was an unspoken void about how life would proceed after July, Webster had just filled it with what he assumed would happen.

"We'd need to discuss something like that." I knew I had been procrastinating about what would happen next, but I could not conceive there would ever be a scenario where I would just pack up everything and go with him. An uneasiness filled the room. He looked shocked.

"I want you to come."

"I will come and see you. For holidays and ... I'll have to earn the money for the fare first."

He left. He sped out of the door and the staircase entrance. There was no sign of him by the time I looked out of the window to see where he was going. I waited for a while but he didn't return. There remained a violent and unpredictable streak within him which frightened me and made me wary of trading everyone I knew for a life 3,000 miles away with just him. I collected up my things and went back to my own room and fell asleep on the bed.

27
Two Gentlemen

I woke with a start and I realised I was due at the Arts Theatre for a technical run through of *Two Gentlemen*.

Roland was in a twitch and not just because I was late. As planned, *Two Gentlemen* was being resurrected for a pre-Edinburgh Festival performance. We'd been given a two-night slot in this professional theatre, filling the gap between two other shows. One had moved out and the next was due in. Roland's success at the student theatre was the amateur sandwich filling between two slices of professional bread. Our simple set meant that we were ideal for these free couple of days and the box office would get something rather than nothing even if they only sold a few tickets. The art deco auditorium was grand and panelled in dark wood; this was a proper theatre and the magnitude of what we were attempting to do was obvious to everyone, particularly Roland.

Phil was back as our stage manager but was having to defer to the professional one who came with the theatre. He was the ideal person to do this: calm, responsible, outwardly happy to be patronised. The 'pros' were giving Roland a hard time, deliberately, and he was not as adept as Phil at dealing with it.

The technical rehearsal is always long and tiresome. Tempers get frayed amongst the performers standing about, amongst the technical staff fiddling with light and sound and without exception between the two groups. Roland was in hyper prima donna mode. Phil and I were enjoying his performance from the wings. "It's good to see you laughing, Roni," he told me. "You looked so sad, like the world was about to end, when you arrived."

"I had my last exam today. I'm a bit tired." Apart from my lack of sparkle in the autumn, Webster rarely noticed how I appeared or asked how I felt. I had the impression that Phil, on the other hand, was not going to be fobbed off by this lame excuse.

As the evening wore on, we became hungry. "Come on," suggested Phil, "let's go and get a kebab." In Cambridge at that time, the kebab shop was the only option for people who found themselves starving hungry and short of money late at night.

We snuck out whilst Roland was flicking his spiky-topped mullet about at some tech who had the audacity to question a particular lighting choice for one scene.

I was a doner kebab virgin; I'd managed to last three years without eating one but now I was throwing caution to the wind. We took our white paper packages, with their flatbreads bulging with meat and random lettuce garnish, back to the theatre. Fortunately, Roland hadn't noticed we had gone. He was now being pressurised by someone from the theatre management to insert an interval into the show because they had become aware that without one takings in the bar would be minimal. "I won't have my work altered," Roland stated emphatically, unaware of the irony that his entire canon was comprised of the adulteration of others' works. His hands were on his hips, always a sign that he was finding standing his ground challenging.

I sank my teeth into the kebab. It was delicious. It was the same effect as eating fish and chips wrapped in newspaper; a kebab straight from the white paper was all the tastier. "It's sort of unbelievably nice whilst simultaneously being a bit disgusting," mused Phil. I began to feel better. He was relaxed and easy to talk to.

Eventually, Roland's negotiations struck a final deal whereby the interval would be longer than each of the halves that preceded and followed it. Management was eager to point out that this meant their audience would still only be at the theatre for just over 90 minutes.

"A longer interval is a good thing, I think," explained Phil. "The more they have had to drink the better the show will go!" He could be amusing, I realised, and, unlike Roland, he had no delusions about the quality of what was going to be presented on stage.

We were in the theatre for two performances. Roland had not brought Frank to the tech rehearsal; he would have been too much of a nuisance pulling at his lead and barking during the sound checks. When the stage manager saw him on the first night he was taken aback.

"There's a 'no animals except guide dogs' policy, so get him out," he ordered. Frank growled a warning at him.

Roland was not to be swayed. "It's impossible. He's in the show. He's got a very important part and is an invaluable member of the ensemble. It's too late to re-cast with something inanimate."

The part of Launce, Crab's owner, had been recast. The actor from the first production had decided that he did not want to continue to oversee the snarling cur. The lad now playing Launce was sneezing constantly and his eyes were running. "I think I'm allergic to Frank and he's bringing on my asthma as well. I need my inhaler," the poor chap wheezed.

"We haven't got time for all that." Roland was adamant. The curtain was about to go up.

The audience was primed. Everyone knew that this show was hilarious and that it was unintentional. From the minute Valentine and Proteus swaggered on in their cowboy waistcoats and gun holsters there were giggles from the stalls.

By the time Launce sneezed his way on to the stage with an unusually reluctant Frank somewhere in the severely truncated Act Two, the audience was crying with laughter. This loud sound unnerved the mongrel, who had been growling and baring his teeth at the stage manager whilst they were waiting to come on. Now he was centre stage he let fly with such force that Launce let go of his lead. Frank barked viciously at the audience, a foamy white slobber dripping from his terrifying jaws. Launce's itchy, puffy eyes watered so profusely that he was almost blind and unable to see where the dog was.

The stage manager bravely came on from the wings to capture him. Frank, who, like all aggressive hounds, had a sense for who was on his side and who was not, snarled before enthusiastically biting into his calf. The poor man let out a howl so blood curdling that the audience was immediately silenced. Phil, with characteristic presence of mind, coolly closed the curtains so the interval began prematurely.

Management was delighted. Not only did they get longer to serve interval drinks, but a good proportion of the audience ordered several stiff spirits to steady their nerves. It was the highest revenue they'd had from the bar all year.

When we left the theatre, I was surprised to see Webster waiting outside the stage door. "Nice to have a stage door Johnnie!" I said.

"What's that?" asked Ferris. He was eyeing Phil and the other boys closely. It wasn't often that I had to explain something to him.

"A groupie, a fan!"

"No-one could be a fan of that pile of shite," he replied bluntly. "That prat Roland didn't mean it to be a comedy." I was unaware he'd been in the audience. Uncharacteristically he took my arm. We were rarely together outside his room, let alone touching. Phil and the others lingered, not really wanting to intervene but feeling they ought to hang about.

"Are you OK, Roni?" called Phil from a safe distance.

"Yes, fine. See you tomorrow," I replied, unsure if this was in fact the case.

Back at college we went to his room where Webster was eager to talk about what had happened earlier. "I didn't know you didn't want to come with me."

"You never asked!"

"I'm asking now."

"It's not that easy, I can't just leave on the spur of the moment."

"You've got nothing planned. Your family will get over it."

I was too exhausted to get involved in a lengthy discussion. We got into bed in silence. I lay facing away from him and presently his arm locked around my waist almost as if he thought I might escape. Despite a numbing sense of tiredness, I was unable to sleep.

The second night at the theatre caused some problems. Frank had been packed off back to the landlady's daughter and it remained unclear whether the stage manager was going to pursue a claim for damages. He was in Addenbrooke's recovering from rabies and tetanus injections and had had several stitches in his leg. He was not returning for the performance. Phil, fortunately, was happy and able to take over.

Roland had had to search all the shops in Cambridge to find a toy dog, which had proved difficult. Eventually, he had to settle for something called a Puppy-Pal from Woolworth's, which was small with long, silky, pink fur and covered in sparkly jewels. It said, "Hello. Please stroke me and I'll love you forever," if you held it at a certain angle. Launce (full of antihistamines, his inhaler in his pocket) was delighted but under instructions not to touch the pink sparkler more than necessary.

The theatre management was in two minds. The show was a sell-out but there had been some complaints. The absence of Frank did something to assuage their worries about a re-run of the 'Wild Dingo Terrifies Shakespeare Lovers' story the *Cambridge Evening News* was already running. In the end, the attraction of increased revenue overcame any concerns they had for their customer base; the show must go on.

It started badly. Phil had to come on stage at the beginning to make the announcement. "Ladies and Gentlemen, tonight, due to unforeseen circumstances, the part of Crab will be played by a Puppy-Pal." A large proportion of the circle, who had chosen the location of their seats wisely, groaned, although a sigh of relief was palpable in the front of the stalls.

The performance was appalling and certain sections of the audience, who had been promised the funniest theatrical experience they had ever witnessed, walked out before the end. Some booed and a very loud and inebriated man in the back row kept shouting, "Where's the sodding dog? Bring on Fido," encouraging a low chant of "We want the dog, we want the dog!"

When it was over Webster was waiting at the stage door again. Conversation on our walk back was strained. "Bet you're glad that's over," he exclaimed.

"A bit. Actually, it was fun. The others are such a laugh."

I knew this was a mistake – but only after I'd said it. No-one would describe Webster Ferris as 'a laugh'. He was many things, most of which I admired and appreciated. He scared and delighted me in equal measure. My feelings, good or ill, about him were stronger than those I had ever felt about another person. His intellect and academic abilities were formidable, he could make me laugh, and he found some things funny, but he wasn't light-hearted or jovial company.

His dark eyes were fixed on me; he didn't often look at me directly. Ordinarily, I caught him taking a furtive glance when he thought I wasn't watching. He spoke slowly.

"*Two Gentleman of Verona,* Shakespeare's exploration of friendship versus love; the conflict between loyalty to friends and submission to passion."

28
Goodbye to all that

Webster Ferris wasn't interested in going to a May Ball. I wasn't surprised. Given it was my last year, I had a tinge of disappointment that this might be my last chance. The one I attended in my first year had been a disappointment and I hadn't bothered in my second.

Phil and some of the other techs had jobs keeping the sound systems and lighting rigs working for the entertainment at some of the balls. At one ball they received extra tickets as part of their payment. Phil got a group of us together to go. I found something simpler than the lilac monstrosity to wear but despite the free pass I still managed to be miserable. It poured with rain all evening and Gary Glitter, performing at the event, had fused the electrics when using his hairdryer in his dressing room caravan and was refusing to go on. The techs had to spend much of the night dealing with electrical problems because of short circuits caused by the weather. In the small hours, I slunk off and returned to Ferris and the bad mood that my attendance had engendered.

The results of our degrees were displayed in glass-fronted cabinets on the wall outside the Senate House. Even then, this was an outdated way of letting you find out how you had performed, but it was a fabulous opportunity for everyone to see just how all their mates had done in return for being exposed themselves.

Had degrees been awarded for nosiness, the biggest proportion of firsts would have gone to the Cocoa Club. They had memorised the results of each subject in minute detail. "How that boy got a 2:1 is a miracle to me," moaned Perfect Penny, who, much to my delight, had proved herself less than perfect by getting one of them herself.

When the results were blazoned on the wall, Webster kept a low profile. That past year, for the most part, he had been much calmer and less obvious about the place. It seemed to me that the outcome of the miners' strike had taken the will to fight out of him, as if his venom was exhausted or neutralised. He had obtained the double first everyone expected, and it was rumoured his papers in his third-year exams had been awarded the highest marks of any since the war. The world of academia lay ahead for him to do what he wished in it. Not an opportunity awarded to me, I might add.

We were still going round in circles about his spur of the moment revelation that I was expected to move to the USA. Webster found it almost impossible to see the situation in anything but a binary black or white way. I didn't need to move to Harvard full time and enrol on a course just so I was allowed to stay in the country in order for us to remain together. It would be harder but certainly not impossible to maintain a relationship with just the Atlantic in between us. I couldn't and wouldn't leave home because he maintained that he could only operate totally without me or completely supported by me. Compromise was not a word in his enormous vocabulary. Despite not knowing the term emotional blackmail, I recognised the essence of what this was.

It came to a head the night before graduation. I explained that there was no way I would be leaving England for good in August with him but that I loved him and would make time and find the money to see him as often as I could whilst he was there.

This was an admission for me. I was almost as bad as him at expressing my emotions. I wasn't sure I did love him. I was ignorant, like Prince Charles, of the true nature of love 'whatever that is'. I certainly felt wild tremors of passion towards him. He made me tingle and my heart raced when I saw him. Was it an adrenaline-fuelled, fight-or-flight reaction he provoked or was this IT? I'm certain my parents didn't feel like that about each other. Surely Nan hadn't had palpitations when she took Grandad a cup of tea when he was spinning his globe enveloped by a cloud of pipe smoke? Yet these were long lasting and, I assumed, successful relationships.

"I want you to be there with me," he said for the umpteenth time. I went back to my room and left him to it. Perhaps once he was in the US he would realise that it might be better just to see how things would turn out. I'd done nothing about getting a job; perhaps putting it off for the moment wasn't necessarily a bad idea? But it was a big step for a twenty-two year old from Barking and one I didn't want to make without consideration.

Mum and Dad had pushed the boat out for Graduation Day. Despite the trip to Cambridge and back being easily accomplished in a day, they'd booked into a hotel – apparently because they wanted to make the most of my big day. I knew the real reason; it was because it had a car park. Dad had been worrying about where he was going to park the Sierra ever since I had explained how the graduations worked. He realised that a large gathering of parents meant a reduction in parking spaces.

I was the first person in our immediate family to graduate from university, but the key issue of the day was the welfare of the Sierra. Mum knew well enough that pandering to his obsession with leaving it in a place where it was both legally parked and unlikely to be stolen or scratched meant there was a sporting chance that they would both be on time and that she would enjoy it. The brief moment when I and four others would each hold one of the Chancellor's fingers and bow theatrically so that our degrees would be conferred upon us would be witnessed. It was almost a bigger deal for them than it was for me.

Only two guest tickets were available for each student so Gran was not included. I had wondered about asking Webster if he could give me his tickets for Gran and Uncle Patrick but decided the interest this would conjure up at home as to the identity of the donor would be unbearable, particularly in the current circumstance where there was a stand-off between Webster and me concerning Harvard. I couldn't risk it. Both Gran and Mum would be like wasps round a jam sandwich trying to investigate a mysterious benefactor with no relatives of his own but sufficient interest in me to give up his tickets.

If any kind of discussion about overseas was discovered, I could imagine Mum would not keep her feelings about potential emigration under wraps until an appropriate time. I did not want to be exposed mid-ceremony in the Senate House by her making a declaration like a person with knowledge of 'just cause or impediment' at a wedding. "That man is kidnapping my daughter against my will." Mind you, most of the students there would have believed it of Ferris.

Extra tickets were not what I wanted. Surely no-one else would have an uncle, furtively having a ciggie round the back of the Senate House, his latest squeeze dangling on his arm complaining, "This ain't much of a date, Pat!". Nor would they have a grandmother with a censorious priest in her wake. "The Good Lord knows, I'll be keeping a strict eye on you, Mrs McNamara, now you're not to be believed…" I wondered if I had become a snob.

Playing 'match the parents to the student' was an interesting game. Unlike school, where your folks had potentially been on daily view, embarrassing you in the flesh since the first morning they delivered you to the gate, this was the first introduction to your family. It was like viewing the stable and pedigree of a racehorse after the seven furlongs were over. Any fabrications you had been maintaining or illusions you had been promoting during the previous three years were exposed.

I spotted a man in slightly grubby corduroys and a tweedy jacket who turned out, correctly, to be the father of an Old Etonian called Tarquin (but known as Stiffy), who was rejoicing in getting the lowest third in the year. I had met some parents of my friends, but graduation was done by college.

I wonder if anyone would have picked Mum and Dad out as mine? Unsurprisingly, Mum had done her hair especially for the occasion. The colour wouldn't have been a clue. She was experimenting with 'antique mahogany', and this deep chocolate, employed to cover up a few greys, was nothing like my own auburn red or her mousey brown. At least she didn't have a hat. There were a number of 'I paid a lot of money for this for our Jacqueline's wedding, so I'm going to make sure I get some use out of it' monstrosities on show. Large feathers, dangling flowers and, in one case, what looked like an entire bowl of cherries dominated the headgear and obscured the views of anyone behind. Dad was wearing his only suit, now a little tight in the waist and with the jacket straining at the buttons if he did it up.

The Cocoa Club moved as one in a gaggle with their parents in tow so it was fun to spot who might be whose parent. The large woman in a flowery creation reaching for a peppermint from her bag every so often had to be Lizzie's mother. The lady with a beaky nose dressed immaculately in a sensible outfit was clearly Penny's mama. A man was walking two paces behind her and had the demeanour of someone who had run up the white flag of surrender in his marriage many years previously. He had to be the unfortunate husband. Some way behind, looking overwhelmed and failing to keep up, was a small unconfident-looking couple who kept apologising. Surely Gill's parents.

We processed to the Senate House as a college group, in subject and then in alphabetical order. Ahead of me, in amongst the Fs and more significantly than I realised at the time, Mary had the pleasure of Ferris's grim face and staring eyes beside her.

After the ceremony there was a lot of fuss with photographs and dads and cameras. They seemed to belong to two groups.

There were those, like my father, who usually just got the camera out on holiday and took pictures from such a distance that the people in the shot were microscopic and unrecognisable. "I think that's your mother on the beach at Clacton. Or it might have been Frinton. It's the seaside anyway." These photographers had an assistant barking out instructions, distracting them whilst they tried to remember what the three simple buttons on the Instamatic were for.

"Mick, take one of Ron with her friend but don't get that lorry in the background or that woman with the big umbrella."

The other kind of David Bailey came with more than one camera, a selection of interchangeable long lenses, tripods, filters and rolls and rolls of film. He'd already prepared a list of the shots he wanted to create and who was to be in them. Cast assembled, he'd take several variations at different exposures, suggesting slight movements of the personnel involved so that the ideal composition was produced. When he went into the bushes or to a dark corner to change the film, various people wandered off which made him furious when he returned.

I have the photos taken outside the Senate House still. The colour has faded, and the sticky squares on the back that stuck them on the page have dried up so when I open the album they fall out like a shower of confetti. But there everyone is, though not necessarily all parts of them – the photographer has decapitated some of them and amputated the feet of others – but the day is preserved within those shots. Not Webster Ferris, of course. He is nowhere to be seen. Like a ghostly apparition which can't be captured on film, he is not even lurking in the background of a single photograph, almost as if he never existed.

Mary's grandmother was gravely ill so her parents left after the ceremony. At the time, I assumed Mary went with them avoiding the next horror which awaited us: the sherry party on the Fellows' Lawn.

I hadn't hidden my background and I wasn't ashamed about

my parents. I was just a bit worried that Mum would be offering hairstyling advice to those who thought their coiffed tresses were perfect already. Dad looked more ill-at-ease than Mum, who embraced the kind of 'do' she'd been hoping to attend for a long while.

I got a bit more nervous when I discovered that Mum saw the ample supply of Amontillado, Fino, Oloroso and cream sherries as an invitation to test all types thoroughly. The more she had, the louder her voice became.

"Try some of this O'Rosso one, Mick," she called out to Dad, who was busy trying to look like he was with someone else. "It's Irish sherry!" Her cackle could be heard by almost everyone within the college grounds.

The Master sought me out deliberately. "Miss McNamara, you must introduce me to your parents. I would like to thank your father for his help over the last year or so."

He took Dad over to the rose bed on the far side where he engaged him in earnest conversation. Perfect Penny noticed this and came over to me because her curiosity could not hold out any longer.

"Is that your father with the Master?" I told her it was indeed. "My mother is desperate for a word with him, but he seems very good at avoiding having to talk to anyone. How come your father is speaking to him?" There was a pause whilst she craned her neck to see if she could catch any of the conversation. "Do you know what they're talking about?"

"Maybe it's my exceptional written papers in the finals," I suggested. Penny looked quizzical. Could she have got it wrong and missed my name amongst the firsts?

"Are you joking?" Penny was one of those people who had to have jokes explained. "Oh look! He's got a pad out now and he's jotting things down. How extraordinary. How can your father have anything to tell him?"

251

I wouldn't have bothered to reply but this last comment annoyed me. "He's his accountant. He's giving him some tips on where to invest his money, I expect."

"Hmm." Penny seemed impressed that Dad had the Master of a Cambridge college as one of his clients and shot back to her mother to share the news.

Extracting Dad from the attentions of the Master and Mum from the sherry table was difficult. She was mid-conversation with Gill's mother concerning the pros and cons of highlights when trying to grow out a fully dyed head of hair in order to go completely grey.

"When you get older, a dark black like yours always looks false because your skin colour changes after menopause," she broadcast. Nearby, several fathers coughed at the mention of the word and blushed. "You want to go gradually lighter and then go for low and highlights, or streaks as some people call them." Gill's mum looked unsure. "You come to The Mayfair Salon and I'll put you right." Mum winked and downed another glass of Fino to emphasise the point. It was definitely time to leave.

When we got back to my room, Roy Ironside was sitting outside my door. I knew at that moment that Webster had gone, escaped during the sherry party. That might have been his intention, but I now know that delivering Roy was the moment when he had encountered Mary. There was a note in the pot in spidery handwriting, 'Please care for me'.

"That's a bit peculiar," Mum said, "Why would anyone give you a bloomin' ugly looking thing like that? It's enormous. I hope you don't think we're having that at home. It's like a huge you know what!" Mum laughed uncontrollably. It was amazing she could string a sentence together given the extensive sherry blending project she'd been engaged in. "Imagine if your dad had one the size of that! And with spikes on."

"Shirley!" admonished Dad, who had noticed a look of horror

on the face of my opposite neighbour, a geeky-looking fourteen-year-old masquerading as a fully functioning adult student. He was leaving his room with some well-ordered luggage and a couple of earnest-looking parents.

"It belongs to a friend of mine," I explained. "He's called Roy Ironside."

"Well, Roy Ironside would do better to give you a bunch of nice flowers than that ugly-looking thing. If it snags my tights I'll be sending Roy Ironside the bill. If it comes home, it's going in your room and I won't be dusting anywhere near it."

"There was a Roy Ironside who used to play for Rotherham," Dad said informatively. I started to cry. "Oh Veronica, you've had a good time here haven't you. I can see you're sad to leave." He gave me a hug. It was just what I needed. I'd like one of Dad's hugs now.

"I expect," announced Mum, "it's all been a bit of an anti-climax, just like when a nice day ended when you were a kid." If Roy was on my doorstep, it meant there was a significant chance my relationship with Webster Ferris had ended too.

Roy had to be wedged into the well behind the driver's seat of the Sierra, between a box of books and my own withered pot plants. He'd already spiked Mum, who, to be fair, had not been walking in a straight line at the time of the incident, and he had almost been left in the hotel car park as a punishment. It didn't help seeing his spiky crown poking up menacingly all the way back to Barking.

To compound my depression, there was some discussion in the following days and weeks which came under the general heading of "what now?" There was no pressure but there were suggestions.

"Girls like you can go into teaching. You could get a job at your old school." I could see Mum's ambitions for me lay clearly not only in the borough but within walking distance of our house. When I didn't leap with excitement at that employment opportunity, she tried another tack.

"I heard there are management trainee schemes at Marks and Sparks for graduates. The pay is good and you get discounts," she explained enthusiastically. There was clearly a degree of self-interest in this suggestion.

Half-heartedly I sent for an application form from the Civil Service. A journey to Massachusetts looked more inviting. Could I do it to them? Not without some subtle groundwork and preparation. Realistically, it looked like I had blown that opportunity. Ferris had left no forwarding address or phone number. I didn't know when he was leaving for Harvard and he hadn't even said goodbye. I had no idea how to get in direct contact with him, if I would ever see him again or if he still wanted to see me.

It should have been a happy and exciting time of my life with the promise of a rosy future ahead of me, but I was very miserable. The only thing on my horizon was the prospect of a trip to the Edinburgh Festival Fringe with *Two Gentlemen,* and even that was looking unsure. Our second evening at The Arts Theatre had been a flop and the cast were dropping out left, right and centre. I wondered if Roland had the ability to come back from this one. Perhaps the Pared-Down Players had performed their last hurrah.

29
Escape to Avalon

The unsuitability of *Two Gentlemen* for a further outing north of the border was obvious. Roland had a venue booked, a deposit on some accommodation and an enviably unwavering belief in himself. He also had several hobby horses left over and a pink sparkly dog. We were still going to go, he told us.

He had devised another Pared-Down show, pruned the cast to the original six of us, plus Phil as our tech, stage manager and props and costumes person rolled into one. The legend of King Arthur (or at least some of it) was to be our summer project. Knights on horseback made good use of the hobby horses and Merlin was getting the Puppy-Pal as a 'familiar'. We'd go to Edinburgh a little early at the end of July, rehearse like mad and then busily hand out flyers on the Royal Mile to encourage people to come and watch so that we could recoup at least some of the money.

The Edinburgh Festival provided an escape for all of us. It was my best excuse for not immediately plunging into the wonderful world of work, a lifetime bringing home discounted goods from Marks and Spencer's or groundhog day retracing my steps to school but living on the other side of the staffroom door.

Steve, Lucy and I sat on the train like excited children, having secured a four-seat-and-table combo with easy access to the buffet car. For this we had to thank Phil in the fourth seat, who had the ability to work out exactly where we should get on the train in order to obtain the optimum seating-with-snacks opportunity.

Mission accomplished, we furnished ourselves with cheese and tomato sandwiches, rock hard pieces of fruit cake in cellophane and disposable cups of scalding hot British Rail tea which only cooled down sufficiently for drinking as we approached Waverley Station. The massive queue at the buffet counter was just part of the fun. For me it was a venture into the unknown.

It was the first time I had been anywhere north of the capital other than Cambridge and a school trip to Cadbury's factory at Bournville near Birmingham. There I had purchased and consumed an unwise number of *Old Jamaica* chocolate bars from the factory shop. The yellow and orange wrapper showed a picture of a three-masted sailing ship besides a Caribbean beach. It was as far away from Birmingham and Barking as a chocolate bar could be. However, the ensuing bout of sickness did not leave me with a taste for exploration.

As we travelled north, I thought of Ferris. I'd heard nothing from him. Nowt from the master of the written word. I'd expected a letter if not a phone call as he had my address and number, but no contact had been made despite what he'd promised. Before graduation, he'd told me he had to clear out the house in Rotherham and give up the tenancy he'd taken over from his mum. The phone had been disconnected long ago. No point in giving me the details, he'd explained. Better if he contacted me directly.

Past Newcastle and along the spectacular Northumberland coast, we caught sight of the island of Lindisfarne. Steve and Lucy had fallen out and then made it up again several times in the nearly 300 miles we had travelled from King's Cross. Steve looked longingly across the water. "Holy Island has been the home to hermits over the years. St Cuthbert spent ten years as one. I can see the attraction," he pointed out plaintively. Phil and I exchanged glances. Fortunately, Lucy had missed this jibe but it was obvious that Steve, incapable of escaping their relationship, was hoping three weeks in close proximity in a small flat in Edinburgh might do the trick for him. If not, he could well discover a sudden calling to a lonely remote rock off the Northumberland coastline on the way home. I thought I might join him.

Phil had completed his postgraduate studies successfully, landed himself a good job somewhere near Oxford and was on good terms with the folks back home in Reigate. Phil might be a bit predictable and dull but he had sorted himself out in a sensible and mature way. He was the only one of us with the prospect of a pay slip at the end of September.

The train took us right into the heart of the Scottish capital, the railway line seemingly in a valley where you'd expect there to be a river. Keeping guard over the station was the castle and several gothic-looking buildings on top of a steep slope. Roland was already in town as were Neil, Ameerah and Danny.

Roland had billeted himself elsewhere, in seclusion from the riff-raff, but the other three were already at our accommodation in the district of Marchmont on the other side of a big expanse of greenery called The Meadows. The area had streets paved with setts, which made a particular and memorable noise when a car went past the tall tenement buildings.

Not that you could hear road noise from our flat, way up on the top floor, accessed by communal stone stairs with an iron balustrade. The reputation of Scots as eaters of deep-fried Mars Bars and guzzlers of Irn Bru seemed irrelevant. Anyone living in these apartments didn't need aerobics or keep-fit classes. Four flights of stairs several times a day would make you fit enough to indulge in as much sugar and fat as you wanted.

There were three bedrooms. Danny and Ameerah took one, Lucy and Steve another and I was allocated a smaller single one. Neil and Phil were to make do with the couple of sofas in the main room. This was luxury beyond what Roland had originally planned. A much larger cast would have had us nose to tail in sleeping bags on the slightly grubby carpet with the prospect of waking up with someone's discarded shoe, or worse, in close proximity to our nose. There were many reasons to be thankful for the demise of *Two Gentlemen*.

Roland had undergone a sea change. *Arthur and the Knights of the Round Table* had no silly gimmicks, no pretentious themes and, although truncated, was a sensible selection of parts of the legend which told the whole story. It was short and had a small cast but, in a surprising flash of insight, Roland had aimed it towards the children's section of the Fringe. We did wonder if only adhering to half of the adage about not working with animals and children might still cast a spell over the performance. Had Roland not learned his lesson from Frank and his snarling jaws?

Ameerah was paralysed with fear when she left the flat. Not because she couldn't face the monstrous climb up again on her return but because she lived in terror of exposure. She'd told her father she was staying with a cousin in Glasgow whilst investigating postgraduate study at the university. He would never have permitted her to stay in the flat with us, let alone share a bedroom with a boy. This was the latest and largest of the deceptions she had concocted in order to maintain her relationship with Danny. The Glaswegian cousin was in on the story, but Ameerah had failed to think of a solution to the problem that she was appearing in a show in public every day for the next three weeks and she had a vast extended family with relatives around every corner.

Danny was escaping his mother's matchmaking and employment agency services. He had also not been entirely straightforward with accurate information about his degree classification. Danny's mum had not been to see the lists on the Senate House walls and had not questioned the staff at his college closely. The actual degree certificate, due by post, could hopefully be kept from her. He was in with a chance that the award of 'top first' (a classification of his own manufacture) would be believed and that the truthful 'lucky to scrape a third' (not an official class but what his Director of Studies had told him) might be consigned to future revelation. Most of the academic staff at Danny's college had had years of identifying parents with whom they did not wish to engage in conversation at the post-graduation reception. Mrs Burgess was without doubt an obvious candidate for this category: her loud voice, visible preening over her son and enthusiastic pursuit of anyone who might prove 'useful' in the future were clear. They all ran a mile and Danny's secret was safe for the time being.

I got a decent part, Morgan le Fay, the half-sister of Arthur as well as a fairy enchantress and witch queen. Not Guinevere, beautiful and richly robed. That was Lucy, of course. Our parents were unlikely to show up. Hers because they didn't know or care whether she was in Edinburgh or not, and mine because they were as likely to visit an arts festival in Scotland as fly to Kathmandu and trek through Nepal.

Danny got the full magician works as Merlin – coloured wig, pointy hat, cloak and stick-on beard – and looked like a low budget children's entertainer, but luckily not himself. Handy if Mrs Burgess opened the certificate-shaped letter addressed to her son and decided to come and find out exactly where he was and discuss its contents with him. He adopted the sparkly pink dog, using its recorded voices when he had short memory lapses in his lines. When we heard "Stroke me and I will love you forever" or "I'm your pal, just tickle my tum" we knew that the magical, supernatural, shape-shifting embodiment of one of the most important characters in the literature of the Middle Ages was struggling to recall the next line.

Ameerah disappeared into yards of blue and green fabric and swirled about as the Lady of the Lake drawing Excalibur in and out of her watery folds at appropriate moments. She painted her face green and blue and looked unlike any person you had ever seen and certainly not the daughter of Mr Shah.

Arthur, however, resplendent in a borrowed Robin Hood costume which Roland had adapted to look knightly, was clearly Neil. It was skin-tight, left nothing to the imagination and was somewhat inappropriate when he was Arthur the (rather advanced) boy. No wonder he could pull the sword from the stone. Neil was delighted with his look and decided it might be useful for the fruitful boyfriend search that he was convinced the Festival might provide. It was an opportunity he was hoping to take advantage of because once back home in Cromer things would be very different. We were performing to children, of course, so Neil chose to wear the Arthur costume not only when he was handing out flyers on The Royal Mile to advertise the show but at all other times.

That left Steve, cheerfully taking on the part of all of the other knights of the round table: Lancelot, Percival, Galahad, and Gawain to name but a few. He galloped his way around the small stage on the hobby horse using a different voice or accent for each knight. For the most part this worked but it was not surprising that sometimes he got mixed up – particularly when he was appearing as more than one knight in the same scene. I doubt the children noticed that he might begin a speech as a Mancunian and then suddenly change into Geordie.

One afternoon he announced, "My sword thirsts for blood!" in the Sheffield Roy Hattersley voice which he kept for Sir Galahad. Then corrected himself, "Shit, sorry… My sword thirsts for blood!" in the Northern Irish of George Best also known as Sir Lancelot. An easy confusion.

There was a short silent pause before a girl in the audience piped up, "That man swored, Mummy!"

I thought the show was going very well. I told Phil so one afternoon when we were struggling across the Meadows with both hobby horses, the Puppy-pal and a bag full of props and costumes, returning from our 3pm performance.

"Oh, come on, Roni," he laughed. "It's better than the Dog Eats Man fiasco but only just."

I was affronted. "We're getting good audiences."

"And we don't rely on repeat business luckily!" Phil seemed to think the whole thing was a hilariously disastrous flop and assumed I did too.

"What are you doing here, then, wasting your time with such a worthless production?" I asked him.

Phil stopped and looked straight at me. I was wearing Merlin's hat-and-beard ensemble as a way of transporting it back to the flat. "You don't know, do you? You just don't notice me."

"What do you mean?" I noticed that Excalibur was falling out of the props bag. We'd be in a difficult position if that got lost.

"I'm here because of you! You're the funniest, most enchanting girl I've ever met. I couldn't bear to say goodbye at the end of term. Roland was going to do the props and everything himself, but I asked him if I could be part of the company."

"You had to ask him? Not many people do that. He's used to begging for help." Strands of Merlin's nylon beard were sticking into my nostrils and to my lips. I tried to blow them away as my hands were full. I knew I should say something sincere and not flippant, but I wasn't very good at that. Phil was just natural all the time. He said what he thought and he wasn't embarrassed. Life wasn't complicated for him. Even then I recognised he was the world's most rational being.

Phil removed my hat, took the hobby horse from me and placed the bag I was carrying on the ground. Then he kissed me. Right there in the open, where anyone could see. Webster Ferris could barely touch me in public. Away from his room, he had only linked arms with me once, that time outside the Arts Theatre stage door, in the dark when he thought no-one was looking but was keen to remind me just where my loyalties lay.

He was kind, Phil, and comforting. He was never in a bad

mood and had a solution for all problems, usually pointing out how they weren't in fact problems after all. I didn't need to guess what was going on with him and he was open with everyone. I think everybody but me had worked out what he thought of me and no-one was surprised when he moved off the sofa and into my bedroom. Steve was delighted because he was chucked out of the room he shared with Lucy on a regular basis if not nightly. There was now a spare sofa for him to sleep on and he could say goodbye to the grubby carpet.

Phil didn't provide the bolt of electricity Webster Ferris seemed to be able to shoot through me. He made me feel good and not anxious. Being close to Phil was like putting on an old warm and comfortable sweater. Everything would be alright when he was there.

It really was fun being in the beautiful city during the festival. We saw some good shows and some bad. We had a steady trickle of customers for ours. There weren't many performances specifically for children, so Roland had backed a good horse in designating ours for young people.

Mary came up to stay with us for a few days and braved the grubby carpet and Steve and Neil's feet. She went off on her own watching shows and worked her way through a list of classical music concerts which were part of the real Festival, not the Fringe, and which the rest of us lightweights hadn't even realised were happening.

"I like Phil," she said approvingly. "He is solid, supportive and level." To me this sounded like the qualities one might look for in a table rather than a lover, but I valued her advice. "You should be careful of being with someone who demands too much from you, who doesn't allow you to flourish as yourself." I wondered what she knew, or what she was surmising about what I thought was my secret liaison in Cambridge. Naively, I thought I had compartmentalised my life. Given what I have learned subsequently it seems that wasn't the case. I wasn't the only one with a so-called secret. As I have learnt, things are never what they seem.

30
Guinevere and Lancelot

The Edinburgh Festival was turning out to be a great thing to have done at the end of my final year as a student. Life in our flat was fun and Phil and I were enjoying watching other Fringe shows and walking around the city.

One Thursday, I remember clearly it was a Thursday, Neil slid up to me after the show with a conspiratorial look on his face. "Could you see into the audience?"

"You know you can't see a thing with that light Phil shines onto the stage!" Phil had only a few lamps at his disposal.

Like many performance spaces used in the Fringe, the venue was primitive and had not been designed as a theatre. It was a hall frequently used for Alcoholics Anonymous and the few attendees who hadn't got the message about meetings being cancelled for the next three weeks turned up and stayed anyway. We let them in free because their loud chortling helped the show move along. There was a small, raised area we used as the stage but the place had a low ceiling, no backstage and was dank and dark. The audience area stretched back with no rake to the seats and so any poor children at the back, particularly those seated behind a burly man from Leith who hadn't touched a dram for the last nine months, could see very little.

"He was there," Neil continued, "sat right at the back, in a dark corner."

"Who?"

"That bloke from your college, Ferris Wheel or whatever he's called."

I hadn't told Neil about how the relationship between me and Webster Ferris had developed. We were good friends and early on I had often entertained him with Ferris stories: about our supervisions and the scary encounters people had around college. I'd hammed it up and exaggerated, so suddenly to announce that I was friendly let alone in a relationship with this unpredictable psychopath would have been odd. Well, that's what I told myself when I wondered why I chose not to tell Neil about the bloody horse head incident or the swimming lessons.

Neil was what we would now call emotionally intelligent. He didn't miss much. He had an antenna for other people's unspoken objects of desire, even if he was hopeless about acknowledging his own to anyone but me. I'd passed Webster Ferris off as a weirdo, just someone who I had to spend more time with than I really wanted, a good supplier of anecdotes for me to tell. I'm not sure Neil believed me, but we kept up a conspiracy of silence.

"Perhaps it was one of the AA lot? A look-alike?" I suggested. My heart was thumping.

"Listen, darling, if that wasn't Ferris Wheel then I'm losing my powers of inspection." Neil was an expert in sizing up every man in the vicinity. He called it 'inspecting'. "I was at the back right next to him, just before I come on to throw Excalibur into the lake." This was a tricky moment in the show when any misjudgement by Arthur could leave poor Ameerah nursing a multicoloured bruise on some part of her body later in the day. "He asked me to give you this." Neil handed me an envelope with Webster's spidery handwriting on the front. 'V McNamara' it read, in a formal kind of way.

"Is it a writ? Or is he inviting me to join the communist party or spy for the KGB?" I tried to laugh it off. Neil gave me what Mum called 'an old-fashioned look'. The note inside was an invitation to meet him at 6pm that evening at the Greyfriars Bobby statue.

"That's bloody odd," said Neil, who had a point. Why hadn't he just waited until the show finished to speak to me? "Sounds like an assignation in some Shakespeare play Roland has adapted for Edinburgh! Have you got to appear dressed as a boy?" I said nothing. "You're not thinking of going are you?" I remained silent. Neil raised his eyebrows. "Please yourself. I'll come with you if you like."

"It's OK." I tried to sound casual. "Don't tell Phil where I'm going, will you?"

As I approached the confluence of roads where the Greyfriars Bobby Bar was I could see Ferris skulking about long before I could see the statue of Greyfriars Bobby himself. The area was busy with tourists and festival goers; if you were looking for somewhere to pass over your microfilm inside a copy of *The Times*, it would have been an ideal place to hide in plain sight.

I'd been trying to work out what I was going to say to him and had several scenarios worked out in my head. He'd just left, without a word, and I'd heard nothing from him since. I'd started a new relationship, reasonable in the circumstances. I didn't like being pressurised and made to feel guilty. He was incapable of seeing things from my point of view. There was a long list of comments I wished to get off my chest before I sent him away with an admonishment he wouldn't forget.

Predictably, things didn't pan out that way. He grinned when he saw me and any anger I was brewing dissolved immediately. He had a black eye. "What pile of shite is Roland pedalling now? The Arthurian legend, his version of *Morte d'Arthur* in twelve pages?"

"Nice to see you too."

"He should have adapted Greyfriars Bobby. He missed a trick. He's got that pink sparkly dog after all; you only need a couple of other characters. One dies of TB early on then you just need someone else to ring a bell whilst another brings out a bowl of food. The dog sits on the grave for fourteen years then dies itself.

Easily condensed into about five minutes of schmaltz."

Webster seemed to know everything. Not only did he appear to have read every book ever written but he knew all sorts of other stuff too. An exaggerated dog myth from Scotland? Yes, he'd know all about it. He retained any information that was fed into his vast brain. As far as I knew he'd never previously been anywhere other than depressed bits of the north and Cambridge.

I wasn't going to let him get away with all that breezy 'I'm so zany and intelligent I don't have to behave like a normal human' stuff. "What is this all about?" I asked. "Notes and invites to meet in weird places? Why haven't you been in touch? Where did you get that black eye?"

"I walked into a cupboard door," he lied. "I wanted you to make a conscious decision to come. I wanted to give you the choice. Besides I thought you'd think it was fun. An invitation to an assignation…" This was a most un-Ferris like concept. He wasn't sensible and reliable like Phil, he was quirky, emotional and spontaneous, but there was an underlying seriousness to everything he did.

"It wasn't much fun when you didn't even write to me or ring up. You left college without saying goodbye, without saying anything. What am I supposed to think?"

"You've been up here most of the time. I didn't know where you were staying. I've been busy sorting things but I'm here now." He seemed excited. That frisson of fear mixed with pleasure sparked through me. 'Sorting things' was a phrase Uncle Patrick used when he was lying or trying not to tell Gran what he was up to.

He suggested we walk round the corner to the graveyard where there was now a little headstone dedicated to the dog. Greyfriars Bobby and the touching tale of the little pooch who loyally guarded his master's grave for fourteen years was still big business. Not only was there a Greyfriars Bobby bar there were plenty of other Greyfriars Bobby marketing opportunities and branding as well. Some American tourists were proudly wearing bright pink Greyfriars Bobby sweatshirts. Perhaps Roland had missed a trick.

Walking round the kirkyard looking at the headstones was certainly an unusual way of re-uniting after nearly a month of silence. We found the gravestone of William McGonagall, the infamously awful Victorian poet.

"Poetry's answer to Roland," he chuckled, "*The stronger we our house do build / The less chance we have of being killed.* What a master of verse he was!" Webster roared with laughter and took my hands. I realised I never knew what he was going to do next. Displays of affection in public? This was both exciting and unsettling.

"Roy is on my windowsill at home," I reported. "Mum is watering him."

"Not too much, I hope. A bit of benign neglect helps him thrive."

"Is that how you think I should be treated?" Webster was pulled up short by this remark. He took an envelope out of his jacket pocket and handed it to me.

He explained he was leaving for the US on Saturday. He had cleared his mother's house and given up the tenancy. He'd sold some things where he could and the envelope had money for a ticket. He thought if I showed up in person at the American Embassy with my passport, I might be able to get a visa then and there. He'd sorted out accommodation and we could see about extending my visa to a student one when I got there.

It was as if we had never had this conversation before. I spoke slowly as I might to someone whose first language wasn't English. "I'm in the show until Saturday 31st August and I'm not coming back to London until the following Sunday or Monday. I can't just leave now, abandoning my parents and family. I'm an only child."

"So was I," he replied. "You'll sort something out."

We found Bobby's headstone. It was fairly new, although the dog had died in 1872. Someone had left some Bonio and a couple of squeaky toys beside it, nutters obviously. Inscribed on the headstone were the words, *Let his loyalty and devotion be a lesson to us all.* Webster seemed to enjoy this epitaph. I couldn't work out if he thought that phrase applied to us and just whose loyalty and devotion was a lesson to whom.

When I returned to the flat later, Phil and Neil were sitting up in the kitchen.

"You've been a long time. It's getting late," said Phil protectively. "Did you have a nice time with your school friend?" Neil pulled a face indicating this piece of information had been planted by him. "You look tired. You haven't been crying have you?" He made me a cup of tea and put his arm round me. "Time to turn in, I think." Phil always went to bed at a sensible time. He didn't sit up most of the night and then regret it in the morning. It wasn't that he didn't enjoy himself, but he just made unerringly sensible decisions all the time. I recognised this characteristic as beneficial for me. I knew he'd made a conscious decision to go out with me. It hadn't just happened, and consequently that made me feel good.

Webster Ferris frequently didn't make me feel good. He made me feel uncertain, incapable and unsure. Did I want to spend my life like that? I was consumed with guilt for lying to Phil about who I had been with. How could I treat him like that?

I thought about Ferris flying out alone to the US, away from everything he had ever known. Why was he doing it? It wasn't as if any universities in England wouldn't willingly have him. It was an escape from his 'it's grim up north' screenplay and an unsettling university experience, I guessed. His Avalon from where he would return at some time in the future.

I hid the envelope of money in my case. I don't know why. I suppose I didn't want anyone asking where I'd got it or, more accurately, who I'd got it from. Perhaps, deep in the recess of my psyche, I knew that in a moment of madness I might use it to buy a flight across the sea.

At the end of the run we were all really tired when we travelled back to London, so no-one said much. It was the 1st of September. Summer was over. University was over. Real life was about to start.

At King's Cross we went our separate ways back to our homes. "I'll call you this evening," promised Phil. Of course, he did. There was no side with him. If he said he'd call, he did. Soon he was off to somewhere near Oxford to start his job.

I fiddled about with a few job applications and filled in the Civil Service form to enable me to sit an exam to get in. I'd thought I'd finished with exams. I went to the travel agent to ask about flights to Boston, just to keep my options open. But there was no communication from the other side of the Atlantic. I expected it might be like that. Ferris was incapable of understanding that I might need to think about my life not just make far-reaching decisions impetuously. I couldn't go with him immediately so he'd interpreted that as I would never be going.

Was he waiting for me to get in touch? To tell him I wanted to be with him, that I'd bought the ticket? Was the ball in my court as it had been with the Greyfriars Bobby assignation? I looked up the address of Harvard University in Barking library – but I dithered about what to write. I needed to be sure.

I was in regular contact with Phil and went to stay with him one weekend. He was renting a little cottage near Abingdon. It was like a proper grown-up house, with stairs and adult furniture. I liked it.

Just as well, really, because sometime in November, I realised I hadn't had a period for quite a while. I bought a home pregnancy test and the result was positive, despite me crossing my fingers on both hands. Fortunately, Phil was delighted.

He came back to Barking and met Mum and Dad. The leaf was

out in the table, the cruet featured as a centrepiece and the 'shall we/shan't we?' tablecloth conundrum was solved. We managed to avoid him sitting on a kitchen chair and, having dined on an upholstered G Plan, he (and remarkably we) passed muster.

Mum and Dad and his parents were surprisingly understanding about a baby being on the way. Even Gran set about knitting all sorts of weird and wonderful garments in neutral shades of mauve and yellow. "I'll not tempt providence by selecting a pink or blue wool." They were mainly for the child's extremities: bootees, gloves and hats. Best of all I could consign the invitation to the Civil Service exam to the bin.

Both sets of parents made it plain that a wedding before the birth was preferable and we went along with that. I very much wanted this to happen. Now I did not want a visit from anyone from Massachusetts or a letter or a phone call to mess things up. I wanted security and stability because I was to be a mother and Phil was the only person who could provide that. He loved me and I loved him, not like a romantic teenager but in a mature and mutually respectful way.

We organised a Christmas wedding and Gran set about designing and sewing a concoction to out-froufrou Diana. It was to be a Register Office ceremony but that didn't put her off. Father O'Connor remained in ignorance, of course. "Sure, he has no need to know. In the eyes of the Church and God it's not a wedding anyways," she protested tactlessly and fortunately out of my mother's earshot. Had I been consumed by the vast frilled and lacy frock she made me, he might have discovered the venue. I expect it would have been in the local paper, 'Pregnant bride smothered by wedding dress outside Register Office. Grandmother says it's the Lord's doing'.

The ceremony took place in a building between our house and The Mayfair Salon, not far from the Lido and my school, with the reception held at the pub next to it. All of them were loci in my former life. Any connections between the royal brides and me ended with a tenuous link to the dress. The back room at the Royal Oak wasn't a glamorous venue but the small group of guests (numbers probably more constrained by the amount of room the dress took up than the size of the function room) had a good time. Not Mary, of course. She didn't come. Now I know why.

So, I never had to make a choice. It was made for me and there were no regrets. Things did change, though, but I wasn't old enough to know that this is always the case.

I moved with Roy Ironside into the grown-up house outside Abingdon and in May of the following year there were three of us co-habiting with the monster cactus.

In time, Dad and Uncle Patrick sold the business to Coral's, Mum relinquished The Mayfair Salon and the new owner renamed it 'Wayvz & Kurlz', which people found difficult to read. He, a George Michael lookalike called Damian, got rid of the stand-up hairdryers in favour of handheld blow dryers only. The interior had a makeover, and the walls were decorated with huge photos of unsmiling models pouting under piles of hair which looked like wild and unkempt hay. Mum's clients, including Mrs Goldblatt, moved elsewhere, and Mum was horrified but powerless. She couldn't bear to walk past so they sold our house, went on lots of holidays and moved to the bungalow in Clacton.

Uncle Patrick flew to Marbella on a short holiday and decided to stay. He picked up a lady-friend with a seafront bar and decided that life on a sunny beachfront pouring the occasional lager and drinking many more was preferable to his dingy flat on the Mile End Road.

Gran alone stayed still, for once, in her flat. She knew she didn't have to keep guard at the window anymore. Even Father O'Connor moved on to another parish. His replacement was Father Flynn, a much younger man who, despite dispensing with some of the more traditional elements of the way the church was run, was charming and knew just how to get the most out of the selfless devotion of Gran and her sort. "Father Flynn, he's a man wiser than you'd think for his years, asked me if I thought…" became her stock phrase.

Life is always in flux. All these other things would have happened whether I had been in Cambridge, Mass. or Barking. I was not the lynchpin of the family that I imagined I was. There might have been a bit of fuss, but life would have gone on. You can instigate change, but you can't prevent it.

In a soppy movie, the picture would diminish into an ever-smaller circle before the words 'The End' covered the screen. But much as I have always wished to inhabit the world of film, I live in the real world where things aren't that simple.

31
Postman's Knock

I still get a pang of excitement when I hear the postman come. It's not only because Arman (we're on first name terms) is devilishly handsome with his stubbly beard and a glossy full head of hair.

It's also because I still hold out the hope of a handwritten letter. No-one writes letters for fun anymore. It's one of the great disappointments of the communications revolution of the last twenty-five years. Fortunately, Arman has other things to stick through the letterbox or hand to me directly if I get there in time. He has a ready supply of pieces of glossy paper with pictures of pizzas or houses with replacement windows on. And barely a day passes without the invitation to look round an apartment which includes 'assisted living', where a friendly-looking woman brings you a tasty-looking meal and another does the hoovering. To while away the afternoon, the lucky residents merely have to choose between a complex jigsaw or a game of cards with friends accompanied by tea and cake. Looks good to me.

I can't put these unwanted communications straight into the re-cycling because I have to sift through them in case there is a bill or a speeding or parking fine lurking amongst them. The last two are always mine, naturally. I try to be quick and open the door to Arman so I can filter them out before Phil picks the post up and gives me another lesson on where the speed cameras are round here. He's never cross, just endlessly understanding about my inability to remember their locations and curtail my speed accordingly. Arman and I have an arrangement. If he notices a PCN or a letter from Thames Valley Police in the pile, he rings the bell. He also does this if there's an oversized publication in the mail. I like to think this is because he finds me fascinating and attractive and wants to chat, but I know it's not.

One day in early October, Arman was grinning when I answered the bell. Along with an offer of two for one on a pizza with something called a stuffed crust was a magazine. Through the biodegradable 'dispose of me in your food waste' wrapping, I could see it was the college newsletter. On the cover was a picture of me. "I couldn't help but notice," he enthused, "you've made the front page. That **is** you isn't it?" He was trying to hide the amusement the image was causing. I don't remember the photograph being taken but there I was, enjoying a cocktail in the bar.

Neither do I remember anyone at the college reunion asking me if I minded being photographed so that the shot could be plastered all over a magazine which would then be sent to every alumnus either in print or digital form. I expect somewhere, amongst the warnings in very small print about the consequences of losing the fob or using more than one tea bag, there was a very small opt-out box which I'd missed.

In the past the newsletter was a small, densely printed booklet in which colour was confined to the cover. It was called *The College Record* which indicated exactly what one might find inside. Amongst extensive obituaries of long serving members of staff and death notices of former students were lists of learned publications written by former and present college members. In addition, there were some dry articles about interesting artefacts owned by the college but not on public display and the occasional poem or reflection by an alumnus. I don't suppose many people read it. My copy generally lurked in the downstairs loo until it got curly and slightly discoloured and I had to admit to myself that it was very unlikely that I would progress further in the turgid article on Byzantine pottery that I thought I ought to finish and chucked it out.

Now it is named *spool!* – a non-capitalised verb or perhaps a noun, exclaiming nothing about its contents or genesis. It has huge, glossy Technicolor pages, interviews with college members in zany fonts with pictures at strange angles and unsubstantiated boasts about the way our college responds to diversity quotas and gender issues much better than all the others. Articles recording gatherings and events are accompanied by photographs of delirious students grinning so madly it looks as if they have been inhaling laughing gas. They all look like models. Where are the tortured philosophy students who are distraught because they can't prove they exist? The miserable loners who can't keep up with all the work they make you do these days? The pale little scientist who never removes his cagoule and blinks when he sees the daylight after emerging from a term in the labs? No photos of that lot. Like all other marketing material, it's phony. A least the Byzantine pottery was genuine and the article informative – if dull.

It is a self-satisfied promotion of the present institution with vacuous articles such as 'Q & A with the Master' (Q: Coffee or tea? A: Neither. Both commodities are redolent of a colonial past. I drink organic kombucha and I avoid milk because the dairy industry is cruel). Inevitably there are various invitations to donate to bursaries and college funds. Any mention of previous students is in the context of either how the college has made them what they are today or how they have generously been welcomed back to see how things have improved since their time. I find it so irritatingly smug that it is out with the recycling almost immediately without limbo in any lavatory, downstairs or otherwise.

When I removed the booklet from its eco wrapping, I looked at the full image in all its horror. I could see why Arman was amused. What was I doing? Leering from one side of the page was my face, grinning manically, my eyes wide as if I'd just sat on a drawing pin. As if in homage to Binka, several cocktail umbrellas and a couple of fluorescent straws were poking out from my hair and from behind my ears. Tom was emerging from the other side of the page with a daft look on his face, but no umbrellas, and he was clinking a tall glass of what looked like vivid blue antifreeze with my balloon glass of neon orange liquid. Out of focus so that their censorious looks were not revealed, but clearly identifiable behind us, was the Cocoa Club.

'Forty years on!' read the banner underneath, 'We welcomed back Tim Pincy and Victoria MacManaman (class of '82) where they celebrated adding a PhD and MLitt to the BAs they achieved in 1985'. We looked ridiculous.

I failed to get the horrific image into the recycling quickly enough. "I told you you'd have a good time, didn't I?" crowed Phil when he saw it. Irritatingly, he had been right as usual. "They've got your names wrong. That chap was called Tom Percy wasn't he?" How could Phil remember that? He wasn't even in our college.

"I have become Victoria MacManaman," I replied, trying to deflect any questioning as to what exactly I might have been up to. I'd been deliberately vague about what had gone on that weekend.

"Thank goodness. I'm glad no one can associate that ridiculous person with me," he laughed.

A few weeks later Arman brought something else. I almost missed it amongst the appeals for money for clean water and donkey sanctuaries and a thick brochure for medical aids – hoists, stair lifts and gadgets to help you put tights on or pick things up without having to bend down.

It was a brown envelope from the college. I was in two minds about opening it, having decided it was either another request for me to remember them in my will or a bill for the unreturned fob from the reunion. This really was a bit much; it wasn't my fault I'd had to leave in a hurry. Fob-location was the least of my worries while the building was slowly being filled with water thanks to Gill, the plumbing and her malfunctioning gadget. Irate, I tore it open and inside was another, smaller envelope.

My mouth went dry and I couldn't swallow. It had an American stamp and the words 'Please forward' above my name and the college address. The spidery handwriting was immediately recognisable. Should I open it or not? Fortunately, I was alone.

My hand was shaking but of course I opened it – how could I not? A handwritten letter – such a rarity.

In embossed print, along the top it read: *'From Professor W Ferris, (MA Cantab, PhD Harvard) Stanford University, Stanford CA.'* I could hardly read it because my heart was beating and my eyes were misting over.

Dear Roni (or is it Victoria?),

I get the College magazine online and was so delighted to see your photograph with the report of the 40th anniversary of your year group entering the college. It seems things have changed quite a lot since the 1980s – particularly at the bar where the sale of cocktails has made it a much more upmarket venue than in our day. Good to see you enjoying a selection of them!

It made me so happy to see your laughing face that I decided to write to you. It's taken me over thirty-seven years to feel joy not sorrow when I think about you and to have the courage to contact you. I don't know how this letter will be received but please believe that it is sent with the best of intentions.

By an extraordinary co-incidence at the beginning of my first term at Harvard I was introduced to another member of our college, Simeon Goldblatt, whom you will remember as he came from Barking too. He had an amusing story, about you and a Boat Club drinks party, which he shared. A short while later he told me that he had heard from his mother that you were engaged. This was a great shock to me, but I should not have been surprised. You had many admirers. I hope this partnership has made you happy.

I can see now that my actions and behaviour in that summer of 1985 were unacceptable. It was a very difficult time for me and, although that is no excuse, I hope it mitigates any hurt I may have caused you. I was frightened about the future, a future which I very much wanted to share with you. I recognised some years ago that, at that time, I was making impossible demands of you. If I had been more patient and looked at the situation from your point of view perhaps things might have been different.

'..if a woman doubts as to whether she should accept a man or not, she certainly ought to refuse him. If she can hesitate as to 'Yes,' she ought to say 'No' directly. It is not a state to be safely entered into with doubtful feelings, with half a heart.'

Jane Austen recognised this and I didn't. Mea culpa.

I never imagined I would be here in the US for so long, but I can assure you that I retain my British passport, do not write color or favor, never use a faucet or an elevator and do not put out the garbage. I'm still following The Millers and have had a succession of Roy Ironsides over the years to whom I talk about their latest defeat. I assume the original went west some years ago.

It is cathartic for me to write to you directly. I have been writing to you and about you indirectly for many years. Please don't think you have to reply. It's my long overdue atonement to apologise. 'The commencement of atonement is the sense of its necessity' – which I know you will recognise as Byron.

I don't know if you will get this letter but I'm trusting the college will have your address correctly (if not your name) and do the decent thing.

I shall be coming over to give a series of lectures at Oxford

University next year and would be delighted to see you and your partner at a location of your choice if you felt that was appropriate.

I hope you are in good health and happy – the photo certainly suggests that is the case.

Affectionately,

Webster

PS Have you still got the money? (That's a joke, by the way).

Only Webster Ferris could write a letter like that, carefully composed, inclusive of quotation and with points for discussion. He alone had got Simeon Goldblatt's name correct. I immediately took it upstairs to the bathroom and locked the door so that I could analyse it without fear of interruption.

Firstly, the photograph. You could only really make out my face, so the 59-year-old body underneath couldn't be inspected. It was taken in artificial light so the pallid skin and grey hairs were less obvious. The cocktail umbrellas in the hair suggested a youthful and jovial demeanour – perhaps not present in reality.

What was I doing? I checked myself. Whatever did it matter what Webster Ferris thought of my appearance? Was I hoping he would have felt regret when he saw what he'd missed all these years? I was getting carried away.

How sincere was all that bit about joy and sorrow? I was sceptical but when I re-read it a little tear fell on my cheek. I thought about Webster a lot; it was not something I shared with anyone, my secret. I didn't feel too guilty. I think about my parents, about Gran and Uncle Patrick all the time. Just because someone is gone you don't forget about them. I'd learnt that. When someone dies they are still with you, their voice telling you things, chastising you even. You don't see them or touch them but they are still there, part of you. Webster's exile to the US was almost like a bereavement. It was entirely plausible that he should think about me often, in the way I thought about him. We didn't see or speak to each other, but he was still there. He hadn't been deleted from my life like Stalin erased Trotsky from that photograph. Initially, I felt anger, even betrayal, when I thought about him, but later, like him, it was generally sorrow. I realised that, unlike him, I had yet to feel joy when remembering him.

Goldblatt's revenge! When Simeon was a second year he would have known Fresher Ferris when he was securing his reputation as the scariest first year in the Fens before mysteriously disappearing for a year. I could just imagine the well-meaning introduction, Stateside. "Hey, Si. Come meet this guy who has just arrived from Ingerland. He's from The University of Cambridge too!" Goldblatt must have been bricking it when he recognised his fellow compatriot was Webster Ferris, probably sporting some unexplained transatlantic black eye. Goldblatt wasn't afraid of bullies, though, and I don't suppose he wasted any time passing on gossip his mother had picked up at The Mayfair Salon. He couldn't wait to tell Webster I'd got engaged to make sure he didn't contact me ever again. Jealous bastard.

After a pause, I reviewed this initial analysis. Simeon Goldblatt had left Cambridge before I ever set eyes on Webster Ferris. Our relationship was so covert that it was extremely unlikely that Goldblatt in the US would have heard even a whisper of gossip about us being together. He had obviously mentioned me when they were stuck for conversation and had resorted to playing the 'who do you remember' game. Unintentional though it may have been, I assumed that his passing on of the news of my engagement was what had prevented Webster getting in touch with me subsequently. How had Simeon exaggerated the boathouse story? Was he laughing about my overindulgence, how I'd lost my underwear and ended up with my pants up the pole?

Had he explained what he was doing when the boathouse caught fire? None of this would have painted me in a good light but I wouldn't have blamed him.

Roy Ironside? The joke about the money? These are very specific things we shared. Were they included to remind me of our closeness? I did feel awkward about the money for a long time. It sat in a drawer waiting for something. I wasn't sure what to do with it. I thought of something in the end.

Roy Ironside lived a very long time. There were a couple of scares when he'd had so little watering I thought he'd finally had it, but he rallied every time. When we had three children and so many possessions that we could barely get in or out of our cottage, we moved house and accidentally Roy got left behind. I was inconsolable when I realised. Phil thought this was an over-reaction but kindly offered to go back and get him. It turned out that Roy was one of the first things the new people had put on a skip they'd ordered to cart away the kitchen we'd saved up for and the rest of the fixtures and fittings we thought we were kindly donating to them but which they obviously couldn't stand. Phil bought me a new cactus, round and squat with softer spines, but it wasn't the same.

I stopped and laughed out loud. Here I was deconstructing the letter, just as Ferris had helped show me how to do with set texts all those years ago. The first sign of joy at his memory? His love of literature was a gift to me. Barking's Biggest Bookworm I might have been, but Webster taught me to understand prose and poetry. I'm still ploughing my way through books, real books with pages, not a Kindle. I love the feel of a book in my hands. It's always hard to re-read the works we enjoyed together or analyse new fiction without thinking of him.

I imagined Dr Bennett, snoozing in his armchair and waking with a start when he sensed the hour was thankfully up. "So, Miss McNamara, what are your final thoughts on the work?"

"I think, Dr Bennett, that regardless of anything else, Webster Ferris really wants to see me."

I can't deny what I'm like. I'm not always proud of it. With the advent of the internet and the stalking possibilities of Facebook and Linked-In there is no way on God's Earth that I have not previously looked up Professor Webster Ferris to see what he is up to. Just as I stalked Simeon Goldblatt and found the fate of his unfortunate cat Veronica, I know about the Prof's stellar career: Harvard, Stanford, publications, books, criticism, accolades and awards. One would have expected no less of the top student of our time. But that's all I do know about him. His private life is shrouded in the mysterious cloak he assumed in Rotherham and which, even living amongst the heart-on-your-sleeve, no-emotions-unexplored or feelings-unbroadcast Americans, remains tightly wrapped around him.

The front door opened downstairs. Phil. Darling lovely Phil, the man who has nurtured and provided for me and our family for so long. The man who keeps the show on the road and indulges me far beyond what I deserve. The person with whom I have spent the majority of my life and with whom genuinely I am very happy. What was I doing? I should have torn the letter into tiny pieces and flushed it down the loo.

"Ron? You upstairs?"

I flushed the lavatory but I stuck the letter in an old box of Tampax in the bathroom cabinet. He wouldn't be looking in there – but I needed to remember to move it before either of my daughters came home.

"There's something wrong with the timing of the engine despite what the garage says. I'm going to have to take it back – again! They're useless, that lot." Phil was taking his shoes off as I came downstairs. He never forgets, so he never traipses mud into the house. I do and it annoys him, but only a bit. "We were low on milk, so I got some."

How would Webster Ferris greet me if I'd lived with him for 37 years? Tedious but useful information about the car and milk supplies? Surely that's how all co-habiting relationships develop? If Phil came in and said, "The car's fucked but I don't care because I've spent all afternoon with my nose stuck in a critique of Gerard Manley Hopkins," I would not only be very surprised but extremely inconvenienced when it came to driving to the supermarket the next day.

I doubt Webster Ferris would notice a problem with the engine. He probably doesn't have a car and hasn't learnt to drive. As for milk, I expect he's still sniffing it when he makes himself a brew. Maybe he doesn't even do that anymore. Perhaps his head is so wedged into several volumes of T S Eliot, Dylan Thomas and Virginia Woolf at the same time that he doesn't notice his tea has white floaty islands in it and smells so rank it makes you gag.

"The problem with you, Ron," Mum used to say when I was drifting off into one of my reveries, "is you need to live in the real world." Phil lives in the real world for me. It's very useful; it means I don't always have to. He frees me in a way a less practical person wouldn't.

The real world had just arrived. In an envelope I'd almost thrown away. I couldn't ignore that letter. It frightened me and excited me in just the same way Webster had done in person. But it was no longer just about me.

32

"The once and future King"

Police Officers deployed in CID, fans of Agatha Christie or those pedants who write to TV companies to point out that the particular model of Bakelite telephone that Jeeves uses to call Bertie Wooster's Aunt Dahlia in episode three of the second series wasn't produced until after the war, will have noticed something. When I described that memorable evening at the Edinburgh Festival there was a small gap in the time-line.

The last time I saw Webster Ferris was in Scotland on Thursday 15th August 1985, that much is true. But I didn't go straight back to the flat after we had stood at the grave of Greyfriars Bobby. With a sudden and unaccustomed enthusiasm for physical exertion, Webster suggested we climb Arthur's Seat, a rocky outcrop which is the result of some kind of volcanic activity I might be able to describe if I'd listened in Geography. It has magnificent views over the city and out to sea – if you survive the ascent.

It was not only a long way up, it was a long way there. One stride of Webster's long legs equalled about three of mine. He grabbed my hand and pulled me all along Cowgate and towards Holyrood, chattering all the time.

When we neared Holyrood Palace, despite the workouts I'd been having climbing up to the fourth floor, I had to have a rest. He told me about Mary, Queen of Scots whose jealous husband Lord Darnley had her secretary David Rizzio murdered because he thought they were having an adulterous relationship during which he had fathered the child she was expecting. Theirs was a world full of intrigue and lies. "Apparently you can still see the blood stains on the floorboards," he told me dramatically. I wondered if this was a message with subtext. Had Neil said anything to him about Phil?

There was a proper path up to the top, thankfully. I could just about still stand to admire the view when we got there. Ferris stood akimbo, legs wide apart and arms on hips, and shouted the names of some of the books and poems he had read connected with the Arthurian tales.

"*The Once and Future King,* T. H. White. *Le Morte d'Arthur,* Thomas Mallory. *The Faerie Queene,* Edmund Spenser. *Idylls of the King, The Lady of Shalott,* Alfred, Lord Tennyson. *Sir Gawain and the Greene Knight,* J. R. R. Tolkien. *Parsifal,* Wagner," he sang out into the Edinburgh evening air. "*The Round Table with Only One Knight,* Roland!" I'd missed his eccentricities.

"How did you really get that black eye?" I asked, but he chose to ignore me.

What happened next is something I have revisited constantly over the years. The sun sets late in the summer in Scotland and just as it began its descent to the horizon we started our trek back down.

I'm filled with a mixture of embarrassment, incredulity and shock to write that, when we came to the part seclusion of a small clump of bushes and a rocky outcrop, we made love vigorously in the open air. At the distance of 37 years, it's almost as if it happened to someone else.

"Come with me," he pleaded. "Now, tonight. If you loved me, you would."

Was I Lydia in *Pride and Prejudice,* running off with Mr Wickham? Were we *Bonnie and Clyde* on the run, or trussed up in crinolines and army uniforms in *Gone With the Wind,* Webster as passionate Scarlett and me as loyal, boring old Ashley?

I was getting carried away again. We'd been over this a million times. I was in the show until the end of the month. I didn't have a visa or a ticket. I'd need to prepare my parents. I couldn't just go.

I told him not to be daft and he came out with some line about not being able to live without me. "You need a better script writer."

His demeanour changed. His face was puce and he was breathing heavily. "Don't laugh at me, Roni. Don't abandon me."

"Oh for God's sake, grow UP!" It was probably the worst thing I could have said to him, this man who had had to grow up whilst he was still an adolescent. He might have been using a corny turn of phrase, but I was the only person with whom he could communicate his emotions.

He got up and snatched his jacket from the ground. I could sense the anger, the vitriolic venom building inside him. For a terrible moment I thought he was going to hit me. He strode off down the hill.

I couldn't keep up with him. I tried for a while but it was clear he wanted to get away from me. I was crying, trying to wipe the tears from my face so I didn't lose my footing. He got smaller and smaller until I could no longer see him. I sat down and sobbed. I hated him so much – just as much as I loved him.

I went back to the flat. I don't know where Webster Ferris went next. He ended up in the USA as planned and he did manage to live without me. I thought he probably would.

When the pregnancy test was positive, I instinctively knew it was his baby. There's no way Phil would have had sex without contraception. Fortunately for me, he did have some statistic about the number of sheaths which are defective. "It's a tiny failure rate but 2% is statistically significant." He seemed quite pleased, actually. His virility had conquered a wall of rubber smeared with spermicide, or so he believed.

As soon as I saw my baby, this boy with thick black curly hair and dark eyes, it confirmed it to me. If anyone who knew Webster Ferris had been asked to draw him as a baby, this is what they'd have drawn. Luckily Phil thought he looked like Uncle Patrick, who was the dead spit of that ne'er-do-well Paddy McNamara senior, a backhanded compliment if ever there was one. Who was I to argue?

"I think we should call him Arthur," Phil announced. My face reddened. How could he know? Had he guessed the place of conception? "It's kind of appropriate given the Edinburgh show, and my grandfather was called Arthur and I was very fond of him."

I have thought about Webster Ferris daily. I couldn't help it. The older his son has got the more he has got to look like him. I don't know if Phil ever has any doubts about whether he is the boy's father. He certainly hasn't passed them on to me. The girls, born after a gap which allowed us to grow up, look like him. "The females are my side of the family," he says enigmatically.

What did I do with the ticket money Webster gave me? It lay hidden in a drawer in its envelope for a few years until I decided to buy Arthur some vintage books, collectable editions of the works whose names his father sang out into the air at dusk the day he was conceived. He says they are what encouraged him to become a writer and, though it sounds like boasting, I'm proud he has been very successful.

Given Arthur's talents and looks, anyone who knew both of us at that time, simultaneously so distant and yet so recent, doesn't need Inspector Morse to work it out.

This unverified but almost certain truth has affected my friendships post university. Mary and I avoided each other because incredibly, as it turns out, both of us were keeping the same secret. Of the Pared-Down Players, Neil alone has met Arthur. My most emotionally intelligent friend has chosen to say nothing – despite surely remembering Ferris's visit to Edinburgh.

And Phil, who has loved and supported the boy? I can only conclude that if he worked it out at some point, he has accepted it. The confessional ball is very much in my court.

33

"The commencement of atonement is the sense of its necessity"

My first part. The beginning which now will influence the end. I can't ignore the bit in the middle, but I feel as if I've been flushed through that blob without touching the sides.

I didn't lie but it's so tempting not to explain everything when you don't have to. I haven't disabused people of what they believed, the assumptions they made when the real facts eluded them. I just didn't correct them. Truth is bent for palatable reasons to spare feelings or avoid offence, but sometimes to swerve responsibility. It suited me not to challenge their narrative. It hid my mistakes and bad behaviour. I'm not proud of that. It just happened imperceptibly without intention to hurt. I kept quiet, or the truth got buried in a better-sounding lie. In truth husbandry I have been most economical.

All this time I have been telling myself that I would never see Ferris again. But he will be here next year and he obviously wants to see me. He deserves to know the truth, as does everyone else; it will be necessary for me to meet him.

Surely Father O'Connor must have moved to a celestial parish by now. If not, he will likely be so old and deaf that he will no longer be able to hear confession. That's a blessing because I have a final admission, one I have only recently acknowledged to myself. There'll be no chance Bloomin' O'Connor will find out about it. Gran would be relieved.

Webster has never been far from my thoughts these thirty-seven years, not only because I have had a visual reminder of him all that time. There is one simple fact which his letter has forced me to confront. I have been yearning for him with an ache which comes from deep within my very being, longing to be with him again all that time.

I want to be with Webster Ferris more than anything else in the whole world. He will be part of my 'end', however it turns out.

And that really is the truth.

Author's Note

If you enjoyed *A Cactus Called Ironside*, please tell your friends and book group. I'd love you to leave a review on Amazon or Goodreads.

You can follow me on Twitter and Instagram for all my book news by going to the following links or scanning the QR codes:

 Instagram: https://bit.ly/KathCrew_Instagram

 Facebook: https://bit.ly/KathCrew_Facebook

 X (Twitter): https://bit.ly/KathCrew_X

Do you want to know what happened next? *Between the Lines* is coming soon, so follow me to be the first to know when.

About the Author

ath Crew has been telling stories since she could first talk and writing them down since someone showed her how to use a pencil. Her active imagination has occasionally landed her in trouble over the years.

She was President of Cambridge Footlights in the 1980s and wrote for and performed in revues whilst at university. As a teacher she wrote for her students and has been a contributor to various publications.

Now she is free of children, her own and those belonging to other people, she is enjoying writing at length for a larger audience. She hopes to entertain with humour whilst not being entirely flippant or lightweight.

Originally from London and a townie at heart, she now lives in Oxfordshire with her husband and a small white dog called Boris. She is trying hard to fit in with life in the country and extend her classification of the natural world beyond a basic 'bird', 'flower' or 'tree'.

Acknowledgements

I am grateful to the following for their early approval and comments: Sally, Pippa, Jean, Sarah, Kath, Paul, Georgie, Mike, Veronica, Caroline and Susie.

Three cheers for Yana for persevering with the dictionary, British idiom and humour and still coming up with a positive response.

Thanks to Alison, Jo, Pete, Jan, Gerry and Andrea for their specialist advice and to Jen for showing me the way forward.

Unquestionably, without the encouragement and long-suffering patience of Hilary, Belinda and Nick, I would not have been able to realise this story in printed form. I am indebted to you all.

Printed in Great Britain
by Amazon